Everything We Keep

A Top Amazon Bestseller of 2016 and
Wall Street Journal Bestseller

Amazon Charts Bestseller

Liz & Lisa Best Book of the Month Selection

POPSUGAR and *Redbook* Fall Must-Read Selection

"This fantastic debut is glowing with adrenaline-inducing suspense and unexpected twists. Don't make other plans when you open up *Everything We Keep*; you will devour it in one sitting."

—*Redbook* magazine

"Aimee's electrifying journey to piece together the puzzle of mystery surrounding her fiancé's disappearance is a heart-pounding reading experience every hopeless romantic and shock-loving fiction-lover should treat themselves to."

—POPSUGAR

"You'll need an ample supply of tissues and emotional strength for this one . . . From Northern California author Kerry Lonsdale comes a heart-wrenching story about fate sweeping away life in an instant."

—*Sunset* magazine

"Gushing with adrenaline-inducing plot, this is the phenomenally written debut every fall reader will be swooning over."

—*Coastal Living*

"A beautifully crafted novel about unconditional love, heartbreak, and letting go, *Everything We Keep* captures readers with its one-of-a-kind, suspenseful plot. Depicting grief and loss, but also healing and hope in their rawest forms, this novel will capture hearts and minds, keeping readers up all night, desperate to learn the truth."

—*RT Book Reviews*

"A perfect page-turner for summer."

—Catherine McKenzie, bestselling author of *Hidden* and *Fractured*

"Heartfelt and suspenseful, *Everything We Keep* beautifully navigates the deep waters of grief, and one woman's search to reconcile a past she can't release, and a future she wants to embrace. Lonsdale's writing is crisp and effortless and utterly irresistible—and her expertly layered exploration of the journey from loss to renewal is sure to make this a book club must-read. *Everything We Keep* drew me in from the first page and held me fast all the way to its deeply satisfying ending."

—Erika Marks, author of *The Last Treasure*

"In *Everything We Keep*, Kerry Lonsdale brilliantly explores the grief of loss, if we can really let go of our great loves, and if some secrets are better left buried. With a good dose of drama, a heart-wrenching love story, and the suspense of unanswered questions, Lonsdale's layered and engrossing debut is a captivating read."

—Karma Brown, bestselling author of *Come Away with Me*

"A stunning debut with a memorable twist, *Everything We Keep* effortlessly layers family secrets into a suspenseful story of grief, love, and art. This is a gem of a book."

—Barbara Claypole White, bestselling author of *The Perfect Son* and *The Promise Between Us*

"With a touch of the paranormal, *All the Breaking Waves* is an emotional story about lost love, family secrets, and finding beauty in things people fear . . . or simply discard. A perfect book club pick!"
—Barbara Claypole White, bestselling author of *The Perfect Son* and *The Promise Between Us*

"A masterful tale of magic realism and family saga. With its heartfelt characters, relationships generational and maternal, and a long-ago romance, we are drawn into Molly's world. While her intuitive gifts may be ethereal, her fears and hopes for her daughter and personal desires are extraordinarily relatable. Woven with a thread of pure magic, Lonsdale crafts an intriguing story of love, mystery, and family loyalty that will captivate and entertain readers."
—Laura Spinella, bestselling author of *Ghost Gifts*

Everything We Left Behind

Amazon Charts and *Wall Street Journal* Bestseller

Amazon Editors' Recommended Beach Read

Liz & Lisa Best Book of the Month Selection

"In this suspenseful sequel to *Everything We Keep* . . . readers will be captivated as the truth unravels, hanging on every word."
—*RT Book Reviews*

"A stunning fusion of suspense, family drama, and redemption, *Everything We Left Behind* will hold the reader spellbound to the last sentence."
—A. J. Banner, bestselling author of *The Twilight Wife* and *The Good Neighbor*

"*Everything We Keep* takes your breath from the very first line and keeps it through a heart-reeling number of twists and turns. Well-plotted, with wonderful writing and pacing, on the surface it appears to be a story of love and loss, but just as you begin to think you've worked it out, you're blindsided and realize you haven't. It will keep you reading and guessing, and trust me, you still won't have it figured out. Not until the very end."

—Barbara Taylor Sissel, bestselling author of *The Truth We Bury* and
What Lies Below

"Wow—it's been a long time since I ignored all of my responsibilities and read a book straight through, but it couldn't be helped with *Everything We Keep*. I was intrigued from the start . . . So many questions, and Lonsdale answers them in the most intriguing and captivating way possible."

—Camille Di Maio, author of *The Memory of Us*

All the Breaking Waves

An Amazon Best Book of the Month:
Literature & Fiction Category

Liz & Lisa Best Book of the Month Selection

"Blending elements of magic and mystery, *All the Breaking Waves* is a compelling portrayal of one mother's journey as she grapples with her small daughter's horrific visions that force her to confront a haunting secret from her past. Examining issues of love, loss, and the often-fragile ground of relationships and forgiveness, this tenderly told story will have you turning the pages long past midnight."

—Barbara Taylor Sissel, bestselling author of *The Truth We Bury* and
What Lies Below

"Love, loss, and secrets drive Kerry Lonsdale's twisty follow-up to the bestselling *Everything We Keep*. *Everything We Left Behind* is an enthralling and entertaining read. You'll be turning the pages as fast as you can to see how it ends."

—Liz Fenton and Lisa Steinke, authors of *The Good Widow*

"While *Everything We Left Behind*, the long-anticipated sequel to *Everything We Keep*, is page-turning and suspenseful, at its center it is the story of a man struggling to discover the truth of his own identity. A man who is determined above all else to protect his family, a man who is willing to risk everything to find out the truth and to ultimately uncover the secrets of his own heart. For everyone who has read *Everything We Keep* (if you haven't go do that now!), this is your novel, answering every question, tying up every thread to an oh-so-satisfying conclusion."

—Barbara Taylor Sissel, bestselling author of *The Truth We Bury* and *What Lies Below*

"With one smart, unexpected twist after another, this page-turner is as surprising as it is emotionally insightful. *Everything We Left Behind* showcases Kerry Lonsdale at the top of her game."

—Camille Pagán, bestselling author of *Life and Other Near-Death Experiences*

"Told through a unique perspective, *Everything We Left Behind* is a compelling story about one man's journey to find himself in the wake of trauma, dark secrets, and loss. As past and present merge, he struggles to confront fear and find trust, but two constants remain: his love for his young sons and his need to protect them from danger. This novel has everything—romance, suspense, mystery, family drama. What a page-turner!"

—Barbara Claypole White, bestselling author of *The Perfect Son* and *The Promise Between Us*

Everything We Give

Wall Street Journal Bestseller

"Fans will not be disappointed in this stunning conclusion to the Everything Series. With Lonsdale's signature twists and turns, nothing is a given until the last, satisfying page. I cried, I bit my nails, and I lost myself in images of wild horses galloping across rural Spain as I journeyed through Ian's past and present. A page-turner about the devastating impact of mental illness and dark secrets on a family, *Everything We Give* is also a story filled with the enduring power of love."

—Barbara Claypole White, bestselling author of *The Perfect Son* and *The Promise Between Us*

"Kerry Lonsdale gives everything away in this final book in the Everything Series, *Everything We Give*. Questions involving an enigmatic woman, the mystery of her name and her identity, and her connection to Ian kick off what is a fast-paced and sensual story of suspense. Like *Everything We Keep* and *Everything We Left Behind*, books one and two in this delectable and layered series, *Everything We Give* is the frosting on the cake, delivering more than one surprise and a total knock-out punch of an ending."

—Barbara Taylor Sissel, bestselling author of *The Truth We Bury* and *What Lies Below*

"Kerry Lonsdale brings the conclusion to the Everything Series to a magnificent ending. Ian's journey through past and present is a trip to remember. A fast-paced thriller with romance and intrigue. Bravo Kerry!"

—Kaira Rouda, *USA Today* bestselling author of *Best Day Ever*

"*Everything We Give* is a satisfying conclusion to this series, which began with a funeral when there should have been a wedding, and ends with the final fallout from the mysterious woman who warned the almost-widow that all was not as it seemed. Lonsdale has woven together a tapestry of characters—Aimee, Ian, James—whose lives are intertwined in ways even they don't entirely know. [It's] both a romance and a mystery, [and] readers will turn these engrossing pages quickly to find out what their final fates [will] be. Fans of this series will not be disappointed."

—Catherine McKenzie, bestselling author of *Hidden* and *The Good Liar*

Last Summer

Amazon Charts and *Washington Post* Bestseller

"An involving story weaves a tale of recovery into a mystery that embraces relationships, danger, and new beginnings."

—Midwest Book Review

"To say that this book is a page-turner is an understatement."

—Criminal Element

"This was a highly entertaining and wildly addictive read that is perfect for summer! . . . Compulsive, sexy and tense."

—*Novelgossip*

"*Last Summer* is one hell of a ride with a heroine who's easy to relate to and a glossy romantic mystery that holds the reader's attention."

—*All About Romance*

"Lonsdale doles out the clues to Ella's lost time in the perfect amount of bits and pieces to keep the suspense going . . . The story was well written, fast paced, and full of suspense. This was a great summer read."

—*Mystery Playground*

"*Last Summer* is utterly captivating and impossible to put down, so strap yourself in for a ride. In addition to being a superb writer, Kerry Lonsdale has a talent for creating complex characters who wrestle with very real situations. *Last Summer* is her best yet, a sly suspense coupled with sizzling romance and unending twists. Lonsdale should be on every reader's radar."

—J.T. Ellison, *New York Times* bestselling author of *Lie to Me* and *Tear Me Apart*

"*Last Summer* is a compelling and chilling suspense that kept me turning the pages until the very end. This was my first Kerry Lonsdale novel, but it definitely won't be my last."

—T.R. Ragan, *Wall Street Journal* bestselling author of *Evil Never Dies*

"Move over, *Gone Girl*, and make way for *Last Summer*, a taut, intricately plotted novel of secrets and lies, love and betrayal. I thought I knew where the story was going, but the final, shocking twist gave me a serious case of whiplash. Just *wow*."

—A. J. Banner, bestselling author of *The Twilight Wife* and *The Good Neighbor*

"*Last Summer* is a deliciously dark and twisty tale that leaves you wondering who you should root for until the very end."

—Victoria Helen Stone, Amazon Charts bestselling author of *Jane Doe*

Side Trip

"Exploring a series of what-if scenarios, readers will thoroughly enjoy this road trip along Route 66 with two curious strangers."

—*Travel + Leisure*

"Swoon-worthy moments and heart-stirring drama . . . A romantic ride!"

—*Woman's World*

"Lonsdale keeps the reader guessing right to the very end . . . with a twist you don't see coming. A great summer read."

—*Red Carpet Crash*

"Lonsdale again takes us on quite a ride through love, loss, and life. Her groupie following will devour this one!"

—*Frolic*

"Smart, sexy, and unexpected—*Side Trip* is everything that makes a novel unputdownable, which is why I devoured it in two days. Kerry Lonsdale's latest demonstrates what fans like me already know: she just keeps getting better and better."

—Camille Pagán, bestselling author of *I'm Fine and Neither Are You*

"Route 66, a convertible, a folk singer, and fate combine to make a confection of a novel in Kerry Lonsdale's *Side Trip*. Scoot into the back seat to watch what happens. What a wild ride!"

—J. P. Monninger, international bestselling author

"Kerry Lonsdale's *Side Trip* is an absorbing, poignant exploration of the road not taken and the pitfalls of failing to follow one's heart."

—Jamie Beck, bestselling author of the Cabots and
Sanctuary Sound series

"Strap in for a fun, musical, and magical ride with characters you won't soon forget. This is easily my favorite of Lonsdale's books. The ending . . . it is one of the most jaw-dropping conclusions I've ever read."

—Rochelle Weinstein, *USA Today* and Amazon bestselling author

"A highly romantic and heart-wrenching story by a writer who rarely takes the expected route."

—Barbara O'Neal, *Wall Street Journal* and Amazon Charts
bestselling author

NO MORE
WORDS

NO MORE WORDS

WORDS

A NOVEL

KERRY
LONSDALE

LAKE UNION
PUBLISHING

Text copyright © 2021 by Kerry Lonsdale Inc.
All rights reserved.

No part of this book may be reproduced, or stored in a retrieval system, or transmitted in any form or by any means, electronic, mechanical, photocopying, recording, or otherwise, without express written permission of the publisher.

Published by Lake Union Publishing, Seattle

www.apub.com

Amazon, the Amazon logo, and Lake Union Publishing are trademarks of Amazon.com, Inc., or its affiliates.

ISBN-13: 9781542019057
ISBN-10: 1542019052

Cover design by Rex Bonomelli

Printed in the United States of America

For Mom

CHAPTER 1

Summer of '95

Charlotte and Dwight Carson unloaded their three children at the Whitmans' lakeside cabin like a courier with a cardboard package. Dwight shook hands with Harold Whitman, and Charlotte helped three-year-old Lily from her booster seat, depositing the little girl with the rosebud lips wrapped around her thumb onto the gravel driveway. She dragged reluctant six-year-old Lucas from his seat, prying his fingers one by one off the door latch while he hollered in her ear that he wanted to go home. Eight-year-old Olivia was the only one who willingly exited the car, inching the plastic thong on her flip-flops between her toes and shouldering her olive-green JanSport backpack. She was also the only one of her siblings smart enough to know that a summer at the lake with a family she barely knew would be a vast improvement over summers spent in day care and evenings with their parents, who, even to Olivia's inexperienced eyes, didn't love each other.

She was nervous, though. She'd never been away from home for six weeks. The longest she'd been without her parents were the four days Charlotte had her and Lucas stay with their neighbor Nancy Merriweather after Lily was born.

Gravel crunched under her flip-flops as she backed away from the car, looking up at the two-story A-frame cabin with the rustic wood siding that would be home for the next one and a half months. It looked tiny under the towering Jeffrey pines. But Rhonda Whitman assured

Olivia the loft had enough room to comfortably sleep Olivia and her two younger siblings.

"Between you and me," Mrs. Whitman conspiratorially whispered last weekend at Olivia's parents' annual summer luncheon, a catered affair with servers in black pants and starched white shirts, "there's enough room to sleep ten kids. We'll swim and play games. It'll be your best summer ever," she reassured when Olivia expressed her reluctance about being away from home for so long.

Olivia had smiled meekly, sipping the one glass of punch Charlotte allowed her before she'd be relegated to her room until the party ended. Dwight Carson was raising money for his congressional campaign, and the important people at the party, including the Whitmans, couldn't be bothered with children underfoot. She wanted to believe Mrs. Whitman, but every summer Olivia experienced so far had been boring. Dwight always seemed to be running for an elected office. Summers were spent going door-to-door, distributing pamphlets, or attending rallies to raise funding for red, white, and blue lawn signs.

Lily sidled up to Olivia, her thumb lodged in her mouth. Olivia felt her little sister's hand inside hers. She threaded their fingers, and Lily leaned into her like Mrs. Merriweather's poodle when she scratched the dog in his favorite spot behind his ear.

Lily was nervous, too. So was Lucas. He wore his brave face but kept blowing out his cheeks and popping his lips. Olivia reached for Lucas's sticky hand, and he surprisingly didn't let go or shove her away. He had complained most of the drive from Seaside Cove, a planned, gated community on the coast just west of San Luis Obispo where they lived. He'd wanted his friend Tanner to come.

"Stop whining. You'll make new friends," Dwight had insisted before going back to his call on his brand-new wireless, scheduling client appointments for the upcoming week. Olivia didn't know exactly what her dad did when he wasn't campaigning, but she once overheard

Charlotte explain to a neighbor that Dwight showed wineries how to operate. His job sounded distinguished to her.

Dwight kissed Olivia's forehead. "I'm going to miss you."

"I'm going to miss you, too."

"I'll call you every day."

A little smile peeked out like sunshine through a cloud as she wondered what she'd tell him tomorrow. They could talk about her new sketches. She'd been drawing *The Lion King* characters from scratch and they looked good to her. She was devouring the Baby-Sitters Club and Sweet Valley High series. Maybe he'd want to hear about the book she'd been reading because she couldn't picture what they'd be doing all day here other than sitting around.

"Be good, Princess."

"I will, Daddy."

He turned to Lucas. "Listen to the Whitmans. Do what they tell you."

Lucas threw himself against Dwight. "Don't leave."

"Summer will be over before you know it. You won't even notice I'm gone." He hugged Lucas, then wrested his arms from around his waist.

Sniffling, Lucas grasped Olivia's hand. She could tell he didn't believe Dwight. From the moment their parents told them they were sending them away, he'd been sure it would be forever.

Dwight turned to leave.

"Daddy?"

"Yes, Princess?"

"Aren't you going to say goodbye to Lily?"

Lily pressed closer to Olivia as if trying to disappear behind her.

Dwight scratched his clean-shaven chin and cleared his throat. His gaze shifted between Olivia and Lily. He stepped closer and patted Lily on the head like Olivia had seen him do with Mrs. Merriweather's dog.

"See ya, kids." He abruptly left and joined Charlotte at the car. Charlotte tossed her head back, laughing at something Mr. Whitman said. They worked at the same real estate firm, which was how the Carsons knew the Whitmans. Mr. Whitman touched Charlotte's arm. He leaned close and whispered in her ear. Charlotte smiled, then folded into the driver's seat, waving goodbye. Dwight got into the car and loudly shut his door. Charlotte drove off, kicking up pebbles and dust onto three pieces of luggage left in the gravel.

Olivia's mouth turned down. Their parents left them in the driveway. UPS had the courtesy to leave packages on the porch and ring the doorbell.

Lily whimpered. Thinking she was sad because their dad didn't kiss her goodbye, Olivia kissed her little sister's forehead, just like Dwight did with her. "He didn't mean to forget," she said.

"Olivia?"

She spun around, tugging her siblings along like spinning passenger cars attached to the center pillar of an amusement park ride.

Mrs. Whitman smiled warmly and Olivia felt better already.

"Are you kids hungry? I made sandwiches. After, we can take the canoe out on the lake."

In unison, three pairs of eyes looked at the lake. Beached on the shore was a colorful assortment of kayaks and canoes. A tire swing hung above the water. A paddleboarder glided across the surface. Mrs. Whitman waved.

Lucas's hand slipped from Olivia's. He scooted away, lured by the water.

"Wait until after lunch," Mrs. Whitman said, and Lucas stopped, heeding the warning tone in her voice. The Carsons lived on oceanfront property. They had a dock with a small motorboat and kayaks, which Dwight took out every weekend. Olivia and Lucas learned to swim while still in diapers. Lily already knew the basics of swimming, enough to keep herself afloat if she fell into the water. But their parents forbade them to go near the shore. Dwight never took them kayaking or on his boat. He thought them too young, the water too choppy. They could fall out.

But this lake was flat and shimmery like the stained glass windows at church.

"Would you like to play in the water this afternoon?" Mrs. Whitman asked.

Lucas nodded, eyes wide, his brave face radiating with excitement.

"Yes," Olivia agreed. Even Lily looked longingly at the lake, the murky water gently lapping the shore. Between two trees hung a hammock. Olivia wanted to sketch there and read her books.

"Wonderful." Mrs. Whitman's smile broadened. She looked over her shoulder. "Theo. Ty. Come help."

Olivia looked up at the Whitmans' kids, who'd been watching their arrival from the front deck slouched over the rail, chins propped on forearms. Both wore swim trunks, their torsos tanned from the high-altitude sunlight.

"Mom," Theo complained, hiding his face.

Mrs. Whitman rolled her eyes. "He can't stand it when I use his first name." She grinned at Olivia.

Olivia smiled shyly. She knew Theo from school. He sat two rows over from her in Mrs. Foster's class. She also knew he hated his first name and insisted everyone call him Blaze. What she didn't know was why. Where did he come up with that nickname?

She liked Blaze. He'd always been nice to her.

"Ty, get Lily's bag," Mr. Whitman instructed. He'd already picked up Olivia's and Lucas's duffels, dusting them off. Tyler, tall for a five-year-old, dragged Lily's My Little Pony roller up the deck steps. The little suitcase bumped along behind him. Lucas followed them inside, eager to eat and change into his swim shorts.

Mrs. Whitman held out her hand for Lily's. "Do you like ice cream?"

Lily's thumb popped from her mouth. "I love ice cream."

"Will you show me your favorite flavor?"

Lily nodded and took Mrs. Whitman's hand, leaving Olivia alone with Blaze. She wiped her palm, damp from Lily's hand, on her light-blue jersey shorts.

"Hi," Blaze said, his hair mussed and feet dirty.

"Hi," she said quietly. She twisted her shirt hem.

He squeezed the back of his neck and nudged gravel with his toe. "Ty and I built a fort in the loft. Want to see?"

Olivia nodded.

She followed him into the cabin with brown shag carpeting and faux wood paneling, and up a wide set of stairs to the loft. What Olivia saw could only be described as magical. Multicolored sheets were draped over ropes that crisscrossed the A-shape room that opened to the house below, creating five small tents. Each tent slept one person. Sleeping bags and pillows had already been laid out so that the head of each tent faced the center of the room. If she'd looked down at the tents from the ceiling, they'd form a five-pointed star. Crescent moon twinkle lights framed the openings of the boys' tents and stars glittered on hers and Lily's. She knew whose tent was whose because someone had taped hand-drawn name cards to each tent.

"You did this?" she asked, dazzled.

Blaze's cheeks pinkened. "Ty helped."

She delicately touched her card. The letters, L-I-V-Y, had curlicues on the ends. Flowers bordered her nickname.

"I made yours," he said. "Ty did Lily's and Lucas's."

Her gaze lifted to the card on the tent beside hers. Blaze's name was written in bold, block letters, the handwriting impatient, not nearly as crisp and lovely as hers.

She looked at their pillows, practically touching in the center. Hers was plain white. His was Mario Bros. She bit her lower lip, her stomach twitching. It felt like hummingbirds flying about, their delicate wings fluttering inside her. She had imagined it would be just her, Lucas, and Lily up there. But this was better, their tent star. Thinking about Blaze sleeping beside her, his head close to hers, made her nervous and shy. But she'd rather be near him than Lucas. Her brother tooted in his sleep. He'd pull her hair and plug her nose just to annoy her. But with Blaze, they could whisper about their favorite movies and books, giggle late into the night about the funny faces their teacher made when she wrote on the whiteboard.

"Kids, come eat," Mrs. Whitman called from the bottom of the stairs.

Olivia smiled. "I like this," she admitted, gliding her fingers across her name card. Mrs. Whitman was right. This would be the best summer ever.

CHAPTER 2

Present Day
Day 1

Blaze was late. It's why he forgot his phone. If he hadn't, Olivia wouldn't have discovered the photo. If she hadn't seen that photo, she wouldn't have spent the afternoon packing his belongings and dumping the boxes and loose articles on her front lawn. A lawn her gardener just finished mowing and edging. She spooked the poor man when a pile of Blaze's Diesel jeans dropped in front of the mower and he almost shredded them. Olivia wishes he had. Then Blaze wouldn't come out of this relationship unscathed like he did last time.

Sal quickly loaded his mower onto his truck and packed up his rake and blower. With a tenuous smile and half-hearted wave, he drove off as Blaze rode up on his Harley. Her soon-to-be ex-boyfriend now faces off with her, in her bedroom, defending himself as if the photo isn't on his phone.

"It's not mine!" Blaze raises his hands in full surrender.

Olivia doesn't believe him. The proof is on his phone, the one he left behind this morning.

She wasn't snooping, not intentionally. She respects his privacy because she expects the same in return. But she's chasing a deadline and her next round of illustrations is due to her editor by midnight. She took a break, her first in seven hours today, because she'd skipped breakfast, missed lunch, and was starving. She needed to eat. While Olivia was munching on a handful of vegan cauliflower puffs in the kitchen, Blaze's phone, forgotten on the counter, pinged with an incoming text. An image flashed, causing her to do a double take.

She brushed her hand on her jeans, wiping off dehydrated cauliflower dust, and unlocked his phone. She'd seen him tap the six-digit code numerous times. She unintentionally knows it by heart because he refuses to access his phone through facial recognition. She calls him paranoid. He calls it being cautious.

Whatever.

Blaze's phone launched and up popped Macey Brown's reaction to Blaze's not-so-private privates: two fat exclamation points in a cartoon bubble.

Blaze had sent his ex-girlfriend a dick pic.

Apparently, while out last night at the bar with his friend Shane, Blaze spent twenty minutes sexting Macey. Their text exchange read like two high schoolers in heat, and Olivia skimmed the entire conversation while trying to stomach her minuscule snack. The texts nowhere near reflect the maturity level of the thirty-five-year-old man Olivia has been dating—*again!*—for almost a year.

Lesson obviously not learned when she dumped him the first time, their junior year in high school.

Olivia fumes.

"Come on, Livy." Blaze turns his wide, calloused palms up. His hands are beautiful in their roughness and wickedly talented in multiple areas. She's going to miss the magic they wield in his metalworks studio and her bedroom.

Her cheeks flush with warmth and she scowls at her traitorous thoughts.

Blaze dares a step in her direction. He arches a brow. His gaze smolders. "You know it's not mine, baby."

"How would I . . ." She stops, exasperated over her own naivete.

A naughty smile frames his jaw.

"Oh, my god," she says, appalled. He thinks she knows it's not his because she's seen his, and touched his, and . . . She is *not* going to let her mind go there.

Olivia stoops to pick up his PUMA high-top, one of the last items she hasn't relocated to the front lawn. She gave him a drawer last year after he and his team finished the remodel on her house, and since then, he's taken over half her closet. He doesn't live here, not officially. Though he's at her place all the time. He has his own house past the country club among the wineries, but she got lax and let him encroach on her space. Until an hour ago she liked having him in it. Who can blame her? The sex is phenomenal. He cooks a mean Bolognese. And maybe, just maybe, dating Blaze let her recapture some of the feelings she lost when summers at the lake house stopped.

She swings her arm back, aiming to toss him the shoe. If he gets anywhere within arm's reach, he'll kiss her, distract her, and before she knows it they'll be on the bed messing up her sheets because she's a sex-crazed monster. She has no willpower when it comes to Blaze's charm, which is why she ended up back in his arms after she'd sworn off men when the last guy she dated back when she lived in San Francisco keyed her Mercedes. Big mistake.

Every time she's opened her heart to someone, even a little, they've betrayed her. Yet again, she's been hoodwinked.

Blaze points a warning finger. "Don't do it. You'll break something."

She underhands the shoe. He doesn't even duck or try to grab for it, her aim is that far off. They both watch the shoe arc across the room like a puma leaping over a narrow river and connect soundly with the bureau top, shattering her favorite bottle of Jimmy Choo.

"No!" She sulks. She loves that perfume, and it's not cheap.

Blaze starts to pick up the glass shards.

"Leave it," she barks, more upset with herself than with him. How could she have been so gullible? He cheated on her with Macey Brown, of all people.

If it weren't for Macey, Olivia wouldn't have broken up with Blaze. She wouldn't have met Ethan.

And Lily wouldn't have run away.

"Whoa, Liv. Chill." He holds up a hand. "Just getting my shoe." He slowly bends over, his gaze locked on Olivia as if she's a wild animal ready to pounce. He picks up the PUMA and tucks the shoe under his arm.

"Let me explain," he begs not for the first time, standing to his full height.

"Please don't." She retreats into the walk-in closet. The other shoe has to be in here somewhere. She nudges her own shoes with her foot and pulls designer handbags off the shelf, leaving them in a heap on the floor. There isn't any logic behind her search, but right now she isn't thinking logically. She wants him to leave, and he won't go anywhere until she finds the cherished mate to his favorite pair of sneakers. But the shoe, like its namesake, remains elusive.

"Liv . . . Liv . . . *Olivia*."

"I'm looking. Damn." She moves aside the laundry basket and returns to the room. "I can't find—"

Blaze holds up the second shoe. "It was under the bed. Hey, baby." He crosses the room to her. "I—"

"Don't 'baby' me." She wags a finger. "Macey Brown? Really?" When Macey's name flashed on Blaze's phone, Olivia felt like she'd been tackled from behind while at a full sprint. It knocked the wind from her, leaving her gasping as decades of old hurt and sorrow flooded her lungs.

"It wasn't me. It was Shane."

Does he take her for a fool?

"Not buying it. We are over."

"The hell, Liv." He looks thoroughly bewildered.

She leaves the room that's starting to smell like a perfumery—and memories of another relationship that soured long before its expiration date. Ethan had gifted her a bottle of Jimmy Choo her first birthday after they started dating. She's been attached to the scent ever since, unable to let it go, like the memory of the way they parted.

Blaze follows her into the hallway toward the front of the house, his step heavy and purposeful behind her. "Shane borrowed my phone last night. How was I supposed to know the asshole would stuff it down his pants?"

Ew. Her face twists. Spare her the visual.

"Not one text mentions they came from Shane. Macey thinks they came from you, that it's you in the photo. From where I'm standing, you sent Macey a picture of your—"

"It's. Not. Mine. Shane borrowed my phone to make a call. And text his dick." He grumbles the last bit.

"Then you should have told Shane to make it clear it wasn't yours." And she shouldn't have thought dating Blaze again would be anything less than complicated, not when they had too much history. What's the saying, evade the flame else you'll get singed? She avoids entanglements for a reason. They hurt. No, they burn.

"I didn't know about it until you called me."

"Why is Macey even a contact on your phone?"

"It's from eons ago."

An object in the front room catches her eye. She veers into the room, her attention on the entertainment system. Blaze dogs her heels.

"She plugged her info in at our ten-year reunion. I never deleted it. I should have. I'm sorry."

Olivia missed that event. She can blame work or living out of the area. She was in San Francisco at the time. But the truth is, she didn't want to run into Ethan. To see him and Blaze in the same room? It would be like holding up a mirror to her past mistakes. If she hadn't allowed Ethan into her life, her little sister would still be in it.

Later she learned that he, too, was a reunion no-show.

"Give me some slack here, Livy. That was years ago. You and I weren't even dating."

"Excuses, excuses."

"You're the one coming up with excuses," Blaze counters. For the first time since his arrival, he sounds more bitter than confused. "You're looking for a reason to end us. You've been looking since the day we hooked up again."

"We never should have gotten back together." But he'd just completed her remodel, and he'd been generous about paying attention to details, making sure there weren't any mistakes and that she was pleased with his craftsmanship. Then on that last night, when he brought over the job completion order for her to sign, he stood in the middle of her brand-new kitchen and shyly asked her out to dinner. For a guy who wasn't the least bit timid, she could tell he'd been working up the nerve to ask her, afraid she'd say no. He'd smiled, and Olivia saw the boy she remembered from all those summers ago. She felt safe. Accepting his invitation felt right, because once upon a lifetime ago they'd fit.

"See? That's your problem," he argues. "You assume the worst of people. You don't trust anyone, so everything you touch or do blows up." He mimes his head exploding.

"Not true," she bristles. Not everything. She was enormously successful as an illustrator at an upstart high-tech company that went public. Thanks to that venture, she "retired" two years ago at thirty-three and moved to San Luis Obispo and into the house her dad sold to her for one dollar as a college graduation present. Dwight had owned the house for years and used it as a rental until she came of age. The place was a dump from several decades of tenants rotating through. But she has since remodeled the house and pursued her dream project: to write and illustrate her own graphic novel series. She's proud of her accomplishments.

Relationships, though? Hers never end well, so best to end this one before it dives further south than it already is.

"Everything's about you," he accuses. "What about me? You're kicking me out, for Chrissake. At least hear me out."

"Too late."

"Come on, Livy. Just last night you were begging me—"

"Shut up!" He doesn't need to remind her how wonderful he makes her feel, not when she's trying to end them, as he so eloquently put it, before he can do any more damage. Her scars already run deeper than the lake they used to swim, holding hands while they floated on their backs, squinting into the sun. She yanks the cord to Blaze's McIntosh turntable from her receiver.

"No! No, no, no." He drops his PUMAs and shoves her aside. "Don't touch my MTI." He carefully lifts the turntable off the shelf and balances the component in his arms before turning to her. "Grab those." He gestures with his chin toward the milk crate of vinyls on the floor.

Olivia heaves up the records and follows him out the front door, her gaze on his backside. He does have a nice ass. She's going to miss looking at that, and him. Too bad she can't trust the man, or anyone for that matter. She's tired of being betrayed. It's like she's walking through life with a neon sign on her forehead: SCREW ME OVER. Picking up the pieces after they break her is exhausting. A part of her is left missing every time. She hasn't felt whole since she broke up with Blaze in high school.

Correction. She hasn't felt whole since her brother, Lucas, ruined their summers at the Whitmans'.

"Don't throw my collection," Blaze tosses over his shoulder.

"I won't." She isn't that much of a bitch.

"Hey, Blaze."

"Oh, hey, Amber," he says when he walks past Olivia's best friend. Amber lounges on the porch steps, making her way through a bottle of pinot noir.

"Thanks for coming," Olivia says to her friend.

"Ah, well, I guess the end was inevitable." As it always is with Olivia's relationships.

Olivia cringes, embarrassed she's such a failure in this area.

Amber smirks. "For the record, I was holding out hope for you guys. But since it's come to this, I wouldn't miss it for the world."

This isn't Amber's first Olivia breakup rodeo. Olivia called Amber right after she'd hung up on Blaze. After that incident several years back that left her with a fat lip and keyed car, she never kicked out a boyfriend without a friend on-site. One day she'll learn to stop inviting men to make themselves at home.

Blaze sets down his turntable on the walkway and Olivia drops the crate alongside. "Careful," he snaps, pulling out his phone. He approaches Amber. "You slept with Shane. Tell Liv this isn't me." He enlarges the photo on his 11 Pro Max.

"Good god. Put that thing away." Amber covers her eyes.

"Screw you, Amber."

"No, thanks. Already got Mike for that." Amber drinks her wine like she's washing down the taste the photo left behind.

Blaze shoves his phone away and turns to Olivia. "What'll it take to convince you there's nothing between me and Macey?"

She glances away. She can't go through this again with him.

"This is it then." Blaze shuffles his feet. His boot heels scrape on concrete.

"This is it," she concurs, ignoring the inkling of remorse churning inside her stomach. She fooled herself into believing they could keep their relationship light, firmly seated on the fun level. She'll miss him like family because at one time, he was family. But she doesn't plead for him to stay. She bites her bottom lip hard so she won't apologize and admit she might be making a mistake.

Amber quirks a brow. "You sure you want him to go?"

"Yes, why?"

She shrugs. "Thought I'd check while there's still time to fix this."

"Whose side are you on?"

"For a guy with a man bun, I kind of like him. And he didn't key your Mercedes."

"Blaze wouldn't have done that. Present fuckup aside, he's too nice."

"Then why am I here? And why are you breaking up with him?"

Olivia quirks a brow. "Seriously?" she asks while at the same time thinking Blaze may be 100 percent accurate. She's been looking for an excuse to break up and Macey handed one to her in the shape of Shane's—

Okay, she's stopping right there.

Either way, a picture is worth a thousand words.

They watch Blaze throw a leg over his bike and the pang of regret in her chest sharpens, though not enough to invite him back or admit she's wrong.

"You forgot your stuff." Amber yells the obvious.

"Sure. I'll pile everything on." He gestures roughly at his ride and straps on his helmet. "I'll be back later with my truck. Don't touch my things." He flicks down the visor and revs the cycle loud enough to scare off a cluster of blackbirds in the enormous pine across the street. He then flips Olivia his own bird and blows out of there.

Olivia exhales loudly. He's gone. And she's free.

She finger combs her hair back, holding the long, cinnamon-brown locks off her forehead, and turns to her friend. Their eyes meet. Amber's brows lift.

"What?" Olivia barks.

Amber fixes her messy bun and refills her wineglass. She makes a contemplative sound deep in her throat.

"You think he was telling the truth," Olivia presumes.

Her friend since college freshman orientation sips her wine. "It doesn't matter what I think."

Olivia settles beside Amber on the porch steps. "He was telling the truth."

"Yep."

She extends a skinny jean–clad leg and pulls out the single Marlboro and lighter she'd tucked in her front pocket before Blaze showed up. She knew she'd need a smoke after he left, a nasty habit she'd picked up in San Francisco when she worked seventy-plus-hour weeks. Something to take the edge off when exercise and sex couldn't. The other side of her California king will be cold tonight and exercise isn't on the agenda. She has too much work to do before she turns into a pumpkin. And that damn recurring nightmare is back. Good thing sleep isn't a priority.

She lights up and inhales. Sensing Amber's hesitation, she exhales a long stream of smoke before muttering, "Out with it."

Amber sighs. "You know Shane's an idiot—whoa." She perks up. "Check out that car."

Olivia looks across the lawn. A pristine, two-door Lincoln Continental pulls up to the curb and rolls to a stop within a hairbreadth of Amber's red Tesla. The driver, an elderly woman with her nose in the air to peer over the dash and her seat pulled forward enough to kiss the steering wheel, shifts the car into park, leaving the engine to idle.

Amber whistles. "Wow. That car's mint. '77 or '78?"

"Something like that," Olivia says absently, watching the people inside the metallic blue antique. There's a kid in the front passenger seat. He can't be older than fourteen. Probably the woman's grandson. They stare blatantly at Olivia and Amber through the open passenger window.

"Are you having a yard sale?" the woman asks.

Laughter bubbles from Amber. "Take the lot of it. It's yours," she says for Olivia's ears only.

Olivia's heart pounds wildly. There's something familiar about the boy. She nudges Amber's thigh, a warning to behave. "No, sorry. Cleaning house."

The woman nods, then murmurs a few words to her passenger. The boy gets out of the car, slides on a backpack, and shuts the door. The woman waves and, after backing up, pulls away from the curb.

"Where's she going?" Olivia asks, alarmed.

The car crawls to the end of the street and turns the corner.

"Did she just leave that kid?"

"Maybe he's a neighbor," Amber says.

Maybe, but doubtful. Olivia hasn't seen him around here.

The boy turns, thumbs tucked under the shoulder straps, and looks up at them on the porch. His chin quivers and Olivia swears his legs tremble.

She inhales sharply. He isn't a neighbor. The brown hair under the flat-billed Padres cap, the almond shape of his eyes, and the slope of his nose, even the hesitant tilt of his head and body stance, tell her exactly who he is. This boy is identical to her baby sister, Lily, when she was his age. A sister Olivia hasn't seen in fourteen years.

"Josh."

CHAPTER 3

Olivia was in her fourth year at the Academy of Art University in San Francisco when her dad made an unexpected visit. Dwight took her to lunch at the Hog Island Oyster Co., and halfway through a bowl of buttery clam chowder, he told her Lily was pregnant.

Olivia was shocked. Her sister was only sixteen. She asked about the father. Did Lily have a boyfriend? Who was she dating? Olivia didn't know, and her mom never mentioned anything. She couldn't say whether Lily ever dated. She was on the JV swim team. She was setting state records. Her practice and travel schedules didn't permit time for dating.

But who was she to say Lily didn't have a secret guy? She and Lily weren't close, not like they had been when they were younger, before Lily drifted to Lucas, leaving a wedge between Olivia and her younger siblings.

Dwight rested a hand over Olivia's and the creased skin around his eyes softened. His gaze dipped to the table.

"What?" she asked, feeling a twinge in her chest.

"It's Ethan."

"I don't understand."

Dwight squeezed her hands. "Your Ethan. He's the father."

"No," she whispered. Her neck and chest heated, tingling in reaction to her denial. "No." She leaned back in her chair, putting as much distance as possible between her and what Dwight was telling her. The clam chowder sloshed around her stomach, making her nauseous.

How was this possible? she wondered, knowing exactly how possible it was. Convenient even. Ethan took the semester off to tend to his mom, who was recovering from an auto accident. He'd been home in Seaside Cove, only three blocks over from Lily.

"Did she seduce him?" Lily must be paying her back for not letting her move in with her and transfer to a high school in the city. Dwight shrugged and her throat tightened around a sour knot of disgust. "Did he take advantage of her?"

"Don't know. She wants to keep the baby."

Olivia looked past her dad's shoulder, not really seeing anything. "Are you going to let her?" She couldn't fathom watching Lily's belly swell knowing it was Ethan's child growing inside.

He shook his head. "I told her she needs to abort it. I can't afford to raise another child. You three kids about bankrupted me."

The whole family knew Lily was an accident, and it didn't take a brain booster pill to figure out the only reason Olivia had a little sister was because her mom didn't believe in abortion.

"What about Mom?"

"Oh, you know your mother. She still resents dropping out of college to support me. She doesn't want Lily to ruin her future. She's trying to persuade your sister to put the kid up for adoption."

"And Ethan? What does he want?" Because Olivia wanted to break up. She was falling apart as their relationship crumbled around them. Ethan's betrayal had cracked their foundation and she wanted to move out and far away before the roof came tumbling down. She'd never recover.

"You'll have to ask him."

She nodded absently, thinking of what she'd say. What could she say? The deed was done. So were they. The tears she'd been fighting not to shed filled her eyes. "Take me home, please."

Dwight did, and after he hugged her goodbye and promised to call later, she flipped open her phone and speed-dialed Ethan.

"How could you?" she accused. "And with Lily!"

"What are you talking about?"

"She's pregnant." She cried. Tears, fat like raindrops during a thunderstorm, fell. Despair swirled like the storm's violent winds. Here she thought Ethan got her. She'd felt happy with him when she didn't think she could after losing summers at the lake and Blaze. Could she have been any more foolish? She never should have opened up to him, or anyone given what Lily had done to her.

"And you think I what . . . slept with your sister?" He sounded appalled.

"Not think. Know. My dad just told me."

"And you believe him."

"Are you saying it's not true?" As if there was the remote possibility her dad lied to her. He loved her, which made her wonder if Ethan ever did.

He remained quiet for a long moment.

"Ethan," she sobbed. "Tell me it's not true."

"Why? You'd never believe me over him."

"Did you sleep with her?"

"No."

"Liar," she cried, beyond reasoning.

"See what I mean?"

"I hate you," she yelled into the phone. Too many people she loved had betrayed her. First Lucas, then Blaze, now Ethan. She should have known he'd eventually break her heart. But Lily? She never saw that one coming.

"Olivia," Ethan said, sounding defeated.

"Don't call again. I don't want to speak with you. I don't ever want to see you again. Goodbye, Ethan."

Years later she'd think back on their conversation and realize she should have waited to call him, given herself the chance to calm down after Dwight left. She also should have waited before she called Lily. But her thumb skimmed across the keypad and pressed the number combo for home. Charlotte answered.

"Mom," she said, her voice watered down with tears.

"Olivia, darling. Did your father tell you?"

"Yes."

"I'm sorry. This must be awful for you. It's difficult for everyone. We need to decide what to do before word gets out. Your father is mortified."

"Where is she?"

"Lily? She's resting."

"I want to talk to her." She wanted to grab her sister's shoulders and shake her until her neck snapped. What was Lily thinking? If she was upset at Olivia, there were other ways to get her revenge. Spray-paint her bedroom. Tear up her magazine collection like she'd done before.

"I'll let her know you called when she gets up. Be gentle with her. She just learned we aren't letting her keep the baby." Charlotte and Dwight couldn't legally force Lily to give up her baby. But if she wanted their financial and emotional support, she wouldn't have a choice.

Olivia ended the call and waited. And waited. Lily never called back. She didn't text either. When the call from her parents' landline finally came through, it was Charlotte. Lily had run away. Charlotte and Dwight had just returned from the police station after filing a missing persons report. Ethan was brought in for questioning, but he didn't have any leads either. The swim team was posting flyers. Everyone was looking for their little girl.

Olivia wanted to feel sad. She expected to feel worried, too. Lily was sixteen, pregnant, and alone. But she couldn't manifest any sympathy. Her tears were spent. She'd buttoned up her heart.

Less than a year later, she received her first annual letter from Lily. Inside the note card was a photo: Josh, his newborn face blotchy and puffy eyelids closed, swaddled in an infant blanket.

———

"Who's Josh?" Amber asks, piercing through the fog of Olivia's shock.

"Lily's son."

Amber stares at her before her mouth falls open. "Your sister Lily?"

Olivia nods. "Get out." Amber softly whistles, her gaze fixed on the boy rooted to the sidewalk.

Olivia snuffs out her Marlboro on the concrete step and stands. Amber joins her, setting aside her wineglass.

"What's your name?" Olivia asks to be sure she's right, that he's her nephew.

Her heart beats faster over that thought. Nephew. Never in a million years did she expect to meet Lily and Ethan's son. "Your name," she repeats when he stares blankly at her. "Who are you?"

His mouth parts and after a few beats, he says, "Josh."

She exhales roughly, feeling shaky. She shouldn't have snuffed out her cigarette. What the heck is Lily's son doing here? And where is she? Olivia looks in the direction the Continental went, waiting for Lily to appear like a desert mirage.

"Come here, Josh." He doesn't budge. She waves her hand, beckoning him closer. "It's okay, come here."

His feet shuffle as if he's debating what to do. He glances from her to Amber and back. His hands tighten on his backpack straps and he takes a tentative step, then another. And another. He stops a few feet from them.

Now that he's closer, Olivia hungrily absorbs his features in the waning evening light. Hazel eyes watch her closely, inspecting. A scattering of freckles dusts his nose bridge, same as they did when she and Lily were his age. Olivia covered hers with a thick layer of foundation during her tween years. She hated her freckles. They look sweet on Josh. He's a good-looking kid. Reminds her of Lucas.

Jesus. Lucas.

Wait until he hears about Josh.

After Lily ran away, Olivia hounded Lucas for details about what exactly went down. He wouldn't tell her. He flat-out refused. Ever since, they haven't discussed Lily. The few times Olivia brought up their sister in conversation, Lucas retreated. He'd disappear into himself or he'd blow her off, ignoring her texts and declining her calls, which wasn't unusual. Ever since he was sixteen and spent six months in juvenile hall, Lucas has been unreliable. Unpredictable, too.

Josh adjusts the pack on his shoulders. His mouth opens and closes and then he scowls, his nostrils flaring with a rapid expulsion of air. Worry wrinkles the narrow band of forehead under the bill of his cap. He looks at Amber.

"What?" she asks, sounding as confused as Olivia feels with his funky facial twitching. He's frustrated about something.

He points at himself. "Josh." He then points at Amber.

"Oh." She smiles. "I'm Amber."

He points at Olivia next.

"Olivia. I'm your mom's sister," she says. "Your . . . aunt." She struggles with the title. It's the first time she's ever referred to herself that way.

The tension in Josh's expression eases instantly. His eyes rapidly blink and Olivia worries he'll burst into tears. As much as she hates who his parents are, she wants to bundle him up and tell him he's safe with her.

Amber thrusts out her hand. "I'm your aunt's friend. Nice to meet you, Josh."

He doesn't reach for Amber's palm, just stares at it. Olivia's chest tightens with worry. Why is he here alone?

"Where's your mom?" she asks.

"I . . ." He stalls.

"Who's that woman who dropped you off?" Olivia looks toward the end of the street again, miffed the lady took off without telling her when Lily would be here, or how long Josh intended to stay.

Josh shrugs.

"You don't know where she is?"

He extends his arm, thumb out. Does he mean what she thinks he means? He hitchhiked his way here? That would explain why Lincoln Continental lady drove off without an explanation. But does Lily know? What if Josh ran away from home?

Wouldn't that be the icing on their dysfunctional family cake? Josh ditching his mom like Lily ran away from them.

Josh's feet shuffle. He looks around her yard, his gaze landing on the front door.

"Why did you come here?" To her house of all places. They've never met.

Josh looks at the ground.

"Is there anything you want to tell me?" she asks. How long is he staying? Where does he plan to go? What's she supposed to do with him? Why the hell isn't he talking? She snaps her fingers below his face. "Josh. Where is your mom?"

"Gone."

Gone? What's that supposed to mean?

"Did she leave you? Or . . . Is she dead?"

Josh's face pales, and Olivia has to fight her anger. How dare Lily die on her before she can beg Olivia for her forgiveness. No, not possible. Lily isn't dead. Olivia refuses to believe that.

"Jeez, Olivia. Take it easy," Amber whispers.

"Sorry." She rakes her fingers through her hair. Nails scrape her scalp. She takes a breath, waits a beat. She didn't mean to frighten him. What Lily and Ethan did was unforgivable, but Josh doesn't deserve her rage. She tries again, tempers her voice. "Did your mom leave you?"

"Don't . . . know." He chews his bottom lip, his gaze shifting around the yard.

Amber nudges her arm. "You're scaring him."

He glances over his shoulder toward the road. Amber's warning sinks in and Olivia swears. "Hey, it's okay. Everything's cool. Why don't you come inside? You can hang out until your mom gets here." She gives Amber a what-am-I-supposed-to-do-with-him look.

Amber comes to her rescue. "Are you hungry, Josh?"

Josh looks at Amber with interest.

"Do you want something to eat?" she clarifies.

"Yes." He looks eagerly between them and mimes eating a hamburger.

"The kid wants a burger."

Olivia taps her finger on her thigh. She wants a smoke. She also needs food. She's been working on deadline and aside from spoiled takeout, her fridge is bare. "Sorry, Josh." She hates to disappoint him. "I don't have—"

"Yes, she does," Amber interrupts with a big smile. "Aunt Olivia has hamburgers."

"I do?"

"DoorDash. He's had a long day. Haven't you?" Josh frowns, cocking his head, then nods. Amber elbows Olivia's ribs. "Give him what he wants. He'll feel much better after."

"All right then. Today's your lucky day." In more ways than she can count. Because by some miracle or fluke, her thirteen-year-old nephew found her.

CHAPTER 4

Olivia invites Josh to follow her and Amber inside the house. He wanders into the living room, scratching his head, leaving the cap askew, the bill tilted. His gaze pans from the floor to the ceiling and along the walls, absorbing everything in between.

The room is a disaster from her whirlwind scrub of Blaze's belongings. Books lie askew on the shelves. Half her Blu-ray collection tumbled to the floor when she picked through movies, dropping Blaze's in a box she dumped out front. Most of the decorative couch pillows are on the floor. She tossed those to pick up his stuff that fell into the cracks: the sock without a mate, the shirt tossed over the couch back that somehow weaseled its way behind the cushion, the used condom that never got tossed because they were both too tired to make it to the bathroom afterward. That one grossed her out. He said he'd taken care of it.

Josh crosses the room to the built-in bookshelf and straightens his cap. The hair covering his nape is a soft brown, several shades lighter than hers, with auburn highlights. He wears his maroon hoodie unzipped and sleeves pushed up past his elbows. There's an image on his graphic tee underneath, but she can't make out what. His hands are in the way. He grips his backpack as if the straps are armrests on an airplane seat and he fears flying. His black skinny jeans, fashionably frayed at the knees, remind her of something Blaze would wear. His black sneakers look new. That's good. Lily doesn't neglect the poor kid, unless Josh stole them. Heck, Lily could have stolen them. She was sixteen and pregnant. Doubtful she went to college. Did she even complete high school? A twinge of guilt for thinking harshly of Lily flickers to the forefront, its flame bright, impossible for her to ignore. Maybe she can't afford clothes for him. She must have struggled to make ends meet. Maybe she still is struggling, and that's why Josh took off?

Or maybe she never did struggle and had help. Ethan honored Olivia's request. He never called her back. He could have been supporting Lily all this time.

Speaking of Ethan, where is he? The last she heard, he's living in Los Angeles but spends more time abroad as a travel journalist. Could Lily be with him now? What if Josh is running away from Ethan?

Olivia's anxiety mounts. She watches him meander around her living room like he's unable to stand still. There are too many unknowns about him, and Olivia is starting to regret she didn't run after Lily when she ran away, or that she didn't try to find a way to reply to her annual notes. Olivia doesn't have any idea about Josh's situation at home.

Josh takes interest in a stack of books she toppled. He stoops and selects one, a coffee-table type of California beaches she keeps for aesthetics over content. He hugs the book close like a security blanket. Okay, not the subject matter she'd expect would fascinate a teenager.

"Are you going to call Lily?" Amber asks. Her empty wineglass and half bottle of wine click together in her hand.

"I don't have her number." For the first time since Lily ran, she regrets the fact she doesn't. She has no way to reach her.

"What about Lucas or your parents?"

"I'd be surprised if they have it. We never talk about her. They don't know where she lives any more than I do."

"San Diego?" Amber taps her forehead to indicate Josh's Padres cap.

"Possibly." The annual note cards Lily sent with Josh's school photo never had return addresses. The postmarks changed every year, random locations along the western coast.

"Are you going to go to the police?"

"Why?" Olivia frowned.

"Lily could be missing."

Maybe that's why Josh came. He needs her help.

She chews her bottom lip. The first inklings that something isn't right drizzle like raindrops, the stain spreading, beckoning her to do something. Amber's right. Highly doubtful Josh's visit is a social call.

"I probably should." But she wants to give Lily the chance to show. She could be on her way at this moment. And Josh needs food. He'll feel more settled and less like a skittish kitten once he's eaten. He'd hide under the sofa if he could.

Olivia taps open the DoorDash app. "Any food allergies, Josh?"

He watches her curiously, then shakes his head.

"What do you want on your burger? Cheese? Grilled onions? Mayo?"

"Yes."

"Yes to what? All of it?"

He nods.

"Mushrooms? Pickles? Tomatoes?"

He nods again.

"Slugs?"

His face draws a blank. After a beat he grimaces.

"Noted. No slugs." She cracks a smile and is almost certain the corner of his mouth twitches. For a moment there, she wondered if he was understanding any of what she asked or if he was saying yes to everything. She frowns at his customized order. He understands her but is slow to comprehend. His speech is broken. Does he have a speech disorder? Was he born this way?

Amber points at the menu on her screen. "Get fries, the curly kind. Kids like fries."

Olivia adds fries to the order. "Want anything?"

Amber shakes her head. "I'm meeting Mike at the hospital cafeteria."

"Sounds romantic," Olivia says of Amber's dinner with her boyfriend, Michael Drake, an emergency physician. "When does he get off?"

"Late. But I'm going home after. I have a ton of emails waiting and a client's books to balance." Amber gave up on her art major and transferred to San Francisco State their junior year to study accounting. "Walk me out?"

"Sure. Josh?" He turns around, the book plastered against him. She almost blurts that he can keep it. She won't take it away. It's okay to chill. He's safe here. Thank god that old woman brought him here and didn't kidnap him. What if that Golden Girl was a human trafficker? Josh could have been forever lost to Lily. As much as Olivia doesn't want to admit it, she felt empty after Lily vanished. Her pang of loss was minuscule to what Lily would feel if Josh disappeared. She doesn't have firsthand experience, but friends with kids have told her nothing compares to a mother's pain when her child is wounded, or god forbid, dies.

She gestures at the couch. "Make yourself comfortable. Bathroom's down the hall if you need it, second door on your left. I'll be right back."

He ignores the couch invite and walks straight into the kitchen.

Olivia gives Amber a look and Amber grins. "Told you he was hungry."

"Apparently." She takes the glass and bottle from Amber, sets them aside, and follows her outside. "Did you really hook up with Shane?" she asks when they reach Amber's Model 3, the rear bumper fortunately unscathed from the Lincoln Continental near miss. Still, Amber checks for damage.

"The nephew you've never met drops on your doorstep and that's what's on your mind?" She runs her hand along the bumper.

"Not entirely. But I understand you sleeping with Shane a whole lot better than the kid hanging out in my kitchen."

Amber opens the driver's-side door. "Go easy on him. He looks like he's had a rough day. You both have."

Olivia's gaze slides to the house with her nephew inside. Nephew. How strange for him to be here. She looks at her lawn and wonders when Blaze will return, kind of wishing he were back already. She'd hate for someone to swipe his McIntosh turntable and record collection on her watch. But he'd help her figure out what to do with Josh. Then she remembers why she overreacted. She doesn't need him. She doesn't need anyone.

"It was one night, by the way. Way before Mike." Amber settles into her car. She pulls a face and Olivia can't help grinning.

"I can't believe you got it on with Shane."

"I can't believe he told Blaze."

"I can. Shane's an idiot."

"Agreed. He also misplaces his phone a lot. Leaves home without it, drops it in the toilet, those kinds of things."

"What a doofus."

Amber starts her car. "Shane's borrowed my phone before."

"Did he text Macey from it?"

"No, but he texts like it's his phone."

Guilt slides through Olivia like an unwanted garden pest, eating away at her conscience. Blaze was telling the truth and she refused to listen. She didn't want to hear that he didn't cheat because she'd have to acknowledge what he was feeling. He was falling in deep with her. She sensed it last night as they lay in bed, their bodies bathed in moonlight and sweat.

He'd arrived drunk after an evening out with Shane. As his hands roamed in all sorts of glorious places, he whispered promises that had her fisting the sheets and eyeing her bedroom door as if she were looking for a means of escape. He wanted to move in permanently. He wanted more than a few dates a week and a night's roll. Did she want kids? They should adopt a dog.

Olivia had gasped and almost bolted for the door. But this was Blaze. Fun, playful, knows-how-to-make-her-belly-laugh Blaze. Alcohol was coursing through his system, playing tricks in his head, loosening his tongue. She closed her eyes and willed herself to relax. He wouldn't remember this in the morning.

Then Macey reacted to the photo Shane sent on Blaze's phone, and the hurt and rejection from years past poured into her like gushing water from a toppled dam. She'd reacted irrationally, especially after what he shared with her last night. She should have known he'd betray her again. Is that why he rambled on while they kicked around the sheets? He felt guilty?

She closes Amber's door and waits for her to ease down the window. "Chat tomorrow?"

Amber smiles. "Definitely. I want details about both guys, the one in the kitchen and the one who'll be back to collect his stuff. Good luck tonight." She drives off, her musical laughter trailing behind.

Olivia looks back at the house, the living and dining room windows ablaze with light against the backdrop of night, and thinks how surreal her day turned. Lily and Ethan's son is up there. What is she supposed to do with him? Maybe she should drop Josh off at Lucas's. He was closer to Lily toward the end before he went to juvie, and Josh might connect more with his uncle than her.

Her phone pings with an incoming text. She glances at the screen. Her Dasher has picked up her order and is on his way.

She returns to the house. Josh is seated at the kitchen table peeling an orange. The rind is stacked in a neat pile in front of him. He breaks apart the orange and shows Olivia a slice. "Peach."

Olivia stares openly. Josh watches her expectantly. She clears her throat, wondering if he's messing with her. "Uh, you know that's an orange, right?"

His chest deflates. He stares at the orange slice with loathing. His nostrils twitch, something that her brother Lucas does when he's angry.

With sudden movement, Josh throws the slice into the sink. The rest of the orange follows.

"Hey, what's wrong with you? That's perfectly good fruit." Olivia collects the orange, leaves it on the counter.

Josh surges to his feet, the chair scraping loudly on hardwood. *New* hardwood. Dammit, her floors are less than a year old. She moves the chair aside and runs her foot over the planks, checking for scratches. Josh scoops up the rind and turns full circle, searching for something. He looks at Olivia, shows her the peel. "Keys?"

"Keys?" She frowns, confused, and he gestures with the orange peel. Her stomach twists with unease. She rubs her forehead. "I don't understand what you mean. You can't have my keys, and throw that away."

He frowns. "Throw," he says, slowly.

"Yes, throw it away," she repeats, cocking her head. "Are you looking for the trash?" She points at the peelings. "Trash?"

A light bulb goes off in his expression. "Trash. Yes."

"Well, we compost around here. The bin is under there." She points at the cabinet under the sink and Josh's face twists up. "Here, it's under here." She opens the cabinet in a rush and shows him the small composting bucket. He dumps the orange peel and backs up, turning away from her as he wipes his face with his sweatshirt sleeves.

She releases a long, ragged breath of relief—she deciphered what he wanted—but then her gaze meets his. His eyes shimmer. Hers widen with apprehension. "Whoa. What's wrong?"

"Hit . . . my . . ." He glances away and drags a hand over his damp eyes.

"Hey, hey. It's okay. What did you hit?" She didn't catch that last part.

He taps his head.

She shirks back. "You hit your head?" She rubs at her throat, trying to make sense of what he's telling her. "When?"

"Before . . . back."

"Before you got here?"

He nods. "Back . . . long before . . . here."

Long before here? She frowns. "You mean you hit your head a while ago?" He nods. "Okay, wow." She backs up and leans against the counter. "Is that why you confused the orange with a peach?" She gestures at the partially eaten fruit.

He nods. "Confuse words. Hard to drive . . . fumble . . . *fuck*." Olivia blinks at the out-of-the-blue f-bomb. He presses his lips tight and exhales roughly through his nose. "Find," he says, finally, and his shoulders droop.

Olivia tries to assemble what he's told her. "It's hard for you to find words?" He nods, his chin tucked into his chest, and she wants to scream at Lily for losing sight of her son.

The poor kid. The simple act of talking must be a mountain of a road bump. Embarrassing, to say the least, given the way he seems to want to curl into himself.

What condition would cause him to confuse words? She'll have to look that up. She could call Mike, which did make her wonder . . . "Do you need a doctor?"

His eyes widened and he shook his head hard.

"Well, you let me know if you do. Okay?"

He shrugs, his head hanging low.

"Here, sit down," she says, feeling sorry for him. She fixes his chair, pats the seat. He can calm down while she gets her own nerves under control. He settles into the chair and she backs away, her hands shaking. She's so unprepared for this. Kids are alien to her. She's never interacted with them let alone carry on a conversation. And this kid can barely get a word out.

Keeping her hands busy, she washes Amber's glass, willing the trembling to subside.

As the wine residue rinses away, a flicker of fear finds its way inside. Josh said Lily was gone. If he's mixing words, he could have meant exactly what Olivia asked out front. Lily is dead.

The sponge drops with a splat in the sink. Olivia has resented Lily for years, but she never wished she'd die. In the back of her mind, she reasoned she'd see her again one of these days. She'd eventually get the chance to let Lily know how much her sister hurt her.

Will she ever come to terms with Lily's demise? Can she without closure? And what is she supposed to do with her son?

She grabs the sponge and squeezes out the water. If something has happened to Lily, she'll have to track down Ethan, because the one thing harder than looking at and talking to his son, knowing Josh or a boy like him could easily have been hers, would be raising him.

The doorbell rings and Olivia startles. Josh tenses, his eyes on the front door like a cat primed to bolt.

"It's only dinner," she says, drying her hands while willing her racing heart to ease up on its drumroll. His gaze moves apprehensively between her and the front door. He slides his legs out from under the table and grabs his backpack. Taking a cue from Amber, she simplifies her words, gestures with her hands. "Food. Burgers." She mimes eating, pointing at the door.

Strained lines leave his face and his body molds to the chair.

"Be right back."

She gets the food and divvies out their burgers and fries. Aside from a few complimentary grunts from Josh, they eat in relative silence. Josh devours his cheeseburger. Olivia picks at her fries, wondering if this is the first meal he's eaten today. Her phone pings with a text to rate her Dasher and she gets an idea.

"Have you called your mom to let her know you're here?"

He shakes his head.

"Do you have a phone on you?"

He bites into a fry and shakes his head again.

That's unfortunate.

"Here. Use mine." She slides her phone across the table. "Give her a call. She must be worried." Lily ran away because she wanted to keep her baby. Either Josh ran away on his own, or something happened to her so they were separated. Otherwise Olivia imagines Lily wouldn't let Josh from her sight, not with his condition.

He stares at her phone.

"Go ahead," she encourages. She taps the screen, prompting him to act.

He frowns and Olivia tilts her head. "Do you know her number? You know, her phone . . . number." She slows the pace of her words but his frown deepens.

"Yes," he says.

"Great! Call her." She inches the phone closer.

He digs into his cheeseburger in no apparent rush to call. All right. She'll try another tactic. She picks up the phone. "Give me her number. I'll call her."

He sends her an empty look, so she mimes dialing and talking on the phone. She looks at him expectantly. "What . . . is . . . your . . . mom's . . . number?"

He sets down his burger and counts on his fingers. His mouth forms shapes. She watches, dumbstruck he has difficulty with numbers, too. "Five . . . nine . . ." He stops. His hands drop. He stares at his food.

"And?" she prompts.

He averts his face. His expression is tight but it doesn't stop his chin from quivering.

"Josh," she says, trying not to sound intimidating. "Did you forget her number?"

He stares at the floor. She taps the corner of her phone against her chin. He might not remember Lily's number, but the fact he tried to give it to her so she could call tells her Lily isn't dead. Otherwise, why would he bother?

36

She wants to melt with relief onto the table. "Where is she?"

He shrugs.

"Can you tell me then why you're here? How did you find me? Who was that woman who dropped you off?"

Josh presses his lips tighter after each question until they've lost all color.

Her own frustration mounts. How can she help him if he doesn't at least try to answer her? "Josh—"

"No."

"Look—"

"No!" He covers his ears and squeezes his eyes shut. "No, no, no."

"Okay, okay. No more questions." Her heart races up her throat, anxiety rising with it, heightening her fear that something terrible has happened to Lily.

Leaning back in her chair, she glances at the microwave clock. It's late. He's tired, and she has work to do. With any luck Lily will be here by morning, or Josh will come around. He'll tell her what happened. Otherwise she's calling the police. Or Lucas. Someone is bound to know what's going on.

Josh lowers his hands and opens his eyes. "Thank . . . you."

She sighs, feeling small because she keeps upsetting him. She slides her phone aside and stuffs a cold fry in her mouth. "You're welcome." His lip twitches as if he's fighting a smile and in him, she sees Lucas. How vibrant was Josh before his accident? Was he like Lucas was as a kid, a rebellious jokester you couldn't help but love? She wishes she'd met Josh before today.

CHAPTER 5

Summer of '97

Olivia was up early, the gray dawn sky visible through the trees. Birds chattered, flitting around the branches. A thin coat of dew sheened the metal dock, the air damp and crisp. She wore a sweatshirt to ward off the chill. As soon as the sun broke over the lake, warming the earth, she would ditch the layer, tossing it over a deck rail until the evening when the temperature dropped and stars brightened. From sunup to sundown, she spent her days in her bathing suit. But not today. It was the first full day of their third six-week summer break at the Whitmans' cabin. This morning Mr. Whitman was taking them on a survival hike, a mandatory excursion if she, Blaze, Lucas, and Tyler wanted to hike in the surrounding forest without him or Mrs. Whitman.

Olivia sat in the hammock, her legs dangling over the side, a sketch pad in her lap. While waiting for the boys to finish breakfast, she'd started drawing Lily as a baby but added a cape and metal wristbands. Her Lily could fly. She was stronger than any of them put together. And her temper tantrum screams could fight evil by breaking windows.

She giggled. Lily didn't need super screams to shatter glass. Her fit last night when she'd learned she couldn't hike with them rattled their ears. Olivia stuck a pinkie in her ear and wiggled it around. Her eardrum still itched. Lily had shrieked directly in her ear when she carried her little sister around, patting her back, trying to calm her down while Mrs. Whitman tried to assure Lily they'd have just as much fun waiting for Olivia and the boys to return.

Olivia toed the ground with her brand-new hiking boots, rocking back and forth. Dwight bought her and Lucas pairs after she blew out her sneakers three weeks into last summer's stay.

The back door slid closed and Mr. Whitman bounded off the deck shouldering an overstuffed backpack. Blaze, Lucas, and Tyler, wearing the ratty old T-shirts Mr. Whitman gave them because he had plans for the shirts and didn't want them ruining their own, followed like weary soldiers who'd been up all night. Lucas hadn't bothered to comb out his cowlicks. She could see a line of white scalp on the back of his head from where his hair swept to the side.

"Ready, Olivia?" Mr. Whitman asked as he passed her on the way to the shore.

"Ready!" She tossed aside her pencil and pad of paper and started to get up. Blaze launched himself onto the hammock, knocking her back. He hugged her waist, keeping her in the hammock.

"It's too early," he whined. "Tell him we want to go tomorrow. He'll listen to you, Livy."

"No way." She, too, was exhausted. They'd stayed up well past midnight, playing card games and giggling in the center ring of their tent star. But she was also excited for this adventure. She read a survival guide on the way up yesterday just for this hike.

"You're mean." Blaze squeezed her tight, holding on as she tried to maneuver her way out of the hammock. His Aquafresh toothpaste breath tickled her nose. She loved the scent on him. She asked her mom to buy the same toothpaste when they returned home last summer. It reminded her of Blaze and the good times they had on the lake.

She smiled brightly.

"What?" Blaze asked, eyes narrowing. He was wise to wonder if she was up to something. She dug her fingers into his ribs. He grunted and squirmed, squeezing into a ball, fending her off with his hands. "Stop!"

Olivia laughed and rolled off the hammock. The sun had popped through the trees and she was already feeling warm. She pulled off the sweatshirt, dropping it on Blaze's face, and straightened the large shirt Mr. Whitman had loaned her.

"Get over here, kids," Mr. Whitman ordered, lake water lapping the heels of his boots.

Blaze groaned and rolled from the hammock. The four of them circled his dad like hatchlings waiting to be fed. She loved how engaged the Whitmans were with their kids, so unlike her parents, who never seemed to have time to interact with them. Except her dad. He spent time with her, usually in his office while he worked. He'd let her sit at his desk and do her homework while he paced the room, making calls.

"Only two rules for today," Mr. Whitman began, showing them two fingers. "Listen and follow orders. You'll learn, we'll have fun, and we'll be back before lunch."

"Yes." Lucas pumped his arm. "Dibs on the blue kayak."

"You had it yesterday," Tyler whined.

"Because I'm older, and you're a baby." He knocked Tyler's shoulder.

"Am not." Tyler knocked him back. He was a year younger than Lucas but just as tall.

Mr. Whitman cleared his throat. "Listen up, kids. I left five empty water bottles lying around. Go find them."

It was a race. They took off in four directions. Blaze found a plastic bottle first. Olivia located one in the bushes. They all met back at the shore.

"Everyone have their pocketknives on them?" Mr. Whitman had given them the knives at dinner last night with explicit instructions on how to use them. Olivia pulled hers from her shorts pocket. They showed him their knives. "Good. We're going to cut the bottles here and make cups." His finger marked a spot on the bottle. "Watch me first." He cut off the base, about a third of the way up the bottle. "See? You try."

Tyler needed help. Lucas took a while, but he finally made a jagged cut. Olivia and Blaze finished at the same time and showed Mr. Whitman their cups.

"What are we doing with these?" Olivia asked.

"Who knows what a compass is?"

Olivia's hand shot up. "It's a dial used for navigation and direction," she answered. She remembered the definition from her guide.

"And what are those directions?"

"North, south, east, west." Blaze yawned. Olivia jabbed him in the stomach midyawn and he gasped. Lightning quick, he snatched her finger and dragged it up to his nostril as if he were going to pick his nose with her finger.

"Ew." She snatched her hand away and he laughed.

"Kids, over here," Mr. Whitman hollered. "Pay attention. Watch this." He filled his plastic cup with lake water and dropped in a bay leaf he'd pulled from his pocket. "Your turn."

They filled their cups and he gave them each a leaf.

"Now for the fun part." He gave them each a sewing needle. "Rub one end of the needle up and down on your shirt one hundred times."

"Whaaat?" Lucas frowned at his needle.

"One hundred times. Let's count out loud."

After a round of funny looks, they did. They rubbed and counted.

"Drop the needle on the midvein of your leaf." He demonstrated, then waited for them to do the same. "What do you notice?"

"My leaf floats," Tyler said.

"They all do, dork." Blaze rolled his eyes with a snort.

"True. What else?"

Olivia frowned and looked at everyone's cups of dirty water. Their leaves pointed in the same direction. She recalled something she'd read in her survival guide and gasped. They'd just magnetized their needles. "They're pointing north."

"Exactly." Mr. Whitman high-fived Olivia and she beamed.

"Smarty." Blaze elbowed her.

Olivia smiled, her insides warming. She looked shyly at her floating leaf. It looked like a canoe and she imagined she and Blaze rowing across the lake this afternoon.

"If this end of the leaf is north and this south, in which direction is the cabin?"

"West," Lucas said.

"Close. Blaze?"

"Southwest."

"Right, son. Remember that, kids. If you're hiking the trails across the street like we're doing and get lost, make a compass. Walk southwest and you're bound to reach the cabin, or close to it. Save your needle, leaf, and cup, but dump out the water. Let's go hike."

Lucas smacked the base of Tyler's cup. The cup flew from Tyler's hand and water splashed his face.

"Lucas," Tyler yelled. He searched the ground. "I can't find my needle," he whined.

"Don't be a baby. Take mine. I don't want it."

Tyler pocketed Lucas's needle and leaf.

"You're going to need those later today, Luc."

He blew his lips, making a raspberry noise, and leaned on Olivia's shoulder. "Nah, I'll just follow you."

"Love you, Luc, but you're on your own." She pushed him off. After reading her survival guide, she couldn't wait to get started.

They followed Mr. Whitman past the cabin, with Mrs. Whitman and Lily waving from the deck and across the street. He took them on a narrow, overgrown trail. Every few hundred yards he instructed them to stack rocks, explaining they'd use them as guides on their way back. Mr. Whitman would stack his rocks, then start walking. Olivia quickly stacked hers before she'd lose sight of him, then take off after him. Once, before she could run off, she saw Lucas swing a stick like a baseball bat. He knocked over Mr. Whitman's rock pile.

"Knock it off, moron." Blaze yanked the stick from Lucas and threatened to punch him. Lucas ducked and ran ahead, chasing after Tyler and Mr. Whitman. Blaze tossed the stick aside. "I know this forest better than my asshole. Let's ditch them and take the canoe out."

Olivia shook her head. "Your dad will ground us for a week." Exactly what Mr. Whitman threatened when he announced their expedition and explained what would happen if they didn't cooperate. She didn't want to be stuck on the deck while everyone else played in the lake. Blaze impatiently tolerated his dad's adventures, but Olivia secretly loved them. Her parents never took time to interact with them on the level Mr. Whitman did. His activities were never dull in her mind.

Olivia ran ahead. Blaze groaned and jogged after her.

After twenty minutes of hiking, they reached a meadow with a creek. Mr. Whitman shared his trail mix and showed them how to filter the creek water so they could drink it. Using their pocketknives, they cut off a strip of material from their shirts. They placed one end of the shirt in the cup with dirty water elevated on a stone and the other end at the bottom of an empty cup.

"Give it one hour and you'll have a cup of fresh water."

"No way." Lucas looked disbelievingly at the contraption.

"Yes way." Mr. Whitman grinned and unzipped his backpack. "Who wants to learn how to build a fire?"

Four hands shot up.

For the next hour, Mr. Whitman taught them how to survive overnight in the woods, tips Olivia had learned in her guide but didn't fully understand. When their filtered waters were ready, much to Lucas's amazement, they boiled the water with the fire they'd made from an egg carton and twigs.

When it was time to return to the cabin, Mr. Whitman announced they were hiking back on their own, one at a time. And they had to keep at least one hundred yards between them, and they couldn't help each other.

"What if we get lost?" Lucas asked.

"Fill up your cups and use your compass."

"Bet you wish you didn't give Ty your needle," Blaze mocked.

"Shut up." Lucas folded his arms and scowled at the ground.

"You'll be fine," Olivia reassured.

Lucas looked at her like he didn't believe her.

"Olivia, you go first." Mr. Whitman pointed toward the trailhead. "Wait two minutes, then you go, Blaze."

Her eyes widened. She nervously looked at the trees edging the meadow. She'd truly be on her own.

"See you back at the lake." Blaze clapped her back, not at all acting afraid. She could do this. She grabbed her cup, filled it with water, and took off at a fast walk. The hike seemed longer returning, but Mr. Whitman had left stone markers at each fork. They helped her until she reached the markers Lucas knocked over, leaving a pile of stones. She had to use her compass. By the time she magnetized her needle, she could hear someone tromping through the brush behind her. She looked over her shoulder. Blaze was closing in.

He cupped his mouth and hollered, "You're slacking, Carson."

"You can't catch me. You're not allowed to."

"Rules, shmules," he yelled, gaining on her. "Dad won't know if you don't tell him." He started running.

Suddenly their hike was a race, because rules or not, Olivia was not going to let him pass her. She took off. Ten minutes later they burst from the trees, gasping and sweating. Her boots and calves were muddy, arms dusty and speckled with mosquito bites. But she won and couldn't help grinning and poking at him.

Blaze playfully smacked away her hands and pulled her into a stinky, sweaty hug. "Good job, Liv."

Tyler crashed out of the trees with a holler of delight. Several minutes later, Mr. Whitman arrived. His gaze skimmed over them and he looked back toward the woods. "Where's Lucas?"

Olivia and Blaze looked at each other and shrugged.

"Didn't see him, Dad."

It took another five minutes for Mr. Whitman to get seriously worried. He dropped his pack on the drive and went inside to see if Lucas had somehow reached the cabin before them.

Olivia chewed her thumbnail, unable to take her eyes off the trailhead.

"Maybe he twisted his ankle," Blaze suggested.

She shook her head. "Your dad would have passed him."

Mr. Whitman returned. "Let's backtrack," he told Blaze. "Olivia and Ty, wait here in case he comes back. Rhonda," he called up to his wife who'd come out on the deck with Lily. "Give us an hour. Lucas couldn't have gone far. But call the sheriff if he doesn't show up within thirty minutes."

"I will," she said.

"Livy, where's Luc?" Lily asked, kicking her legs between the deck rail slats.

"He's playing hide-and-seek," she said, not wanting to worry Lily. Her little sister would have another meltdown and Olivia didn't want to deal with her temper tantrum, not when she was worried about her brother. Where was he?

Mr. Whitman and Blaze disappeared into the forest. Ten minutes went by, then twenty and still no sign of Lucas. Olivia paced the driveway. She chewed the cuticles off her thumbs. Lily whimpered from her spot on the deck. She knew something wasn't right.

Five minutes before Mrs. Whitman was to call the sheriff, gravel shuffled behind Olivia. Someone poked her shoulder blade. She turned around and shrieked. "Lucas!"

"Where is everyone?" he asked like it was no big deal for him to suddenly show up.

Olivia hugged him. "Where've you been?"

"Hiding in the canoe. I was going to spook you guys but you were taking forever."

"You idiot!" She thrust him away from her. "We've been looking all over for you. We thought you were lost. Mrs. Whitman was going to call the sheriff."

"Why? I've been here the whole time."

"Oh, thank goodness." Mrs. Whitman came rushing down the steps. She hugged Lucas. "We were so worried."

Lucas grimaced, his cheeks reddening as he realized the joke he'd tried to play on them didn't go over well.

Mr. Whitman and Blaze returned an hour later, panicked. When they found everyone safe inside the cabin, and after Lucas explained he thought the trail was boring and made his own, cutting the distance in half so that he arrived before everyone else, Mr. Whitman knocked back a finger of scotch and grounded Lucas for twenty-four hours. The following morning, he took Lucas back on the trail and made him find his way home the right way, insisting he pay attention to the trail markers.

For the rest of their summer visit, Olivia was grateful Lucas didn't pull any more pranks, even though she knew he wanted to. But whenever he started to get that mischievous, rebellious look in his eye, Olivia glared at him. She didn't like him ruining their adventures. If the Whitmans couldn't trust them to be on their best behavior, Charlotte had told her, they wouldn't invite them back next summer. Olivia needed these summers at the lake. It was the only time she genuinely enjoyed herself. She felt like she was part of something. A real family.

CHAPTER 6

Olivia strips off her sheets that smell of Blaze and her insecurities, memories of summers at the lake lingering like his scent. But it's thoughts of Lucas that have her shaking the pillow so hard from its case that she almost knocks over her bedside lamp. Her brother was never reliable. Deep down she knows she can't count on him, but her fingers are crossed he'll step up and help with Josh when she calls him. He's Lily's son. That should motivate him.

A toilet flushes in the bathroom. Olivia looks toward the door and the unfamiliar sound where Josh is getting ready for bed. He's the first guest to use the spare room since the remodel. He reminds her of a lost puppy, all big feet, floppy hair, and baggy sweats. She found a pair of Blaze's in the dryer when she noticed Josh didn't have a change of clothes. He was going to sleep in his jeans.

If he was planning to run away, wouldn't he have packed smarter? He doesn't even have a phone. Can Lily afford one, or is she strict? Maybe she never gave him one. Or he could have lost it when he lost his mother.

Olivia needs to find her. Or, she thinks, her limbs feeling shaky, find out what happened to her.

Looking back at the empty bed she feels a little empty herself, like something, or someone, is missing. And she's not sure if the feeling stems solely from knowing Blaze won't be staying with her tonight, or if it arises from Lily. Her whereabouts are a mystery.

Making her way to the laundry room, she pauses outside Josh's room. The door is ajar, the bedside lamp on, dousing the room in soft light. Showered and dressed in her old Nine Inch Nails concert shirt and Blaze's gray sweats, Josh flips through the coffee-table book he's been attached to since he stepped into her house. He skims through the pages like he's glossing over the words and photos. Is he looking for something? What if he can't read? Can he even write? Her questions sound ridiculous about a thirteen-year-old, but if he mixes words and has trouble with numbers, he reasonably could have other issues, too.

Olivia eases away from the door so she doesn't burst in and bombard him with questions. She upset him earlier, and frankly, she's a little freaked he'll flip out again.

She starts a load of laundry and retreats to her office, where three life-size prints of her superheroes lord over her workstations: Ruby, Titian, and Dahlia, fully suited in their red-and-silver superhero outfits. Two sisters and a brother, each capable of wielding energy in their own way. They're close like she and her siblings used to be. And very protective of each other, in a way the Carson kids never were.

They should have been.

The thought fills her with remorse. Instead of waking her computer to tweak her panels and fine-tune her digital art frames, she veers to the cabinet behind the drafting table where she sketches her rough layouts and removes the well-worn Juicy Couture shoebox from the bottom drawer. Inside are Lily's letters, all twelve of them. They arrived every September without a return address, postmarked from various cities throughout the western states. Lily either moves around a lot or someone mails the letters on her behalf. She doesn't want to be found.

But Lily always found Olivia. Somehow, she learned that Olivia now owned their parents' first house. She always sent the letters here, and the current tenant kindly forwarded the letters to Olivia in San Francisco.

This year, the letter never came. But now that Josh is here, she wonders if there's a connection between his sudden arrival and the lack of a letter. What if Lily *is* missing? It explained why she didn't send one.

The letter and photo should have arrived two weeks ago, around Josh's birthday and the beginning of the school year when Lily would get Josh's school picture. At first, Olivia thought the letter was late. She reasoned her sister finally came to her senses and stopped shoving pictures of her and Ethan's little family in Olivia's face. Every year Lily would drift to the back of Olivia's mind, no more than an echo of a previous life, and then *wham*. A letter would arrive with Josh's latest photo, along with a note where Lily expounded on everything about their son. When he was younger, Josh loved to build forts and act out fantastical adventures, much the way they used to do summers at the Whitmans'. Josh's interests shifted to the outdoors as he entered his tween years. He spent most of his free time at the nearby skate park. Olivia has resented Lily for fourteen years. She's resented her parents and Lucas because nobody will talk about the stains that, according to Dwight, smeared her dad's reputation and ended any further chances of a political career. But she'll always remember the little girl who held her hand when she thought their mom was abandoning them that first summer at the lake house.

And her letters.

They're a constant reminder that her relationship with Lily isn't fractured. It's nonexistent. They're an annual reminder that Olivia seals herself off from everyone.

Because she's masochistic, she opens an envelope from the middle of the small pile and Josh's picture floats to the floor. Leaning over, fingers stretching as they walk along the hardwood, she picks it up. It's his third-grade school portrait. He was a cute kid. She remembers thinking when she first saw the photo that when he grew into his looks, he'd be striking like Ethan.

She wishes she could pick up the phone and call Lily. She also wishes, looking up at the prints on her wall—stunning and powerful—that she and Lily had a relationship different from what it was. But Lily wasn't the easiest person to get along with once the lake house summers ended. Olivia had gone from dating Blaze to Ethan, and Lily gravitated toward Lucas since Olivia was rarely around. They drifted further apart than their five-year age difference. But Lily did have a knack for spoiling Olivia's plans, and even her possessions. The prom dress incident was one event Olivia refuses to forget. It left enough of an impression that Olivia wonders what she'd done to Lily for her to act so carelessly with a dress she knew wasn't only expensive, but would be a highlight of Olivia's senior year.

She can picture the embellished light-blue dress she never had the chance to wear as clearly as Josh's arrival this evening. Floral embroidery decorated the plunging neckline bodice and floor-length A-line skirt. The dress sparkled, and when Olivia found the dress at a boutique online, Charlotte took her to the exclusive bridal shop on State Street in Santa Barbara.

For months the dress hung in her closet, tailored and pressed and ready for her big night. She was going with Ethan but secretly hoped Blaze, who would have Macey on his arm, would see what he'd lost. Her. But three days before the event, Olivia came home from school and found the dress missing.

Lily, who'd been gawking at the dress like an obsessed fan of Zac Efron, denied taking it, even though their mom had seen her in Olivia's room trying it on.

"I told her to take it off and put it back," Charlotte said, leaning into the mirror as she applied the mascara their neighbor Jean St. John had recommended. She jammed the wand into the bottle and lifted a shoulder. "You know how your sister is."

Charlotte thought Lily looked up to Olivia. Rather, she looked up to Lucas. Her sister was also a liar, because Olivia asked Dwight about the dress when she didn't find it in Lily's closet. Her dad tilted his head toward his home office window that looked out onto the yard, the garage with the overhead apartment visible to the side. "That wasn't you outside wearing a dress a bit ago?"

"No!"

"I swear I saw you a few hours ago, twirling about. You looked real pretty. You ran upstairs to the apartment. Blue dress, right?"

Olivia about died. "That wasn't me."

She ran across the yard and up to the one-bedroom apartment where the furniture left behind by her grandmother Val sat unused under a blanket of dust. Olivia stood in the center of the main room looking for where Lily could have hidden the dress. The sun shifted and light leaked through the blinds, spilling across the floor. A shimmer of blue across the room caught her eye.

"No!" Her sister had crammed her $350 prom dress into grandmother Val's antique shipping crate.

Olivia stumbled across the room and threw open the lid. She clutched the dress to her chest and inspected every square inch, from the sequined, embroidered bodice to the torn, mud-stained skirt hem. "Nooo. No, no, no." Fat, ugly tears dripped off her chin. How could Lily be so cruel? Prom was in two nights. There wouldn't be time to salvage the dress.

Olivia flew down the stairs and ran to Lily's room, the dress clutched in her arms. She threw open the door. "How could you?" She shoved the dress between them. "It's ruined!"

"I . . . I . . . ," Lily stammered. Colored pencils rolled from her hand onto the floor. Her eyes sheened.

"Explain yourself," Olivia yelled.

"I don't understand. I didn't do anything."

"You did. Daddy saw you."

"Saw me where?"

"Out back, dancing in the mud. In. My. Dress!"

"Not true. Daddy's lying. I swear." Her chin quivered, and for a moment, Olivia wondered if their dad did lie. Then she saw Lily's hands. She grabbed her wrist and twisted her hand so they could both see the dirt caked under Lily's fingernails.

"Liar!"

"It's paint," she cried.

"I don't believe you. I'll never believe anything you say, not when the proof is right there." She gestured at Lily's dirty hands and left the room.

Olivia slaps the lid on the pink shoebox. Something about that memory doesn't sit right with her. It feels different than before, but she can't pinpoint what. Nudging the box aside, she drags her keyboard forward. She's about to search the National Crime Information Center website to see if Lily or Josh have been reported as missing when a car door slams, drawing Olivia's attention away from her computer.

Blaze is back.

The urge to run outside and straight into his arms has her pushing away from her desk. She wants to tell him about Josh. She doesn't know the first thing about kids. He'll help her figure what to do. Then memory kicks in and her stomach knots. He's no longer hers. But he'll listen. He might even help, though she doesn't deserve it, not after the scene she made earlier today.

She meets up with him as he's loading a floor lamp into the bed of his truck.

"I'm surprised you came out," he says, his back to her.

So is she, but she regrets how she handled herself. It wasn't fair of her to accuse him of cheating. "I'm not looking to get back together if that's what you're thinking." The snarky comment slips free before she can tell him about Josh.

"Just to ship me off." His tone has an edge.

She cringes and gives him the shoebox she used to pack his toiletries. He drops the box in the truck bed. It lands with a thud.

She tries again to tell him about Josh. "Blaze—"

His hand is a stop sign between them. Words lodge in her throat. He leans against his truck and rests an elbow on the bed ledge. "You forgot how well I know you. You end things before you get too close."

"I do not," she says, defensive, even though that's exactly what she did.

"I should have seen this coming. We were getting close." His smile is sad. "Not everyone is out to break your heart, Livy."

She purses her lips and crosses her arms. "This never would have worked out. We shouldn't have gotten back together." Then she wouldn't have had to worry about her heart in the first place.

"I bought a ring, Liv."

Air rushes from her lungs. She shifts back a step.

"Didn't expect that, did you?"

No, she didn't. Her chest strains and she feels a weird scratchy sensation at the base of her throat. "I wish you didn't tell me."

He tilts his head. "Why?"

If she'd known he was this far into them she would have ended it sooner. She keeps her gaze fixed on the truck behind him.

He rubs the back of his neck and expels a long sigh. "I've never lied to you, and I'm not going to start now. Even in high school I didn't lie. I fucked up, that's for sure. It killed me seeing you with Ethan, knowing you were with him because I screwed up."

It was late in their junior year, after the Whitmans divorced and the doctors diagnosed Rhonda with lymphoma, that Olivia caught Blaze between the library stacks making out with Macey Brown. She broke up with him immediately, right there in the library. Blaze pleaded for months that he'd made a mistake. She almost reconsidered until he started dating Macey officially. Then she met Ethan.

"You never would have been with him if I hadn't hurt you." His face tightens and nostrils flare. He averts his face.

She stares at him. Where is this coming from? Blaze isn't an emotional guy. That's why she liked dating him. Everything about him was light and fun and wicked good. She should have known a casual relationship was impossible with their history.

"You had no clue," he says.

None that she was brave enough to admit being aware of. She shook her head.

"Were you aware at all of how much I care about you?" She looks at the ground. He laughs at himself. "Of course you were. Why else would you call it quits?"

"Blaze, I'm—"

"What would you say if I proposed right here?" He runs over her attempt to apologize.

"Now?" Her voice squeaks. Nervous perspiration dampens her armpits. She moves an involuntary step back.

"Thought so." A sad smile curves his full lips. "Until you get over whatever's holding you back, no one's got a chance with you. You won't let anyone in."

She doesn't want to. She has every intention of flying solo from here on out. But it still bites when he calls her out. "You're saying I'm a bad person."

"Don't twist my words."

"You think I'm horrible." She's the one who treated him horribly, but she can't stop the outpouring of accusations. She wants him hurting as much as she has in the past.

"Liv." He says her name with an air of impatience. He cups the back of her neck and brings her forehead to his lips. He kisses her and she wrenches from his grasp. "Hope you're happy."

"I am happy," she snarls. Emotions seethe. Forget it. She doesn't need his help with Josh. She just wants Blaze to leave so she doesn't feel worse than she already does. Get this over with already.

He just laughs. "See you around town." He pulls himself up into his truck and drives off.

"I'm not a bad person," she screams after his truck, flipping him off. He might be looking in his rearview mirror. "I am happy," she mutters when he turns the corner. She has a beautiful home with a resort-like backyard. She was incredibly successful in her career. She's pursuing her artistic aspirations as a graphic novelist and she's been quite successful with that, too. Her first book was a bestseller. With Blaze gone, she can get back to her life without the risk of someone screwing her over.

But dammit, she's on her own again with Josh. She rubs her cheeks. *Smooth, Liv.* She just keeps flying off the handle and landing in shit stew. Blaze's proposal blindsided her and she freaked out. Now she needs to resolve what to do with her nephew. By herself. She also wants a smoke. But she checks on the kid first.

Despite the late hour, light spills from under Josh's door. She lightly knocks, and when he doesn't answer she cracks the door to find him fast asleep. She tiptoes across the room to turn off the lamp and glances at his bare head. "What the—?"

He lies on his side, knees bent, and sheet pulled up to his waist. He snores gently and a frown mars his forehead as he dreams. The Padres cap rests on the pillow beside him, his hair flopped to the side revealing a crescent-shape surgical scar, the staple indentations visible.

She lurches upright and back. Whatever happened, Josh had hit his head hard enough to require surgery. Did he have a brain bleed? A hematoma? Given how pink the skin is, the procedure was more recent than what Josh described as "long before . . . here."

What happened to him?

CHAPTER 7

Day 2

Lucas arrives exactly at noon. Right on time.

"You look like death warmed over," he tells Olivia when she greets him at the door.

"I *was* going to offer lunch." She covers a yawn as she tightens the sash to the silk robe she wears over a hot-pink camisole and navy silk pajama bottoms. She was up late searching for Lily, who hasn't been reported as missing. Same with Josh. And neither one of them has any social media accounts. They're ghosts on the internet. Discouraged, Olivia closed the numerous open windows and spent the rest of the night finalizing her latest panel of illustrations, which she emailed to her editor at 4:30 a.m. She then slept through her 8:00 a.m. alarm only to be startled awake three hours later. Josh broke a dish. She spent the next hour pacing in front of the window, wondering when Lily would pull up. Would she just get here already?

"Where is he?" Lucas wipes his boots on the doormat.

She tilts her head toward the kitchen. "He's eating lunch." Opening the door wider, she lets her brother inside. She called him in a panic after she saw Josh's scar. She gave him the rundown on their nephew: his unannounced arrival, his strange communication quirks, the surgical incision on his head, and her opinion about the situation. Josh either ran away from Lily or something happened to their sister. Could she be in trouble? Should Olivia wake up Josh and take him to the ER?

Lucas didn't think so. Their nephew was walking and talking and Lily was bound to show. Lucas promised to swing by during his lunch hour when Olivia begged for his help.

"How much time do you have?"

He glances at his Fitbit. "I'm due back on the jobsite in forty-five."

"Do you want something to eat? I made grilled cheese and tomato soup." Not from scratch. She isn't that good in the kitchen. She poured the soup from a can and had to scrape a bit of mold off the cheese. Later, if she remembers, she'll put in a grocery delivery order.

"Gonna feed me after all? Nah, I'm good. Grabbed a sandwich on the way over." He shrugs off his paint-stained hoodie, drops the sweatshirt over the back of the living room couch, and pockets his keys. Blue paint speckles the backs of his hands, discolors the fingernails he's clipped to the quick. She resists insisting he scrub his hands before he touches anything. Dry, brittle cuticles hug the nail beds, an arid desert at the end of a plateau of tanned skin. Lucas makes his living as a commercial painter, a job far off course from the architect career he once wanted and neglected to pursue.

"Has he said anything more this morning?" he asks.

"Not really. He doesn't talk much." It doesn't come easy for him from what she's seen. He gets frustrated and clams up. "He spent the morning drawing. He's good, borderline gifted."

"Like Lily." He glances toward the kitchen. "She used to do that, remember?"

She nods. Lily would while away hours filling up the pages of her sketchbooks.

"What do you make of what I said last night?" she asks.

"About?"

"Lily. Do you really think she'll show?" she asks, feeling a sour twinge flip in her stomach like a fried egg in a pan. She's losing hope by the minute. Wouldn't her sister have been here by now? "She hasn't been reported as missing. I looked. I need to decide what to do with Josh."

Lucas lifts his hands and shrugs.

"You've got nothing?" Her spine bows on a sigh of frustration. Sometimes she wants to knock the indifference out of Lucas with his kayak paddle. "What if we can't find Lily? What if she doesn't show up or we never find her? What am I supposed to do with Josh? Put him in school? Do I call Ethan and tell him to come get his son? What if he doesn't want anything to do with Josh?"

Lucas puts up his hands. "Take a breath, Liv. Let me meet the kid and I'll give you my opinion."

"Don't say anything about his head," she says with an air of protectiveness she shamefully admits she hasn't felt in eons for her siblings.

"Even if it's staring at me like I have spaghetti coming out my nose?"

"He wears a hat, Luc. He's self-conscious. And go easy on him. He understands most of what we say, but he responds better when we talk slow and use fewer words."

"Whatever." He slides his hands into the side pockets of his paint-speckled canvas pants. "Do you still believe Ethan's the father?"

"Yes." She folds her arms. Dwight's never lied to her. When he dropped her off at her apartment after he told her Lily was pregnant, he said he had pictures of Ethan and Lily in Ethan's truck. He didn't bring them, unsure how Olivia would react to his news, but he offered to send them when he returned home. Give him a call and he'd email them. She never asked. Hearing about Lily and Ethan was heartbreaking, but seeing them together? She couldn't bear it.

His brow arches. "You gonna call him?"

She grimaces. She doesn't want to but will probably have to if she doesn't get a lead on Lily.

"Tell you what," Lucas says. "I'll meet Josh, see if I can get anything out of him. If not, you call Ethan."

"Fine."

"And he's not coming home with me." He gives her a look that he knows what she's been thinking.

"Come on, Lucas," she whines. "You and Lily were closer. And you're a guy. Josh will relate to you."

"You aren't the only one with a social calendar."

"That has nothing to do with it." Though she is busy with a looming deadline. "It's just—" She stops.

"What?"

She hugs her sides. "It's weird having him here."

"Because he's Ethan's son?"

"That and because of how everything went down." Josh is a reminder of the years she lost so much: summers at the lake because Lucas screwed up, the breakup with Blaze, Lucas returning home so different from when he left after serving time, Ethan cheating on her with Lily, and Lily running away. Those were Olivia's dark years.

Lucas scratches his scalp. "Look, I doubt he'll be here long. For all we know, Lily's right behind him."

"I hope you're right," she says, despite feeling that something is seriously wrong. The statistics she read last night aren't promising. Over six hundred thousand people go missing every year in the US alone.

Lucas toes off his work boots and nudges them against the wall. "Take me to him."

She leads Lucas into the kitchen ripe with smells of melted cheese and toasted bread. Josh sits alone at the large farmhouse table, hunched over a pad of paper. He's furiously sketching a townhouse complete with palms and shrubbery and a skateboard abandoned on the postage-stamp front lawn. He grips a blue graphite pencil and scratches at the paper with long, spirited strokes. His backpack rests at his feet, the pockets zipped closed, and for the first time since his arrival she wants to know what he has in there aside from art supplies. No phone, apparently. What about a wallet with an ID card? And where is the townhouse he's drawing? Is that his?

She stands opposite Josh and waits until he registers her presence. She doesn't want to startle him like she did this morning when she flew into the kitchen after the dish crashed, forgetting he was here in her semiawake stupor. He yelped. She screamed. She then spent several minutes reassuring him she wasn't upset about the broken dish, not really, since he apologized profusely. He helped pick up the larger fragments, then took the broom from her. He wanted to sweep up his mess.

Lucas rounds the table and stands behind Josh. He studies Josh's sketch, the details of which are stunning for his age, from the precise alignment of the asphalt shingles to the grain patterns in the wood porch railing. Lucas points at the roofline. "Great rendering, but your pitch is off. Your windows aren't to scale either."

Olivia glares at Lucas. Not a good introduction, bro.

Josh drops his pencil and leans back in the chair. He cranks his neck to look at Lucas. His gaze finds hers. Questions swirl in his mind. She can see them reflected in his eyes, taking shape in his mouth. He doesn't utter a word, only exhales lightly and tugs on his bottom lip.

Her throat clamps tight. He's so like his mom. Lily tugged her lip, too, when she was nervous.

"Josh, this is your uncle Lucas." She paces her words, hoping he understands.

Lucas thrusts out his hand. "Nice to meet you."

Josh stares at Lucas's hand hovering above the drawing. His eyes widen. For a split second she tenses, ready to put him at ease. But he slides his palm into Lucas's, surprising them both. Josh lifts his eyes, Lily's eyes. He smiles. Lily's smile.

Her chest tightens along with her throat as she realizes how much she's missed Lily. Has she always felt this way? Did she bury her longing so she didn't have to acknowledge that Lily's departure left a hole in her heart, despite her betrayal?

Lucas's cheeks inflate before he expels a loud breath. Her gaze meets his and she knows he sees the similarity, too. He pulls out a chair and sits. "He looks like her." Then as if remembering Josh has ears, he redirects his comment to their nephew. "You look like your mom."

Josh's mouth turns down. His fingertip nudges a pencil.

"I'm her brother. Let me show you." Lucas extends his leg and tugs his wallet from a deep front pocket. He opens the wallet and skims his thumb over bills, a foil condom (Really, Luc?), and receipts until his thumbnail snags on a photo. He shows Josh the picture.

Curious, Olivia peeks at it. A younger version of her, Lucas, and Lily stand on their dock, the wind whipping their hair, the bay's gray water in the backdrop. It's the last photo of the three of them, taken with their dad's Nikon. Charlotte gifted him photography lessons one year for his birthday and he took that camera everywhere. At the time of that photo, Olivia had come home for Christmas break. Lucas had already moved into the apartment above the garage and looked as apathetic as ever with his scowl. He and Dwight were not getting along since Dwight hadn't hired an adequate defense to keep Lucas out of jail like his friends. Olivia didn't know. Lucas wouldn't tell her. Lily is the only one smiling, like she has a secret. Olivia knows exactly what her secret was. She was sleeping with Ethan behind her back, and she is sure Lily was pregnant with Josh in the photo and had yet to realize. Lily ran away from home four months later. Olivia tore up her copy of the photo two weeks after that.

"You still have this?" she asks, amazed Lucas has been carrying it all this time. How sentimental, and so unlike him, given how he feels about their family. They look so young in the picture, back when everything had started to implode. Lucas had returned home after serving time for shoplifting. Their father had to cancel his third campaign for Congress because of the bad press. And Lily was on her way to becoming a statistic as a teenage mom.

"Yep. Here." He gives the photo to Josh. Lucas points to each of them. "That's your aunt Olivia, me, and your mom. You look like her, same chin and eyes."

Josh looks at the picture for a long time before returning the photo. "Where?" he asks, looking at her expectantly.

"That was taken at your grandparents' house, where your mom grew up."

"No, where?"

"Seaside Cove, about ten miles from here." Olivia points west.

"Where?" Josh says with more force.

"Do you mean where is your mom?" She looks at Lucas. "We're hoping you can tell us."

Lucas slides the image into his wallet and tucks it back into his pocket. "Is she coming to get you?"

Josh's face is blank.

"Did she send you here?"

He shakes his head. Olivia and Lucas share a look. "So, she doesn't know you're here?"

He shrugs.

"Where did she go?" Lucas asks.

"Gone," Josh says.

Lucas's brows lift. "Gone where?"

Josh tugs his lip.

"Where'd she go?"

"Gone," Josh repeats.

"Yeah, but where?"

"Gone . . . gone. Gone!" He wipes his arms in front of him.

Olivia grasps the chair and whispers, "He thinks she's dead." His eyes shine with fear, and her body tingles with it. Why would he have tried to give her Lily's number last night if he knows she's not alive to answer her phone?

"We don't know that." Lucas glances at her. "Did she leave you?" he asks Josh.

"Gone," Josh shouts. He shoves the table and unexpectedly stands. Empty dishes from lunch rattle and pencils roll to the floor. He shoulders his backpack and stomps from the kitchen. The front door slams.

"Where's he going?" Olivia moves quickly. Lucas follows. They run to the living room window. "Thank god." He's still here. He drops onto the bottom porch step and buries his face in his hands. His shoulders shake.

"That went well," Lucas drawls. "I'll go talk to him."

She grasps his forearm. "Not yet. Let him chill." Drives her nuts when people press her to talk and she's not ready. She watches Josh through the window and her heart tugs. Poor kid.

"He needs his dad, not me." Lucas gives her a murderous grin. "Got Ethan's number?"

She flips him off.

Lucas chuckles. He jams his feet into his work boots and crouches on the floor to tie them. "What does he mean when he says Lily's gone?"

"I think he thinks she's dead."

"I know, you said that. I'm not convinced." Lucas grunts, standing. He picks up his sweatshirt and throws it on his shoulder. "He doesn't know what happened to her."

She hopes he's right. "What makes you think so?"

He shrugs. "Gut feeling. I'll sit with him for a bit, see if he tells me anything, then I got to get back to work."

Olivia pulls her hair off her face. Lucas is right. She shouldn't jump to conclusions. Josh confuses words. Lily could know he's here. She could still show up.

She walks with Lucas to the door. "Thanks for trying."

"Anytime." He opens the front door. "Hey, how's Blaze?"

She quirks a brow. "Like you care?" His grip tightens on the knob and she glances away. Yeah, that wasn't nice of her.

"Sorry. It's over." Or she thought they were. Blaze sent two texts before she woke this morning. She deleted them without reading. After the way he left last night and what he said to her, what more could he want?

"Huh. I liked you guys together. Well, good luck with Ethan." He claps her shoulder.

"Go to hell."

The door shuts on his laughter.

CHAPTER 8
LUCAS

Lucas settles onto the porch step beside the kid. Josh scoots over, making room, and, face averted, he roughly drags his sweatshirt sleeves across his eyes and under his nose. His jaw tightens and lips thin as he pretends not to cry.

I get it, kid.

There were many nights as a teen when Lucas had to fake a smile so his parents could feign life was good. That their underage son hadn't been sentenced for stealing beer with the handgun his friend had brought to the scene of the crime. Or that the other crime committed behind bars never took place. Well, hate to break it to them. What the Carsons let people see was fake news. His upbringing was not a fucking Hallmark movie as his parents wanted everyone to believe.

Josh takes one of those deep post-cry inhales where the lungs sputter like a tailpipe. Lucas starts talking because he doesn't know what else to do to put the kid at ease. He yammers on about Lily and Olivia and growing up on the water in Seaside Cove, which was cool. He kayaked and surfed after school. He still hits the water when he can.

He has no idea if Josh understands. He's rambling. But the kid seems to be listening. He likes the pictures on his phone when Lucas shows him. He laughs at some of Lucas's stupid stories from when he played Pee Wee football and he and his teammates ran around the field like bobbleheads with their enormous helmets. And when Lucas tires of his own stories, he prompts Josh to return to the house, hating what the kid must be going through, his emotions close to what Lucas experienced. Fear recognizes fear.

"Check on your aunt. She won't admit it, but she's worried about you."

He gives Josh a fist bump and waits until he returns to the house. The instant the door closes, the smile he Gorilla-Glued to his face vanishes. He ambles to his truck, settles in the seat, not bothering to clip the belt, and drives off. He makes it two blocks. He jerks the truck to the side of the road and kicks open his door. He walks round the front and vomits in the gutter.

"Fuck."

Lily.

Her son looks so much like her at that age it hurt to look at him. Lily shadowed Lucas everywhere. She'd wait for him after school and he'd walk home with her. She sat on the floor at his feet doing homework while he watched TV. She'd wait for him at the dock until he returned from his morning row.

Lucas swipes the back of his hand across his mouth and looks up. An elderly woman watering her lawn, the green hose hanging like a limp dick from her hand, glares at him, her mouth pinched like a wrinkly asshole. Oh, yeah. He isn't hitting approval ratings with her anytime soon.

A toddler on a trike has stopped nearby. Her little feet push against the sidewalk, rolling the trike back and forth. She points at him. "Mommy, that man's sick."

"What have I told you, honey? It's not nice to point." Her expression wary, the mother shoots him a look of warning not to mess with her or her child. She moves to stand between him and the squirt in a skirt as if he's a predator.

He scowls, returning to his truck, and searches through the center console for his bottle of clonazepam. He pops the chill pill and washes it down with a mouthful of tepid water from a plastic bottle the experts say will give him cancer. Like he gives a shit.

The toddler watches him through the window. He guns the engine, stopping short of laying on the horn. The toddler clamps her hands over her ears and screams, rattling his own ears. Holy hell, she's got lungs. The mother's face turns as red as his grandmother's cooked beets and she yells at him. He can't hear what she's saying over the noise of his truck and her daughter's shrieks, but he's sure it isn't nice.

Shifting into gear, he yanks the truck away from the curb and heads back to work.

CHAPTER 9

Olivia watches Lucas and Josh with interest through the living room window. When Lily ran away, Olivia called Lucas. Had he seen Lily with Ethan? Did Ethan ever come by the house? Did he know he was seeing Lily? And what happened the night she ran away? Had she been planning to run? Did Ethan sway her to leave when their parents forced Lily to choose between an abortion or adoption?

Lucas hadn't seen them together. Ethan never visited. He wasn't there the night Lily left, and he didn't know if she'd been planning to run. He's not a mind reader. He also didn't know where she went and he didn't care.

Olivia told herself she didn't care either. Dwight blindsided her with the news, that was all. How did she not see this coming? But what equally baffled her was Lucas's indifference. He wouldn't agree to keep her posted on what was happening at home, or the leads Dwight and Charlotte had on Lily's whereabouts. Lily wanted to keep the baby. Let her.

She chews a hangnail on her thumb. What are they talking about that's keeping Josh rooted to the porch? He'd been ready to bolt. She saw the wild look in his eyes when he fled the kitchen. If it weren't for Lucas, Josh would have been around the corner by now, swallowed up by traffic, trees, and retail stores. They would have lost him before she could get her keys and start the car, which would make everything about this situation easier. It would be like he was never here.

But then she'd never find out why he came. They might not find Lily without him.

If she's still alive.

Lucas holds his phone so Josh can see the screen. The living room window is open, and she hears Josh's occasional laugh, a name drop from Lucas, and a description of a project he's been working on. He even smiles at one point, though on him it's more of a sneer.

Lucas has rarely smiled since his junior year in high school. Seeing a hint of the one he gives Josh is monumental. Flashes of the vibrant, talented little brother always pranking them and looking for laughs come into focus. He taped Blaze's hand to his forehead while he slept, keeping her in giggles for most of the morning. The tape left a red mark just under Blaze's hairline. Lucas stuck a rubber snake in Tyler's shoes left outside. Olivia can still hear Tyler's scream when he stuck his foot in his shoe and Lily's laughter when they realized it was fake.

Lily was the only one who escaped Lucas's pranks. He protected that girl better than a left tackle protected his quarterback's blind side.

Longing tweaks the muscles in her chest, tightens the skin around her eyes.

She wants that little brother back, unburdened of the hand life dealt him. He should have been an architect. He should have played football at a PAC 12 university. He should have completed high school magna cum laude as a first-string tight end. And Lily should have completed high school and gone off to college. She would have studied art and design and competed on the swim team. Olivia is sure she would have earned a full-ride scholarship, she was that good. But at some point near the holidays, Lily's life intersected with Ethan's, and Olivia's twenty-one-year-old boyfriend slept with her sixteen-year-old sister, and she took off with their baby.

She promised Lucas she'd call Ethan, dreading that she must. First, she needs to locate his number.

Her phone pings with an incoming text, startling her. Blaze. Again. Talk about déjà vu. Is he going to pester her like he did last time?

After their breakup in high school, he'd wait for her by her locker in between classes. He'd lean against her car after school at the risk of getting kicked off the soccer team, just for the chance to talk to her. She wasn't replying to his emails or returning his calls.

She deletes Blaze's text without opening the message and calls Amber. Her friend's perky nose and curly hair lights her screen.

Olivia paces away from the window. "Hey," she says when Amber picks up.

"I was going to call you. How'd it go last night with Josh? Did you find out why he's there?"

"No. He doesn't talk much," she says, turning back to the window. Lucas and Josh carry on their one-sided conversation. Lucas talks and gestures. Josh smiles and nods. He isn't the easiest kid to talk to, but Lucas makes it look easy. "He doesn't have a phone on him and he can't tell me her number; otherwise I would have already called Lily." She briefly explains Josh's challenge with words and numbers.

"What about his backpack? Does he have a wallet?"

"That did cross my mind. Lucas is here. He's talking with Josh. He might find out something. Hey, do you know what Ethan's been up to?"

"Ethan Miller, your ex? I don't, why? Oh, wait. He's Josh's dad. Are you planning to call him?"

"I'm concerned about Josh's medical issues. He should be with his dad, don't you think?"

"But he came to you. I can ask Mike to look at him. He's asleep at the moment and has another shift tonight, but I'll ask him to call you when he gets the chance."

"Thanks, I appreciate that." She'd feel better knowing what she's dealing with. Should she be worried about his condition worsening? "I still want Ethan's help with Josh."

"I don't know if that's a good idea, Liv. What if he's never met Josh? What if Lily and Ethan didn't keep in touch after she ran away? Josh might not know who his dad is. Or Lily told him someone else is his dad? What if she's married and that guy adopted Josh?"

Olivia squeezes the taut tendons in her neck. Amber's right. She could be removing the lid on a potential custody nightmare. But if Ethan's been part of Josh's life, or even just paying child support, he'll know how to reach her. And if he hasn't been in touch with her, Olivia wants to know why he didn't pursue Lily after she ran away. She took his son away from him. The Ethan she thought she knew never would have let that happen.

"He might know where Lily is," Olivia explains.

"I don't have his number, but Pete might." Ethan's best friend from high school. "He follows me on Insta. I'll DM him."

"Thanks."

Amber promises to text Ethan's number as soon as she gets it and Olivia ends their call just as Josh comes in the front door. He looks at his shoes. "Sorry I . . . hop." He squeezes his eyes shut. "Ran."

Her heart knocks around her chest. "That's okay. You've been through a lot."

He nods. "He said . . ." He points at her. "Help."

Olivia frowns, deciphering what he's attempting to tell her. *Lucas said you'll help*, comes to mind. She switches her phone between hands, back and forth. "I will. I'll help you find your mom." And his dad. This kid needs to go home. "So, um . . . what did you and Lucas talk about?"

He shifts from one foot to the other. He cocks his arm back and pretends to throw a ball.

"Football?" she guesses and he nods. "Do you play?" He shakes his head. "Do you watch on TV?" He nods. "Favorite team?" If she can get him talking, he might remember something about his mom and share.

He licks his lips and doesn't attempt to find the right word. He holds two fingers by his head like horns and bends at the waist, looking up at her.

Charades. Crap. She sucks at games. And it's killing her he has to resort to hand gestures to communicate because words are lost to him. Lily must be going crazy thinking Josh is wandering around alone. Is she aware he's missing? Is she alive to even wonder?

She clears her throat, focusing on Josh so the pit in her stomach that gets bigger with every thought of Lily stops aching. "Okay, I got this," she says, playing along. "Buffaloes?" Josh looks appalled and she swallows a laugh, holds up her hands. "Sorry. My bad."

He hunches over and blows air out his nose.

"Rams?"

He grins and holds out his fist.

Of course. Ethan's favorite team. Figures. But she bumps his fist anyway.

He gestures toward the kitchen and she supposes he wants to go back to his drawing.

"Sure, fine. I have to send some texts." She shows him her phone. "Hey, Josh." He turns around. She gestures at his backpack. "What've you got in there?"

His throat ripples and she swears he pales a little. "Stuff."

"Do you have a wallet? Anything with your address on it?" He shakes his head. "May I take a look?" she asks, approaching him, hand outstretched for the backpack.

He backs up, fear shimmering in his eyes again. "No."

"Okay." She stops, showing him her palms. "You'd let me know if you have something that would help with your mom, right?"

He frowns. Her question confused him. He points over his shoulder at the kitchen.

She waves him off, plotting to search his pack when he's sleeping and feeling guilty she has to. "Go ahead. I'll join you in a sec."

He goes to the kitchen to do whatever and she fires off a text to Lucas.

Details

He replies within a few minutes.

We talked.

AND...?

And nothing. Cool kid.

That's it?

Lucas...

She adds a frustrated emoji.

Kid clammed up when I asked about Lily.

Which meant what, exactly? Does he clam up because he's scared, or is he scared and clams up? What does he know? What did he see? He could be in shock.

The less Josh tells them, the more she wants to know what happened. They really must find Lily.

Before she can ask Lucas his opinion, he texts again.

Tip, prince-sis. Don't ask about Lily.

She bristles at his nickname, a mockery of their dad's pet name for her. What is she supposed to do in the meantime? Sit on her ass? Lily could be hurt or injured. She could be dead. What then? How does she tell Josh his mom is never coming for him?

How are we supposed to find out where she is?

He'll tell us in his own time.

But you said he doesn't know.

Olivia waits for the three dots to shimmer.
Lucas???? (adds angry emoji)
He doesn't reply. He's done.

CHAPTER 10

Olivia sits in her backyard, firepit lit, burning through her second ciga-rette. She leans forward, arms braced on her knees, and flips her phone end over end. It's late. Josh is asleep. His second night with her. Over twenty-four hours and still no word from Lily. Olivia can officially file a missing persons report, which she could have done the moment Josh arrived, but will do first thing in the morning, depending how her call goes with Ethan. Amber texted his phone number a short bit ago.

Nerves tap-dance in her stomach and shorten her breath. Her hands are shaking. It's the same sensation she felt before she jumped off a thirty-foot cliff while river rafting in the Sierra Nevada foothills. His number is underlined in Amber's text. All she has to do is tap the link, but she can't motivate herself to call him. If she flew off the handle when she saw the texts from Macey on Blaze's phone, how will she react when she hears Ethan's voice?

This isn't about you, she tells herself. Think of Josh. He needs his mom. Hopefully, his dad knows how to reach her. *If* Ethan is his dad. She swallows the knot of doubt left over from her conversation with Josh.

Before he went to bed, Olivia asked him if he's met his father. Not in person, she deciphered from his stilted explanation.

"Is your dad Ethan Miller?" she asked.

He shook his head.

"No?" She stared hard at him to see if he was lying. Maybe Lily told him someone else is his dad. "Who is your dad? What's his name?"

He tugged his bottom lip. "His name . . . name . . ." He stopped. "I can't . . ." His arm flopped to his side. He scowled and went back to his sketching.

"Can't remember or can't say?" she prodded, ducking to see his face when she noticed his fists. His cheeks had darkened. His expression drooping into one of defeat. She asked him to write his father's name. He gave her gibberish on paper.

Anger was a gift ribbon curling through her limbs, its sharp edges scraping the underside of her skin like paper cuts. Josh's face hadn't lit up with recognition when she mentioned Ethan's name. Why would Lily lie to her own son about Ethan? Unless Ethan isn't the father.

One way to find out.

Olivia takes a final drag and snuffs her cigarette in the ashtray. Ethan has one social media account, an Instagram profile of photos from his travels. He's been all over the world. They talked about traveling together after college. He'd write. She'd paint. They'd keep shallow roots, living a nomadic life. But she's now firmly planted in the house her parents, hoping she'd return to the area, sold to her for a buck, and Ethan is a respected travel journalist. She read a few of his articles when she searched him.

Did he think about her? Did he gaze across the Black Sea, or turn his face into the wind while sailing around Crete, and wish Olivia was at his side? Did he ever take Lily with him?

Bitter, Olivia clenches her jaw, squeezing her phone. She misses the idea of them, and despises that she feels that way. Lily stole her chance to experience the world with him.

She needs to cease stalling and call him.

Olivia brings up his number. He answers after the second ring.

"Olivia?"

Her breath catches, startled by the sound of her name in his voice. Her number hasn't changed since college. His has because she accidentally called him once when she dropped her phone. An automatic recording notified her that his number had been disconnected as she fumbled to end the call before he answered.

"Yes." The sour knot in her throat expands.

"Is that you?"

"It's me."

A short pause. A brief, dubious laugh. "It's really you." He almost sounds happy to hear from her. That's unexpected. Another pause. "How are you?"

"Ethan." His name feels odd on her tongue. Tight and inflexible, like a muscle that hasn't been worked in a long time. "Josh is here," she announces.

"Josh who?"

She frowns into the phone. Is he playing games? "Your and Lily's son."

"I don't—" He stops and the line goes quiet. "You still think I'm the father?"

Olivia unconsciously draws a cigarette from the box. Dwight has pictures. He didn't lie. Lily did. She even lied to her son. "Something happened to Lily. Josh needs you."

"Is she all right?"

"I don't know. We're trying to work that out."

"Where is she?"

"I was hoping you'd know, or that she'd be with you."

"Olivia, I haven't seen Lily since my last year at Southern Cal."

The cigarette drops to the ground. A chill makes its way up her arms. Her skin tingles. "You didn't know she ran away?"

"Yes. But I didn't think—she never came back?"

She swallows roughly. "You didn't go after her?" The question comes out as a breathless whisper, heavy with shock. He'd wanted kids. If Josh is his, he wouldn't have let Lily take their son from him. He would have chased her around the world insisting on visitation rights. At the very least, offer financial support. That's what she assumed he did.

At a loss for words, Olivia supports her head in her hand. All these years she's believed Ethan betrayed her. Is it possible she's been wrong? Was Dwight wrong? If so, who's in Dwight's photos?

Josh's father.

She needs to ask her dad for those pictures.

"Where are you?" Ethan asks.

"SLO. I remodeled the house Dad practically gave me and moved in."

"I know the one. I have back-to-back meetings tomorrow. I can be there tomorrow evening. Seven okay?"

"Seven's fine," she states, stunned he wants to visit. Maybe he's ready to admit Josh is his and wants to do so in person, because she's not ready to believe the alternative: Josh isn't his. He never betrayed her.

———

Olivia stands just inside Josh's room, nursing a scotch. Blaze left behind the bottle. Josh breathes evenly, the sheets kicked to his ankles. The ceiling fan above rotates on the low setting. She thought she'd look for a wallet in his backpack, save them both from the frustration of him attempting to answer her questions when she'd asked before to see it. But he hugs his backpack like a koala with her cub.

Olivia leaves the room before he senses her presence and wakes up. He'd open his eyes and think her a creepster.

It's a quarter past midnight. She should sleep. She was up late the night before. She should also start working on her next series of panels. Instead, she replenishes her scotch and peers out the living room window into the dark void, willing Lily to pull up. She's too frazzled after her conversation with Ethan, which means she should work. Illustrating soothes her, and she needs her rest. She and Josh have an early day tomorrow.

In her studio, she gathers a handful of charcoal and her sketch pad, intending to draft a rough layout. Bare feet take her into the living room where she plunks onto the buttery soft couch and sketches a face from memory. The drawing slowly evolves from Lily's features with her sprinkling of freckles and auburn hair into a full-body action scene: Dahlia Crimson of the Crimson Wave, complete with shimmery pantsuit and streaks of electricity emanating from her palms. Defined brows dip low over intense, fiery eyes. Luscious red lips scowl as she delivers justice. The sketch is rough and done in black and white, so it's not obvious Dahlia's outfit shimmers or that her powers emit a low hum. But Olivia knows, and to her, Lily is Dahlia, wielder of electricity, mistress of energy, adept at manipulating natural forces. The glue of the Crimson trio.

She was always stepping in whenever she and Lucas didn't get along. Their arguing upset her. Maybe because their parents didn't get along.

Their childhood home has a wine cellar, a narrow eight-by-four-teen-foot room with concrete walls down a steep set of wood steps. Without the wine racks, the room that Lucas dubbed "the pit" could easily pass as a solitary confinement prison cell. It was darker than dark, lacking a window or second exit. The build-out was done under the table, nothing about it according to code. Though the room boasted a state-of-the-art cooling system to control temperature and humidity for the wine. And their parents had a lot of wine.

As a winery management consultant, when he wasn't a wannabe politician, Dwight traveled throughout California and up into Oregon and Washington, working with wineries for weeks at a time evaluating and redeveloping their processes and procedures. The vintners often paid a portion of Dwight's fees in trade, and her dad would return home with cases of wine, which he stashed in the pit. She and her siblings weren't allowed inside without first letting someone else know they were going down. Lucas had once locked in their dad. He said it was an accident, but Dwight had been livid. He grounded Lucas for two weeks.

Despite the weird rules around the pit and how eerily dark it could get, Olivia stored her acrylics and oils with the wine. It was a temperature-controlled environment. But one afternoon, she unlocked the door and flipped on the light to find Lily huddled at the bottom of the steps, her eyes bloodshot and swollen. She whimpered, her lips blue from the chill.

At first Olivia thought Lily fell down the steps, but her little sister slowly stood and dusted her pants. Her legs weren't broken or ankles sprained. She seemed to be in one piece.

"What are you doing here, weirdo?" Olivia asked, coming down the steps.

"Mom—" Lily stopped, her gaze veering to the door. A shadow fell over them. Charlotte stood in the doorway. Lily's jaw tightened.

"Come here, Lily."

"What's going on?" Olivia looked between them.

"Lily," Charlotte warned.

"Nothing," Lily mumbled, moving past her. Lily trudged up the steps, her shoes leaden. When she reached the top, Charlotte moved aside. As her youngest child passed, she grasped Lily's arm. They exchanged words, harsh, heated whispers. The only thing Olivia could make out was Charlotte's question, "Are you ready to talk?"

Lily jerked her arm from Charlotte's grasp. She started to shut the door.

"Hey, I'm down here," Olivia yelled.

"Hurry up," Charlotte sharply ordered.

Olivia did, collecting her paints. She jogged up the steps, flicked off the light, and bolted the door. Looking back, she wonders why she never stood up for Lily. She should have asked Charlotte why she locked Lily in the cellar, a punishment she never doled out for her or Lucas. She also should have checked on Lily when she heard her little sister crying herself to sleep. There were many times Olivia should have just stopped and seen her sister for who she really was: a frightened little girl trying to fit into a family that never went out of its way to embrace her.

CHAPTER 11

Summer of '99

Twelve-year-old Olivia reclined in the canoe, her head propped against the starboard side and her legs, golden brown from a summer in the sun, draped over the port side. The aluminum gunwale bit into the back of her knees and the life vest dug into her chin, making her sweat. She wanted to take it off, but that would be against the Whitmans' rules. If they rowed more than fifty yards from their dock, the life vests had to stay on.

Olivia was baking hot. So was Blaze, seated to her left in the stern. He paddled aggressively, his face flushed a deep red. Sweat sheened his forehead and dripped into his eyes. Lucas took up the bow. His back muscles rippled as he timed his strokes with Blaze. The guys were taking them to a private inlet. They'd been swimming there all summer, out of the Whitmans' sight and Lily's and Tyler's incessant pleas to hang out with them.

When they reached the inlet, Blaze and Lucas dropped their oars in the boat and shed their vests. They stood, the canoe tilting violently side to side, and jumped into the lake. Water splashed, dousing Olivia.

"Hey!" she yelled.

"Get in, Liv," Blaze hollered, treading water.

Unzipping the vest, she sat up slowly, not wanting the day to end. It was their last one at the lake. Underneath, her racerback bathing suit top was drenched through. She finished off her bottled water and clambered over the gunwale, dropping into the cool water. It felt so good against her heated skin. She surfaced with a sigh and floated on her back, eyes closed. If it weren't for Lucas and Blaze making so much noise, she could fall asleep. She loved the damp smell of the lake, the scent of pine along the shore, and the sound of the water lapping against her ears. She could feel her hair floating on the surface, a halo around her head. The water tasted mossy and disgusting, but she didn't mind when she'd accidentally swallow a mouthful because she was having a good time.

The guys swam ashore and climbed a fallen tree, walking along the trunk. They'd been doing it all summer, they no longer needed to hold their arms out to balance. With a whoop, they cannonballed into the water.

Lucas yelled for her to join them. She waved them off, lethargic from the heat. Temperatures had to be in the upper nineties, and since it was their last day, she just wanted to chill. It would be another year until she could spend a day doing nothing.

They were supposed to be at the cabin helping to close the house for the summer season. But they'd slipped out when Mr. Whitman ran an errand, sneaking past Lily and Tyler. Tyler would beg to come, and Lily would tattle.

"Cannonball!" Lucas launched in Olivia's direction, drenching her with water. She ignored him, used to him leaping over or even on her. Sometimes he tried to pull her under with him. Today, she just wanted to pretend their summer wasn't over, that their parents wouldn't be there tomorrow morning to take them home. Last year was hard. Dwight and Charlotte argued about everything. Money, politics, and Lily. Charlotte pressed for Lily to receive the same treatment as Olivia and Lucas. Dwight argued they couldn't afford to send a third child to private school. They could barely afford two.

A gull flew over her before diving into the water. Lucas swam back to shore and Blaze took his turn jumping off the tree trunk.

How much trouble would they get in if they skipped their chores and swam here all day? A lot, she was sure. She'd give the guys another fifteen minutes before she insisted they row back. She didn't want to jeopardize their invitation to return next summer. It wasn't worth it.

She didn't know how long she floated while the guys messed around before she sensed someone nearby. Lurching up, she saw Blaze treading beside her. He cocked his head for her to follow. He swam to the canoe and lifted himself up, arms folded over the side, his legs dangling in the water and back exposed to the sun. Olivia went to the other side so the canoe wouldn't capsize. Facing him, she rested her chin on her fists.

"I wish we didn't have to go back tomorrow," Blaze griped.

"Me either," she said.

"Who'd you get for first period?"

"Ms. Keenan." Class schedules were mailed this week and Olivia asked Charlotte to open hers when she spoke with her mom last night. She'd crossed her fingers all summer hoping she'd get Ms. Keenan. She was younger than the other teachers and cooler, too. She didn't lecture. She taught English class like a book club. Olivia had never participated in a book club, but her friends said Ms. Keenan sat them in a circle and they discussed books. She even encouraged her students to act out the scenes. Her class was the only thing about school Olivia was looking forward to. That and cross-country. She was going to try out for the team if Charlotte and Dwight didn't make her babysit Lily after school like they did last year. Her parents pretended they had money, but Olivia knew that wasn't the case. Dwight wanted Charlotte to sell more homes. Charlotte wanted him to pick up more winery clients. She even overheard her father smash a chair when Charlotte learned Grandfather Gilbert never wrote her back into his will. Olivia has no idea why. Her mom wouldn't tell her when she asked once. She's never met her grandfather. She heard he was sick for a long time, but he must have been a mean person to do that to his own daughter.

After her parents received that news, they fired Lily's nanny and had Olivia stay home with her instead. It wasn't Lily's fault, but she started to resent her little sister for taking up all her free time. Summer break couldn't have come fast enough, and it had been wonderful spending these last six weeks thinking only of herself. She didn't have to constantly worry about Lily. Mrs. Whitman watched over her.

Olivia lazily twirled her legs in the water. The sun scorched her back. "Who'd you get?" she asked Blaze.

He made a face. "Mr. Rivers." He was old and crabby and five years overdue for retirement. Olivia pouted with him.

They compared schedules and sulked when they realized they didn't share any classes. Last year they sat next to each other in fourth period science.

"This year's going to suck." Blaze rolled his chin on his arms, squinting against the sun reflecting off the metal boat. His nose was peeling, the new skin a bright pink.

A chill skipped across Olivia's bare shoulders like a pebble across the lake's surface. Her ears pricked. She lifted her head. "Where's Lucas?" The lake had gone awfully quiet. She listened for his splashes and heard nothing.

Blaze looked behind him at the shore overgrown with brush. "He's probably taking a piss."

Olivia shielded her eyes with her hand and squinted at the shore. Usually she could see the guys when they peed. Much to her disgust, they didn't venture too far into the bushes. She couldn't see Lucas at all.

"I don't see him."

"Lucas," Blaze yelled. "Stop dicking around."

"Lucas!" Olivia shrieked. Her heart thumped fast. She swam to Blaze's side of the boat to get a better look. "He's not up there." Where could he have gone? She didn't see him wander past the log they'd been jumping off. But then she hadn't been paying attention. "Go find him," she told Blaze.

Blaze groaned an objection, but he swam to shore. Olivia hoisted herself into the canoe, almost tipping it over as she clambered aboard. She flopped into the hull like a fish and scrambled into the stern seat. Picking up an oar, she paddled toward shore, searching the water as she hollered for her brother.

The idiot was always joking around, and he'd been pranking them all summer. This was probably no different, but Olivia hated it. Even Blaze was getting annoyed with Lucas's stupid stunts. They'd gotten into trouble more than once when Lucas made them late for dinner or forced them to stay out past curfew because they couldn't find him. This time, though, she hoped he was pulling a prank and wasn't on the bottom of the lake.

"Please be okay. Please be okay," she chanted. He'd better not have drowned. Lily would be devastated. Olivia would kill him all over again just for dying on her. Why was he always causing trouble? The Whitmans wouldn't invite them back if they constantly worried about Lucas.

"He's not here," Blaze shouted.

"He has to be. Where could he have gone?"

Blaze shrugged.

"Get in. Hurry." She paddled to shore and Blaze climbed aboard.

"Look there." Blaze pointed at the tree they'd been using as a diving board. "See if he's under there." He grabbed the other oar and they backpaddled around the tree. A spiderweb of brittle branches extended over the water and dipped below the surface like bony fingers.

"Do you think he's hiding?" Blaze asked as they drifted by.

If he was, Olivia couldn't see where. The space was too small and tight, even for a beaver. "Go look."

Blaze glanced at her over his shoulder like she was mad. But she saw his fear, too. They were both starting to think the worst.

"Please," she pleaded, trying not to cry.

Blaze set down the oar and dropped into the water. He sank below the surface and came up for air on the other side of the tree. "I don't see him. He's not here."

He has to be. "Keep looking." She wasn't ready to give up. They couldn't. She wouldn't lose her brother.

Blaze took a deep breath and went below. Olivia stood in the canoe to get a better look. Legs braced, she balanced in the boat. Blaze came up for air again and again.

"Any luck?" she asked.

He shook his head and she started shaking. She felt sick and prayed out loud they'd find him alive. She'd never been so scared.

Blaze disappeared below the surface and she counted to thirty. It was the longest thirty seconds in her life before he surfaced beside the canoe. She released the breath she'd been holding and almost cried. Their eyes met.

"He's not here," he said.

"Don't say that," she cried.

"We should get my dad."

"No! He's here. He has to be. We can't leave him."

"Liv—"

A loud roar burst behind her with a wave of water. Olivia felt herself going over. She sank below the surface, kicking and twisting. A hand grabbed her under her shoulder, fingers digging into her armpit, hauling her up.

She gasped when she surfaced.

"You okay?" Blaze asked.

"Yeah." She sputtered, wiping water from her eyes. Turning around, she looked back at the canoe. Lucas sat in the middle seat hugging his sides, laughing.

"Fucking idiot," Blaze grumbled.

"You should have seen your face." Lucas pointed at her.

"Where've you been?" she asked, her teeth chattering. She was still in shock. They'd almost lost him.

"Watching you doofuses freak out."

"Asshole." Blaze swam to the canoe.

"That wasn't funny." Olivia swam around the stern, hoping she was hidden from view. She was about to burst into tears. She really thought he'd drowned.

Blaze pulled himself into the canoe. "We're late. Let's go back."

In their haste to return before anyone noticed they were gone, they forgot to put their life vests back on. Olivia paddled aggressively, throwing off their rhythm. She was furious with Lucas. This time he'd gone too far. Lily and Tyler were waiting on the dock. Mr. Whitman watched for them from the deck.

"We're screwed," Lucas muttered.

"It's your fault we took so long," Olivia hissed.

"There you are," Tyler said when they were within earshot.

"We've been calling and calling and calling," Lily added.

"Blame Lucas." Olivia got out and stomped down the dock.

Lucas followed, giggling. "You should have seen your faces. Lucas! Lucas!" He mimicked Olivia.

"Not funny, douche." Blaze was angry. But not as angry as Olivia. Blaze wouldn't lose his summers at the lake. His parents owned the house.

"Lucas, where are you?" Lucas teased, dogging Olivia.

Olivia snapped. She tackled Lucas. They rolled in the dirt. Two years older, she was taller and stronger. She ended up on top and started swinging. Lucas tried to block her arms, but he was laughing too hard until her fist solidly connected with his jaw.

"Ow!" He howled.

"You could have died!" She hit him again.

"Get off, Livy. Don't hurt him." Lily tugged Olivia's hair, trying to pull her off their brother.

Olivia pushed her away. Lily landed hard on her rear and burst into tears. "You're an idiot," Olivia shouted at Lucas. She was angry and scared and sick and tired of his tricks. "You're going to ruin everything."

"Stop, Livy. You're hurting him," Lily wailed.

"He deserves it." She cocked her arm and then she was soaring away. Her feet kicked air as she swung in Mr. Whitman's arms. He deposited her roughly on the ground.

"That's enough." Mr. Whitman helped Lucas to his feet. Lily ran to Lucas and clung to him. She wouldn't let him go.

"You're mean, Livy. Don't hurt my brother."

"He hurt me first." Olivia wiped off the tears she just noticed she'd been shedding. Dirt smeared across her face, stinging her eyes.

"Explain," Mr. Whitman ordered. He was looking at Blaze but three sets of eyes dropped to the ground.

Several hours later, after Mr. Whitman got the full story from them, after Blaze and Olivia finished putting away the outdoor recreational toys in the storage shed, and Lucas had cleaned the toilets because he finally admitted he'd been hiding under the log the entire time just to spook them, Olivia passed the Whitmans' bedroom on her way to take a shower. The door was cracked and she heard them mention Lucas. Holding her breath, she turned her ear toward the door. She knew she shouldn't, but she couldn't help eavesdropping.

"This isn't the first time he's disobeyed your orders and endangered their lives," Mrs. Whitman accused.

"He's a kid. Kids do stupid shit."

"Theo thought he'd drowned. Imagine what that would have done to him if Lucas's joke had gone wrong. Theo would have been scarred for life."

Mr. Whitman sighed loudly. "All right. I'll talk to him."

"Talking doesn't work with a kid like Lucas. You need to call Dwight. Lucas needs to be punished."

He did, but Olivia feared they'd all be punished.

"Now, now. It's their last night here. We have a whole year before they're back."

"I don't know if I want them back."

Olivia pressed her back to the wall and looked up at the ceiling. A tear unraveled down her cheek. The Whitmans didn't want them back, exactly what she feared. Stupid Lucas. He ruined her summers.

"Theo's had a crush on Olivia for two summers. You want to punish him, too? The kids will be older next year, wiser. Lucas will settle down."

"Let's hope so," Mrs. Whitman said.

He will, Olivia thought. She'd make sure of it.

"Any more pranks from him and they aren't welcome back," Mr. Whitman said. "We'll talk more later. I have to straighten the garage."

Olivia's face hardened. She wanted to rewind what Mr. Whitman said about Blaze liking her, but her anger overshadowed her own infatuation for Blaze. She marched upstairs and found Lucas inside his tent, flipping through a comic book. She tore off his tent and tossed it aside in a tangle of white cotton and twinkle string lights.

"Livy!"

She kicked him in the ribs.

"Oomph." He rolled to his side and into a ball. "What was that for?"

"Do you want to spend summers stuck at home?"

"No," he whined.

"Neither do I. You prank us again and the Whitmans won't let us come back."

"Not true."

"True. I heard them talking."

Lucas's face paled. "I was just having fun."

"It wasn't fun to us. Knock it off."

Lily stuck her head out of her tent. "Why are you always being so mean to Lucas?"

"He deserves it."

"Livy, apologize."

"Never!" She left the loft with fingers and toes crossed. Lucas had better not have ruined next summer.

CHAPTER 12

Day 3

"Olivia."

She opens her eyes and squints against the morning glare. Sunlight pours into the room. More glaring and sharper than the knife slicing her brain in half. She'd consumed one too many whiskeys while sketching her panels. Dahlia Crimson took over the scene, taking her off track. She veered off course from the plot her publisher approved, getting lost in memories of Lily and Lucas.

Her dreams were also wild, a recurring nightmare she's had since she was five. She's a little girl, alone on the beach. The sky is black as sin and the waves oily and angry. The wind howls like a pack of wolves. The scene is perfect for a bedtime horror story until it morphs into her own personal thriller. Her parents rise from the water, their hair and clothes drenched. Moonlight reflects off the blade Dwight tightly grips. Sometimes she sees a body floating offshore. Charlotte is distressed, as if she fears for Olivia's life. Her viselike grip clings to Olivia's upper arms, holding her in place. Her mouth moves, but Olivia can't hear her over Mother Nature's rage. She can't make out the words. But she senses it's a warning. She woke several times during the early morning hours drenched in sweat only to fall back into a fitful sleep.

She rolls onto her side, exhausted. The suede underneath her cheek is cool. Birds chirp outside the window she neglected to close. The scent of burnt toast wafts from the kitchen. Why is Josh up so early?

Josh.

She rubs her face, muttering into her hands. She wanted to be at the police station first thing.

"Olivia." The sharp order jolts her fully awake. She looks up into Lily's face, but older, and augmented. Charlotte had a recent Botox injection. Her bee-stung lips purse.

"What are you doing here, Mom?" Olivia's throat is Velcro scratchy and dry as an empty motel pool. She peeks at the pack of cigarettes on the table. She'd burned through half the box. Normally, she limits herself to two smokes a day. She feels gross. But the past thirty-six hours have put her on edge.

"I want your opinion on my dress before I meet Nancy. I have another in the car, just in case. Did you sleep on the couch?" She sniffs, her chin lifting. "What is that smell?"

"Burnt toast?" Olivia guesses.

Charlotte's nose crinkles. "You've been smoking again. Do you know what that does to your skin?"

Olivia stifles a yawn and swings her legs over the side of the couch. "How'd you get in?" She doesn't remember leaving the door unlocked.

"That boy in the kitchen." A dish clatters. Charlotte swings her head in that direction. "Who is he?" she asks curiously. "He wouldn't tell me."

"He doesn't talk much." Olivia stands, stretching her arms overhead. Her back aches from sleeping on the couch. Cool air kisses her torso where the fitted shirt from yesterday rides up. Before Olivia can explain about Josh and Lily, Charlotte heads for the kitchen. She turns back to see if Olivia is following.

"Really, Olivia. You slept in your clothes?"

She grunts, hitching up her jeans, and decides it's best to ignore her mom. Olivia is already running late. She doesn't have time to get into it with Charlotte, who never hesitates to dole out large helpings of advice when Olivia's plate is already full.

She pads barefoot into the kitchen to check on Josh, worried how he fared in the face of Charlotte. She'd told him to be ready first thing and is surprised he didn't wake her. The microwave clock reads 8:54. They should have been at the station by now.

Josh sits at the table eating jellied, burnt toast. The paring knife from her parents' wedding set, the one they gifted her with the house, stabs a cube of butter. She remembers when she found the set in the attic. She told Dwight about it and he brought the knives down, dusted off the block, and presented them to her. She recalls the way her parents exchanged a look as if the set held memories from the early years of their marriage when she'd like to believe they once got along. It was a wedding gift after all.

A sketch pad and pencils sorted by hue are laid out within Josh's reach. He smiles at her.

"Morning, Josh," she says.

"Hi." He shoots Charlotte a nervous glance.

Olivia grinds beans. While water heats in the electric kettle she grabs a to-go tumbler from the dish rack. "Sorry we're running late. You should have woken me up."

"Tried."

Charlotte peers at him like he's finally showed some manners. "You do speak. Olivia, aren't you going to introduce me to your young friend?"

Her back to her mom, she gently rests the tumbler on the counter and realizes she's stalling. Each time Olivia brought up Lily, which wasn't often over the years, Charlotte shut down the conversation. She flat-out refuses to discuss Lily. Talking about her is too painful, she claims. In Charlotte's eyes, Lily abandoned her, which is why Olivia didn't call her mom about Josh. She knew Charlotte wouldn't willingly discuss her. But now she's here. And she would have eventually heard about Josh through her or Lucas. Or Dwight. Her dad was bound to call soon.

Olivia takes a breath and turns around. Charlotte arches a brow, waiting. Olivia closes the distance between them and rests a hand on her arm. "Mom, this is Josh, Lily's son. Your grandson."

Josh gives Olivia a funny look before staring openly at Charlotte. He struggles to speak. Charlotte pales, and for a heartbeat Olivia thinks she's going to pass out, which happens when her nerves inch up the anxiety meter like mercury in a thermometer. The hotter the topic, the higher the temperature. Charlotte's hand flutters to the thin gold chain with the pearl drop. A gift from Olivia last Mother's Day. Charlotte replaced the diamond Dwight gifted her ten years ago for their anniversary. Lucas says unless they're arguing, they aren't talking.

"You okay?" Olivia asks.

The kettle boils behind her and clicks off. Charlotte's arm drops. "I'm late," she whispers. "Come with me." She rushes from the kitchen.

Josh slouches in his chair. He nudges toast crumbs with his fingertips. His gaze swings to her, then back to the table as if he doesn't want her to catch him looking at her. He might have been hoping Charlotte could help them find Lily. Olivia does.

She touches his shoulder. "I'm going to check on her. Will you be okay?" He nods and she smiles faintly. "Be right back."

Olivia finds her mom in her bedroom. Charlotte studies her reflection in the full-length mirror, turning side to side. "Are you all right?" She enters the room. "Trust me, he was the last person I ever expected to see."

Charlotte's complexion is waxen. She doesn't look at Olivia. "This dress. What do you think?"

"Mom, Lily is missing."

Charlotte stares at her, lips slightly parted. Her fingers touch the white patent belt at her waist. She rotates the belt and gently clears her throat. "The dress, Olivia. Please. I'm late," she whispers with forced calm.

Charlotte is scared. Her arms tremble. Olivia recognizes the onset of a full-fledged panic attack. She's learned the best way to help her mom get her emotions under control is to not force the subject. Folding her arms, she leans against the wall. "Who's the designer?"

"St. John. I picked it up yesterday in Santa Barbara. Which reminds me." Charlotte visibly relaxes. She even smiles. "Jean is finally selling her house."

"Jean St. John?"

"Mm-hmm. She hired me as the listing agent."

Uneasiness curdles in Olivia's empty stomach. "Is that ethical?"

Charlotte looks down at the dress as if a stain magically appeared. "What do you mean?"

"Jean's husband, Benton, the one who drowned. He was stabbed like what, eight times?" The St. Johns lived a few doors down from the Carsons and he was murdered six months after they moved in. When Benton's body washed ashore, Dwight had been a suspect. All the neighbors had been questioned, but the publicity tarnished Dwight's campaign. He pulled out of the race. That was thirty years ago. Jean moved to Texas ten years ago, but she's been leasing her house. Olivia is amazed she'd hire Charlotte as her listing agent given their history. "Don't you feel weird working with her?"

"Hush, Olivia." Charlotte glowers at her. "We don't talk about that. You know better."

Olivia sits on the tufted bench at the end of her bed and drags a pillow across her lap. The summer Benton St. John died was a dark summer for the Carson family. The St. Johns have always been a sore subject for her parents. Around that time was the first of three congressional campaigns that never came to fruition. Charlotte always resented Dwight for being incapable of delivering what he promised before they married: a prestigious lifestyle. They'd mingle in the same political circles as California's family dynasties. But if Charlotte can work with Jean St. John, she should be able to talk about Lily.

"The dress, Olivia. Please," her mom begs, her expression vulnerable. "What do you think?"

"Where are you going?"

"The Cliffs. Nancy's wearing a Beaufille."

Olivia chews a hangnail. "The dress looks fine."

"But does it make me look good?"

Charlotte's vulnerability becomes more apparent as it navigates across the terrain of her cheekbones and jaw, softening her skin. She looks young for her age. She's fifty-seven but can easily pass for midforties. Olivia sighs. "You look beautiful." She can only hope she looks half as gorgeous as her mom at her age.

Charlotte turns back to the mirror. She adjusts the clasp on her belt, taking it in a notch. Her eyelashes dust her cheeks and she smooths the front of the dress, flattening the creases that formed during her drive here.

"What is it?" Olivia asks gently, sensing Charlotte's mood shift. Is it sinking in she just met her grandson? Is she finally registering something could be seriously wrong with her youngest daughter? Olivia glances at the clock. She and Josh need to get going.

"I think your father's cheating on me," Charlotte whispers as if Josh can hear them from the kitchen.

Olivia yanks off the cuticle with her teeth. "What makes you think that?" Again. This isn't the first time Charlotte has suspected Dwight's having an affair. She grows edgier the longer he's away. Olivia wonders as she always does why Charlotte hasn't left him yet. They haven't gotten along for years.

Her thumb stings. She kisses the tip and presses her tongue to the bead of blood.

"He's not returning my calls."

"It's conference season. He's busy," she says, coming to her dad's defense. "When is he due home?" Between clients and exhibiting, Dwight's been on the road for over a month. Olivia had lunch with him the day before he left. When he's not traveling, which isn't often, they meet for lunch once a week. He'll call her several times a week while on the road. He'll probably call her today or tomorrow.

"The last time we talked he said this week. But he keeps changing the date on me."

"That doesn't mean he's sleeping around."

"But we didn't have sex the last time he was home, and it's not like I'm unattractive. I work hard and pay good money to look this nice at my age."

Money they don't have, Olivia notes.

Charlotte takes a breath. "Your father should appreciate what I do for us. I have a perfectly healthy libido, too. My vagina isn't dry like Nancy's. Did you know she has a subscription through Amazon for vaginal lube? It comes every two months, like clockwork. I wonder what she needs it for. It's not like she's hosting Tupperware parties for Magic Mike. Anyway." She waves dismissively. "I have needs and your father's been neglecting them."

"God, Mom. Stop!" Olivia smashes her face in the pillow. That was way too much information. An image of Nancy and Bruce Merriweather getting it on in every room of their house shines overly bright in her mind.

Charlotte glances at her watch again. She gasps. "I have to go. Talk later?"

"Mom, Josh . . ." She follows Charlotte out of the room.

Charlotte opens the front door and stops. She turns around and her eyes hold on to Olivia's. Fear ripples through them before she blinks away the emotion. She grasps Olivia's wrist and lowers her voice. "I'm worried about Lily, too. But don't tell your father about Josh. He can't know he's here."

Goose bumps speckle her arms. "Why not?"

"Please, Olivia. Don't press me. Trust this is for the best." Charlotte's phone chimes. She checks the screen. "It's Nancy. I have to take this. Hello, darling," she says, walking to the car. "I chose the St. John. Yes, it's stunning, perfect for brunch. You'll love it."

CHAPTER 13

"I need to report someone missing," Olivia tells the clerk at the police station an hour after Charlotte rushed off to brunch. After Charlotte's announcement, she debated following her mom outside. Olivia and Dwight are close. He calls her at least a couple times a week. He takes her to lunch on Thursdays when he's not traveling. How's she supposed to keep him from finding out about Josh? More so, why?

With any luck, she won't have to worry about it. Josh will be back with Lily before Dwight returns. Olivia doesn't know if Lily is missing or dead, but she can't spare the time and wait for her sister to make an appearance.

"Adult or child?" the man with the short-sleeve dress shirt buttoned to the collar asks. He barely looks up from the paperwork fanned across his desk.

"Adult. A woman. My sister."

"How long has she been missing?"

"At least thirty-six hours."

"Name?"

"Lily Carson. She's thirty. No." Olivia calculates on her fingers. "Twenty-nine years old."

The clerk looks up. He impatiently taps his pencil. "Your name."

"Oh, sorry. Olivia Carson."

"Have a seat, Ms. Carson." He points the pencil tip at the waiting area where she had Josh sit upon their arrival. "An officer will be with you in a moment."

"Thank you," she says, tapping the countertop, jittery. Her gaze sweeps the waiting area. It's the first time she's been inside the station. She was young when Benton St. John was murdered and out of town when Lily ran away. The police came to her parents. Except that time they took Dwight to the station after Benton's body was found. He was a suspect. Her dad's been inside these walls before. Same with Charlotte when they filed Lily's first missing persons report.

Since Olivia wasn't living at home, the only thing she knows about what happened the night Lily ran is what her parents told her, which wasn't much. Olivia felt removed from the entire situation, her emotions detached. She compartmentalized the pain of Lily's betrayal just so she could function. But standing here inside the station with Lily's son, the boy Olivia's little sister protected by giving up the security of family and home, makes everything much more real.

Josh is alone. Lily is missing. And oddly enough, Olivia blames herself. Lily might not have run if things had been different between them. She wouldn't have slept with Ethan.

She settles beside Josh on the vinyl couch. She inhales, her lungs expanding east to west, then exhales slowly through rounded lips, willing her nerves to calm. She needs to be strong for Josh. He clasps his hands between his thighs. His knee bounces, making Olivia even more antsy. She rests her hand on his thigh. He stops, but a moment later, starts cracking his knuckles.

"Josh." Anxiety rolls off him, blending with her own. His elbows land on his thighs, and chin dipped, he plays with the bill of his cap. "The police are going to help us. It's okay."

He nods. "Want to clean . . . uh, find her."

"We will."

Magazines featuring local businesses litter the table in front of them. The county paper is open to last week's cop logs, a listing of burglaries and break-ins. A woman's voice crackles over the speaker system, pricking Olivia's ears. An Officer Curbelo is requested to report to the front office. The station smells like a Lysol-and-hand-sanitizer bouquet, cleaner than a hospital. Olivia drags a magazine across the table and glosses over the pages, not necessarily reading, just keeping her hands busy. She has the same issue on her living room cocktail table at home.

Josh twists his wrists. One pops and Olivia grinds her teeth at the noise. She tosses the magazine on the table.

"Ms. Carson?"

Olivia looks up at a young female officer, hair pulled back in a tight knot at her nape. She extends a hand with blunt nails. An Ironman watch adorns her wrist. "I'm Officer Tanya Curbelo."

"Olivia Carson." She shakes Tanya's hand.

"If you'd come with me."

Olivia stands, gesturing for Josh to follow.

Tanya leads them to a small windowless conference room with a circular table and four chairs. She settles into the chair facing the door she closed behind them and invites Olivia and Josh to take the seats opposite her.

Josh drops his backpack on the floor. Olivia sits beside him, her purse on her lap.

"How can I help you today?"

"My sister is missing."

Still, she thinks. Technically, Lily's been missing since she was sixteen.

"How long has she been missing?"

Fourteen years.

She clears her throat and drops her purse on the floor. "Thirty-six hours, at least." Olivia's gaze swings to Josh. "Sound about right?" Josh nods and Tanya quirks a brow that looks like it was hair sprayed in place. "That's when my nephew showed up at my house. This is Josh," she introduces. "Josh, Officer Curbelo. She's going to help us."

He lifts a hand in greeting before it flops back on the table.

"Hi, Josh. I'm sorry about your mom. I'll do my best to help you find her. How old are you?"

"Three . . . tenth . . . no." He counts his fingers.

"He's thirteen. He struggles with numbers."

Tanya's gaze meets Olivia's, but she doesn't say anything. She flips open the cover on her tablet, revealing a keyboard, and props up the device. "Let's start with her basics. Name, age, and where she was last seen."

Olivia lays her hands flat on the table. Her thumbs tap the plastic surface. "I don't know where she was last seen."

"Who was the last person to see her?"

"Josh. I think."

"Where did you last see your mom?" Tanya asks Josh.

He frowns, looking at his hands. "The road."

Tanya's gaze slides to Olivia and back. "What road?"

"The one . . . the one . . . we . . . I . . . walked . . . and I . . . then she . . ." His frown deepens and he lightly bangs his clasped hands on the table.

Olivia feels his frustration as her own. The details that can help them find Lily are trapped inside his head or hanging on the tip of his tongue. She rests her hand over his.

"Josh had an accident a while back that makes talking a challenge. I've noticed nouns and verbs give him the most trouble."

"What happened?" Tanya asks.

"He hit his head."

Tanya looks at Josh for confirmation or a reaction, Olivia can't tell.

"Josh?" the officer prompts.

"I fell."

Olivia watches Tanya process this information, fearing how this might play out. Falling is the most common excuse in the book to explain away bruises and breaks when someone is abused. Was he?

Could he have been running from someone and was separated from his mom?

"Is that true, Josh?" Tanya's voice takes on an authoritative tone.

Josh is quiet. He tugs his bottom lip.

"Josh." Olivia gently touches his shoulder. "Answer the officer." She wants answers, too. If there's someone out there who might harm him, she needs to know about it. She promised him he's safe with her.

He shakes his head.

"You didn't fall, or you don't want to answer me?" Tanya moves aside the tablet and folds her hands on the table.

"Not . . . fall."

"What happened then?" she asks when Josh shakes his head again. Josh shoves his hands in front of him.

"What's he doing?" Tanya looks at Olivia.

"I don't know," she murmurs with mounting alarm.

Josh repeats the gesture and Olivia softly gasps. "Did someone push you?" she asks as a sickening feeling balloons in her stomach. Josh nods. "Who?"

"My . . . my . . . your . . ." He looks at Olivia, silently begging for her to understand.

"I don't know what you're trying to tell me. I'm sorry."

Josh presses his chin into his chest and her heart breaks for him. "We'll talk about this later. Let's focus on your mom, okay?" she suggests as her mind races with possibilities. Did he get into a fight? Was he attacked? If so, is that person still a threat?

Tanya repositions the tablet, her fingers hovering over the keys. "When you find out what happened, you let me know if this is something that should be reported."

"Oh, I will," Olivia agrees. She lays her hand on Josh's midback, a protective gesture that doesn't feel as foreign as she'd expect.

Tanya nods, satisfied, and taps the keyboard. "What's your sister's name?"

"Lily Carson."

"No," Josh says firmly.

The hand on Josh's back tenses. Olivia looks at him. "No? That's not her name?"

"Not . . . Lily."

She stares at her nephew. No wonder he gave her funny looks whenever she spoke Lily's name. "She changed her name?" Of course Lily would. She didn't want her family to find her. That also explains why Lily is a ghost on the internet. Olivia feels a lightness in her chest as her pulse races. They're getting closer. They'll find her now.

"Not Lily. Her name is." He stops all of a sudden and inhales roughly through his nose. "Can't . . . can't . . . don't say." He pounds his forehead with his fist.

"It's okay. It'll come to you." Her words are rushed. Olivia's teeth dig into her bottom lip. She's sitting at the edge of her seat.

Josh nods, but his mouth takes on a doubtful twist, and she tries not to let his disappointment douse her hopes. Lily is out there. They only need her name. He cracks his knuckles.

"What's Lily's date of birth?" Tanya asks, steering them back to the report.

Olivia tells the officer and Tanya's frown deepens as she reads what's on her screen. "Is your sister Lily Carson of 398 Sundial Court in Seaside Cove?"

Their parents' address. "Well, she was. Have you got something?" Olivia leans forward to see what's on Tanya's screen.

"Says here she was reported as a runaway fourteen years ago."

"I know. My mom filed a missing persons report. They never found her."

"But he found you." Tanya points at Josh.

"I don't know how."

Tanya's gaze mines Josh's. Olivia sees the questions flicker across the officer's face, but something on the screen grabs her attention. Her brows lift into her hairline.

"Is your brother Lucas Carson?"

Olivia briefly closes her eyes and silently curses. She found Lucas's record. "Yes."

"And your father—"

"Is Dwight Carson. Yes, yes, I know." They both have records.

"He was a suspect in the St. John murder, which is still unsolved," Tanya adds, and Olivia detects a hint of accusation, as if Olivia is wasting the officer's time.

She peeks at Josh, worried how he's taking this news. He gapes at the officer. "Everyone on that street was questioned. It wasn't just my dad. It wasn't just him," she says to Josh.

"But the St. John case wasn't the only one for him."

Olivia wants to disappear under the table. Her family is an embarrassment. "I know," she mutters. The night Lily ran away Wes Jensen, a boy in Lily's algebra class, drowned just off their property. Olivia was away at college and Charlotte was a wreck after Lily ran. All she knows is Wes was last seen walking up the Carsons' driveway. Dwight was brought in for questioning, but there wasn't enough evidence of foul play. Wes's case was ruled an accident. Old news that Josh doesn't need to hear about his mom.

"Your family has had a few run-ins with the authorities."

Tell her something she doesn't know. "Can we focus on Josh's mom?" She tips her head in her nephew's direction. He doesn't need to hear their family's dirt, and frighten him more than he already is.

"Here's the deal, Ms. Carson." Tanya closes her tablet. "Your sister is an adult and has every right to go missing."

"She left her son," Olivia argues.

"She wouldn't be the first."

"What if she's hurt or dead? We think something happened to her."

"Gone," Josh adds.

"Do you have evidence of that?"

Olivia leans back in her chair. "No, but—"

Tanya lifts a hand, stopping her. "Unless there's evidence of foul play, Lily, or whatever name your sister is going by, is a grown adult. There isn't much we can do. Without a last-known location or home address so we can target the right community for potential witnesses, the report is useless. Over half a million people go missing every—"

"I know, I know." Olivia props her elbow on the table and rests her forehead on her fingers. "There's got to be something we can do. I've got her son. We need to find her."

"What's her home address?"

"I don't know."

"Hmm."

"He does, but he hasn't been able to tell me." Olivia glances at Josh, who's staring at the table. His body vibrates, coiled tight. He grinds his teeth. She's as desperate as Josh to find Lily. Her sister might have slept with Olivia's boyfriend, but Josh doesn't deserve to be separated from his mom, no matter the circumstances.

"What about region?" Olivia points at Josh's ball cap. "He's from the San Diego area. Right, Josh?" He nods, and she looks hopefully at Tanya. "Does that help?"

Tanya flips open the tablet. "Tell you what, Ms. Carson. We'll file a courtesy report and distribute to the San Diego law enforcement agency. Without her legal name and address, or a last-known location, it won't do much good."

"But it's something. Right?" She looks at Josh again. He's frowning, bouncing his fist on the table. A new worry bubbles up in her. "What's wrong?"

A noise vibrates in the back of his throat and her heart speeds up.

"If you can get the address," Tanya says, jerking Olivia's focus back on her, "I can contact local law enforcement to do an in-person wellness check. They'll send out an officer to knock on her door and talk to her neighbors. Likely, she'll show up in a few days. Most do."

"And if she doesn't?"

Tanya pushes back from the table, ready to leave. "Find her address. Talk to her friends. Someone is bound to know something. When you do find out more, come back." She pushes her business card across the table.

Josh swipes it onto the floor. "No! Fuck, no!" he explodes like he did the other day with Lucas in her kitchen. He pounds the table with his fists and lunges at Tanya. "Fuck you. You . . . hop . . . help."

Tanya leaps back from the table, hand on her holster.

Olivia jumps in front of Josh, heart clogging her throat, eyes huge. Liquid hot panic heats her chest. "Whoa. He's just a kid."

Any emotion Tanya might have shown melts off her. She turns her blank expression on Olivia. "Ma'am, calm your nephew down."

"We're sorry. He's upset. He just wants to find his mom. Josh." She turns to him.

He kicks the chair. "Fuck, fuck, fuck. She help. My mom . . . mom . . ." He cries out. "She's gone. Gone!"

"It's okay. It's okay. Let's go home. We'll solve this." Josh stomps from the room. Olivia grabs her purse and his backpack. "Thanks for your time, Officer," she says over her shoulder and follows Josh out of the station.

She meets up with him in the parking lot. He circles the car, pacing. While he blows off steam, she lights a cigarette. "I'm sorry she couldn't help."

He jabs a finger at her. "You promised."

"I did. But I need your mom's name. The police can't find her—*I* can't find her—until we get that name. What is it?"

His mouth tightens until his lips turn white, head shaking. Then he lets out a roar of frustration. Folding his arms, he leans against the passenger door and sulks.

"Josh." She drops the cigarette, crushing the butt, and waits until he looks at her. "I'm not giving up. You'd better not either."

CHAPTER 14

Olivia met Ethan Miller the first day of their senior year in high school. He took the empty seat behind her in American Government. It took him two weeks to work up the nerve to talk to her, even though she smiled at him every day. But it takes him less than twenty-four hours to show up after she called. He arrives promptly at seven, as promised, and all the way from Los Angeles.

Despite her looming doubts that he's the father and wondering whether Lily lied to Dwight to spite Olivia, Ethan's offer to visit, his willingness to drive up here with just one phone call after fourteen years, leaves her with the impression he either knows something about Lily he couldn't share over the phone—wishful thinking on her part because she's starving for information—or he is Josh's father and he wants to meet his son.

She's been eager to talk with him all day. After the police station, she tried to reach him only to remember he was in meetings.

Now Ethan is standing on her porch, swathed in artificial light, and he looks like a memory from her past, with the creases that bookend his full mouth like parentheses when he flashes a smile after she opens the door. Arms loose at his sides, hands in his pockets, he regards her with an open expression. He wears a black tee and cognac utility pants, his tawny hair mussed from running his hands through it, something she remembers he does when he's stressed. She can see the grooves left by his fingers. It's the only sign he shows he might be as nervous as her. But that smile, his mouth, those eyes . . . him. They always made her heart sprint like she was catching up to him. This time, that reaction is noticeably absent, and her heart races for a different reason: Josh. She wants to know what Ethan knows.

She invites him into the house. "Thanks for coming."

"Of course." Ethan's presence fills the entryway. He's the last person she expected to set foot in her house. He scans the room, taking in the changes since he was last here. He once spent a weekend helping Dwight repair the drywall in between tenants. His gaze eventually finds hers.

"It's good to see you again, Olivia."

"You too." If anything, it's good to know she doesn't feel for him the way she used to.

Josh enters the room, lured by their voices. He looks expectantly at Olivia. She'd told him earlier a friend was visiting. He might know something about Lily.

"Ethan, this is my nephew, Josh," she introduces.

If Ethan has any reaction to meeting his son for the first time, he doesn't show it. He offers Josh his hand, his smile friendly. "Ethan Miller. Nice to meet you."

"Josh. Same." Olivia notices his grip is solid, but his eyes waver back to her. They glimmer with expectation. "He . . . help?"

Ethan's pale blue eyes find hers. His brows draw together.

"We're hoping you might help us find Lily." She answers the question she knows he wanted to ask.

Ethan slides his hand into his pocket. "I'll try my best."

"Thank you." Josh's relief is visible.

"Josh, why don't you finish your movie while Ethan and I talk out back?" He's only thirteen, and after what happened at the police station, she doesn't want him to overhear anything upsetting and explode again.

Josh hesitates, clearly reluctant to leave the room.

"I'll come get you if I learn anything new, promise."

He nods, and after a moment he retreats to the living room, where he left the latest Marvel release on pause.

"Let's talk outside."

She leads Ethan through the kitchen and out to the back. Her yard is an oasis, thanks to Blaze and his team. Raised garden beds on the left. A firepit to the right. A ten-seat pastoral table underneath a pergola covered in jasmine draws the eye to the center of the yard. Wind chimes Blaze crafted sway in the light breeze. Any other given night she'd find the rustic music relaxing. But not tonight. She's too wound up. Her drive to discover what happened to Lily too pressing, like a palm on her back shoving her forward.

Closing the slider, she digs into her pocket for the lone cigarette and lighter she keeps on her like a security blanket, or the stuffed lamb she couldn't give up as a child and kept into adulthood. Putting some distance between them, she lights the Marlboro with shaky hands and takes a long draw. The nicotine she's craved since this morning in the parking lot rushes into her system, taking off the edge. Ethan scrutinizes her, but he doesn't comment. Another draw and the trembles stop.

"Here's the deal," she begins, turning to him. "I don't know if Lily is dead or missing. I haven't seen her in fourteen years. Josh showed up alone. I have no idea how he found me or what happened."

"Have you asked him?"

"Of course I have. Do I look like an idiot?" His chin dips, eyes widen, and she swears. She's fried, and anytime she tried asking Josh, he'd get flustered. "Sorry. It's been a trying couple of days." And she can't let her anger at their history take over. "He can't talk. I mean, he can, it's just not easy for him."

"What do you mean?" His concern is genuine.

She gentles her tone. "He had an accident sometime before he arrived. He hit his head. Look, you apparently knew Lily a lot better than I thought you did," she says, spite leaking into her voice.

"I meant what I said. I haven't seen her since college."

113

"And Josh isn't your son," she says, sarcastic. She flicks off the ash head.

"No, he isn't. And I didn't sleep with your sister. Are we really doing this? I can leave." He starts for the door.

"Wait," she says before he grasps the handle. She looks at him for a long moment, lips pursed, until she sighs, admitting what her gut has wanted to tell her for fourteen years. She's just refused to listen. "I know—" She clears her throat. "I know you're not."

His arm falls to his side. He slowly turns back to her. "What changed your mind?" he asks, cautious.

"Josh."

She drops the cigarette on the ground, something she never does in her backyard, and grinds the butt with her heel, her eyes never leaving his, as painful as it is to face him while admitting a truth she should have explored over a decade ago. Swallowing her nerves, and her pride, she lets her gaze wander his features, searching for any similarities to the boy inside her house. So much of Lily is in her son, but Olivia didn't see a speck of Ethan in him, in looks or mannerisms. Kids can look nothing like their parents, but there is something else, something stronger than the intuition telling her Ethan isn't the father.

"Josh knows who his dad is, and it's not you," she explains. "And you wouldn't have let Lily run away with Josh if he was yours."

"No, I wouldn't have." Ethan closes the space between them. "But I can take a paternity test if you still doubt me."

She shakes her head. "Not necessary." Josh has been traumatized enough. Last thing he needs is her swabbing his mouth to prove something she's sure isn't true.

Looking back, it's more reasonable Lily lied to their father than it is that Ethan cheated on Olivia with her. Lily had a history of lying. Why not go out with a bang? She was pretty upset with Olivia when she wouldn't let Lily move in with her and Amber in San Francisco.

Olivia presses fingers to her forehead. Imagine if she'd paused years ago and thought through what Dwight told her about Lily. If she hadn't overreacted. She would have realized sooner Lily was lying. She wouldn't have broken up with Ethan. Unfortunate, yes. Her life could be quite different than it is today. She and Ethan could be married, a thought that doesn't excite her, another surprising realization. So is another: she wouldn't have dated Blaze again. And that thought feels like a dry wind over desolate land. Her arm drops to her side and she shivers from the unexpected tide of loss. She misses him.

"My dad said he has photos of you and Lily."

"It isn't me."

"I don't think so either." Lily could have staged it with someone who looks like Ethan, knowing Dwight would demand to know who the father was. Whoever is with Lily in those photos is either Josh's father, or someone Lily used to cover for him.

"I never touched your sister, Olivia. I saw her walking home from work once when I drove past. I offered her a ride."

Lily had a job? "She wasn't allowed to work." She didn't have time, not with her swim schedule.

"That's why she was walking home," Ethan says. "Dwight wouldn't let her use the spare car."

Olivia's mouth pinches. That sounds like Dwight. For reasons she can't understand, Dwight never connected with his youngest daughter. He didn't treat her equally to Olivia and Lucas.

"Why didn't you tell me this before?"

"You didn't give me the chance." His words are bitter.

Anger weaves through her. "So it's my fault."

"Yes. No!" He cuts his hand through the air. He heaves, exasperated. "We weren't talking, Olivia. About anything. I was overwhelmed with school and stressed about my mom. You, well . . . I had the impression Mom's injuries bothered you. I gave you space."

Olivia looks away, regretting how she'd behaved and that Ethan had her pegged, tacked to the board like a memo he'd deal with later. No wonder he'd let her go so easily. But what he was going through with his mom at the time was like watching Blaze with Rhonda all over again when his mom was going through treatment for lymphoma. Olivia tried to comfort Blaze and he cheated on her. Rather than trying to be there for Ethan, she'd pulled away without realizing she was doing so.

"I'm going to check on Josh." She rushes into the house to clear her head. She needed space, and they need to get back on topic. This visit isn't about them and a past she can't repair. Because she *is* at fault. She's the one who reacted without gathering facts.

As soon as the door closes, she notices how dark and quiet the house is. The lights and TV in the living room have been turned off. Same in the kitchen. Olivia flips the switch. Recessed lights bathe the quartz counter Blaze helped her select, noting the overhead lights gave depth to the intricate work of mineral veins that wove through the slab. Down the hall, the faint *thump-thump* of the washer tosses Josh's single set of clothes. He asked earlier about washing them. She finds him in his room, lying on his back in the center of the bed, staring at the ceiling. The single bedside lamp casts a golden circle of light over one side of the bed and the floor below the nightstand. He's still wearing Blaze's sweats to bed.

Knocking gently to get his attention, she smiles at him, relieved he's cozied up in the room. His head lifts. He looks at her expectantly.

"Nothing yet. You okay?"

He plops his head on the pillow. "Yes."

"Need anything?"

"No."

She nods slowly, wishing he could give her the answers she needed. She wishes she had all the answers for him. "I'll be in the kitchen if you need me."

He rolls to his side, giving her his back.

Olivia closes his door as her phone buzzes in her back pocket. The sound tells her it's a text from Blaze. She ignores it and texts Lucas, asking if he'd take Josh shopping in the morning. She wants to pay Charlotte a visit. Dwight never cared for Lily. Her pregnancy was one more stain on his campaign, and Josh must be a reminder of his failures. That's why Charlotte doesn't want him to know about Josh. But Olivia wants to know if that's all. Is there another reason Charlotte wants to keep Josh from Dwight? Is it related to Lily being missing?

Olivia returns to the kitchen intent on pouring a whiskey before rejoining Ethan when she notices Josh's backpack leaning against the table leg. For the first time since his arrival, the pack is out of his sight.

With a glance over her shoulder, she drops the pack on the chair and rifles through the compartments. She finds gum wrappers and broken pencils in the front pocket, a Hellblazer graphic novel in the middle pocket. She flips through the book, wondering if it's appropriate for his age. She returns the book and pulls out this month's issue of *Thrasher Magazine*. Pictures have been cut out, leaving windowless frames in the pages. They trigger a memory.

Lucas gifted her a subscription to *Apollo* for her thirteenth birthday with the money he saved from mowing lawns. Olivia renewed the art magazine every year. She treasured the issues and kept them stacked in her bedroom. Once, during her senior year, she came home from school to find her collection missing.

Afraid her parents tossed the issues, she sought them out in the living room where they spent the evening after dinner. "Who took my magazines?"

Charlotte, legs curled on the couch, looked up from the book open on her lap. "I haven't seen them." She licked her finger, turned a page. "Maybe it's for the best. They made your room look messy."

"Did not. Dad, what about you? Have you seen them?"

Dwight peered over the front page of the *Wall Street Journal*. "Have you checked with Lucas or Lily?"

"Lucas knows how much they mean to me. He wouldn't have touched them."

"Must be Lily. You know how she is," he murmured.

Charlotte glared at Dwight like she was trying to will him from the house.

Olivia tossed her hair and left the room, leaving her parents to bicker. When she was young, it used to bother her how Dwight treated Lily like she was a lesser member of the family. But lately Olivia had seen his point. Ever since Olivia beat up Lucas at the lake, Lily had been nothing but a nuisance to her.

Olivia pounded on Lily's door.

"It's unlocked," Lily said.

She pushed open the door and stopped short. Lily sat in the middle of her bed with dozens of *Apollo* issues and a pile of cutout pages. Large shears snipped a photo in the most recent issue. Olivia knew the issue because she'd been saving the magazine to read Bae Lee's interview. She was Olivia's favorite contemporary ceramics artist. Her work was a smart juxtaposition of classic and modern craftsmanship, and Lily was cutting out Bae's face. Shredded paper and torn issues littered the floor like a street after a parade.

"My magazines! What have you done?"

Lily flinched. "Daddy said you didn't want them anymore."

"Liar. I just saw Dad. He would have told me that. You should have asked me."

"My project is due tomorrow. You weren't home."

"Doesn't mean you can go into my room and take them." She scooped up the nearest issues, salvaging what she could.

Lily grabbed for them. "Hey, I need those."

Olivia moved out of reach. "They're mine." She flipped through a magazine. Pages were missing, others had windows to the page behind. Her body tightened with rage. "You ruin everything."

"I do not."

"My prom dress?"

"That wasn't me!"

"Liar." Their dad had seen her dancing in the backyard while wearing the dress.

Olivia gathered up the issues Lily hadn't touched and stopped in the doorway. "Stay out of my room. Better yet, stay out of my life." She slammed the door.

The glass slider closes. "Hey."

Olivia yelps. Josh's spiral-bound notebook flies from her hands, the memory of Lily leaving her shaken. She presses a palm against her sternum and catches her breath. "You scared me, Ethan."

"Sorry. Came to check on you. Thought you'd forgotten me."

She momentarily had.

He picks a dingy white envelope off the floor. "You dropped this."

"What is it?" She takes the envelope and reads the handwriting on the front. Her heart seizes. "It's from Lily." But it's addressed to Olivia. The envelope must have fallen from Josh's notebook. It's old, crinkled and worn; the ink faded. Whatever Lily sealed inside, she did so some time ago. Why didn't she send it? Why does Josh have it? Did Lily give it to him to give to her? If so, why hadn't he passed it along?

"Are you going to open it?"

"Absolutely," she says, impatient for answers about Lily and why Josh is here. She grabs the letter opener and slides the blade under the sealed flap.

Inside are two documents, a power of attorney and Josh's birth certificate. Her gaze dives to the father's name field. It's blank. She shows Ethan.

"Maybe she doesn't know who it is."

"Did you see her with anyone? Did she ever mention a name to you?"

He shakes his head. "There's another possibility."

"What's that?"

"She doesn't want anyone to know who he is."

He's right. If Lily were protective enough of Josh to run away before he was born, she would be protective of the father. "Why so secretive? What was she afraid of?"

"I wish I knew."

Olivia skims the birth certificate. "Well, I know now why Josh is a Padres fan. He was born in San Diego." She flips to the power of attorney and a heavy feeling that can only be described as responsibility settles in her belly. "She appointed me as Josh's guardian in the event of her death." The first thought that crosses her mind is that Lily is, in fact, deceased. Then she reads the next line. Lily granted Olivia short-term guardianship in the event she goes missing. "Who puts that in a POA?"

"I haven't seen that before."

Olivia ponders the possibilities and each one is no less concerning than the last. Did Lily have a stalker? Is that why she's missing now, or did she run away at sixteen for reasons other than wanting to keep Josh? The document is old, notarized only a few months after Josh's date of birth. Her gaze snags on the attorney's phone number in the letterhead. Finally, someone she can call.

She refolds the documents and slides the envelope in her back pocket. Ethan opens the sketchbook Josh left on the table and Olivia is anxious for him to leave so that she can follow up with the law firm.

Ethan flips to the next page, the beach scene Josh sketched that morning. He put a lot of work into the drawing, the detail on par with the townhouse he drew yesterday. Since then, he's added a shadowy figure by the right margin. "Who's that?" she murmurs, peering closer. She thinks about Lily's "if I go missing" clause.

Olivia stills, moistening her lips. "I went to the police this morning to file a missing persons report. The officer told me Lily will probably show up in a few days."

"I bet they say that about everyone who goes missing."

"She said most missing adults do eventually show up," she conveys, fixated on the shadowy figure in Josh's drawing. She can't take her eyes off it. "I don't think Lily is going to. She would have been here by now."

She packs up Josh's backpack with shaky hands. It takes her three attempts to zip closed the largest pocket. "Is there anything else you can think of that might help?"

He shakes his head. "I'll let you know if I remember something."

She nods slowly. Ethan wasn't that much of a help, but his visit wasn't exactly a waste of time. Without him, she might not have found the envelope in Josh's bag. She no longer has to wonder what would have happened to them if she didn't break up with him. They wouldn't have lasted that long after college graduation. Their love wasn't deep enough, she sees that now. She probably would have ditched him somewhere between Australia and Asia during their trek around the globe.

"Do you mind calling it a night then? It's late and I want to look up that law firm."

"Sure. Call if you need anything from me."

She nods, distracted, and walks with him to the front. When she opens the door, it occurs to her he has a long drive home. "Do you want a coffee or something?"

He shakes his head. "I'm just down the road. I'm staying at Caroline's rental in Pismo." His sister. "Been there all week working on an article."

"Oh." He's close. No wonder he invited himself over. He was probably more curious than courteous.

A truck passes the house, same make and model as Blaze's. She feels a dull pinch in her chest, at first thinking it was him, then fleetingly hoping he doesn't drive by. He'll see Ethan's car and know she has company. He might get the wrong idea. She doesn't want to hurt him more than she already has, then remembers she doesn't care.

"Actually, do you mind coming over tomorrow?" She's anxious to jump on her new lead and they didn't have a chance to delve into his relationship with Lily. He might have overheard or seen something he thought insignificant but could be monumental for her and Josh. "We can talk over dinner."

Ethan's shoulders push back, the only sign of his surprise at the invite. "Sure. I'll pick something up."

"Great." She doesn't have to worry about cooking. She probably wouldn't have time anyway, not with their schedule tomorrow. "Night, Ethan."

"See you tomorrow." He lifts his chin and makes his way to his car.

She doesn't wait for him to drive away. She bolts the door and jumps on to her computer.

CHAPTER 15
LUCAS

Day 4

Lucas backpaddles with a double blade until he slips the kayak into the current. He follows the shoreline as he's done since he was a kid. He'd struggle to keep pace with Dwight, trying to impress him as if the man earned the #1 Dad in the World award. There was a time when Lucas would have purchased a hundred of those cheap plastic trophies and filled Dwight's office.

Now, Lucas can outpaddle, outrun, outmaneuver, and outsmart his dad. He made sure of it. Because one of these days he's going to run. Not from Dwight or the law, but from Lily. When she returns, he can't face her. And she will return. Josh found his way here; it's inevitable.

He maintains a punishing pace, cutting the carbon blade into the water. Left, right, left, right, stroke after stroke. He wants his arms to burn and body to sweat so he knows that he feels, that he's capable of caring.

He didn't care when he watched Lily run away. He had been so jaded after his stint in juvie, abandoned by his own father, that he witnessed the clusterfuck of events go down and he didn't lift a finger to stop Dwight. By the end, Wes Jensen floated in the bay and Lily was gone.

Lucas rounds a bend and his house disappears from view. He might be thirty-three and living with his parents, but he's not a failure to launch. After witnessing Dwight threaten Wes, he kept close to protect his mom. Who knows when Dwight will go off the rails again?

He grunts and paddles harder, digging into the water. The kayak skims across the surface like skates on ice. The wind rakes its nails across his face and tunnels up his nose, shoving the rotten smells of sun-warmed algae and decomposing fish into his lungs. Like food scraps down a disposal.

He glides past a family of four out for a leisurely row. They wave. He ignores. Something he's good at doing. He doesn't have to answer to anyone or make excuses for being a pathetic asshole.

A few days after Lily ran away, when Dwight had been called in for questioning about the drowning of Wes Jensen off their dock, Lucas cut across the back lawn from his apartment above the garage to the shore. The best way to evade the constant stream of police cars and nosy neighbors was to avoid them. Put his head down and carry on as if nothing extraordinary had happened.

He rounded the back deck and heard weeping. Looking in that direction, he saw Charlotte. Bundled in a wool blanket on a patio chaise, his formidable mother appeared small and fragile, a flower wilting in the April mist.

He mounted the deck and sat by her feet. She reached for him, hand on the blanket, palm up. After a moment, Lucas wove his fingers with hers. He wanted comfort from her as much as he wanted to comfort her. Out of character for him, but he didn't give a shit.

"You don't have to hide from me, Lucas. I know you saw your dad with Wes the other night," she whispered.

Lucas could have stopped them, but he hadn't. His jaw ticked. He could still hear the echo of the shot that went off when Lily tried to wrestle the rifle from Dwight.

"Your father doesn't know you were watching. Keep it that way. Best no one knows."

He moved to extract his hand. Charlotte's grip tightened. "I'm trying to protect you, Lucas, like I've been protecting your little sister. It's not your fault she left. She didn't have a choice. You saw what your father did to that boy. I worried he'd harm her, too. He was incensed about her pregnancy. I'm the one who helped her run away even before your father told her to go." Lucas's eyes widened and she leaned closer. "I've wondered if your father did something to Benton St. John."

He tilted his head. "What?"

"Our neighbor. Remember him?"

"Barely." Benton was murdered when Lucas was three.

"It's just a feeling. But after what happened with Wes, that feeling's back. That poor boy. I couldn't see from the window, but I heard him. I know he was here. Then he wasn't. What did you see?"

Something he'd never be able to forget. Guilt over his failure to act on Lily's behalf crept through him, making itself at home. It wouldn't leave anytime soon. He should have stormed the scene, ripped the rifle from Dwight's hands, shot him in the chest, and dumped his body in the ocean. Lily would have no longer feared him, and she wouldn't have had to run away.

"Nothing I want to talk about," he said.

Charlotte squeezed his fingers. "He's not the man I married, Lucas. His failed campaigns have changed him. Our tight finances have made him bitter. And Benton St. John, your father was different after Benton's body was found. I don't want to find out what else he's capable of." Her voice quavered. She clung to his hand. "Wherever Lily is, she's safe, safer than if she'd stayed."

Lucas studied their linked hands. Charlotte's knuckles were ghostly white against her skin. She was shaking. Her trembles ran up his arm. He vowed to keep her safe. Whatever her reason—possibly fear Dwight would come after her, or the feeling she had no escape. He'd read an article about emotionally abused spouses and their belief there was no way out—she wouldn't leave Dwight. But Lucas wouldn't allow him to harm anyone else, no matter the cost.

"Give me your word, Lucas. Promise you won't tell a soul about anything you saw. They can't arrest your father. He knows things, things I can't share, please understand that." She squeezed his hand with a bruising grip.

"All right." He agreed for no other reason than his mom asked it of him. If she believed his silence kept her safe, then he'd keep quiet. For now.

"Thank you," she whispered.

He stood and kissed her forehead. "I'll take care of him when you're ready. I'll persuade him to leave us for good. Just give me the word." He now had leverage over Dwight. *Sorry, Mom.* But if Dwight's arrest meant he'd be out of their family picture, he'd tell the world what his father did. Paybacks were a bitch.

Lucas reaches the halfway point of his morning row and rests the paddle on his lap. The kayak bobs with the swell of the ocean, lulling him into a false sense of peace. His shoulders burn and biceps ache. His breathing comes long and deep.

He should have picked up Josh and taken him shopping. He'd promised Olivia. But he can barely look his nephew in the eye knowing he didn't come to Lily's aid when she needed him. His baby sister ran because she believed she shot Wes Jensen. He should have told her otherwise.

A lone seal swims under his kayak. He leans over and stares into the water's murky depths. How easy it would be to tip over and sink below the surface. End the noise of horrific memories in his head. Nobody would find him. Would anyone care?

Lily would if she were here. She'd berate him for thinking such ridiculous thoughts.

But it's thoughts of her and how she must have persevered all these years that keep him from capsizing. She's stronger than them all. Olivia's Dahlia Crimson. He paddles home at a PR pace, the wind at his back.

CHAPTER 16

"You are a godsend." Olivia meets Amber on the walkway and takes the grocery bags off her hands.

"I have more in the car."

"How much did you buy?" Olivia asks. Amber's trunk is open and filled to capacity. Olivia's never purchased that much food. It would spoil before she could eat her way through it.

"You're feeding a teenage boy." Amber returns to her car and Olivia takes the groceries to her kitchen.

After Lucas failed to show this morning to take Josh shopping, she called Amber, complaining about her brother. Nothing new. Lucas is unreliable. He avoids responsibility like a venereal disease. But it's been a stressful few days and she didn't need Lucas adding to it. She should have known he'd flake. She shouldn't have mentioned Lily added him as Josh's secondary guardian on the power of attorney if she couldn't fulfill her duties. Amber, bless her, offered to pick up groceries when Olivia mentioned she hadn't had the chance to place an order.

Olivia leaves the groceries on the kitchen island and meets Amber at her car. She eyes the bags. There's no way two people will consume this much food in a week. Less than that if they find Lily sooner and Josh can go home.

"Trust me," Amber says. "I see how much my clients with teens spend on groceries. It won't go to waste." She hands Olivia an over-stuffed paper bag. The bag rips and Granny Smith apples roll down the drive. "Yikes!" Amber chases after them. "They're going to bruise."

Olivia's phone rings. Distracted, she answers, expecting it's Lucas with an excuse. "I've been trying to reach you all morning. You were supposed to pick up Josh hours ago. Where are you?"

"Uh . . . Olivia?"

She swears and glares at her screen. Blaze. Her first instinct is to tell him about everything since they last spoke: her parents, Lily, Josh, even Ethan. But it's no longer her place to unload on him, even if up until the other day he's been her source of comfort when she's in a bind.

"Sorry. Thought you were Lucas."

"Everything okay?"

Far from it. Nothing's been normal since she broke up with Blaze. Her world was balanced with him in it. She's been teetering since she knocked him out of it.

"Fine. What's up?" she clips, juggling the torn bag so nothing else falls out.

"I've been trying to reach you."

"I know. Look, I'm really busy." Amber takes the bag from her with a head tilt. Blaze, Olivia mouths. "Can we talk later?" she asks him without bothering to find out exactly what he wants to discuss. She just wants to get off the phone, and not because she doesn't want to talk to him. The more she's thought about the other day, the more embarrassed she is about her over-the-top reaction. Blaze didn't deserve the way she handled things, or her lack of respect toward him. She owes him that apology she tried to give him the other night when he cut her off, and he deserves to hear it face-to-face. And maybe, she thinks, her conversation with Ethan fresh on her mind, she was wrong to end their relationship. She should have listened to Blaze. They should have worked through her concerns—and her insecurities—she reluctantly admits. But not right now.

"I'll swing by tonight," he offers.

"Sounds good." She ends the call and pockets the phone.

"What did he want?" Amber asks as they take the remaining groceries into the house.

"To talk."

She grins. "Knew it. You're going to get back together."

"Mm." She's not ready to commit to that.

Josh is rifling through the bags on the center island. He looks up when they enter the kitchen. "Hungry."

"I got something just for you." Amber pours him a cream soda over ice and digs out a box of extra toasty Cheez-Its. Olivia has never seen a kid look so happy.

"Aunt . . . O . . . has . . ." He gestures at the pantry. "It's . . . empty."

Olivia grimaces and he grins, taking his loot out back where he's been hanging out all morning, filling his sketchbook. He's been obsessively drawing pictures of where he lives. But without a city or street address, his home can be anywhere along the southern coast. She's confident they'd find Lily quicker if he could read, but he complains words make him dizzy. The letters aren't in order. They swirl around the page.

She glares at Amber. "Are you trying to kill him?"

"Huh?"

"Carbs and sugar. That's the worst thing you can give him."

"Your pantry is a teenage torture chamber. You smoke, but you have the most boring, bland food on the planet."

"It's healthy. Please tell me you bought something healthy." She peeks into a bag, afraid of what she'll find.

"What's going on with you? Aside from Lucas being Lucas. You're wound up," Amber says, unpacking groceries.

"When am I not?" She rips open a bag of dried fruit and pops an apricot to take the edge off.

"More than usual," Amber says.

Olivia eats another apricot and pulls out a stool. She sits at the island and gives Amber the rundown of the past few days from the police station and Charlotte's odd remark about Dwight to Lily's power of attorney in Josh's backpack and Ethan's visit.

"Hold up." Amber raises her hands. "You saw him?" Olivia nods. "That must have been . . . interesting."

"Very." She never expected to speak to Ethan again, let alone see him. Amber knows their history. They were roommates and she was there after she broke up with Ethan over the phone. She even broke out the box of Kleenex and chewy chocolate chip cookies as they binge-watched *Alias* because Olivia couldn't sit through a teary rom-com. When Olivia questioned if Dwight might have been wrong, Amber agreed he couldn't have been. Why would her dad lie about the father of Lily's child?

"Surprisingly less dramatic than I thought it would be. We were both civil, and . . ."

"And what?" Amber closes the fridge.

"He's not Josh's father."

Amber leans her elbows on the island. "You're sure?"

Olivia nods. "Josh says he knows his father. It isn't Ethan. But Ethan did offer to do a paternity test to prove it."

"Is he going to?"

She shakes her head. "It's not necessary."

"You believe him," Amber adds as Olivia picks through the apricots.

"I believe Josh. But I knew it the moment they were in the same room." Intuition kicked in. The feeling was overpowering. Josh and Ethan aren't blood relatives. "Their hair color is similar, but that's where it ends. Lily lied about Ethan. I'm sure of it. My dad must have really pressured her for a name."

"What are you going to do? Wait for her to show up like that police officer thinks she might?"

At a loss, Olivia shrugs. Last night she sent an email to the address on the POA and immediately received a failed-to-deliver message. When she tried the phone number, she reached a disconnected-number recording. A quick search online showed the law firm went out of business years ago, and there isn't any information about who took over their cases. Olivia was crushed. That law firm should have led her directly to Lily.

"The police aren't much help yet. They need to know where she lives or where she went missing—otherwise the missing persons report is useless. We're stuck with a courtesy report that doesn't even have the right name."

"What do you mean?"

"Lily changed her name." Olivia closes the dried fruit and nudges the bag aside. "Josh couldn't tell us at the station. He still hasn't told me. I'm going to work on it with him later, after we go to my mom's." Since Lucas bailed on shopping, Josh will have to tag along. "I want to know why Mom's worried about my dad. She might know something about Lily." Olivia also wants to locate those photos on Dwight's computer. He's obscenely organized and saves everything, so it should be easy.

"Is Mike working?" she asks, wondering if there's a work-around with Josh's speech impediment. Can he improve enough while he's with her? Is there something she can do to speed up his recovery? Can he recover?

"He never called?"

"Not yet. I thought about taking Josh to urgent care, but after what happened at the police station, I didn't want to chance stressing him out. I mean, aside from his speech issues, he seems fine physically. Can we see if Mike answers his phone?"

"Sure." Amber pulls out her phone. She moves next to Olivia and FaceTimes Mike. "Hi, hon," she says when his face appears. A two-day scruff covers his jaw, a mask hangs off one ear. Amber met Mike a couple years ago when she sliced open her hand while breaking down boxes. They met in the emergency room, but it wasn't until a few weeks later when they ran into each other at the grocery store that she asked him out. "How's your day going?" Amber asks.

"Long." He rubs an eye. "Just sat down for a break." He shows her a coffee mug with two Shih Tzus in bows. His mouth twists sideways. "Not my mug."

Amber grins. "Cute."

Olivia chuckles.

"Real quick, hon, I'm at Olivia's."

Olivia waves when Amber tilts the phone toward her. "Hi, Mike."

"Hey, Liv."

"Remember what I told you about her nephew?"

"Yeah, yeah, yeah." Mike perks up like Amber's presented him a new patient, which isn't really the case. Olivia understands whatever Mike tells her isn't an official diagnosis. But at this point, anything he can share about Josh's condition, possible therapies he can use to improve, would be a blessing.

"Sorry about your sister," he says. "Have you heard anything yet?"

Olivia shakes her head. "We're working on it."

"Best of luck. Tell me about your nephew. Josh, is it?"

"Yeah." Olivia scoots closer to the phone. "At first he told me he fell, but when we were at the police he said he was pushed." She tells him about the surgical scar on his head and how he mixes, even forgets, words and numbers. "He called an orange a peach and trash, keys."

"How is he physically? Any balance issues, dizziness?"

Olivia shakes her head. "None that I've seen."

Mike listens, rubbing his palm on his chin. When she finishes, he folds his arms on the table and leans forward. "Sounds like he had a brain bleed."

Amber sharply inhales. Olivia glances at her. That's what she thought when she first saw the scar. She can't imagine what Josh has been through, or Lily for that matter. His accident must have been a mother's worst nightmare.

"How serious is that?"

"Very. It can be fatal. But your nephew seems to be in luck. They caught it in time. A neurologist would have performed a burr hole drainage surgery." Mike goes on to describe how Josh probably had small holes drilled into his skull to release the pressure. A piece of his skull might have been removed to clean up the hematoma.

How tragic.

Olivia feels the unexpected burn of tears. A pinch in her chest aches behind her ribs. She glances over her shoulder and looks out the window where Josh sits at the table, worried he could fall over at any moment while under her watch. Her heart beats faster. He shouldn't be here with her. He should be home with his mom and under her care.

Amber nudges her elbow. "What's wrong?" she whispers.

"Worried about Lily. Do I need to bring him in?" she asks Mike.

"Not necessarily. Once the staples are removed and the incision has healed, there isn't much need for follow-up. Every case is different, of course. Has he complained about headaches? Any vision issues?"

"He can't read. He says it hurts his eyes and the letters are jumbled."

"That would be the aphasia."

"The what?" Amber asks.

"Aphasia. It's a residual effect of his BTI. Sorry, brain trauma injury," he says when they frown. "You can look it up, but it's basically the brain's inability to retrieve the right word. For instance"—he brings his mug into view—"he knows this is a mug and he knows what he's supposed to do with it. But ask him to tell you what it is and he'll say something else, like car or tree."

"He gets frustrated when he tries to talk." She gets frustrated when he can't.

"I imagine he would."

"Will he always be this way?"

"Hard to say. Aphasia can last several days to months. More extreme cases like those with stroke patients can be permanent."

"Is there anything I can do to speed up his recovery?" He needs to be able to tell her what happened.

"What about Melanie?" Amber asks.

He frowns. "Who?"

"Your friend Melanie."

His face lights up. "Yeah, yeah, yeah."

"Who's Melanie?" Olivia asks.

"She's a speech pathologist Mike knows from the hospital."

"She might be able to meet with you if Josh is going to be around for a while," he offers.

"Thank you," Olivia says, feeling more relieved than she expected to. She didn't ask to be in this situation. She has no idea what she's doing.

"I'll text her number. She might have some ideas that you can work on with Josh now."

"He draws a lot," Olivia says. "Can that help?"

"Great idea. He can show you what he wants to say."

Olivia nods, taking notes in her head. She can barely wrap her mind around everything she needs to consider to keep Josh safe and healthy. Clothing, food, doctors. How did Lily manage this when she was sixteen? Olivia briefly closes her eyes, feeling a flood of mad respect for her baby sister.

The hospital intercom on Mike's end crackles. He looks past his phone. "I have to go."

She thanks Mike for his help before the screen goes dark, grateful to have a sense of what Josh has been facing, dragons bigger than any thirteen-year-old should have to slay. Armed with this new information, she hopes she can help him communicate. At the very least, help him find his way home.

CHAPTER 17

After lunch and Amber has left, Olivia takes Josh to the mall, exactly where she didn't want to be. Every moment she's not focused on Lily is a moment she isn't looking for her. But Josh needs clothes. She's nervous. Will he explode like he did at the police station if a salesclerk asks his clothing size and he says *turtle* instead of *medium*? Will he take off like he almost did the other day with her and Lucas if she asks too many questions? *Which shirt is your favorite style? What color do you like? How's the fit? Short sleeve or long?* But once they arrive, she realizes her worries are unfounded. When Josh understands why she brought him, he leads her straight to his favorite store and combs through the racks as if he, too, is tired of wearing the same socks and underwear. Within fifteen minutes he has an armful of clothes, and when he can't stop saying thank you, she wants to buy out the entire store.

While Josh tries on jeans and tees, Olivia researches his condition. She doesn't learn much more from what Mike told her other than there are multiple types of aphasia that affect speech, reading, and writing to varying degrees. Aphasia doesn't affect intelligence, but it can influence comprehension. That would explain why Josh takes his time answering her questions. No wonder Josh doesn't talk much. She wouldn't either if she thought she sounded stupid when the wrong word popped out.

She watches his feet below the dressing room door, wishing she could call Lily and let her know Josh is safe. It's a miracle he found her and didn't end up in a dumpster somewhere. Olivia shivers from thoughts of all the dangers Josh could have run into.

The dressing room door opens and Josh appears. He gives her several shirts and a couple pairs of jeans, and for the first time since he arrived, she gives his shoulder a playful knock. "You did good," she says of his selection, and he smiles.

A short time later, Olivia parks in front of her parents' house, a sprawling ranch near the end of Sundial Court in the private community of Seaside Cove. When her parents purchased the beachfront property, Dwight wanted to build a home to boast about. He was a politician in the making with an image to uphold. Charlotte didn't want to see the neighbors from her windows. Olivia believes her parents never recouped the life savings they invested. Their financial woes were built into the framework. The house is a showcase.

Olivia cuts the ignition and Josh unclips his seat belt. She puts her hand on his arm, her eyes on the surveillance camera under the porch eave, Charlotte's warning kicking back in a lawn chair in the front yard of her mind. "Wait here." Dwight never looks at his surveillance footage, and from their current distance, parked on the side of the road, he won't be able to make out Josh's face in the car. But she doesn't want to risk that Dwight finally figured how to work the system Lucas insisted he install and sees someone else is in her car. He'll ask who it is. She restarts her car and finds a music station she thinks he'll like. "I won't be long."

He lets go of the latch. "Mom?"

"Yes. That's why we're here." She pats his knee and exits the car.

Olivia lets herself in through the front. Her parents rarely lock the door. They live in a gated community and Lucas resides in the apartment above the garage. Her parents have always had a false sense of security Olivia found out of place. Granted, it was thirty years ago, but there was a murder at the end of their street.

She heads for the kitchen, following the scent of baked goods, only to stop when she rounds the corner. Her mom, arms in the air and wearing nothing but an open purple silk robe, swivels her hips. Back and forth, she dances around the kitchen. She twirls and her eyes meet Olivia's. Charlotte shrieks, stumbling backward. She lands on her rear.

"Oh, my god." Olivia clamps a hand over her eyes and turns away from the kitchen. She can't unsee that. "It's Saturday. Aren't you supposed to be getting ready for a showing?" She peeks over her shoulder only to squeeze her eyes shut. The image of her mom, rear in the air, scrambling to stand, burns onto the backs of her eyelids. "Sorry. I should have called."

"You should have knocked." Charlotte huffs and Olivia hears her tying the robe's sash. She braves a look. Charlotte glares at her.

Olivia picks up the noise-canceling headphones Charlotte dropped. "You wouldn't have heard me." She puts the headphones on the counter.

"Lucas bought those for me."

She knows. Lucas told her. He was tired of Charlotte's complaints when he blasted his music or tinkered with his antique trucks in the driveway, revving their motors.

"Where is he?" she asks, wondering about the excuse he'll give her for bailing on Josh. His truck isn't in the drive.

"He's on the water."

Olivia's gaze wanders to the shore out back where Lucas beaches his kayaks. All three are beached near the water. "I don't think so."

"Then I don't know where he is. Give me that, will you?" Charlotte points behind her.

Olivia grabs the bath towel draped over the back of a kitchen chair.

"What brings you here?" Charlotte wraps up her hair.

"I've been thinking about what you said about Dad. Can we talk about Lily?"

"Is her son still with you?"

"He's in the car."

"Hmm." Turning to the counter, Charlotte transfers freshly baked cookies into a plastic storage container. "Your father will be home in a few days."

Olivia steals a cookie and bites into it, frowning. A thought clicks into place like a Scrabble tile that earns her enough points to win the game. But this combination sinks like lead in her stomach, leaving a heavy weight inside her. "Dad's in San Diego."

"Mm-hmm."

"Josh was born in San Diego."

Charlotte seals the lid on the container. "What are you implying?"

"Maybe it's just a coincidence." But Olivia can't shake the thought.

"What is?" Charlotte asks.

"Josh is here, Dad's there, Lily's missing. She could be dead."

Charlotte's complexion blanches. Hurt skates the rims of her eyes. "Olivia, please. Don't talk like that. I've coped without Lily because I picture her out there alive and thriving. Don't convince me otherwise." Her face cracks. She retreats to the kitchen sink and flips on the faucet. Water pours into the sink. She stares at the dirty dishes, but Olivia doesn't think she sees them.

"I don't like it either, Mom, but we have to consider all possibilities. Josh may be with me for a while. Dad's going to find out. Why can't he know about Josh? Do you think he'd hurt him?" Olivia doesn't believe so, not physically. Dwight and Lily had their disagreements, but he never laid a hand on her. He'd also get angry at Olivia, and usually because she deserved it, but he never struck her either.

"You were away at school. You didn't see him before Lily ran. The rage in him. I'd never seen anything like it, Olivia. He was so upset about Lily's pregnancy that she ran away. She left me. I don't want to risk it."

Was he upset enough to never stop looking for her all these years? A coldness seeps into Olivia like fog creeping in from the bay. Her hands turn to ice. It's not a coincidence that he's in San Diego. She's positive. "He found her, didn't he?"

Charlotte drops the sponge she soaked. She slowly turns to Olivia when something outside draws her back. "Who is that?"

Olivia looks outside and curses under her breath. "It's Josh." He's heading toward their private dock. What's he doing? She told him to stay in the car. "I'll get him."

"Take him home, Olivia. He can't come in the house. Your father's security cameras."

Too late now. Olivia tries not to feel alarmed. "Dad never looks at the video footage." He can barely log into his computer. Twice she's tried to walk him through the app on his phone and he never got the hang of it.

"He does too." Charlotte wrings her hands.

And he will if he has reason to look through the footage. Olivia watches Josh mount the dock. Her limbs tingle as adrenaline courses through her extremities.

"Get dressed. I'll see what he's up to." After closing the french door behind her, Olivia dashes across the yard. "Josh, wait up."

He's hauling, his pace a reminder that he's Lily's son. Lily was quick, whether chasing Lucas in a game of tag, breaking records in the fifty-yard freestyle, or running away from home.

She catches up with him at the end of the dock. Hands stuffed in his hoodie pockets, shoulders rounded against the wind, he gazes over the choppy water.

"I told you to wait in the car. What are you doing here?" She gasps, short of breath.

"Looking for you. Saw that." He points across the bay toward the sleepy ocean-side town of Morro Bay.

"That's Morro Rock," she says of the massive volcanic rock dominating the coastline. Behind the geological formation, three four-hundred-foot-plus smokestacks left over from an old power plant tower over the Pacific coast. Her inspiration of the source of the Crimson Wave's power. Every day she looked out her bedroom window at this view. So did Lucas and Lily. "Cool," he says, showing no sign of leaving.

"We should go. Come on." She'll ask Amber to stay with him and come back later.

Josh looks up at the house. "Mom?"

Olivia glances over her shoulder. "She's not here, I told you that."

He shakes his head and points at her.

"Me? Oh, my mom. She's inside."

Josh starts walking toward the house.

"Where are you going?" She chases after him. "Josh, stop." She tugs the sleeve of his new sweatshirt. He gets too close to the cameras, Dwight will have a clear picture of his face.

He turns around. "My . . . mom." He points at the house.

"Like I said, she's not here." How many times does she have to explain this? "I was asking my mom about yours when we saw you out the window."

He holds his hand at his waist. "Mom . . . girl . . . bat . . . rug." He smacks his forehead repeatedly. "Little!"

"I don't—" She stares at his hand. "Do you mean *little girl*?" He nods vigorously. "Yes, you're right. This was her home when she was little."

"See?"

"See what? Her room?"

He nods.

How does she tell him no? He'll ask why. He's probably curious about his mom's childhood. Did Lily share anything with him? She left behind her clothes, artwork, scrapbooks, and journals.

On a slight gasp, Olivia looks up at the house.

Charlotte's kept Lily's room unchanged for years. She's also kept the door locked as if it was too tempting, yet too painful, to look inside.

What if Lily wrote in her journal about her pregnancy and where she was thinking of running away to?

She might have named the father. Olivia still believes Josh's father might know how to reach Lily. He might even know where she could have gone.

"Keep your head down."

He gives her a funny look and she huffs impatiently. Yes, it's a weird request. "Just do it. I'll explain later."

CHAPTER 18

After Olivia confirms Charlotte is in her room getting ready for work, which gives her plenty of time to scour Lily's room and get Josh back to the car, she puts a finger to her lips for Josh to be quiet and leads him into the kitchen. Olivia searches for a tool to unlock Lily's door. "Found it." She shows Josh the paper clip. "Follow me."

At Lily's bedroom door, she shapes the paper clip into a somewhat straight wire and jams the makeshift device into the doorknob, working the lock. As she does, she wonders how Josh will react when he sees his mom's childhood room. How will *she* react? She's so used to the door being closed that it's as if the room hasn't been here all these years. As if Lily was never a member of the family. Something was going on between Lily and their parents that Olivia failed to recognize when it mattered. Not only that, she failed her sister. If Olivia had helped Lily when she needed it, they wouldn't be in this mess. Lily's bedroom wouldn't be the empty space everyone tiptoed around. Josh would have grown up surrounded by family. Olivia has so many regrets.

The paper clip misses the notch inside the knob and Olivia mutters under her breath. Will Lily's room smell the same? Warm, fresh, and feminine from her favorite perfume? Or will the air be stale like Olivia's memories of Lily have become? They aren't as clear anymore, and after talking with Ethan last night, she wonders if everything that occurred between her and Lily happened the way she believes.

The paper clip slips from the knob and scrapes her thumb. "Ow." She's horrible at breaking and entering. She sucks the tip, glancing back at Josh. He's halfway down the hall looking at the framed photos on the wall. He makes a noise.

"What is it?" she asks, miffed. She thought he was right behind her.

He points at a photo and tries to speak, but the words stick to his tongue like wet sand on a damp bathing suit. He punches the air and roughly points at the photo, begging her to understand. Olivia motions with her hands for him to be quiet, glances back at her parents' bedroom door, and makes her way over to him and studies the family portrait that has his attention. The photo was taken Olivia's senior year in high school during Dwight's third and last campaign. She was seventeen, Lucas fifteen, and Lily twelve and a half. Big brown eyes fill Lily's face. Braces hug her teeth. A flat chest doesn't deter from her budding beauty.

Josh squeezes his eyes shut and bangs his head with his fists. He's literally trying to beat the words out.

Familiar with his signs of distress, Olivia pockets the mangled paper clip and gently touches his shoulder. "Look at me. Josh, hey," she says, urging him to come with her outside before Charlotte hears them. The fresh air and openness will calm him down. They can return later.

His eyes snap open and he makes a grab for the photo. "Shh. Don't do that," Olivia loudly whispers. She slaps a hand to the frame so the photo remains mounted. "Take a breath, Josh. Relax and talk your way through this. What's wrong with this picture? Are you looking for your mom? She's right here, see?" She prompts him like she'd read about for people with aphasia. Spell out the words. Give them the chance to speak.

His face reddens and a word pops from his mouth like a truck backfiring. "Bad."

"The photo or the people in it?" Olivia's gaze rakes over the family portrait. Charlotte had wanted a magazine spread when *SLO Life* featured her as a top real estate broker in the county. *California Living* used the same photo when the publication featured a sneak peek inside their custom-built home during Dwight's campaign. Taken in the backyard, Dwight and Lucas wore tuxedos. They looked dashing in black with their silk ties. Charlotte, along with Olivia and Lily, wore champagne gowns with all the sparkle and glitz found at an Oscars after-party. Their dresses shimmered in the golden hour sunlight. Wind cut across the yard at the perfect moment, ruffling Lucas's hair and lifting her cinnamon locks and Lily's long auburn tresses off their shoulders the moment the photographer snapped the shot. A glamorous pose that rivaled that of any family of status. The photographer won a coveted award for the photo. Dwight posted the image on the About Us page of his corporate website. The photo, along with the accompanying articles, cemented the Carsons as a family to watch, much to Charlotte's delight. *How I wish my daddy could see me now*, Olivia recalls her mom remarking on more than one occasion about the grandfather Olivia had never met.

If people could see them now.

What a mess the Carsons have become.

"Bad." Josh jabs at the glass. The photo swings on its hook.

"Careful." Olivia fixes the frame. There's a larger version of this photo above the living room fireplace, but Charlotte will still have a conniption if anything happens to this one. It's her favorite of all the portraits in the hallway.

"Bad." Josh knocks her shoulder, pushing her back.

"Hey." She stumbles against the wall.

"Bad. Bad." He yanks the photo off the wall, ripping out the nail along with. Drywall dust sprinkles to the floor like snow.

Charlotte comes out of her room, tucking a pale-blue blouse into cream slacks, her makeup partially applied. Only one cheek has been rouged. Her lips are unadorned, making the color above her eyes stand out. She looks waifish, like a model in a designer label ad. "What's going on?" She stops when she sees Josh. "Why's he here?"

"Bad," he yells, showing Charlotte the photo.

"Put that down," Charlotte roars, her face deathly pale.

Her reaction sends a ripple of fear through Olivia. Where's this coming from?

Olivia grips Josh's arm. "We need to go."

He shakes her off, "Bad, M-m-man!" He spits the word. Rage fills his eyes. Something else churns there, too.

Heart pulsating in her throat, Olivia looks at the photo. There's only one man in the picture because Lucas is just a kid, not much older than Josh: her dad.

She asked Charlotte earlier if Dwight found Lily. Her mom didn't have the chance to answer her. Josh interrupted them.

But Olivia has her answer now.

He was pushed by a *bad man*.

Her daddy attacked his grandson. *Her* nephew.

No. Olivia shakes her head. Josh has to be confusing Dwight for someone else. Her dad would never intentionally harm anyone. It has to have been an accident. Olivia feels as shattered as broken glass.

Josh grips her arm. His blunt nails dig into her skin. She winces. His mouth forms nonsensical words.

"Come on." She takes the photo from him. "We're going home." Charlotte yells behind her to save her photo. "It's fine, Mom." She finds the nail on the floor and shoves it back into the wall. She hangs the photo, even straightens it as her world crumbles into dust finer than the drywall flakes on the floor.

Josh finally blurts what he's been struggling to say. "Run!" He pivots, his backpack scraping along the wall. Frames crash to the floor, including the family portrait. Glass shatters.

"My pictures!" Charlotte's cry is shrill. She folds to the floor.

The front door slams and another crash follows.

"Now what?" Charlotte exclaims.

Olivia hurries to the entryway. Josh slammed the door hard enough to shatter the side window. She feels like she's looking at her heart. It's in pieces on the floor. Her dad, the man she admired her entire life, is a bad man. Josh wouldn't have reacted so violently if it wasn't Dwight. He wouldn't be as scared as he is.

Through the open pane, she sees him pace the length of the car, arms folded, head down. He drags the back of his hand across his eyes and glares at the house, only to quickly look away. Olivia watches him, stunned, her head shaking in disbelief. Her throat is so thick with unshed tears that the air gets trapped. Her lungs strain.

"Help me, Olivia." Charlotte tries to salvage the frames.

Olivia looks from the door to her mom, torn between her and the tormented boy outside.

"Olivia." Charlotte barks her name when she's too slow to react. "Do something."

"I'll come back later." Josh needs her. Charlotte only needs a broom. She runs to the car. When she reaches Josh, she grabs his elbow, startling him. He takes a swing at her. The back of his hand connects with her cheekbone.

She rears back, palm cupped over her cheek. "Ow." She rubs the burn from her face. "What was that for?"

Josh points at the car. "Go."

"I'm not leaving you." He's scared and confused. She won't walk away from him, especially now that she has a sense of why Charlotte warned her about Dwight. Did she know? Does she know where Lily is? Was her sister running from Dwight when she and Josh separated?

"Go." He reaches for the passenger door, and she realizes he's telling her he wants them to leave.

"All right, we'll go." He opens the door and drops into the passenger seat.

She starts to close his door and stops. "That man in the picture, you sure you've seen him before?" she asks with trepidation, hoping she's wrong. That he's wrong, and he's mistaking Dwight for someone else. Josh nods. "He's my dad, your grandfather."

A tear rolls down his face. "I know."

Olivia feels a sting in her eyes. It hurts to breathe, like she's cracked a rib. "When did you meet him?"

"Before." He touches the spot on his hat that covers his scar.

Before his head injury

Olivia glances away. *Oh. God.* She takes a breath. "Did he push you?" She needs his confirmation.

He nods, then shakes his head.

"You aren't sure?" She frowns, and a beat later, he shrugs.

"Didn't see."

She cocks her head. *Didn't see what?*

"You didn't see who pushed you, but you think it was your grandfather?"

He shrugs.

Jittery, she drums her fingers on the window edge. He isn't positive. It's still possible he's confused Dwight with someone else.

She could call her dad and ask why he's in San Diego. Does it have anything to do with Lily? Does he know where she is? Is she missing because of him?

Is she running from him?

Did he hurt Josh?

Disbelief wedges between her doubts and what she witnessed inside like a book on a stacked shelf. She can't think of anything that would motivate Dwight to pursue Lily after fourteen years. Unless Lily knows something about him that just came to light, but what would that be?

Benton St. John comes to mind.

No, she won't believe that either.

One phone call and she could get the answers. But would Dwight tell her the truth?

It's Ethan. Your Ethan. He's the father.

Maybe Dwight's the one who lied.

No, no, no. Not possible. He wouldn't have done that to her. He knew how devastating a lie that would be, how much it would hurt her.

Olivia shuts the door and rounds the back of the car. She roots around the bottom of her purse for her Marlboros and lighter. It takes three attempts to light the cigarette, her hands shake that badly. She looks back at the house, tempted to return and ask Charlotte what she knows about Dwight and Lily. But her mom's too worked up about the damage Josh did. They'd just talk in circles. And Josh is upset and wants to leave.

Taking a long drag on the cigarette, she shakes her head. Josh has to be wrong. Charlotte must be exaggerating. Olivia's dad isn't a violent man.

But he was a suspect in an unsolved murder case, she reasons, her mind taking a U-turn back to Benton. A person of interest in a drowning that was eventually ruled an accident. What if there's more to those cases than what she read?

Charlotte would know.

Olivia starts walking back to the house and hesitates midstride. She needs to talk this out first. Amber will help her make sense before she worries herself to death that her beloved daddy is a murderer who might have attacked his grandson. The thought sickens her.

"Stop." *Just fucking stop.*

Her mind is taking her down rabbit holes.

Juggling her phone and cigarette, she brings up her call history. When she sees Blaze's name in the queue, he unwittingly flashes to mind and ash singes her finger. She fumbles the phone. It drops in the grass.

"Hello? Hello? Liv, you there?"

She hears Blaze's voice among the grass blades. Her finger must have brushed his name in her attempt to grab the phone before it flew from her grasp. Her impulse is to kiss her phone. Blaze would listen; then he'd tell her that her line of thinking is flawed. Dwight's had his share of hardships. His reputation has received its dents. But he's a good man.

"Liv, I know you're there. I can hear you breathing."

She presses the phone to her ear. "Sorry. Called you on accident."

"Wait. Don't hang up. Something's wrong." He must have caught the mania in her voice.

She closes her eyes, counts to five. Breathes. "Nothing's wrong." She tempers her voice, hoping she sounds normal.

"I can tell it's not nothing. What's going on? Talk to me, Liv," he asks, and she almost caves when Josh throws open his door.

"Go now."

"We are," she tells him, then says to Blaze, "I have to go."

She ends the call and dials Lucas, leaving a message when he doesn't pick up. "Call me. It's urgent. And check on Mom when you get home. Josh shattered the front window. She needs it fixed." She looks back at the house and the window to Dwight's home office. "Do me a favor. Ask Mom about Lily. I think she and Dad know where she's been living."

Ending the call, she stares at the window. Lily's address could be there, in a file or on his computer. She has to delete the video surveillance of Josh anyway. She also wants to find Dwight's photos. If Olivia can find Lily's address, Officer Curbelo can call in a well-neighbor check. Better yet, she can drive there herself. Someone has to know where Lily went.

Olivia drops the cigarette butt, snuffing it with her heel, and settles into her car. Josh keeps his face averted, chin propped on his hand, his backpack on the floor between his legs. Her gaze drops to the pack. "You like graphic novels?" she asks, thinking of the Hellblazer book in the center pocket.

He looks at her peculiarly, pulling on his bottom lip, and a vise tightens around her ribs. Such a Lily gesture.

"Will you draw me your story? Show me what happened to you and your mom? How you got here? Draw any place you think your mom could have gone, like a friend's house, or places you traveled to. Make it like a graphic novel if you want." That way, she might understand the pictures without him having to explain. "She's out there, Josh. We're going to find her."

His hand drops in his lap. "Okay."

She starts the car and swipes the tear that found its way over her cheekbone. Her family has its share of dysfunction, but damn. This is ridiculous.

"Sorry," he says, pointing at the house.

"Don't be. This isn't your fault. None of this is." But she intends to find out whose fault it is. This time, she won't jump to conclusions, something she's prone to do. As was Dwight.

CHAPTER 19

Summer of '00

Four weeks into their sixth summer at the lake, thirteen-year-old Olivia, Blaze, Lucas, Tyler, and Lily, who was already eight, walked into Decker's Market. The artificially chilled air blasting through the store, a tidal wave of cold relief, spilled out the entrance, mixing with the hot, dry mountain air. The door slid closed behind them and they sighed in unison, their bathing suits stiff from dried lake water and skin sticky with thick layers of water-resistant sunscreen. The market was always a welcome relief after walking the half mile in flip-flops on a hot asphalt road under the early afternoon sun. But fifteen minutes of discomfort was worth the treat at the end.

"Lily, come with me," Olivia said. Lucas was up to no good. He was in a mood, bumping shoulders with Tyler. He knocked Tyler into a bread display. A few loaves dropped to the floor. Lucas laughed and kept on walking. Tyler haphazardly put the bread back and ran after Lucas.

Lily started to follow.

"I'll buy your ice cream today," Olivia enticed. Lily only had in her pocket what their dad gave her at the beginning of the summer, which wasn't much. And her allowance was minuscule compared to what she and Lucas had earned at her age. Their dad justified it by saying Lily had fewer chores than they had when they were eight. Olivia didn't think that was true. Lily's chores kept her just as busy as them on Saturday mornings. But who was she to argue with their dad?

"Meet up in five," Blaze said, as if they needed reminders to meet at the icebox like they'd been doing all summer.

Decker's Market was as old as the lake and still owned by Mr. Decker, the grandson of the original Mr. Decker. It was a quarter of the size of the supermarket back home, but the store had everything, from fishing tackle to sun hats and beach towels. It even had a ride-on horse out front that took two quarters. Neil Diamond, Mrs. Decker's favorite, always played on the ceiling speakers.

With coins in their pockets, they went their separate ways, Lucas and Tyler to the toy section in back to see if the new Hot Wheels Mr. Decker ordered had come in. Blaze went straight to the drink section. He'd chug a Red Bull and pay for the empty can so he could toss it before they left the store and his dad wouldn't know he was drinking the stuff. Olivia took Lily to the magazine rack. Mr. Decker kept office supplies on the bottom shelf. She needed a new pad of paper for her sketches.

Lily flipped through a comic book left over from two summers ago. "There's nothing new."

Olivia showed her *Seventeen*. "Try this." The latest issue came in a few days ago.

Lily opened the magazine to an advice column on pimples. Her eyes glazed over. "Boring. I'm going to check on Luc." They could hear him and Tyler laughing a couple aisles over. Lily returned the magazine to the rack.

"Stay here. Lucas is being a—" A cold can pressed against the back of her neck. She shrieked and whirled on Blaze. "You!" She playfully nudged his shoulder. He got her every time.

Blaze laughed; then his arms roped around her and he kissed her, right there in front of Lily. He smelled like coconut and sweat, and he tasted like the most thrilling ride at Six Flags Magic Mountain. Her pulse pounded in her ears.

Kissing was new, all tongue and saliva, and they did it any chance they could get when they were alone. But they weren't alone this time. They were in the middle of the store. People who knew the Whitmans could see them. If Harold and Rhonda knew their friendship was now fueled by lust and hormones Olivia and Blaze barely understood but couldn't get enough of, they'd separate the girls and guys in a heartbeat.

"Ew. I'm outta here." Olivia heard Lily's flip-flops recede. They smacked the tile floor until they faded away. She tore her mouth from Blaze's, gasping. He grinned, his chest heaving.

"That wasn't nice." She pointed at the Red Bull in his hand and noticed he was tenting his swim shorts.

"Shit." He grabbed a magazine and held it in front of his shorts.

Olivia's face felt like an inferno. She didn't know whether to be embarrassed for herself or for him, so she left. "I'm going to find Lily."

Lily was at the icebox with Lucas and Tyler. As Olivia approached, she saw Lily stick her hand into the freezer just as Lucas started to slam closed the lid. Tyler smacked his hand to stop the door. "Watch it. You okay?" he asked Lily.

She showed him the chocolate ice cream sandwich she'd selected. "Got it."

"Heard you were sucking face." Lucas pretended to make out with his forearm.

"Jerk." Olivia smacked the back of his head as she passed him. He snorted a laugh. "Thanks a lot, Lily." She stuck her tongue out at her sister, opening the icebox, and selected a Drumstick.

Blaze came around the corner and grabbed a missile pop. His lips would turn red, then bright blue, and they'd all be making fun of him before they reached the cabin. Olivia noticed he'd stuffed the Red Bull in his pocket to hide the residual effects of their kiss. He dropped a possessive arm around her shoulders. "Ready to head back?" he asked everyone.

"Yeah, let's bounce." Lucas led their pack to the market's single checkout line. Mr. Decker worked the cash register. They showed him their ice cream, Blaze's Red Bull, and piled their change on the counter. Lily murmured her thanks to Olivia for covering her.

"That all?" Mr. Decker asked.

"Yes, sir," Blaze said and the rest nodded.

"Are you sure?" Mr. Decker looked straight at Lucas.

Lucas glanced at Tyler, then Olivia. He nodded at Mr. Decker.

"Care to empty your pockets, Lucas?"

Lucas's throat rippled. "No."

Mr. Decker's gaze moved over them before landing back on Olivia's brother. He picked up the phone by the cash register. "Empty your pockets or I call the police."

Lucas gulped.

Olivia's skin tingled all over, and she wasn't even the one in trouble. "What did you do?" she loudly whispered at Lucas.

"Nothing. Shut up."

"Show him, Luc." Their ice cream was melting.

"There's nothing in my pockets," he said angrily.

"Honest, Mr. Decker. I saw him," Lily said in a little voice. "He didn't take anything."

Mr. Decker hesitated. He returned the phone to its cradle. "Follow me. All of you."

The trek to the small office at the back of the market seemed like the longest walk Olivia had ever taken, even longer than the walk to the market from the cabin.

Mrs. Decker was sitting behind a desk with a couple monitors.

"Dot, play that recording," Mr. Decker said, closing the door behind them. The office was cramped and stuffy. He turned one of the monitors so they could see. "Gather round, kids." They huddled closer.

On the screen was a black-and-white image of the market. Olivia could see people in the aisles, moving about.

"There's Lucas." Lily pointed. "And me! Look, I'm on TV." She grinned.

"I've been watching you all summer, Lucas. You take things off the shelves and stick them in your pockets, but you always make sure you put them back before you leave the store. They're little things you might not think I'd notice have gone missing until I do inventory at the end of the month."

Olivia squinted at the screen. Mrs. Decker replayed their shopping trip and Olivia saw that Mr. Decker was right. Lucas snagged three items and returned them someplace else in the store. And then he snagged a fourth and followed Tyler to the icebox. Anger spiked. Her hands fisted. She hadn't realized what Lucas had been doing; otherwise she would have said something to him. Now he'd dragged them all into hot water.

Blaze gently touched her lower back. Their eyes met. His burned bright. He was fuming.

"So far, Lucas, you've been good," Mr. Decker was telling them. "But I knew one day you'd be tempted enough to walk out of the store without putting it back." He dipped his hand into the large front pocket of the market apron he wore and pulled out a torn Hot Wheels box. "Found this on the floor."

Lucas's face drained of color. Olivia's stomach bottomed out. Mr. Decker's order had finally come in and Lucas couldn't resist.

"Lucas," she lamented.

Mr. Decker gestured at the screen. "Dot here watched you open that box. She didn't see you put the car back. Show me where it is out there and I'll let you go. Can you do that for me?"

A tear rolled down Lucas's face. He shook his head.

"Give me the toy, son."

Lucas's chest expanded with a large inhale. He reached into his swim shorts and took out a yellow Mustang. He hadn't been lying.

The car wasn't in his pockets. He'd stuffed it into the netted underwear attached to his shorts.

"Dude." Blaze cupped a hand over his mouth.

Mr. Decker didn't call the police. He called Mr. Whitman, who picked them up in his minivan.

Olivia slammed her melted Drumstick into the trash and climbed into the rear seat of the van. Lucas started to follow her and she stretched her legs out on the bench seat. "You're not sitting next to me."

"I didn't mean to take it," he mumbled. He didn't need her to tell him she was pissed.

"Don't talk to me." She crossed her arms and looked out the window, recalling the conversation between Harold and Rhonda she overheard last summer. This was it. Lucas finally screwed up big-time. The Whitmans would send them home. They'd never invite them back.

Dwight Carson arrived just before sunset. He declined Rhonda's invitation to stay for dinner and packed his three kids' luggage into the trunk of his Cadillac. Lucas had been quiet all afternoon. He knew he'd ruined summer and that everyone was upset with him. Dwight was going to ground him until school started. Good, Olivia thought. He deserved it.

She was in tears. Nothing she said could change Dwight's mind to let her stay, even when the Whitmans offered to drive her home when he said he wasn't making a second trip. Harold and Rhonda had only asked him to pick up Lucas. But Dwight and Charlotte worked. They needed Olivia to watch her younger siblings.

Lucas dropped into the back seat and slammed his door. Olivia was about to get into the front seat when she saw their dad block Lily from getting into the car. Arms folded over his chest, he towered over Olivia's little sister. Lily backed up a step. He moved forward.

"Did you see Lucas stealing?" he asked, his tone stern.

"No." Her face fell. "Yes," she whispered after a moment. She looked at the ground.

"You should have stopped him."

"He always puts the stuff back," she said, near tears.

"It's not her fault," Lucas defended.

"You stay out of this. I don't want to hear a word from you, young man." Dwight turned back to Lily. "And you." He dropped a hand on her shoulder and squeezed. Lily winced. "You had a chance to stop him and you didn't. This is as much your fault as his."

"But I didn't do anything. I was with Olivia." Her sister's eyes found Olivia's over the roof of the car.

Olivia should have stood up for Lily. Their dad was being unfair. But she was too upset with Lucas. She shook her head and got into the car.

"You're grounded when we get home," Olivia heard their dad tell Lily. "And I'm cutting your allowance for the rest of summer. Now get into the car."

Lily climbed into the back seat sobbing. Dwight slammed her door. He sank into the driver's seat and started the car. Olivia pulled a tissue from the caddy and dried her eyes, blew her nose.

Dwight patted her knee. "This isn't your fault, Princess." Olivia shredded her tissue. She wanted to tell him it wasn't Lily's fault either, but tears clogged her throat. She was on the brink of being a blubbering mess and the Whitmans were watching them.

"Cheer up," he encouraged. "I'll take you to lunch this weekend."

Olivia didn't want to go to lunch with her dad. She wanted to grill hamburgers with the Whitmans and kayak with Blaze.

Dwight backed out of the driveway. It would be two weeks before she saw Blaze again. Olivia was going to miss him and swimming and campfires. She turned around and watched the cabin shrink in size as they drove away. In the back of her mind, she knew this would be the last time she'd visit the lake house.

CHAPTER 20

LUCAS

Glass shards crack under Lucas's work boots. Typically, he'll remove his shoes before entering his parents' house, or any house, for that matter. They're filthy, caked with sawdust and paint. Who knows what else his soles pick up when he's mangling bushes and tromping flower beds while painting a home's exterior? But Olivia left him a message several hours ago and their mom still hasn't swept the mess.

That kid has an arm if he can break a window from slamming the door.

He'd make a great quarterback, Lucas thinks, reaching for the broom Charlotte left leaning against the wall. But he stops short of comparing Josh's potential to the skills he let waste away.

Light from the chandelier overhead ricochets off the glass while he sweeps, making the scraps shimmer. They remind him of the broken window at the convenience store after the bullet he accidentally shot off shattered the glass. The shards refracted the market's fluorescent lights like sunlight on the ocean's surface when he was forced to his knees and handcuffed.

His jaw hardens and hands tighten on the broomstick. He hates how something as mundane as sweeping glass easily sends his mind there, to that night. How the handgun he wrangled from Tanner went off, blowing out the window and the front windshield of his car. How his football teammates ditched the place, and him, leaving him to take the fall.

Lucas sweeps the pieces into a dustpan and drops the shards into the pail Charlotte put by the door after Olivia and Josh left. He still hasn't heard the full story from her. Only that Josh came unglued when he saw the picture of Dwight. What has his old man gotten himself into now?

Propping the broom against the wall, he reaches for the measuring tape he brought with him. He quickly measures the window frame, committing the numbers to memory, and leaves the house. He calls Dan at the local glass shop and puts in a rush order for a replacement. He then grabs a piece of scrap plywood leaning against the side of the garage from another project and saws a piece to cover the window. When he's nailed the board in place, he finds Charlotte in the kitchen, scrolling through her iPad. Old photos rest on the table beside her elbow, their broken frames in the trash.

"You're all set," he announces, opening the fridge. "I put in an order for a replacement. Dan will bring it by in several days and install it." He grabs one of Dwight's Coors Light. Piss water. But he still pops the top and guzzles a third. "What happened?"

"Josh saw your father in a photo. He broke everything on his way out."

"That's what Livy said. Do you think Dad found Lily?" He knows Dwight hadn't thought about Lily for years until that reporter came sniffing around a few months ago about her high school swim record.

"He must have."

"I didn't think he'd actually go looking for her." The man put on a good show after Lily ran. He could barely speak his youngest's name without tearing up. But Lucas knew it was an act.

"Neither did I." She sorts the photos she salvaged from the broken frames, measures their sizes with a plastic ruler that has her real estate agency's logo.

He crosses his arms and leans back against the counter. "Do you know why?" He's regretted he never lifted a finger to help Lily. She needed him, even relied on him, and he walked away.

Charlotte sets aside the ruler and photos. "I wouldn't possibly know what he wants with her after all this time," she says in a low voice.

"Do you remember what you told me the day after Lily ran?"

"That I worried he'd harm her?"

He shakes his head. "You said Dad knows things. What kind of things, Mom?" He's always wondered if it had to do with the St. John case. Charlotte once told him she suspected his dad may have had more involvement than he let on. She covers her mouth and looks away. The skin on the back of his neck tingles. "That reporter a while back, Dad said he was asking after Lily. He asked about the St. John murder, too."

A tear unspools over her cheek. The skin underneath shimmers. Lucas drops to his knees and takes her hand. The gesture feels foreign to him. It's been years since he tried to comfort her, or sought reassurance from her, or anyone, for that matter. But his mom has put up with so much from Dwight. "Does Dad have something to do with that? Did he murder Benton? You told me once you thought he did."

Charlotte looks troubled. She stares at his big hand, trembling. "Lily overheard your father and I arguing about what to do with her. You know he wanted her to abort. He started going off about money again. His campaigns came up and then, I don't know how, he brought up the St. John murder. Everything he hated about our marriage came gushing out. It was the worst argument we ever had. I thought he was going to strike me, he was blinded by rage. I'm not sure he meant it— good Lord, I hope he wasn't serious—but he told me he'd kill Lily like Benton if she didn't get rid of the baby."

Lucas sees red. "But did he kill St. John?" If he could hang Benton's murder over Dwight's head, he could get rid of his father for good. Let the authorities lock him up. He'd get a taste of the medicine Lucas was forced to swallow in his cell. Life isn't glorious behind bars.

"I don't know. He went out for a walk the night Benton died," she cries, squeezing his hand. "I couldn't take the risk he'd harm Lily. I told her to run away to a place he'd never find her, somewhere he'd never look. But Woo, that poor boy. He came over when your sister was packing and your father went nuts."

"Dad knows she overheard you arguing?"

"He isn't sure how much. He's always wondered. And he's always worried she'll talk."

Dwight probably thought she had talked when that small-time reporter came sniffing out of the blue, asking about Lily and her time with the Seaside Cove High swim team.

Their eyes meet. For a man whose image is everything, Dwight would want to tie up loose ends. Lucas fears Lily might be one of those ends.

He lets go of Charlotte's hand and stands up. He guzzles the rest of his beer. "Let me see," he asks of the photos.

She stands up from the table and gives him the pictures. She goes to the counter and pulls a tissue from the box by the house phone, dabs her eyes.

He flips through the photos. His junior year photo, the last class picture he took because he was in juvie during senior portraits. The next photo is their family portrait, the one that must have flipped his nephew. Dwight stands proudly on the right, Olivia on the left and his mom seated in front. The last picture is of Lily playing on the beach looking cute in her green one-piece with the ruffle skirt. She couldn't be older than six. He thinks how vibrant she was at that age; then he thinks how lonely and frightened she must have been when she left them. His throat burns with remorse like it's been scalded with coffee.

He quickly flips back to the family portrait. "Do you remember what I promised you the day after Lily ran?"

Charlotte wipes her nose and looks at him curiously.

"I said I'd get him to leave for good. Look at us. Look what we've become. Our family is a mess. His campaigns have drained your finances. You've mortgaged the house several times over. At this rate, you'll be making payments long past retirement. His drive to save his reputation, to bury whatever he's done, will only hurt you. Let me bring him around to leaving us. If you want to divorce him, and I think you should, I'll convince him to sign the paperwork. You'll finally be rid of him. Lily can come home."

"It's too much, Lucas." She shakes her head. "I can't ask that of you."

"You're not asking. I'm offering."

"No. I won't risk him hurting you, too."

He looks at the tile flooring. "He can't hurt me more than he already has."

Charlotte's face falls. She rests a hand against his hard cheek. "I tried to talk him into hiring a better lawyer for you."

"I know," he whispers.

"I'm sorry about what happened to you when you were . . . when you . . ." She presses the crumpled tissue against her lips.

When he was arrested for armed robbery. He finishes the thought for her. His cellmates ensured his six-month stay was no vacation. He carries the emotional scars to this day.

"Where's Dad staying?" he asks, anxious to get on the road, to put an end to Charlotte's misery.

"I can't tell you. I won't be responsible for whatever it is you plan on doing." Her false lashes brush her cheeks and a drop of moisture hangs on the tips like a desperate man who's run out of options. He lets go and he's gone.

"Don't tell me." He smiles sadly and reaches for a small memo pad and pen. He puts them in her hands. "Write it down," he says, barely audible.

"Lucas." Her gaze lowers to the items in her hands. Her lower lip trembles and hands shake. But he doesn't have to ask her twice. She opens the pad to a blank sheet and scribbles the hotel name and city. She rips off the paper, folds it twice, and puts it in Lucas's palm. She closes his fingers around it. "Be careful."

Lucas kisses her forehead and heads for the front door.

She follows him. "When will you be back?"

"Don't know."

"You will be back."

"Sure, Mom." He gives her a gentle smile and softly closes the door. He waits for her to flip the lock. He's been telling her she needs to keep the door locked when she's home alone. Dwight's security cameras are shit. They can't prevent someone from walking in.

The bolt flips. Nice to know she's finally listening to him.

CHAPTER 21

As soon as she arrives home, Olivia prints off two dozen of the panel templates she uses for her own illustration work, gathers a fresh supply of drafting lead, and calls Josh into her studio. Renewed hope and a fresh sense of urgency has her setting him up at her drafting table, and like a penciller translating a graphic novel script into visual form, she instructs Josh to illustrate what he's been through, how he got here, and maybe, just maybe, what happened to Lily. The least she wants to know is where and when Lily drops out of his story. His script is in his head. But a picture is worth a thousand words. With luck, through his artwork she can extract the thousands he hasn't been able to vocalize.

When she turns around, Josh isn't listening. Riveted, he stares at the Crimson Wave prints adorning her wall. Her superheroes are quite intimidating in life-size form, all sinewy muscle and glossy attire.

He points at Titian and says, "Uncle . . . ?" He waits, looking at her.

"Uh . . . yeah. Lucas. That's right," she says, unsettled, amazed at his intuitiveness. He picked that up fast. Not many of her friends have caught on to the physical similarities between the Crimson Wave and the Carson siblings. Lucas has yet to comment, but she knows her drawings unnerve him. She's seen him study the prints like he's looking in a mirror and isn't keen on what he sees. Olivia senses Lucas doesn't believe he can live up to the man he has the potential to become. She fleshed out Titian with young Lucas's most positive traits. His fierce protectiveness of the young and weak. His humor and wit. The prankster. Traits he's lost over the years after he lost himself. How she wishes more than ever that she knew what happened to him in juvenile hall. She wishes she'd made the effort to reach out to her siblings rather than feeling sorry for herself because they didn't seem to have interest in her.

Her parents have chosen to ignore how obviously she modeled her characters after her siblings. Her heroes shine a spotlight on their family's flaws. The Carson siblings never were as tight as the Crimson Wave. As much as she wishes for it, she wonders if they ever will be. Is it even possible?

Olivia used to believe they grew apart after their summers stopped at the lake. They no longer spent weeks on end relying solely on each other. But these past few days, with her breakup with Blaze and Josh's arrival, she's been thinking a lot about those summers, and her relationship with Lily and Lucas in general. Instead, those summers pushed them apart. They took sides. As Lucas's pranks escalated, so did Olivia's temper.

Olivia scoffs. She probably sounded like their father. A thought that now disgusts her given what she's learned about him.

Lily gravitated from her side to Lucas's, because in Lily's eyes Lucas could do no wrong. She was too young to understand their brother's antics took away the one thing Olivia looked forward to most of the year.

No wonder Olivia's temper flared like Dwight's anytime Lily or Lucas upset her. She was disappointed and despondent. She grieved because the decision had been out of her control. And she felt betrayed.

Olivia nods at the younger version of Lucas on the wall. "His name is Titian."

Josh points at her likeness. "You?"

She nods. "Ruby."

He then stares at the youngest Crimson. Olivia yanks a pen from the mug on her desk and rapidly clicks the end. What's going through his mind? Does he see his mom's likeness as well?

"She looks . . ."

"Like your mom. Yes."

His face scrunches up. "Some."

"I didn't have a recent photo when I created her. Her name is Dahlia." And she's how Olivia imagines adult Lily. Wise, beautiful, kind. But she doesn't hesitate when she executes justice. "Your mom's name used to be Lily. Lily May. She was born in May and named after that month's flower. Lily of the valley."

Josh watches her with open interest, absorbing every word.

"She didn't tell you much about her childhood, did she?"

He shakes his head. "Doesn't like . . ." He presses his mouth flat.

"She didn't like to talk about it or didn't like her childhood?"

He stares at the floor.

"Josh?"

His mouth turns down as if he's ashamed of how his mom feels about her family. "Both."

Olivia looks down her length. She pulls off a loose hair clinging to her shirt. She could have done something about the way the family treated Lily and she didn't.

"What name does she use now?"

"Sun . . . no. Jim." He scowls. His nostrils flare with a stream of hot air.

"That's okay. It'll come to you."

"Know it, but can't—"

"Say it." They'll have to figure another way.

Josh turns his attention back to the wall. He widens his arms to encompass the three prints. "What?"

Olivia guesses he's asking who the characters are. "The Crimson Wave. The superheroes from my graphic novels."

His mouth opens. "Your? No . . . way."

"Way." She can't help smiling at his reaction. Like a kid at Comic-Con. Wouldn't that be the dream, to sign at the biggest comic book convention around? She'd buy tickets for Josh and his friends. She'd even invite Lily and Lucas if they were interested.

Josh crosses the room to her bookcase. His gaze darts over the spines before glancing back at her. "Where?"

He can't read the titles. She can only imagine how frustrating that must be.

She drops the pen and pulls two books off the shelf. "Books one and two. I'm working on three." She shows him the covers and hands them off.

"Cool." He hugs the books and looks at her with stars in his eyes.

"Yes, you can keep them."

"I will . . . rip . . . read . . . when better." His smile wavers like he's apologizing for the fact he can't read. She stops short of pulling him into a hug, afraid if she makes a big deal it'll only embarrass him further. It would her if their roles were reversed. Instead she smiles warmly. His gaze returns to Dahlia, his longing unquestionable, and another realization dawns. Can Olivia be any more selfish? She's been fixated on Lily and hasn't once considered how Josh must be coping.

She picks up the pen again and starts clicking. She points it at Josh's hat. "I saw your scar."

Color flushes his neck. "When?"

"The other night. You were sleeping. Your hat fell off."

His free hand flies to his hat.

"Is that from when you were pushed?"

He nods and she swallows the bile that rose faster than the bestseller clutched in his hands rose on the charts. Her dad might have done that to him. He could have damaged Josh for life.

"Do you have headaches? Feel dizzy at all?" She asks the questions Mike suggested.

He shakes his head.

"That's good," she murmurs, relieved. "Will you tell me if you do get any?"

He nods. "My mom . . . she . . . mom . . . flew." He grunts and stops talking, looking at her like he does when he wants her to understand what he's trying to say without having to say it. He'd rather not talk than sound stupid.

"Sorry," she whispers regretfully. This time, she doesn't understand what he's attempting to explain.

Josh grimaces and again she wants to hug him. She doesn't, afraid she'll get attached, only to have Lily keep him from her once they find her. The POA and Lily's annual photos in the mail aren't enough to satisfy Olivia she won't only lose Lily again. She'll lose Josh, too. No point letting him in if he's only going to leave.

"So, um." She clears her throat and drops the pen on her desk. "Sit here." She pulls out the chair in front of the drafting table.

Josh stuffs the graphic novels into his backpack and drops the pack at his feet. He sits and her phone vibrates with an incoming call. She peeks at the screen and her limbs go cold. It's Dwight.

"Um . . . okay," she mutters, distracted. "Pencils there. Paper here. Draw whatever comes to mind. I'll be right back." She leaves Josh and goes to the kitchen, her phone vibrating like a kid with a temper tantrum. She sets the phone on the kitchen island, appalled she won't pick up the phone because she can't. Not now. She'd left her dad a message this morning, but that was before Josh's reaction to his picture. Dwight will know something isn't right just from the tone of her voice, and she's never been able to lie to him.

His face lights the screen, a photo she took when they walked across the Golden Gate Bridge several years back before she moved out of the city. The phone dances on the quartz countertop until the call drops into voice mail. As much as she wants his side of the story, Josh's safety and Charlotte's warning keep her from reaching out. She needs to protect her nephew. That's her priority.

The new voice mail icon appears and Olivia plays the recording.

"Livy, Princess. Daddy here. I'm still in San Diego at the wine symposium. Gorgeous here. Weather is perfect. I was just talking to your mother and you came up in conversation. But you always do." He chuckles and she tries not to feel alarmed. *Don't overreact.* She gives herself a pep talk. Charlotte won't tell him about Josh. He still doesn't know. "I got to thinking we haven't done lunch in a while, you and me, like we used to. I'll be home in two days. Call and let me know when's a good time. I'll make reservations. You pick the place. Got to run. Love you, Princess."

The recording ends and Olivia immediately calls Charlotte. Questions race through her mind as the phone rings. What did they talk about? Did she tell him about Josh?

The doorbell rings. "Now what?" she wonders out loud, peeking out the front window. Ethan waits on the porch with a smile and groceries. She opens the door and stares at him like he's a ghost.

"Hello? Olivia, are you there?" Charlotte's voice spills from the phone.

"I'll call you back, Mom." She ends the call and Ethan's smile fades.

"Forget about dinner?"

She peeks at her phone screen and balks at the time. "Lost track of time. Sorry."

"I can come back later." He starts backing up.

"No, no. Come in." She hasn't thought about dinner. Josh must be starving, and she's eager to learn anything about the days and months leading up to when Lily left. She takes a bag from him. "It's been a long day, that's all." She leads him into the kitchen.

"I brought steaks," he says when she starts unloading his bags. At least she doesn't have to think about what to cook. "I saw the grill out back last night. Hope you don't mind."

She hesitates before dropping a bag of potatoes on the counter. "Of course not." Blaze might. He treated the grill as his own.

"Where's Josh?" He looks around the room.

Her gaze follows his, eager to see what Josh will show her. "He's in my studio drawing. Remember Amber?"

"Yeah, I do. How is she?"

"Good. She runs her own accounting firm. Dating an ER doc. I talked to him this afternoon and he told me he thinks Josh has aphasia. I read that the best way for him to communicate when he can't talk is to draw. He's drawing what happened to Lily."

"That's smart. Hope it works."

"Same." She crosses her fingers.

Ethan uncorks the wine, and she turns on the stereo to drown their voices so Josh doesn't overhear them in case Ethan shares something disturbing. Evening jazz pours from the speakers throughout the house.

Ethan pours two glasses. "What?" he asks when she doesn't take the wine he offers. His eyes mine her face. "Did something happen today?"

She hesitates, debating how much to tell him. They'd been close once, but she doesn't know him anymore, a strange sensation given the years of anger and hurt. After all that happened, the lack of emotion she feels for him is a revelation. She tilts her head. "Did Lily talk about our dad with you, other than he wouldn't let her use the car for work?"

He sips the wine. The creases on his face deepen like tire tracks in dirt. "God, that was a long time ago, but now that you mention it, she—" His gaze lifts past her. "Hey there, Josh."

Josh stands in the doorway, hands tucked into the front pockets of his dark-washed skinny jeans. Ethan gives him a fist bump. "Hungry?" he asks.

"Yes," Josh says.

"Hope you brought your appetite. I'm grilling steaks."

His face brightens and he vigorously rubs his stomach. Olivia smiles, grappling with her impatience. She wants to know what Ethan was going to say.

Ethan looks at Olivia, his expression apologetic, a promise to pick this up later when Josh isn't around. "I'll put these on the grill, then we'll talk."

The doorbell rings.

"I'll get it. Josh, why don't you help Ethan," she suggests, already on her way to the door. She looks through the peephole, wondering who is selling what on a Saturday night. A lone figure holding a motor-cycle helmet and a bottle of Fireball fills her view. His leather jacket fits snugly over his torso.

She presses her forehead against the door and groans. Blaze. She remembers the apples rolling down the driveway. Distracted, she'd agreed for Blaze to swing by tonight to talk.

She opens the door, ready to apologize. Their issues will have to wait.

"Hey, Liv." Blaze smiles and displays the bottle like a trophy.

"Blaze—" She senses movement behind her. Blaze looks beyond her. His eyes widen, then sharpen. He stands taller and grips the helmet like he wants to chuck it over her head.

"What the fuck is Miller doing here?"

CHAPTER 22

"Theodore," Ethan greets. He lifts his wineglass.

Blaze grimaces at the sound of his given name and looks between Ethan and Olivia, taking in the scene, which is entirely misleading, worse than what he would have interpreted had he driven by the house last night. Wine in her Zalto glasses. Soft jazz playing over her wireless system. The dim lighting because she hasn't had the chance since they arrived home to turn on all the lights. Her chambray shirtdress with the three-quarter sleeves. Would he believe she's been wearing the dress all day? But when Blaze had called earlier, it completely skipped her mind she'd already made plans with Ethan. She can only imagine what he must be thinking. He'll truly hate her now.

Blaze scoffs. "Is this a date?"

"He's just visiting," she says.

Blaze narrows his gaze.

"How've you been, Theo?" Ethan offers his hand.

Blaze reluctantly takes it. "Fine. How long are you in town?"

"I leave tomorrow."

"Good." Blaze's face sours.

"Will you give us a moment?" she asks Ethan.

"Come on, Josh. The steaks won't grill themselves."

"He's using my grill?"

Ethan slides him a look. "Your grill?"

"That's right, Miller. I live here." As if to prove his point, Blaze moves farther into the house, nudging her aside.

"Not anymore you don't, and the grill's mine."

"I picked it out."

He looks at her as if her announcement is the most ridiculous thing he's heard. But he doesn't hide the hurt that deepens the grooves around his mouth.

She rests a hand on his chest to guide him out the door. It takes effort not to curl her fingers into his shirt. His body is warm under his biker jacket and she wants to lean into him, tell him everything that's happened since she broke up with him. She wants to express what she's been thinking about them. She owes him an apology, but not with an audience. If she didn't think Ethan could help in her search for Lily, she'd ask him to leave now. But if Blaze doesn't go, Ethan might clam up, and she'll get nothing from him.

Searching his face, her eyes asking for his patience, she lowers her voice. "Can we talk tomorrow?"

"Wait a sec." Ethan clues in. "You're dating Theo?"

"Yes." She closes her eyes. "No," she says softly. Not as of several nights ago.

Blaze is grinning down at her when she opens them, as if he can tell she's fighting her feelings for him. He knows she's realizing that she made a mistake.

Josh, lurking off to the side, coughs into his hand. "Awkward."

He couldn't be more accurate.

Blaze gives Josh the once-over. He smiles. "Hey, I'm Blaze. You are?"

Her nephew surprisingly stands taller when she'd expect him to recoil from such a direct question. "Josh."

"This your kid, Miller?"

"No, he's Lily's son," Olivia answers for Ethan. As far as she knows, Blaze isn't aware she thought Lily's son was Ethan's. They weren't in touch when she was in college and Blaze was in the army. And over the last year they never got around to why she and Ethan broke up. Blaze didn't ask and she didn't volunteer. It was a period of their lives they glossed over like a countertop sealant. Between Blaze's parents divorcing, his mom's lymphoma, and Olivia's family drama, they didn't let those years bleed into their relationship.

"Not . . . Lily," Josh says.

"He's not her son?" Blaze looks to her for clarification.

"We think Lily changed her name," she says.

His brows shoot up. "To what?"

Josh opens his mouth. "Peanut." He then swears. His neck and cheeks flame. He starts to back out of the room.

"Josh, stay. It's okay."

Blaze covers his mouth with the back of his wrist and studies Josh, mildly shocked. "She here?" He looks at Olivia, searching. Questions are clouds crossing his face, different shapes and sizes. She senses he wants to ask why, but more than that, he wants to know how she's faring. He knew Lily, and while they weren't together when Lily ran, Blaze would know Josh being here, standing with them in her entryway, is a big deal.

"No. Josh is staying with me for a bit." She has so much to tell Blaze, she's practically bursting to share.

Screw it. Ethan can wait.

"We'll be back in a few." She grabs Blaze's elbow to draw him out front but his boots remain firmly planted. He sets down the Fireball on the table by the door and gives Josh his hand.

"Nice to meet you. How's your mom?"

"Umm . . ." Josh gnaws his lower lip.

"Is she okay?" Blaze asks when Josh struggles to answer. He pivots to Olivia. "Where is she?"

"We don't know." His eyebrows rise and she picks up the Fireball. "I'll explain everything. Just come with me."

"You have my PUMAs."

Those darn shoes. Dropped and forgotten when he elbowed her aside to get his McIntosh turntable. She tossed them in her closet when she cleaned up after Josh had gone to bed his first night here.

"They're in my room. I'll get them," she says, but Blaze is already on the move. He strides through the entryway, his gaze locked on Josh. He checks him out from ball cap to black Vans, lingering on Josh's face until he's forced to look away or else he'll walk into the wall.

Josh unconsciously touches his cap as if Blaze can see through it to his scar.

"Go help Ethan with dinner," Olivia says in a gentle voice. "I won't be long."

Fireball in hand, Olivia follows Blaze into her room.

"What were you thinking?" she asks of the liquor. "You'd get me drunk and into bed?" She should be mad at him for asserting his way into her home, and her life. But she's grateful he's here, even if for a short bit.

"I don't need to get you drunk for that." He looks out the window that has the perfect view to her outdoor kitchen. The backyard is lit up. She can see Ethan and Josh trying to master the grill Blaze personally installed. She expects to see the cocky smirk that always riles her, but when he turns around, the look on his face is anything but that. He appears troubled.

"What is it?" she asks, the skin along her hairline tingling.

He meets her in the middle of the room. "I'm worried about you."

"Because of Lily?"

"Her and because I care about you. Your call this afternoon. It scared me."

"I'm okay."

His brows drew closer. "You sure?" She nods, tight lipped. "Tell me about Lily. What's going on?"

"She's missing."

"Hasn't she always been?"

"Yes, but it's different this time. Josh showed up here on his own. He says she's gone, but I think that's the word he's using for missing. I'm starting to think she didn't run away this time. Josh is injured. He hit his head a while back. That's why his speech is confusing. I'm worried there's a connection between his injury and Lily's disappearance. Because of his impediment, Josh has trouble explaining what happened. He gets worked up and starts talking gibberish. For all I know, Lily could be dead," she explains. Tears threaten to spill as an invisible load lifts off her shoulders. Her chin trembles.

"Hey there, what's wrong?" He tucks his finger under her chin.

She steps out of reach, undeserving of his tenderness, ashamed she behaved so irrationally. He'd betrayed her long before, and her reaction was instinctual. But now she wonders if the one man she's trusted most and looked up to her entire life has been the one lying to her all along—her father. Her world crumbles further, as if she has more bricks to spare. You think you know someone until you learn something new and realize you didn't know them at all. There are new pieces to their puzzle and the finished image isn't anything like the original on the box lid.

"Dwight's in San Diego."

"What does your dad have to do with this?"

"Josh was born in San Diego. I think that's where he lives now, or somewhere nearby." She tells him about Josh's arrival, the police station, the visit from Charlotte, and Josh's reaction to Dwight's photo this afternoon. He carefully listens to every word, his features softening. He'd pull her into his arms if he weren't holding his helmet or was afraid how she'd react. She can tell he's not taking any chances that would push her further away.

"That's when you called me?"

"Yes."

He whistles. "Shit, Liv. I would have come earlier. Wait. You aren't saying your dad pushed him?"

She feels like someone scooped out her heart and let it melt on the hot pavement. Her back buckles from the hollow space left in her chest. "I don't want to believe it, but yeah, I think that's what I'm saying."

"Liv, baby, no," Blaze cups her neck and leans his forehead on hers, and Olivia wants to melt into him. It feels wonderful to have him touch her again, even if only to soothe. "He's not like that. Yeah, he was a dick toward Lily, but that's quite an accusation. You're missing something."

"I hope so."

"What's all this got to do with Miller?"

"Blaze." She drags out his name. Of course he'd circle back to Ethan. His gaze narrows. "Are you sleeping with him?"

"Give me a break." She huffs. She doesn't have time for his jealousy. "Nothing's going on." Her gaze slides out the open window. Ethan is finishing up the steaks. She owes Blaze an answer, but this is a much longer conversation. "Look, I just want to question him about Lily, that's it. He leaves town tomorrow."

She retreats into the closet for Blaze's PUMAs and joins him at the window. He intently watches the guys outside.

"I'll call you tomorrow and tell you everything, promise." She tries to give him his shoes. He doesn't take them. He turns to her, the motorcycle helmet hanging from his hand. He gently bounces the helmet against his thigh.

"I've been thinking about the other night. I overreacted."

He overreacted? "You were mild compared to me."

"I get it. You don't trust easily. I hurt you once and now you're overly cautious. Nothing wrong with that."

"You were my first," she murmurs, as if that made his betrayal much worse. Maybe it's one of the reasons she's overly sensitive when it comes to him. They've never openly talked this past year. She wanted to keep it light and fun and uncomplicated. But now, everything she held back from him wants to pour out like a tipped carton of juice.

"You were mine. I was young and stupid." He fits a hand to her face, and his touch feels like a long-missed kiss. He's her magnet, her refuge amid the unrest in her life. She unconsciously leans into him, needing him more now than ever before.

"I saw Macey's texts and it was high school all over again." It was losing summers with the Whitmans, her close relationship with Lucas. It was losing Blaze. It was Lily leaving.

"I know. That's why I want to give you a second chance."

"Me?"

"Us. I mean us." He chuckles, rolls his eyes. "See? Stupid."

"You're not stupid." He's braver than her, the way he dove into their relationship like he did after all he's been through. His estrangement with Tyler because Blaze had been in the service when Rhonda was most ill and Tyler was left to care for her. The sudden death of his father. Rhonda's year of suffering after the doctors tried everything. He also sees right through her to the heart of her issues: trust. Rather, the lack of it. She's a little slow on the uptake when it comes to letting people in.

Blaze plays with the ends of her hair. "I gave you a free pass to call me stupid. Take it."

He's trying to be funny, but her suspicious mind has her peering at him cautiously. "Are you saying this because Ethan's here?"

He shrugs, noncommittally, then quickly holds up his hands. "No! I mean, no."

She scoffs and pushes the soles of his shoes into his chest. He grabs the sneakers before they drop. "Good night, Blaze. We'll talk tomorrow," she says, making her way to the door.

"This has nothing to do with Miller."

"Thanks for the booze." She gives the bottle a shake. "You can show yourself out."

"I still plan to propose to you."

She stops. The air snags in her throat as she waits for the claustrophobia that comes knocking whenever she thinks about opening herself up to someone, which she'd have to do in a marriage. When she starts feeling that pressure, that's her sign to get out before she gets screwed over. But she doesn't feel it with Blaze.

He's behind her, his warm breath on her neck. "I still plan to be the one to hold you at night when you wake from your nightmares, all sweaty and panting." He draws a finger down her spine. "I'm going to be there because you want me there. I know you, Liv, better than anyone. Give us another chance," he whispers by her ear and she shivers. She wants to, more than anything, surprisingly. But she's been selfish her entire life. Her love life needs to take the back burner for the moment. Josh needs her. And if Ethan can remember anything that can help her locate Lily, Olivia needs to find out what that is before he leaves town.

She moves out of reach. Yes, they need to talk some more. A lot more. But not right now. Her focus needs to be on Lily and Josh, not her love life, or lack thereof.

"Then let me help you with Lily."

"How?"

"However you need me. I'll make calls. You tell me. But don't feel like this is all on you. Leaning on someone isn't a sign of weakness. And baby, you can lean on me all you want." The corner of his mouth draws up and a little smile curves her lips.

"Okay. Let's talk tomorrow." Given how unreliable Lucas is, she could use his assistance.

"Good. I'll be waiting." Blaze kisses her temple, then slowly squeezes past her in the narrow doorway. He nods at the Fireball clutched in her hand. "Keep Miller's paws off my bottle. That's ours when you're ready. We'll get stupid drunk and fuck like horny teens."

"Jesus, Blaze." Her face heats. She follows him to the front door.

"Keep our bed warm for me, baby," he says loud enough for anyone in the house to hear. He blows her a kiss and lets the door slam behind him. The windows rattle as if to emphasize his point.

Movement in her peripheral vision draws her attention to the kitchen. Ethan hovers in the doorway, tongs in hand.

"Steaks are ready." He smirks because he probably overheard most of that.

She smiles tightly. "Great."

———

Twenty minutes later, after the potatoes are cooked, Olivia admits she doesn't have an appetite. By the looks he gives her, Ethan can tell her mind is far from him. He agrees to leave when Olivia asks him. She has more pressing matters demanding her attention. She walks him out.

"What were you going to tell me, back in the house before Blaze showed?" she asks when they reach his car.

He presses a button on the key fob and his engine starts. He turns to her, his expression solemn. "Lily didn't tell me she was pregnant. I wasn't supposed to know. She didn't want anyone to know. But I picked her up from work and a pregnancy test fell out of her bag. She wouldn't tell who the father is. Trust me, I asked. She also refused my offer to help. I should have told you, but she asked for my confidence, and I—" He shrugs, regretful. "I kept my word."

Olivia chews her lip. He would have. That's the Ethan she knew, not the guy she thought he was when she believed he cheated on her with her sister. He also isn't the great love she once believed he was and lost.

He lays a flat hand on his chest and taps his fingers. "I, uh . . . I overheard you and Theo talking. Sorry, the window was open. You were talking about your dad and it reminded me of something. Lily was scared."

"Of my dad?" Fresh horror seeps into her like mist under a door. She tried to get Blaze to convince her she's wrong about Dwight. But the facts are adding up against him, flashing light on a man she thought she knew.

"She worried what he'd do to the guy who . . ." He rolls his hand. "The father. That could explain why she left the name blank on the birth certificate."

Olivia digs her fingers under the long hair covering her neck and scratches her scalp. Dwight really didn't know who Josh's father was.

"Anything else?"

He nods. "I once noticed bruises on her legs. Another time she winced like her back was hurt. She got pissed at me for helping her up into the truck. She didn't want me to notice. She was in pain."

Anger flares brighter than stadium lights. Was her dad beating Lily? "Jesus, Ethan. Why didn't you tell me back then?"

He has the gall to look guilty. "You're right. I should have." He splays his hands. "She swore Dwight wasn't hurting her. But she was doing something that scraped up her legs."

"Like what? Sneaking out her window at night to visit her mystery boyfriend?"

As she says it, Olivia realizes it's plausible. There were plenty of nights she snuck out her window to meet Blaze at their pier. There was a juniper bush under her window. She wore jeans even during the summer months just so the shrub wouldn't tear up her calves.

Ethan shrugs and she scowls, more irritated with herself than him. If she'd let Ethan more fully into her heart, he would have come to her about Lily. Lily would have come to her.

She had, she reminds herself.

Guilt makes another pass through her like a car circling the block for a perfect parking spot, looking for a place to settle in.

Ethan taps the curb with the toe of his trail shoes before meeting her eyes. "The police questioned me after Lily ran away. That's how I found out she did. I would have called you, but I felt somewhat responsible for her leaving."

Not as much as Olivia did. If anyone's to blame, it's her. But Ethan's remark reminds her she'd been lied to.

"Did my dad ever contact you after we broke up?" If Dwight believed Ethan was the father, he would have confronted him.

He shakes his head. "Only the police."

Olivia stares at him as the last bit of hope she had about her dad burns out. *He* lied to her, not Lily. She cups a hand over her mouth and closes her eyes.

"Are you okay?"

"I'm not sure," she murmurs, looking back at the house where Josh is safe inside. For now. Dwight returns in two days. Two days to find Lily or she and Josh will have to leave. Dwight has been known to show up unannounced, and he will show up. If he's capable of lying to her about Ethan, whom he knew she loved at the time, and can push Josh hard enough to cause a brain bleed, who knows what he'll do when he realizes Josh is here? Who knows what he's already done to Lily? Dwight is dangerous. Unpredictable. She doesn't know this man.

Ethan touches her arm and she flinches. His expression is sympathetic. "I wish I knew more."

So did she. But what he did tell her helped. He confirmed she can't trust her dad. He reaffirmed Lily needs her, more than she ever has before.

"I leave for Malta in the morning, but I'll reach out if I think of anything else."

She nods, biting her bottom lip to stop it from trembling.

"Will you be okay?"

"Yeah." She pushes her hair off her face and plugs in her smile, even though she's screaming inside. "Yeah, I'll be fine."

CHAPTER 23

Day 5

Olivia pushes her shades up her nose and crouches in her car across the street and two houses up from her parents'. Lucas texted this morning that Charlotte doesn't know Lily's address. His next text told her to stop asking Mom about their sister. She's emotional. Lily's a sensitive subject and Olivia's stressing her out. Which is why Olivia finds herself hiding in her car as if she's casing the neighborhood. She needs to get inside Dwight's office to find Lily's address without Charlotte around. She also wants to search for the photos Dwight said he had of Lily and Ethan to see if she can tell who Josh's father might be, as well as review yesterday's surveillance tape. How visible is Josh's face? The recordings autodelete after six days, but Charlotte mentioned Dwight does watch them, and that's a chance Olivia won't take. He'll be home tomorrow.

This time she left Josh at home with Amber.

Through the rearview and side mirrors, Olivia watches Charlotte load her Mercedes trunk with A-frame signs: OPEN HOUSE. She adds a bag of flyers and a plastic container of freshly baked cookies to the back seat before settling into the driver's seat. For a few minutes, she touches up her mascara and lipstick, then reverses out of the driveway. Olivia waits until her mom turns the corner before she pulls into the drive Charlotte just vacated.

She lets herself in through the unlocked front door, grateful Charlotte believes a gated community and security cameras keep her safe and home invaders out. The window hasn't been replaced, but is boarded up. She wonders if Charlotte is still steamed about the damage. She also wonders how often she thought about her youngest daughter, out in the world, alone with an infant. How devastating that must have been for her. No wonder Charlotte avoids talking about Lily. Her heartache must be unbearable.

Granted, she wanted Lily to put Josh up for adoption, but she had Lily's best interests in mind. Charlotte never finished college. She met and married Dwight. Olivia suspects Charlotte has resented that decision. She pushed for her children to earn degrees. It wasn't a question that they would. Olivia is the only one of the three who achieved that milestone. Olivia surmises Charlotte took it personally when Lily ran away. She took with her Charlotte's hopes and dreams for her artistically talented, athletically inclined daughter.

The house smells of the cookies Charlotte just baked, melted chocolate chips and butter. Even though Olivia has plenty of time—Charlotte isn't expected to return until after 5:00 p.m.—she rushes to Dwight's office, feeling sick to her stomach. She's let herself in before, has so many fond memories of watching her dad work in his room, but she's never invaded his personal space under false pretenses, especially now that she suspects of him what she does.

She drops her hobo purse on a chair and rounds his desk. He's a neat freak, so she should be able to locate what she needs quickly. Still, her hands shake when she boots up Dwight's computer. Dishonesty makes her physically ill. For once, she's the betrayer.

"Hurry, hurry," she whispers to the room. His computer is an old Dell, and the unit takes its sweet time waking up. She rubs her hands together, looking around the spartan office she spent many hours in while growing up. When she was a kid, she'd do her homework on the floor while Dwight made his late afternoon calls. Her gaze latches on to his Rolodex. He still uses that? She rotates the wheel, landing on C. The front door slams and she almost falls out of the chair.

"Olivia? Olivia, are you here?"

Olivia's stomach drops.

She stabs the computer's power button to shut it down and stuffs the Rolodex in her bag. It's unwieldy, but she needs something to point her to Lily. Shouldering her bag, she gives the computer a look of frustrated longing. Dwight's contact list will have to wait. Charlotte appears in the doorway as she's walking out. She flips her hair over her shoulder and slaps on a smile. Charlotte's gaze volleys from Olivia to Dwight's desk. The fan on the archaic computer whirs. Olivia's heart runs a marathon around her chest.

"Hey, Mom," she says, her smile strained. "Thought you were gone."

"What are you doing here?" Charlotte asks.

"Uh . . ." She flounders for an excuse, looking back at the desk to see if she left anything amiss other than the Rolodex she lifted. "I, uh, can't find my wallet. I think it fell out of my purse when Josh . . . you know . . ." She hitches her purse higher on her shoulder. "Don't you have a showing?"

"I do. Forgot my phone." Charlotte turns to leave, but her gaze snags like a shirt on a doorknob, hooking onto the naked space where Dwight's Rolodex had been.

"What?" Olivia asks innocently when Charlotte peers at her shoulder bag.

"What are you doing in your father's office?"

"I thought you might have put my wallet in here." She twists her watch on her wrist and looks at the time. "I have to go. Josh is waiting." She tries to move past her mom.

"What's in the bag?"

"Nothing." She pushes her purse behind her back. "Talk later?"

Charlotte moves aside, letting Olivia past. She gets halfway to the door when she stops. The way her mom suspiciously looked at her triggers a memory. She's seen that look on her before in her dream.

Olivia turns around. "Do you remember that nightmare I had as a kid?" she asks, walking back to Charlotte. "Dad was knee-deep in the water?" His shirt was bloodied, and although the dream was blurry, she swore he carried a knife. Moonlight glinted off the blade. Her mom stood beside him, hair and clothes drenched. She eyed Dwight suspiciously before running to Olivia, where she fell to her knees and grabbed her hands. Olivia felt her desperation. She woke gasping almost every time.

Charlotte lifts her chin. "What about it?"

"It's back. Actually, it never stopped really. But there's more to it now, like the story's continuing, or I'm remembering something I forgot. I don't sleep so I don't dream. I'm so tired," she explains. Her mom can help make sense of her dreams. Dwight always encouraged her not to put too much faith in them. But isn't there some truth buried in recurring nightmares?

Charlotte twists the pearl on her necklace. "I'm sorry to hear that. Have you tried drinking tea?"

More like bourbon and a cigarette. Olivia shakes her head.

"Lemon balm works for me. What is it, dear?" Charlotte untucks Olivia's collar stuck under her purse strap.

"Josh thinks Dad might have pushed him. He hit his head. That's why he has trouble talking." The idea Dwight attacked Josh horrifies her every time she thinks about it.

Charlotte's skin above the neckline of her blouse dulls to a pale peach. "Not possible. Your father wouldn't . . . I mean, he has a temper . . ."

"He's not sure, Mom. I didn't think Dad was capable of it either. But I can't stop thinking about that dream and what you said about not letting Dad know Josh is here. It makes me think he is capable. Please tell me I'm wrong." She needs to know that she is. She has to be looking at this all wrong. The father she knows can't be that monstrous.

"It's just a dream, Olivia." Her voice is paper-thin.

"Maybe. But I think we both know Dad found Lily. What's her address?"

Charlotte weaves. She puts a hand on the wall. "I don't have it."

"But Dad does. Let me look." She gestures at his office. "He'll never know I was in here."

"No." Charlotte's eyelids blink rapidly before fluttering closed. She gasps softly and like thick paint poured over canvas, she crumples to the floor. Olivia feels out of breath and can only imagine what was racing through Charlotte's mind. Is she that scared of her husband?

"Mom." Olivia catches her before she knocks her head on the hardwood floor.

It only takes a few seconds for Charlotte to rouse. Olivia sees when her mom brings her into focus. "Darling." Charlotte looks around her. "You saved me."

"Caught you just in time. It's been a while, hasn't it?" The first time Olivia recalls her mom fainting was years ago when her parents had been arguing at the dinner table. Grandmother Val had just passed away and Dwight was incensed Charlotte didn't inherit even a dime with pocket lint, nothing but old furniture that they stored in the garage apartment. He pounded a fist on the table, shook his other in her face, and Charlotte dropped to the floor. Mayhem ensued. Lily cried in her high chair. Lucas called 9-1-1, and Olivia held her mom's hand. Olivia had never been so afraid for her mom. Dwight adjusted Charlotte's head onto his lap and begged her to forgive him. The ambulance took her to ER, the doctor examined her, and she was released later that night with a diagnosis and prescription for anxiety. Charlotte, it would seem, has an innate fear of confrontation whenever the subject makes her uncomfortable. She literally shuts down.

"Sorry I pushed you about Lily." Olivia cradles Charlotte's head, now seeing what Lucas said in his text. Discussing Lily stresses out their mom. Olivia's only just realized how sensitive Charlotte is about her youngest. "How are you feeling? Light-headed?"

Charlotte moans softly. She tries to stand.

"Take it slow." Olivia helps her to her feet and walks her into the bedroom.

"My pills, darling." Charlotte points toward the bathroom, wiggling her fingers. "They're on the shelf."

Olivia helps her onto the bed and goes into the bathroom. The top shelf is cluttered with prescription bottles. Lopressors, anti-inflammatories, anxiety meds. Olivia twists the bottles so the labels face outward.

"Which one?" she asks.

"The clonazepam."

The same med she's seen Lucas pop when he doesn't think she's looking. Sheesh. Her family is a hot mess of anxiety. Locating the bottle, which is almost empty, she pours a glass of water and takes both to her mom. Charlotte sits against the headboard. "You should stay home and rest." Olivia gives her the pill and water.

"Can't." Charlotte washes down the medicine. "Several interested buyers are touring the house. We're expecting at least two offers by this evening."

"Promise you'll take it easy?"

Charlotte's gaze jumps upward.

"Mom."

"Yes, yes. I will. Happy?" She gives Olivia the empty glass and stands, smoothing the creases from her skirt.

Charlotte follows Olivia onto the porch, and this time, she bolts the front door. Charlotte's way of telling Olivia to leave Dwight's office alone.

"Mom?" Olivia turns to her, her voice intentionally gentled. "I know Lily hurt you when she ran away, and I know you don't want to ask Dad for Lily's address because he'll ask why, am I right? You want me to keep Josh safe. To do that, I need to know what happened to her. How they separated." Charlotte's lips purse. She looks down at the keys in her hand. "If you think of anything at all that'll help me find her faster, call me, okay?"

"Of course, darling."

CHAPTER 24

LUCAS

Lucas nurses his second draft beer, his attention on the lobby escalator and elevators. The five-star hotel is packed with vineyard managers, owners, and everyone who supplies them. Between the wine expo and another technology seminar downstairs, the place is buzzing, exactly the way Lucas needs it. He can fade into the background. Move with obscurity in case the baseball cap and reflective shades don't cut it. But hey, this is SoCal, land of the famous and state of the rich. Anyone who is someone is trying to hide.

He shifts his weight on the firm barstool to ease the ache in his lower back. He's not one to sit for long periods, or even hang in one place longer than necessary, and he's already been here for almost three hours, waiting, watching. If he leaves now, he risks losing sight of Dwight. And his vantage point to the guest elevators is perfect.

He glances at his watch. It's almost 6:00 p.m. The expo's sessions end in a few minutes. Dwight should be making his way up the escalator at any moment. He'll go straight to the elevator. He likes to freshen up before he hits the bar and on the women. He's so predictable. And Lucas will be right behind him, dogging him to his room where they'll have a brief chat. He's no longer wanted at home. Find his own place or Lucas will tip off the police. Yes, Wes drowned. But he fell off the dock because he'd been running from Dwight. Lucas watched the entire confrontation between Dwight, Wes, and Lily from across the yard. Dwight found the boy in Lily's bedroom. He was convinced he impregnated his daughter.

The woman seated beside him settles her check and gathers up her clutch and phone. "Nice not talking with you," she says, sliding off the stool. Lucas grunts. She tried to engage him in a stimulating conversation about cannabis storage containers with automated locking systems and facial recognition. She even invited him upstairs to do a few lines of the hard stuff. As if he'd do anything that risks landing himself in jail. That's one ride he'd never risk repeating. He doesn't care how gorgeous she is, or how luscious her coral pink lips would look locked around him. Instead, he ignored her. So what? He isn't here to socialize, over drinks or under the sheets.

He senses her walking away rather than turning to watch her, as hot as she looks in that fitted black pantsuit and sheer pink blouse. His gaze is sealed on the escalators. Where are you, old man? He drums his fingers on the bar top.

Someone takes the vacant stool beside him. Lucas can smell his stale body odor and the cheap cologne that fails to cover up the unpleasant stink before he catches a glimpse of the man from the corner of his eye. He's middle-aged with thinning gray hair. His plaid shirt is wrinkled and beard untrimmed. He orders a shot of vodka in a gruff voice, then orders a second before he tosses back the first. The bartender serves him a glass of water with the third shot.

"You here for the conference?" the man asks after he empties the last shot and nudges the glass away. He elbows Lucas's arm when he doesn't respond.

Lucas grinds his teeth and gives the man a dark look. The man's unfazed.

"Which conference?" he repeats with curious, weary eyes that have seen too much in a short time. Lucas recognizes the haunted look.

Lucas's gaze narrows. He takes in more of the man's appearance. The swollen skin around his eyes. The crumbs in his beard, leftovers from lunch or a snack. "None," he answers.

The man nods. He puts out his hand. "Scott."

Lucas gives him a short nod, ignoring the hand. He hails the bartender and orders a refill.

"I'll have the same," Scott says. "And two more shots. One for me and my buddy." He jabs a thumb in Lucas's direction. "Today was hell. Hoping to forget everything about it."

Not Lucas. He needs to keep a level head. But Scott seems to have a different plan in mind.

"I just got back from the hospital. My mother . . ." Scott chokes up, then drains his water.

Lucas closes his eyes and calls on his patience. He's not an ideal sounding board. He pushes away the shot the bartender leaves in front of him.

Scott puts down the empty glass dead center on the paper cocktail napkin. He absently spins the water glass as he talks. "My mother just died. She was sick for a long time. I was ready for this, I guess as much as anyone can be when you know you're going to lose a parent." He rubs his eyes.

Lucas thanks the bartender, paying her in cash, and drinks his beer. He turns his attention back to the escalator and bank of elevators, only half listening to Scott.

"Why do people make confessions on their deathbeds? They feel better. They want forgiveness. I get that. But what about us, the ones they've left behind?" He looks at Lucas in earnest. "We're left feeling miserable, confused, and—" He gulps his beer. "Angry. I'm really, really mad. My mother, she was a trial. Whose mother isn't? But she loved us, me and my two older sisters. There were four of us. We had a baby brother. Freddie. We called him Freddie. Cutest little kid. He died when he was two. That's what our parents told us. We grew up believing he got sick and died. They took him to the hospital and never brought him back. But that's not what happened. You know what they did? Do you know what my parents did to my little brother?"

Lucas doesn't know, and he doesn't want to care. But he can't help listening to his story. Parents could really do a number on their kids, and Scott's wounds are making his feel more fresh. Lucas removes his sunglasses, pinches the inner corners of his eyes, and hears himself asking, "What did they do?"

"They sold him. They sold my little brother." Scott's eyes sheen and he looks away.

Well, damn.

"Your mom confessed that?" Lucas asks, appalled. Though his own dad has a laundry list of sins.

Scott nods. "They couldn't afford four mouths to feed so they gave one of us up. One less mouth, she admitted. Tubes were coming out of her and she could barely breathe. But she got out that confession. They gave him up for six hundred bucks. I don't know what to do." He sounds miserable.

Movement near the escalator pulls Lucas's attention to the lobby. People flow off the escalator and Dwight's right in the middle of the pack.

Lucas swipes up his wallet and shades, downs the remainder of his beer. "Go find your brother, Scott. You'll regret it for the rest of your life if you don't." As he's regretted not going after Lily. Lucas gets up and leaves. He doesn't look back. By the time he reaches the bank of elevators, he's already forgotten Scott and his dead mother's confession.

Lucas stands a couple feet behind Dwight. The old man chats up wine nonsense with a colleague. Lucas thinks of what happened to him while he was in juvie and how Dwight blew it off when Lucas confided in him. *Deal with it, son.* Lucas has been dealing with it. The memories, the torment, and the shame. Burying fists in his jacket pockets, he lets the anger that's been simmering below the surface flare.

The elevator doors slide open, people pile in, and Lucas keeps his head ducked. He's the last one to step inside. He turns his back to the elevator interior, faces the lobby, and waits with everyone for the doors to slide closed. The bell dings.

"Four, please," someone behind him asks. Lucas pushes the button. "Fifteen," says another.

"Ten," says Dwight, and Lucas slowly smiles. He obligingly pushes the button.

CHAPTER 25

Josh is in her studio, hunched over his panels, when Olivia arrives home. Only a few blank templates remain, he filled up most of them. His attention to detail is exquisite. It reminds her of his mom. Olivia would come home late from her dates with Ethan to find Lily awake, doodling with her colored pens. She was always creating a new comic. Furry little animals with big eyes and cute tails that made her and Lucas laugh. Cats, squirrels, raccoons. You name it, she drew it. Olivia would linger in Lily's doorway. Deep in the zone, Lily never knew she was there, how Olivia debated asking why they weren't as close as they used to be. Had Olivia done something to drive a wedge between them? She wishes she'd asked, but was too afraid she'd realize the fault was her own.

Olivia flips the corners of Josh's panels like pages in a book. Her thumbnail snags on a panel. She slides it from the stack. It's a profile of a woman with bright red hair and a young boy in a car. Huddled off to the side is a group of women. They watch the woman and boy. "Is this you and your mom?"

Josh lifts his head from his work. He wiggles a pencil between his fingers. "Yes."

Olivia studies Lily's profile. It's only a drawing, but strange nonetheless to see a more current rendering of her sister. She's beautiful in Josh's eyes. But she's also angry. Her brows dip low. There's a crease between them. Josh stares out the window, scowling like the teenager he is.

"Where are you here? What's happening?"

Josh points at the building he drew. It looks like a gymnasium. He gestures at his desk. "Like this."

Olivia tilts her head. Gym. Desk. "Is this your school?" She takes a guess and he nods. "Is your mom dropping you off?" He nods again. "Why's she angry?"

He thumbs his chest. "At me." His gaze drops to the desk. "Forgot stuff. Didn't hear . . . listen. Started." He waves his arm around the room.

"Are you saying this is when everything started?"

He shakes his head. "I . . . started it."

"Josh. Hey." She crouches beside him. "Look at me. This isn't your fault."

He shrugs listlessly.

She touches his arm, wishing she could come up with a stronger argument so he didn't blame himself. But she doesn't know how he and Lily separated and why it happened in the first place.

"Everything will work out. You'll see."

Josh shrugs again and goes back to his drawing.

Olivia pushes to her feet. "I'll be in the kitchen if you need me."

Amber's at the table dipping carrots in hummus. A book is open on her lap. She drags her feet off the chair she was using as a footrest and sits up when Olivia enters the kitchen. "How'd it go?"

Olivia digs out her prize and plunks the Rolodex on the table. "I stole it from my dad's office."

Amber snorts. "That was productive." She flicks through the cards. "Man, I haven't seen one of these in years."

"My mom came back. I didn't have a chance to get anything I wanted." She thinks of the empty thumb drive in the side pocket of her purse.

"I can't believe you've gone all Charlie's Angel on your dad." Amber frowns. Olivia told her earlier what she was after at her parents' house. "I don't see Lily in the Cs or Ls."

Olivia isn't surprised. She grabs a flavored S. Pellegrino from the fridge and pops the top. "I think she changed her name," she says, sitting beside Amber. She sips the spring water. "Josh has tried to tell me, but so far, no luck."

"You've got a lot of calls ahead of you if you plan on reaching out to everyone in here."

"Just the women in the San Diego area, if there are any." She rotates the Rolodex. Most cards are female. Olivia recognizes many as Dwight's clients or people he met campaigning, names Olivia has heard over the years.

Amber leans back and nibbles a carrot. "What does Daddio want with Lily?"

"Ding-ding-ding. That's the question of the day." Charlotte never really told her.

"Maybe he wanted to let her know she's welcome back home."

"Then why is Josh afraid of him?" Before she left for Charlotte's she told Amber about yesterday's visit with her mom and why she needed to go back.

"Good question." Amber drags a carrot through the hummus. "What are you going to do if you can't find Lily?"

"I will find her," Olivia says, adamant. The other possibility is too disastrous to consider.

"But if you don't. What if she's dead?"

"She's not dead." She slaps a hand on the table. Lily is not allowed to die before Olivia has the chance to make up for being a sad excuse of a big sister. If it's the last thing she does, she will reunite Josh and Lily. She owes her sister after turning her back on her before. She catches Amber's wide-eyed expression. "Sorry."

Olivia leans on the table and presses the cool can to her cheek. She thinks of the power of attorney document on her desk and her mood turns somber.

"What is it?" Amber asks quietly and her mouth turns downward, reading Olivia's conflicting emotions. "You're afraid."

Olivia rolls her lips over her teeth and nods.

"What are you more afraid of, not finding Lily or getting attached to Josh?"

She scoffs. Amber cocks her head. Olivia sighs. "Both." Josh will think she betrayed him if she can't follow through on her promise. And if she can't find Lily? It will be like losing her all over again. Only this time she cares, and it'll hurt that much more.

Olivia puts the Rolodex back in her purse and notices an old iPhone at the other end of the table. "Whose is that?"

"Mine, an old one. Mike ran into his speech pathologist friend at the hospital and got some app recommendations. I downloaded them."

"Great." She perks up with interest. She'd been waiting for Mike to text her the pathologist's number. Now Josh can work on his speech. If he makes some immediate progress, he can explain more about what happened to Lily. She picks up the phone and the screen awakens with a photo of Josh smirking. Amber took the picture in Olivia's backyard. She can see the pergola Blaze built behind him. His expression is corny and she chuckles.

"It doesn't have cell service. I tapped into your Wi-Fi."

Olivia returns the phone and searches the kitchen, unsure if she's hungry, or even motivated to fix a sandwich. A bouquet of peonies she didn't notice before brightens her kitchen island.

"Did you bring those?"

"Blaze. He scared the shit out of us. We were out back and I couldn't tell it was him in the kitchen."

"Sorry about that. He should have called first." And returned his house key. She'd also promised to call him today.

"They're pretty," Amber says.

Olivia sniffs the flowers. They're beautiful. Perfectly imperfect, like her and Blaze. He's never given her flowers. The gesture is oddly romantic. Her stomach feels like a ballerina twirling. A hint of a smile adds a curve to her lips.

"He's so in love with you, Olivia."

"I know." She really hurt him and sensed that much last night when he saw Ethan.

"He was also very curious about Josh."

That gets her attention. "How so?"

"He asked a lot of questions, like where he's from, and all that."

Her heart rate speeds up. Josh could have had another anxiety attack and she wouldn't have been here for him.

"Did Blaze find out anything new?"

Amber shakes her head. "Josh was mixing up his words pretty bad. Nothing he said made sense. But he kept his cool."

"Good."

"Blaze wanted me to remind you that you promised to call him."

"I know." She rubs a peony petal between her fingers. "I think I'll pay him a visit instead." She owes it to him to have this conversation face-to-face.

"Thought you might say that." Amber settles back in her chair and kicks up her feet. "Take your time. I've got my book."

———

Blaze opens his door wearing a shirt with a Harley-Davidson logo and faded jeans clinging to his hips, looking not at all surprised to find her on his porch. His hair is loose, tousled, and falls above his shoulders, his feet bare. "I asked Amber for you to call, but this is better." He grins, his mouth pulling wide and tugging on her heart.

She shows him her hand, palm up. "Key, please," she says gently before she gets distracted and forgets.

He gives her a sad smile and reaches for the key chain on the small circular table by the door and twists off her house key. He presses the key into her palm. "Your car wasn't there. I didn't think you were home."

"You shouldn't come over without calling first, not while Josh is staying with me." She's worried about his safety and Blaze showing up unannounced might scare her nephew.

"I know." He runs a hand over his head, holding the hair off his face. He leans an elbow against the jamb. "I'm still getting used to our new arrangement."

They don't have an arrangement. Whatever this is now between them is her fault, and she should repair it. She *wants* to repair them. She studies the key in her palm and runs her thumb over the sharp teeth. "Amber tells me you talked with Josh."

"Cool kid."

"Did he tell you anything?" she asks, hoping he gleaned something she has yet to find out.

Blaze moves back and lets her in. "Everything okay?" she asks, noticing the bewilderment tweaking his brows.

He closes the door. "I think he's Ty's kid."

"Your brother?" she asks, stunned.

"Maybe." He scratches the back of his neck.

Lily never shared anything beyond friendship with Tyler as far as she knew. Olivia thought they lost touch when they lost their summers. And Tyler never asked about Lily when she was over at Blaze's house when they were dating.

"Explain," she says.

"Not sure I can. It's a hunch, Liv. I was in the army at the time. Ty got himself into some trouble and skipped town for a bit. Pissed off my mom."

"She was still sick then?"

He nods. "It was near the end. When I heard Lily ran away I wondered if it had anything to do with Ty. They left around the same time."

"He came back, though. Wouldn't he have stayed with her if it was his kid?"

"That's why I'm not sure."

"Ask him." At this point, anything is worth a shot. Tyler might know where Lily ran off to.

"I doubt he'll answer, but I'll try." After Harold's sudden passing, he left their properties in both Blaze's and Tyler's names. Blaze wanted to remodel and sell. Tyler couldn't let them go. As far as Olivia knows, Blaze has been renting out the homes waiting for Tyler to change his mind. But the two have been at odds since before Harold passed. Tyler resented Blaze for leaving him to care for their mother. She had a live-in nurse, but Tyler took the brunt of responsibility between the two brothers. He was living at home, attending classes at a local JC because their mother needed constant care and Blaze wasn't around.

"Where is he, by the way?"

"Milan, Singapore, who knows." Tyler's a financial wiz with some big-name tech company Olivia can't remember. Blaze once told her Tyler splits his time between San Francisco and New York, but he's essentially all over the place.

She follows Blaze into the sparsely furnished great room at the back of the ranch house. A recording of the Angels vs. Astros game from earlier in the week is paused on the big-screen TV. In the kitchen, the dishwasher runs.

Blaze picks his phone off the couch and calls Tyler.

"Wait." She grabs his forearm, her mind on her dad. He ends the call. "Don't mention Josh. Lily kept the father's name off his birth certificate for a reason. She might have been protecting him. Until I know why, the fewer people who know where he is the better."

"What do you want me to say?"

"Tell him it's a family emergency and we're trying to reach Lily."

He drags a hand over his bearded chin. "You know, I could move back in if you're worried about his safety. Keep that bed of yours warm."

She rolls her eyes. "Call your brother."

He smirks and presses the phone to his ear. "Ty, it's Blaze. Call me when you get this. It's urgent." He hangs up and tosses the phone onto the couch. His face softens and he lightly skims his fingers along her jawline. "You doing okay?"

She feels his touch all the way to her toes and her face crumples and her defenses fall. "I'm sorry. I screwed up. I got scared. I never should have assumed anything about you and Macey." It feels good to admit what she feels, to finally be real with him, and to herself.

He traces the shell of her ear, tucks back her hair. "I wouldn't cheat on you, Olivia. I learned my lesson." His mouth angles up into a half smile.

She realizes that now. "I know. I'm sorry."

"Enough for me to keep my key?"

"Blaze . . ." She rolls her eyes and he chuckles.

"It's okay to love me. You told me once, long ago. You can tell me again."

That once was a couple weeks before he hooked up with Macey, and he didn't say the words back. Granted, they were sixteen, but it left an impression that's rippled through her other relationships, including those with Lily and Lucas. She's always hesitated to express her true feelings.

His demeanor softens, but there's still a cocky edge. He presses a thumb to the corner of her eye, absorbing the moisture she didn't realize was collecting there. "Where's Josh?"

"Home, with Amber."

He tucks a finger under her chin and coaxes her face up until their eyes meet. "Stay."

"I can't." She wants to clear her head before they restart anything. She wants a future with him, but she's still scared. She won't plunge into their relationship if there's the chance she'll walk away when it gets too serious. "I have to go."

She turns to leave and almost makes it across the room. But Blaze is the exercise band pulling the muscled limb back into place. She feels terrible for treating him unkindly, and she's missed the hell out of him. Who is she kidding? Blaze is her family. He's where she belongs, her safe harbor.

Turning back, she walks straight into his waiting arms. She clings to him, her raft in her sea of unrest. Lifting to her toes, she hooks her arms around his neck and kisses him. He sweeps her off her feet as if he's afraid she'll change her mind and walk out the door. Abruptly, he breaks their kiss, lifts his head. "You sure?"

She cups his cheek. Emotions soar like birds surfing air currents. "Yes."

CHAPTER 26

Arms around her shoulders and hooked under her knees, Blaze carries Olivia to his bedroom. His mouth tangles with hers. The kiss is wet and sloppy because he's multitasking: walking while devouring her like they've been apart for months rather than days. Olivia grasps his head, desperate with need. Desperate to forget everything since she went batshit crazy on him the other day. She sucks his lower lip and Blaze groans, stumbling into the wall. He grunts, almost dropping her.

"I can walk." She tries to shimmy from his arms.

He holds her closer. "Uh-uh. I've got you."

They enter his room and she expects him to toss her onto the bed in typical Blaze I'm-going-to-fuck-you style. But he lets her legs drop while holding her close. She slides down until her feet gently land on the carpet. He then slips her sweater off her shoulders, lifts her shirt over her head, and peels off her jeans, all the while kissing her. Her lips, underside of her chin, the soft skin between her breasts, her hip bone. She can hardly catch her breath. By the time he sheds his clothes, she's clawing at his chest, urging him to go faster. "It's been five days." She feels the urgent need for a distraction, put the worry and pain that's been plaguing her on pause, even if only for a momentary reprieve. But he's taking his sweet time and it's messing with her head.

He backs her up, moving with her. "Seems longer."

Her calves bump against the bedside, and with a gentle nudge from Blaze, she falls back onto the covers. He crawls up her, the bed dipping under his weight, and settles between her legs. Blowing right past foreplay, he smoothly enters, sighing like he's returned from an extended trip overseas. "Been too long."

She urgently raises her hips, begging him to lose control, but he doesn't take the hint. He draws back and pushes in achingly slow. He does it again, and then again.

"What are you doing?"

He lifts his brows. "Umm . . ."

She pats his rear. "I know what you're doing. But why like this?" she asks, her arms coming around him. So. Excruciatingly. Slow. He's tormenting her.

"You mean like this?" He demonstrates with another slow withdrawal that drags a moan from her. She feels every inch. "As in why aren't we banging the headboard against the wall or trying to break the bed?"

"Yes, yes." She laughs. Her hips move in sync with his, finding the new-for-them rhythm he's set.

His big hand cradles the side of her head. His eyes bore into hers. "I'm making love to you."

She blinks. "Why?"

A low laugh vibrates his chest. "You look so serious." His mouth quirks, the right side pulling up higher than the left. "Because I love you?"

She clasps his head with both hands and searches his face. His declaration is a balm to her soul. She feels like he's the only person she can trust, the one she can truly open up to. "You love me."

"I do." Blaze kisses her nose before his eyes darken. He picks up the pace, drawing a guttural sigh from her.

And just like that, the tide shifts. Her head tilts back and a low moan replaces her smile. She clutches his back and grips the sheets. Their energy swells and problems fall away, leaving nothing but him and her in pursuit of the same endgame. That moment of bliss.

Afterward, they lie on their backs, breathing heavily, staring at the ceiling. His hand finds hers among the sheets, and she says, "That was . . ."

"Incredible? I was thinking more like epic. Or mind-blowing. But incredible will do." He scratches his chest and she laughs, because he's right. *Incredible* is an inadequate description as to how he made her feel. There was an added layer tonight, as if an invisible barrier lifted and suddenly there was more of him. More of them. It wasn't just physical. He made her feel treasured. Adored. No longer alone.

"You love me," she whispers, letting the words roll around her mind, find their place.

From the corner of her eye, she sees his head turn on the pillow to look at her. "I never stopped."

"That night at the beach when you tossed my shoes in the bonfire. You said 'loved.' Past tense." It was fall of their senior year, the first bonfire of the season. The varsity football team had beaten their rival the night before and most of the class wanted to celebrate. Olivia was there with Ethan. Blaze had brought Macey, and he was drunk. With Macey hanging on his arm, he'd confessed that he'd loved Olivia. Appalled, Macey stomped off. But when Olivia told Blaze to have Macey take him home, he plucked her white canvas Keds from the sand and tossed them into the fire before stumbling off.

"I was angry. Sorry about the shoes. Guess I owe you a pair." He laughs like a devious little boy and shows her three fingers.

He's confessed his love three times. "When was the third?"

"The *first* time was at the lake house."

She rolls to her side, facing him. He does the same. "Was that the time we were fishing?" They'd been thirteen, their last summer there. They fished from the end of the Whitmans' dock. Blaze dropped a worm in her hand and said that he loved her. She laughed in his face and pushed him into the lake. It was the morning before Lucas was caught shoplifting. They'd been so young.

"Our last summer there," Blaze murmurs. His fingers skim her hair. Thick emotion pushes its way up her chest. She rolls out of bed.

"Where are you going?" Worry laces his voice. He sits up.

"Getting some air," She pulls on her jeans and shirt and pads barefoot to the great room. She rifles through her purse, grabs her smokes and lighter, and goes to the porch. She lights up and takes a long pull. Blaze's house resides on top of a sloping hill and his view goes for miles. Homes are scattered among the rolling landscape of San Luis Obispo's backcountry, lit up like earthbound stars. The evening is quiet, absent of cars and music, a neighbor washing dishes in the kitchen. Sounds she hears in the suburbs. Her gaze follows the horizon's dusky sky. Lily is out there, somewhere. Alone, she imagines, frightened for Josh. The only family she has.

Blaze joins her and drops his biker jacket over her shoulders. "Those things will kill you."

She snorts. Unless stress finds her heart first.

"I love it out here." So peaceful. "Why'd you always sleep at my house?"

"You were there." He leans his weight against the porch rail beside her, his back to the view, and crosses his arms. "Why'd you leave?" He tilts his head toward the house.

Because everything she's been fighting to ignore wants to be heard. "Those summers at the lake house were the happiest ones I had. They just went away. I felt like I lost your parents. Lily wanted nothing to do with me because Lucas was being an ass and I had no problem telling him so. Then he wouldn't stop screwing around. Every summer he did something stupid until your parents finally got fed up. I overheard them talking. It's his fault. He took those summers from us. I pushed him away. Lily too. Then I found you with Macey."

"So you pushed me away."

"When I saw you together, I felt like I'd lost everything about those summers. They were well and truly gone." She looks up at the now black sky and takes a long drag on her smoke. "My dad told me Ethan was the father of Lily's baby. He's not, but for years I believed so."

Blaze whistles. "Shit. That's why you broke up?"

She nods. "After we did, Lily ran away. I shut everyone out. Since then, I've been in one worthless relationship after another."

"You and Ethan were pretty close."

She picks up his hand and traces the deep grooves in his palm. His skin is rough near his wrist, dried out from his work. He loves to build, and she should have realized he's as strong a foundation to her as the ones he pours. "Never like you and me."

His hand skims up the side of her arm, cups the back of her nape. "Stay with me tonight."

She tugs his shirt hem. "You know I can't. Josh. Besides, I'll keep you up all night."

His mouth parts and she suspects he's about to make a wisecrack when his brows draw together. "Nightmares again?" The one that makes her edgy. The one that now carries so much weight given what she's learned about her dad.

She puts out the cigarette in the ashtray he keeps on the porch for her like a water bowl for a stray cat. She always comes back.

"They've been more frequent since Josh arrived. Stress, I guess. I haven't been sleeping."

"Same dream?"

"Always." The nightmare gave her the idea to create her Crimson Wave superheroes. They'd go to battle for her. "I've been wondering if there's some truth to it. What if it really happened?" Something she's never worried about before. Dwight always convinced her it was *just a dream* when she sought his comfort.

"You're still thinking he has something to do with Josh."

She nods. Outside of Blaze and Amber, Olivia goes to her father when she needs advice. Right now, she doesn't even want to call him, let alone see him. Fear for Josh and what might have happened to Lily has her frozen. She can't rely on him, and that feeling has left a hollow ache in the center of her chest.

"I can stay with you," he says, quietly.

"No, I'll be fine." She puts her hand on his chest. He's solid, her rock. Her thumb rubs the bare skin above his neckline. "I guess I had to lose you to realize I love you," she whispers, feeling as much as hearing his breath catch.

"You never lost me, Olivia." He kisses her forehead, letting his lips linger on her cool skin.

"I have to go. Josh—"

"I know." He nuzzles her neck and whispers his good night.

———

It's almost two in the morning when Olivia ventures into her studio, unable to sleep as much as not wanting to, restless about the past few days. Amber left hours ago with her book tucked in her purse and a smile plastered to her face. Her friend didn't ask what went down at Blaze's. She knew, thanks to Olivia's flushed cheeks and fluid movement. So relaxed she practically floated into the house.

But her euphoria post-Blaze wore off quickly as she roamed the darkened rooms waiting for the text that he'd heard from Tyler.

She flips on the light, settling onto the swivel chair, and draws Josh's stack of panels across the drafting table. She should wait for Josh to explain them, as best as he's capable, but she's desperate for answers. She flips through them. Page after page shows Josh with friends, skateboarding at the park or cruising the mall. And Lily, with similar coloring and eyes to her character Dahlia. She's there, too. But so is someone else, a shadowy figure, his features undefinable, always lurking. Always watching. He's in every sequence, panel after panel. Dread expands through her like an incoming fogbank, slinking into every limb, spreading her fear for Lily. Josh too. Could this shadowy figure be looking for him?

The deeper she gets into the stack, the darker Josh's illustrations become. Shattered windows, flights of stairs, a crumpled body. She can't tell if it's Josh or Lily.

A strong compulsion forces her to look outside the darkened window to see if she's being watched. Her thoughts arrow to the worst. Lily is dead. And from the looks of Josh's illustrations, her end was tragic. And preventable. Guilt consumes her. Pain stabs her.

No, she's not dead.

She'd sense it, wouldn't she? Josh would be grief-stricken, inconsolable.

Chilled, Olivia leaves the panels in the order she found them. She'll ask Josh to explain them as best he can in the morning. Or Lily can. *When* they find her. She wants to hear her sister's story.

Olivia leaves her studio. She needs a stiff drink and a smoke. Turning on the kitchen light, she rummages through her purse, then yanks open drawers until she remembers she tossed her Marlboros when she returned from Blaze's. A half-hearted attempt to quit cold turkey. She pulls out the bin from underneath the sink and sifts through soiled towels and crumpled food-stained plastic wrap. So much for trying to kick the habit.

Her fingertips touch the lighter the same instant her phone buzzes. She slams the cabinet door and answers her phone.

"You up?" Blaze asks, his voice gruff.

"Hey, you. Yeah, can't sleep." She's been on edge since before she walked into her studio.

"Me either. I heard from Ty. Mentioned there was a Carson family emergency and you were trying to reach Lily."

Hope blossoms. "And?"

"He doesn't have her number," he says, crushing her. "Says he hasn't spoken to her since high school. He was curious about said emergency. I didn't tell him anything." He exhales loudly. "I don't know what I was thinking. Josh isn't his. Nothing would have kept Ty from his kid. Sorry to get your hopes up."

"That's okay." She pinches her nose bridge, near tears. Josh's panels unnerved her. "Thanks for trying."

"Anytime. How's your headspace?"

She rinses and dries her hands. "Forecast says partly cloudy." She told him she loves him, and she does.

Blaze chuckles. "I'll take that over stormy. You rocked my world tonight."

He definitely tilted hers. Though her life has been off-balance all week. Her elbow lands on the table and her forehead in her hand. She looks unfocused at the table, frustrated, and notices Josh's sketch pad. It's open to the beach scene with the pier he's been working on. So is her coffee-table book, the one that fascinated him his first day here.

"Talk tomorrow?" she asks, peering at the location printed underneath the photo that Josh's sketch is almost an exact replica of. Oceanside, California.

Olivia feels a rush of excitement.

"Good night, Liv."

"Night." She ends the call and cups her mouth. She wants to yell and wake Josh up. Did he just tell her where he's from?

CHAPTER 27

LUCAS

The elevator is stuffed with talking heads, packed shoulder to shoulder like a can of sardines. It smells as ripe as one, too. Stale sweat mixes with cheap department store cologne and has the metal box reeking worse than Lucas's gym shirt after a grueling workout. Though the odor isn't as pungent as his juvie cellmate after a dinner of canned beans and corn. He can tolerate the air in the elevator.

Lucas watches the numbers on the panel above the door light up for each floor, cautious of his surroundings. Camera in the upper right corner. Another hidden in the button panel. He only gives them a sliver of his face.

The door slips open every few floors and guests spill out. Each time, he tightens his fist and the artery in his neck throbs like an embolism. He braces his legs as people nudge past, feeling queasy. He hates cramped spaces and wills the buttons to light faster. Tugging the visor lower over his forehead, he keeps his back to the two men left. His old man and the guy he's shooting the shit with. Something about in-state distribution growth.

Damn, the man could talk. He'd yak on the phone through dinner if Charlotte let him. Dwight could talk himself out of anything, and Lucas wouldn't put past him that he talked himself out of St. John's murder and his involvement in Wes Jensen's drowning.

The tenth-floor button lights up like a joint. Hands jammed in his hoodie pockets, Lucas steps off the elevator. He goes straight to the lobby phone and pretends to make a call, watching for Dwight in his peripheral vision. The old man and his buddy make plans to meet at the bar downstairs. Dwight claps him on the shoulder and they part ways, with Dwight heading right. Lucas drops the receiver in the cradle and follows, his work boots eating up the tacky carpeting.

With each step he grows more enraged. Dwight swings one of those canvas bags they hand out at conferences, whistling like a Looney-fucking-Tunes character who doesn't have a care in this messed-up world. Whistling as if Lucas's mom doesn't believe he stabbed the neighbor and got off. Lucas is convinced. He saw what the man is capable of the night Lily ran away. He aimed a gun at his own daughter. Beats him why Charlotte can't see it, or why she hasn't left him. What's Dwight's hold over her?

One thing's for sure, he didn't protect Lily from their dad before. He intends to do so now. If Dwight is giving her and Josh trouble, he'll put an end to that.

Dwight stops at a door and slides his key card into the slot. He ducks into his room as the woman in the room across leaves hers. Talk about shitty timing. She smiles at Lucas. He averts his face and keeps walking, right past Dwight's room and straight to the stairwell. The metal door bangs open and slams shut behind him. He got what he needed, for now. Dwight's room number. He'll come back tonight. Might as well let the old man enjoy one more evening at the bar because he won't want to show his face at home when Lucas is done with him.

CHAPTER 28

Day 6

Olivia's phone vibrates on her nightstand, drawing her from the cold, windy shore of her nightmare. The surf still rages in her ears. She wipes her damp hair off her forehead and reaches for the phone.

"Hello?" she croaks, her head foggy. Her dream still lingers in the recesses of her mind like a reluctant child who won't leave the room.

"Got your call."

"Lucas?" She glances at the clock, miffed she slept through her alarm again. It's just after nine. She'd wanted to be on the road by now. Swinging her legs off the bed, she sits up. "Where are you?" Her irritation works its way into her tone. She's still upset he bailed on shopping the other day. He hasn't returned her calls either.

"On a job," Lucas says after a beat. His voice lacks inflection. She can't tell if he's tired, down on himself, or flat-out doesn't care, as if calling her is an inconvenience. Knowing Lucas, it's the latter.

"You okay?"

"Yeah. Yeah, I'll be fine." He doesn't sound certain to her. "Oceanside, eh?"

Last night, Josh couldn't sleep and found her in the kitchen. She'd asked if he lived in Oceanside. Bleary-eyed, he'd nodded. But he doesn't believe Lily would have returned home. When Olivia asked why, he tried to explain, only to get flustered when he spoke gibberish. But the one thing she did understand was that he and Lily didn't have a choice. They had to leave home.

She still asked him to draw what happened so she'd have a clearer picture. Josh took her to the studio and showed her one of the panels, five rectangles stacked like books. A series of illustrations depicting a lone woman on a barren highway except for one oncoming car. In one rectangle the car clips the woman. In the last rectangle, Josh drew the car's taillights. The woman, though, is gone.

"Is this your mom?" she asked, horrified. He nodded. "Was she hit by a car?" She could be seriously injured.

"Don't know."

"Did you see her get hit?"

He shook his head and touched his ear. "Heard," he said after a brief struggle to get out the word.

"You heard it happen?"

He nodded.

"Josh, my god." She grabbed his arm. "Where did she go?"

His lower lip quivered. "Gone."

"Did the driver take her away?" An even more horrifying thought than Lily being hit.

"Don't know."

"Did you look for her?"

He nodded. "Gone."

"Josh." Her features softened, and she touched his shoulder, her heart breaking for him. That's what he meant the day he arrived. He didn't know where she went, or if she was alive. She was just gone when he went back to the scene. Where'd he been? What had he been doing? That wasn't clear in his drawings. But it was apparent someone was after them. They were being followed.

Lily could have been abducted, or the driver could have taken her to the hospital. Dazed, Lily could have returned to her car and driven away without Josh. Any number of scenarios could have occurred.

She took a deep breath. Okay, they'd figure this out. She leveled with him. "We're going to find her."

Which is why they're driving to Oceanside. Puzzles aren't easy to solve, even harder when the pieces are missing. But Olivia doesn't believe like Josh does that Lily wouldn't have returned home after she and Josh separated, assuming she was physically capable of getting back. But someone, a neighbor perhaps, is bound to have seen Lily before they left. Someone has to know where they were going. If they can get into the house, there might be clues. And the more information she can bring back to the police, the more details she can add to Lily's missing persons report. They'll find Lily that much sooner.

"I want to talk to her neighbors," she says to Lucas. "Josh might be able to get us into the house." There isn't a house key in his backpack, not that she saw the other night. She goes into her closet and gets down her overnight bag. "Have you heard from Dad at all?" she asks, intent on finding out when exactly he'll be home today. She hasn't replied to his voice mail, and thankfully he hasn't yet called back. "Lucas? Did you hear me?" she asks when he doesn't respond.

"Yeah, no." He roughly clears his throat.

She stops midstride across her room, bag in hand. "Are you okay? You sound a little strange."

"Fine," he says tightly. "What do you want?"

She'd left him a message last night detailing her suspicions about their dad, all while trying not to have an emotional breakdown. She doesn't know what he wants with Lily, but suspects he found her. Dwight could be the shadow man in Josh's drawings. He might have accidentally or intentionally pushed Josh and hit Lily. He might be the one who followed them out of town. He could be the reason Josh is here and Lily missing.

"Am I being crazy?" she asks.

"About Dad? No."

Olivia drops her bag at her feet and jams her hand into her armpit. She bites her lower lip hard, holding back the scream building in her lungs. She isn't crazy. Lucas sees it, too.

She slinks onto the tufted bench at the end of the bed. "Did you talk to Mom? What did she tell you?" Her questions are barely above a whisper.

"Not much more than what you've told me." He pops his lips.

The skin on the back of her neck tightens. He's lying. "Lucas . . ."

"Not now, Liv. If you don't need anything, I've gotta go."

"Wait! Text when Dad gets into town." She doesn't want Dwight surprising her with an unannounced visit.

"That all?"

"Keep me posted on his whereabouts." She starts stuffing clothes in her bag, shirts, jeans, a dress. If she doesn't find Lily in Oceanside and Josh comes back with her, they'll stay with Blaze. She can't hide Josh from Dwight forever, but she'd feel better if someone is looking over her shoulder while she's looking out for her nephew.

"Will do." Lucas ends the call.

Olivia quickly showers and packs and meets Josh in the kitchen. Already dressed in jeans and a tee, his hair every which way, he frantically searches his backpack, upending it on the table. He sorts through magazines, books, and sketch pads, holding them up, fanning the pages as if hoping something falls out. She knows exactly what he's looking for.

"Are you looking for a white envelope?"

His head snaps up.

"I have it."

"Mine."

"But it was addressed to me."

"Give back."

If his eyes weren't wild and frightened, she'd say no. Lily named her his guardian. She needs to hold on to the originals. "I'll make a copy." She retreats to the studio, copies the birth certificate and power of attorney, then gives him the originals.

"My mom—" He shuts his mouth and shoves the envelope in his backpack.

She takes a wild guess. "She doesn't know you have it, does she?"

He shakes his head, which explains why he didn't want to show her what was in his backpack.

"Josh?" He zips closed his pack. She waits for him to look at her. "Did your mom tell you about me?"

His mouth turns down. "Not much. Only your . . . frog . . . box. Ugh. Name."

Just her name. Olivia tries not to feel hurt, but it's impossible. Her chest aches. Lily probably hasn't told him anything about her family. And why should she? They turned on her. But like any kid his age, raised by a single mom, he had to have been curious. He went looking for answers and came across Lily's old files. Olivia's pulling straws here, trying to find the missing pieces. But it makes sense to her.

"Is that how you found me?" She gestures at the envelope in his backpack. "Did you show that to the woman who brought you here when you couldn't find your mom?"

His eyes shimmer. "Yes," he whispers.

"Do you know how lucky you are that you did find me?" She cups her mouth. The odds alone make it a miracle. What if he hadn't snagged his mom's paperwork? He could be anywhere by now, lost to Lily forever. And Olivia would have never known.

Josh nods, his shoulders slumping. Olivia watches as the weight of the past few days bends him over. Tears flood his eyes. She doesn't ask for permission or overthink what she's doing. She pulls Josh into her arms and he falls apart.

His body shakes with deep guttural sobs. Her shoulder is drenched within seconds and tears bite her eyes. She doesn't bother wiping them away, because even though Josh is miserable, her heart feels a bit fuller.

She's so glad he found her. Rubbing his back, Olivia whispers a prayer Lily won't keep him out of Olivia's life. Because she's becoming attached to Josh.

———

An hour later, Olivia parks in front of her parents' house. Josh fiddles with the phone Amber gave him. He lifts his head and looks outside the windows when he notices they've stopped. He sees the house and panic peeks around the corners of his eyes.

"He's not here," she reassures. Dwight never arrives home early when he's coming from out of town, and Charlotte's Mercedes is the only car in the driveway. "I'll be quick. Just stay in the car this time."

"Okay."

Shouldering her purse with Dwight's useless Rolodex, she exits the car and calls Amber.

"I need a huge favor. I'm returning the Rolodex. Call my mom and distract her." She needs time to download her dad's contact list. While she hopes Josh recognizes landmarks and can direct her to his house, Oceanside is a decent-size town. She'd rather have an address and not waste time driving around. Besides, she also needs to delete yesterday's surveillance and copy his photos. If the trek to SoCal is a dead end she needs to pursue Lily through Josh's father.

"What should I say?" Amber asks.

"Pretend you're in the market for a new house?" That'll keep Charlotte busy.

"I just bought one."

"Investment property, then. Ask for a referral to an interior designer. You'll think of something. Please? Just keep her on the line for ten minutes or so."

Amber makes a noise in her throat. "Ten minutes max. I have a new client coming into the office."

Olivia reaches the porch. "You're a lifesaver. I owe you a lot for this week."

"Yeah, you do, and you will pay up."

Olivia can only imagine what scheme Amber will rope her into. A night out at a Western bar riding a mechanical bull was her last brilliant idea. She was sore for a week.

"Give me a minute or two. And heads-up. She was a hot mess yesterday."

Olivia disconnects and presses the front door latch only to find it locked. No thanks to her unannounced arrival yesterday. She rings the doorbell, then rings again when she doesn't hear Charlotte approach, and wonders if she should be worried. She's about to call her mom when Charlotte finally answers the door.

"Olivia," she says with genuine surprise. Dark circles from smeared mascara hold up her eyes. Her hair is unkempt. "What are you doing here?"

"I was in the area. Thought I'd check on you." Her gaze sweeps up Charlotte's wool pants and white tailored blouse. The buttons are out of alignment. The skin above the collar is flushed and damp. Olivia gestures at the buttons. Charlotte detests when she's not put together.

"Oh." Charlotte fixes her blouse.

"Is, uh . . . everything okay?"

"Mm-hmm." Her mom runs her hand over the column of buttons, then folds her hands at her waist. She smiles at Olivia. "I'm fine, darling. Yesterday was just a . . ." Her hand flutters in the air. "Blip."

"Good. I'm glad." Olivia's phone vibrates. She reads the text from Amber. Now?

"Sorry, have to respond. It's my editor." The lie sours in her mouth like a green apple–flavored hard candy.

Yes. She quickly types. Call the landline. Charlotte will have to leave the door to answer the phone.

It rings in the kitchen. Charlotte glances over her shoulder into the belly of the house. She starts to close the door but Olivia steps into the house. "Go ahead and get that. I have to use the bathroom."

She lightly touches her lips and glances back toward the bedrooms and Olivia thinks she'll ignore the call, but Charlotte sighs dramatically.

"All right. Make it quick. I have . . . an appointment."

"Thanks." Olivia walks briskly toward the guest bathroom. When Charlotte disappears into the kitchen, she veers into the bedroom wing and Dwight's office. The surveillance system monitor and keyboard are in the closet, but she goes for the computer on his desk first.

"Amber, it's been a long time. How've you been? How's the new house?" Olivia hears Charlotte exclaim from the kitchen as she returns the Rolodex to its spot, aligning the base inside the square free of dust on Dwight's desk. Settling into his chair, she plugs her thumb drive into the USB port and powers on the computer.

She glances at the time as the computer wakes. "Keep on talking, Amber," she murmurs. When the prompt appears, she types the same password Dwight has used since she was in high school and she helped him set up his new desktop. With every computer upgrade, he always reverted to the same: Princ3ssO*

Bless her daddy for always cutting corners to make his life simpler. She scoots forward and gets to work.

"I know of the perfect property for you." Charlotte's voice carries down the hallway. She sounds closer, as if she's poking her head out of the kitchen, wondering what's taking Olivia so long in the bathroom.

"Stay in the kitchen," she whispers, exporting Dwight's contacts.

The musical lilt Charlotte gets in her voice with the prospect of a new deal trickles down the hallway like a bubbling brook. Olivia tries not to feel too bad that she's playing her mom while she copies over the photo file from fourteen years ago. She reasons she's doing her mom a favor. Talking about Lily heightens Charlotte's anxiety. Best she doesn't know what Olivia's up to. She doesn't want to cause her mom further worry.

"Why don't you come into my office tomorrow? Does ten in the morning work for you?"

Olivia removes her drive. Before she can slide open the closet door to access the surveillance, a door down the hall, in the opposite direction of her mom, slams. Her head snaps in that direction. *The hell?* That came from her parents' bedroom.

Her arms start to tingle with fresh perspiration. She didn't think Dwight was home. Lucas would have texted her.

If that idiot forgot . . .

Olivia powers down Dwight's computer, and with one look back to check that she left everything in order, she walks toward her parents' room. If her dad's home, where's his car? He always parks in the drive. Unless . . .

Does Charlotte have company? Is *she* cheating on Dwight?

"That was your friend Amber," Charlotte says from the other end of the hallway.

Olivia yelps, pressing a hand to her chest. "Don't do that. Seriously." She gasps. "You scared me."

"What were you doing?" Charlotte looks past her.

"I was checking on a noise." She gestures at the bedroom door.

"Hmm. Not sure what you heard. No one else here but me."

"I wasn't thinking . . ." Her face heats. Okay. She was. Maybe her mom is lonely. That's something she can understand. Dwight's away more than he's home, and they don't get along.

Olivia smiles awkwardly, feeling sorry for her mom. Her husband is negligent, possibly abusive, and she lost a daughter. Charlotte starts backing away into the foyer. "So, Amber. She's looking to invest in some property."

"She mentioned that last night." Olivia doesn't meet her mom's eyes. Charlotte finds the prospect of helping Amber exciting and

Olivia resists confessing it's a ruse, especially after all her mom has been through.

"I'm glad she called you," she says with forced enthusiasm.

"Me too. I have the perfect place in mind. A cute little beach cottage that'll make a killing as an Airbnb." As she's talking, Charlotte's gaze wanders to Olivia's noticeably less bulky hobo purse. Olivia's stomach sours with guilt. She tucks the purse behind her arm.

"I should go. I'm glad you're feeling better today."

"I am. Thanks for checking on me." She smiles and opens the front door. Olivia steps outside into the bluebird-sky morning. "Oh, is . . . Josh . . . is he still with you?"

Olivia turns around. "Yes. He's in the car. Why?"

"I was wondering if you've located Lily yet."

She shakes her head. "I'm trying, Mom. Anything you know of that can help me out? Did Dad tell you anything?"

Her expression draws a blank. "I already told you. He hasn't. We don't talk about Lily."

"Okay," she says. "I'll call you later."

"Of course, darling. Have a good day." Charlotte shuts and bolts the door.

Olivia texts her thanks to Amber, then notices a silver Audi parked across the street. She glances back at the house, wondering who the car belongs to. If she didn't suspect what she does about Dwight, she'd be livid over Charlotte's hypocrisy. But as her view of her dad has changed, so has that of her mom. She's starting to see her in a new light. Charlotte should divorce Dwight. He doesn't respect her at all, and she's done so much for their family, especially him. All those years she helped him with his campaigns, organizing fundraisers, traveling door-to-door with the flyers she designed and ordered.

"Hey, Josh," she says when she gets into the car and starts the engine.

He sets aside his phone and rubs his eyes. Olivia's noticed he can only spend so much time working on the aphasia apps before he loses focus or his eyes tire.

"Ready?" he asks.

"In a bit." She drags out her laptop and plugs in the drive, hopeful he's kept it updated. It doesn't take long to realize Dwight's contacts are a bust. He doesn't have Lily's address, at least not on file. She jabs her elbow against the door, frustrated. Josh watches her, wary.

"Hey, Josh, anything you remember about your address would be a huge help," she says, scrolling through the contacts a second time on the off chance she missed something.

He points out the windshield. "It's like . . . that . . . big . . ."

"Like what?"

"That."

She looks out the window to the small grove of eucalyptus trees behind the house. The treetops peek over the roofline.

"Eucalyptus? Is that the name of your street?"

"No. Like."

"Like?" she asks, trying to decipher his meaning. "You mean like a tree?"

"Yes."

Olivia quickly launches her map app and brings up Oceanside. Quite a few streets are named for trees. "Ash, Pine, Oak . . ." She lists them off out loud.

He grabs her arm. "Pine!"

"You live on Pine?"

He grins. "Yes."

Well, damn.

"Good job, Josh." She gives him a fist bump. "Let's get going. We have a long drive ahead."

CHAPTER 29

Summer of '01

Through Dwight's office window, Olivia watched Lucas and Lily play basketball in the driveway, envious they hadn't invited her. He was teaching her how to line up a shot. He'd already taken her kayaking that morning and taught her how to paddle since their dad said he didn't have time to teach her.

Olivia chewed off a hangnail on her thumb. Lily hadn't asked for her help in a long time. She always went to Lucas and only sought Olivia when she needed something, like to raid her closet for the sweater Charlotte just bought her, which Lily returned with a tear in the armpit and insisted she didn't do it. Aside from the one time she wore it to a movie with a friend, Lily swore the sweater had been folded on her dresser the whole time, and it didn't have a hole when she took it off.

Olivia didn't believe Lily. Holes didn't magically appear. Lily threw a temper tantrum when Olivia pressed that Lily owed her a new sweater.

What had she done to make Lily act so mean? What happened to that sweet girl who held her big sister's hand, looking up to her with brown eyes as sweet as warm chocolate cake? Olivia didn't know.

She spat out the hangnail and covered a yawn, hating this summer. The Whitmans hadn't invited them to the lake house. She was missing Blaze, and missing out on hiking, canoeing, eating too many Popsicles, and roasting marshmallows with him over their bonfire. And it was all Lucas's fault. Idiot had to get caught lifting a Hot Wheels car. Their dad didn't know, but he was stealing again, a Bic lighter here, a jerky stick there. He bragged about it the other day when she overheard him talking with his friend Tanner. She was tempted to tattle on him, but she wasn't mean like Lily. Lucas would get his comeuppance one day; Olivia was sure of it.

Behind her, Dwight smacked his computer monitor.

"That won't help," Olivia said without looking back at him. Lucas just tried to give Lily a high five and she jerked her hand away at the last second. Now Lily was laughing as Lucas chased her across the driveway.

Olivia yawned again, as much from weariness as to quell the pull in her stomach. She wouldn't invite herself to play. She didn't want to join them outside. She'd probably be bored anyway.

"It's so damn slow," Dwight complained. "Time for an upgrade."

"Try defragging it." Mr. Whitman taught her that trick last summer when his computer was sluggish while she played a video game.

"No time." He was leaving in a few hours, visiting winery clients from Temecula up to Calaveras County. He'd be away for a couple weeks. "Your mom will be home late. She has her Women in Real Estate thingamajig." Olivia knew he wanted to be out of the house before Charlotte returned. Avoiding her was better than getting into another argument about how much he was spending. "Keep an eye on your brother," he said.

"Lily too?" she asked absently, tugging a hangnail with her teeth.

"Hmm. Yeah, her too." His fingers rapped the keyboard. The computer's fan whirred as the unit powered down, his third attempt to reboot, but the computer kept freezing.

"They don't need me," she muttered. They seemed to be doing fine on their own.

"Do I detect some animosity?"

She shook her head—she'd never admit it—and turned away from the window. "Here, let me do it." She approached the desk. Dwight vacated his seat. Olivia rubbed her eyes and sank into the chair.

"Tired, Princess?"

She nodded. "Nightmare again. Couldn't fall back to sleep." That version of her dad who invaded her dreams scared her.

Dwight stood beside her. He casually eased his hands into his side pockets, his gaze out the window. "It's just a dream. Nothing to be afraid of."

"I know that."

Olivia rebooted the computer and waited for the password prompt. She scooted aside. "You want to enter it?"

"Go for it." He nodded at the keyboard. "It hasn't changed."

She logged on and started the defragmentation to free up more space.

"I notice you've been watching your brother and sister. They're pretty close, aren't they?" he asked, packing his briefcase. Olivia nodded. "What about you and Lily? Still get along like you used to?" She shook her head. "Sorry about that, Princess. Maybe things will change when you get older."

She wasn't sure about that. They were drifting apart faster than two kayaks caught in the tide.

He dropped a hand on her shoulder. "My brother and I were never close. I survived. You will too. Don't let them bother you. Just worry about yourself and you'll be fine. You only need to rely on you."

"And you, Daddy?" she asked, looking up at him.

"Always, Princess. I'd never turn my back on you. In fact, you come to me anytime, no matter the problem. No matter how much trouble you're in. I'll be there for you. Those dreams get worse, you see me," he instructs, trying not to look bothered. But Olivia can tell he's concerned about her. Or maybe he's concerned about the contents of her dreams. He told her once when she was scared or hurt, so was he. If she was sad, he felt sad, too.

Her smile was heavy. "I will."

He gestured at the monitor. "How long is that going to take?"

"Long. You can finish packing. I'll stay here." She didn't need to watch it, but what else would she do? Her friends were on vacation. She was too young to get a job. And naps were for babies.

Dwight dropped a kiss on her head. "You're the best daughter ever."

"Love you." She lifted a hand when he left the room and doodled until something better came along. She drew a picture of her dad with a cape and left the sketch on the desk. He'd see it when he returned and know that she thought of him as the best dad in the world. Her superdad.

CHAPTER 30

They make good time to Oceanside. Olivia takes an exit that points them toward the Pacific. She eases down her window. Josh does the same. The air smells of salt and diesel. Traffic, congested and noisy, moves slowly. She drops the visor to block the glaring afternoon sun as they inch toward the beach.

Josh leans as far forward as his seat belt allows, anxious to get home. His knee bounces and his gaze swings everywhere, taking in the scene. Concrete and palm trees. Cyclists in flip-flops on beach cruisers. The blue-gray ocean ahead where the water swirls like her emotions: hope that Lily is home, worry that she isn't, and the fear she's been abducted, injured, or killed.

"Recognize anything?" She keeps her emotions and thoughts in check so she won't alarm Josh.

"Yes." He gestures at the windshield. "Go."

They reach an intersection and Olivia takes a left at the light. Pine is several blocks up. She goes to make a turn and a car cuts her off. She's forced to continue straight until they come to a dead stop at a construction zone. Pylons line the painted median. A sign flashes about traffic delays. Cars idle bumper to bumper. The navigation system vocalizes her route correction.

Olivia's hands drop to her lap. She weaves her fingers to keep from fidgeting. Her head leans back against the rest. "This shouldn't take too long."

Josh pivots, looking out the rear window. "There. Go back." She hears the anxiety in his voice, sees it in the upward tilt of his brows.

"We can't turn around until we pass this." She leans right to see how far back they are but can't see anything beyond the truck in front of them.

Josh groans, exasperated, and flings off his seat belt.

"Keep that on. We're still driving." But Josh is out the door, shouldering his pack before she realizes what he's doing.

"I'm going." He shuts the door and rounds the rear. "Follow."

Follow him? She can't. She's stuck.

"Josh! Get back here," she yells out the window. He jogs across the street and her heart does an erratic dance. "Shit," she mutters.

Her phone rings. Amber's contact information brightens the dash monitor. Olivia taps the call answer button. "Amber, oh, my god. I'm stuck in traffic and Josh just ditched the car." She looks behind her to see where he went, cursing that the cars ahead haven't moved. Her heart rate is jacked, constricting her chest. She can't see him anywhere.

"Where are you?"

"Oceanside. Josh lives here." She quickly updates Amber on Josh's sketch and the matching photo in her book.

"Wow. Okay. Can you pull off to the side and park?"

"No room. Wait. Hold on." She has to get out of this roadblock.

Olivia looks over her shoulder, then makes a U-turn. The front bumper knocks over a pylon. She rolls over the tip of another. A glance in the rearview mirror shows several pylons rolling in the opposite lane. Navigation adjusts its course to Lily's street.

"Okay. I'm clear. Driving now."

"Can you see Josh?" Amber sounds worried.

"No, but I know the general direction where he went. Sorry, did you call for something?"

"Yeah, I have news but it can wait. Will you be home tonight?"

"Late." She turns onto Pine and coasts up the street. "Anything urgent?" she asks, half listening, her attention on the apartment buildings and townhouses she passes. Josh couldn't have gone far.

"It can wait. Good luck down there. Call me when you're back in town."

A flash of red matching Josh's backpack pops into her peripheral vision. "Will do." She ends the call and double-parks.

"Josh," she yells, running across the street. He's impatient to see his mom, she gets that. But his stunt was reckless. What if he was already inside one of these apartments? She wouldn't have been able to find him. Just thinking about losing him has her lunch turning over in her stomach.

She mounts the steps of the tiny porch to a townhouse that looks identical to the one Josh drew and Lucas critiqued. Josh picks up a small clay pot with a dead plant and cocks back his arm.

"Whoa, whoa, whoa." She grabs the pot before he hurls it through the window.

"Not here," he says angrily.

Lily isn't here.

Olivia sags against the door, even jiggles the latch. She peeks through the window and sighs her disappointment when she can't see past the blinds.

"I know. We talked about that." She reminds him of what they discussed. On the way down, Josh's hope inflated. His eyes brightened and he grew more restless. Maybe she was there, he told her in broken speech. If she isn't, Olivia explained they'd talk with the neighbors, ask if anyone knew where Lily and Josh were headed. Maybe someone has seen Lily since she lost Josh.

She sets down the pot, brushing dirt from her hands. "There are other ways to find her." Ways that don't involve breaking and entering and setting off the alarm. Her gaze darts to the sticker in the window.

Coastal Alarm Co. She'd rather not waste time held up at the police station talking herself out of a breaking and entering charge.

Josh probably already tried, but she checks the door latch. It's locked. She also rings the bell and feels let down when Lily doesn't answer.

"Is there a spare key lying about?"

He shakes his head. "Used to. Not since he—" He presses his lips tight.

"He what, Josh?" And, he who? Is Josh talking about Dwight?

"Can't." He taps his forehead, then punches the house siding.

He can't call up the word.

Olivia breathes through her teeth and backs away. She's tempted to grab his shoulders and shake the words out of him. They'd drop at their feet as though a thief were emptying his coat pockets because those words stuck in his head are gold. They're the answers she needs to end this outrageous week.

"Was there someone harassing your mom? Is that why she removed the spare key? Is he the shadow man in your drawings?"

"Yes."

A chill seeps into Olivia's limbs. "Was it my dad, the bad man?" Her stomach heaves at the thought.

Josh looks at the ground. His shoulders shrug.

"You want to blame him, but you're not sure it was him."

He lifts his head and nods, meeting her gaze.

Who else can it be if not Dwight? What sort of trouble was Lily in?

She heaves a sigh and looks around. This drive can't be a complete bust. "Okay. Is there another way in?"

"Come." He leaps off the porch and she follows him to the garage.

Josh punches in a code on the remote opener. The door doesn't budge. He punches in another code, swearing when the door still doesn't open. While he tries to sort the number order, Olivia backs up to get a better view of the townhouse. Two floors with ocean views given the direction of the windows on the second floor.

How in the world did a sixteen-year-old pregnant runaway who didn't finish high school afford a place two blocks from the beach in SoCal? Even if she's leasing, it can't be inexpensive. What does she do for a living? Someone must be supporting her.

She thinks of Josh's father, whoever that is, which reminds her to look at the photos she copied over from Dwight's computer. And that reminds her she hasn't heard from Lucas. He hasn't texted that Dwight arrived home.

Something else is odd, too. Dwight hasn't called or texted since his voice mail the other day. Normally he would have tried to reach her again, especially since she didn't call him back. She doesn't know whether to be concerned or relieved. Or maybe she should be wary. Could he already know Josh is with her?

Olivia checks her phone to see if she missed any messages, but everything has been read.

"Josh?"

Olivia turns around. Two doors up, an older woman in a paisley athletic-style sundress unpacks groceries from her car. She returns a bag to the trunk and approaches them.

Josh waves. "Hi, Ms. . . . . hi."

"Where's your mom?" The woman's gaze shifts to Olivia. "Where's Jenna?"

"Who?" Olivia asks.

"Jenna Mason."

Josh runs to Olivia and grabs her arm. "Jenna . . . Mason. That's . . . that's . . . Mom."

"Jenna Mason?" Olivia tilts her head. She's heard that name before. "The animator?"

"Mm-hmm." The neighbor eyes her warily. "And you are?"

"If Jenna's who I think she is, I'm her sister."

234

———

"I have no idea where they were going. Jenna didn't tell me," Glenny Ross says over a bowl of macadamia nut ice cream in her kitchen. Glenny invited her and Josh inside for the treat when Olivia asked her about Lily—Jenna. They could talk inside. As soon as Glenny mentioned she hasn't seen Jenna since the morning she and Josh packed up and left, the same day Josh arrived at Olivia's, Josh grumbled, "Told you so" and took his ice cream to the back patio to play with Glenny's terrier. While she unpacked the groceries, Glenny explained Jenna and Josh moved into their townhouse two years ago, and for the most part, Jenna keeps to herself. Most of what Glenny knows about Jenna she gleaned off the internet. Jenna never shares anything personal.

"I was outside when she was packing the car to leave," Glenny explains in a warm voice. Her eyes are a faded blue and hair long and gray, streaked with silver. She hooks a hand around her hair while she talks and drapes it over a shoulder. Her limbs are lean, athletic, and skin sun soaked and aged. "She asked me to watch the place and call the police if I noticed anything suspicious. That was six days ago."

Olivia thinks of Dwight. "Do you have her number?"

Glenny shakes her head. "I know I should have asked. But it was early. The sun was just coming up. They were in a rush and I was running late. Other than the other day, we hardly speak. I don't see her often because of my hours. I own the ice cream and coffee café down by the water."

Olivia probably knows more about Jenna Mason than Glenny, since they're in the same industry. Jenna is the award-winning creator and animator of *Tabby's Squirrel*, a cartoon about a quirky elderly woman with coke-bottle glasses and frazzled white hair named Tabitha and her pet gray squirrel. The curious critter gets into all sorts of mischief and Tabby into trouble. Jenna came onto the scene about eight years ago when quitting the high-tech industry was only a spark of an idea in

Olivia's head. The Crimson Wave wasn't anything more than doodles in sketchbooks, unfinished illustrations on her computer. But Jenna's YouTube channel was gaining in popularity. The artist, though, is a mystery. The Sia of animators. As far as Olivia knows, the public hasn't seen Jenna's face. Her social media profile pictures are animated caricatures, and her publicist oversees her handles. All communication is funneled through the one-woman publicity firm, from what Olivia was able to gather during a quick search while Glenny scooped ice cream. She already sent the publicist an email when she couldn't locate a phone number, stressing her concern about Lily.

"Can you think of anyone who might know where Jenna went?"

"Not sure." Glenny shakes her head. "I don't see visitors other than Josh's friends. But even they haven't been around lately, not since the accident."

"Josh's head?"

She nods. "You know kids. They came around for a little bit after. I'd see them skateboarding out there in the street when I came home. Josh wasn't allowed to."

His activities were probably medically restricted.

"When did all that happen?" Olivia asks.

Glenny taps her chin. "A few months back. That sounds about right."

Olivia nudges her bowl aside, the ice cream turning to soup. Her stomach rolls like small waves when the tide's coming in. How long has Dwight known where Lily is? What on earth could he want from her? Does he have any compassion at all for Lily and Josh? She looks out the back window. Josh rolls a ball past the dog. The terrier chases it. "What was he like before?" she asks.

"Wild. Disobedient. Those boys smoke pot under the pier. I see them from my shop windows. His father isn't around," Glenny says as if that's the reason Josh is the way he is. "After, he was different, as you can see." Her gaze swings to Josh and holds on. "He's quiet."

Olivia would say depressed. "You mentioned the police. Was Jenna in some sort of trouble?"

"Not that I'm aware of, though we did have a man sneaking around. He was a pervert, peeking in our windows. I called the police on him once. I think others did, too. The police came several times. Whoever it was left. I haven't seen him in some time."

Heart pounding, fingers mentally crossed she's wrong, she opens her photo app and pulls up a picture of Dwight. "Do you recognize him?"

Glenny frowns at the photo. "Not sure. Wait . . . yes. If he's the same man, he visited Jenna once, maybe more. Hard to say."

Olivia's hand trembles when Glenny gives back her phone. She wishes she'd been wrong about Dwight. But Glenny is the second person to confirm Dwight found Lily. "When did you last see him?" she asks, rattled.

"Weeks, maybe months ago."

"Nothing more recent, like last week?"

"No, sorry. I can't confirm that."

"Can you describe the other guy, that peeping Tom?" Olivia wonders if he has anything to do with Lily's quick departure. Could he be the shadow man in Josh's illustrations?

"Never got a good look at him."

That is not what she wanted to hear. Same with the fact Dwight has been in contact with Lily.

———

After Olivia and Josh leave Glenny's, they knock on neighbors' doors. Josh grows increasingly agitated with each visit. "Don't know her," he'd say with each person Olivia tried. Those home and who know of Jenna confirmed Glenny's observations. They recognized Josh, who'd play catch and skateboard with his friends in the street, but Jenna kept to herself. Most didn't realize she'd left town or that she's missing.

Over dinner at a taco stand by the beach, Olivia fires off another email to Jenna's publicist, this time begging the woman to call her. The matter is urgent. Olivia also exchanged numbers with Glenny. Glenny would reach out if Jenna returned home.

Olivia debates spending the night. They could visit Josh's school to spread word they're looking for Lily—rather Jenna. They could check the local hospitals and police department, but it's likely Lily and Josh weren't anywhere near here when they separated. If they were, why didn't Josh just go home?

Her mind keeps veering back to Dwight. He's potentially dangerous but he could be the last person who saw Lily. Olivia is deeply convinced. She and Josh could spend the night and more time looking, or she could rally Lucas, and they could confront their dad. She could get her answers. Lucas would help her make him talk. It's a risk, but she'll leave Josh in Blaze's care. Dwight will never know he's with her.

Plan made, Olivia decides to drive home.

On the way out of town, they stop at a CVS for road snacks and drinks. Olivia caves and buys the Marlboros she's been craving all day. Josh settles into the front seat, listening to music. She lights up as soon as they leave the store and stands beside the car, burning through the mix of tobacco and chemicals that are wreaking havoc on her lungs. But she doesn't give a shit. Her sister is—as Josh put it the day he arrived—gone, and their dad is likely behind her disappearance.

Olivia's fingers tremble as she waits for the nicotine hit. She texts Lucas, first asking him if he's heard anything from Dwight, then tells him he's a dick for not texting anything all day. Dwight should be home by now. Lastly, she tells him to meet her at the house tomorrow. They're going to confront their dad together. She then calls Blaze.

"Hey, been thinking about you all day."

She inhales, and her exhale is a long sigh. "It's so good to hear your voice."

"Rough day?"

"Long." She'd texted that morning she and Josh were driving to Oceanside. "I have a favor," she asks.

"Name it."

"Will you search for a Jenna Mason? Find out if a missing persons report has been filed. And call the hospitals in the San Diego area. See if they have a patient by that name." Lily could be in a coma or physically incapable of returning home.

"Wait, wait, wait. Are we talking about *the* Jenna Mason, that cartoonist you like?"

"Yeah." She's laughed out loud a time or two watching Lily's three-minute animations.

What a trip. To think Lily was right there all these years and Olivia didn't know it. But did anyone know Lily was Jenna? Did she legally change her name or is Jenna a pseudonym?

"She's Lily?" Blaze asks, stunned. "Holy shit."

"I'd make those calls but Josh is with me in the car. I don't want him to worry."

"Say no more. I'll take care of it."

"Thank you." She rubs her shoulder. Blaze gives the best neck massages. She could use one. Her upper back is tight from driving all day and the added stress of finding Lily and comforting Josh.

"Driving home tonight?"

"We're about to head back."

"Do you want to stay here?"

Relief is a warm blanket of embrace. "Would that be all right?"

"I'd prefer it. I'll wait up. I love you."

"Love you too." She marvels at how easy the words come to her when she says what she feels.

CHAPTER 31

Blaze is kicked back on a porch chair when Olivia and Josh arrive at his house shortly before midnight. Lately, Olivia has been a night owl. She's just waking up around this time, running on nerves and nicotine. Tonight she's physically exhausted. While she's crushed Lily wasn't home, she did come back with something: Lily's new name and confirmation Dwight has been in contact with her.

Blaze stands when they mount the steps. "Hey." His mouth is by her ear, his voice drowsy. He kisses her cheek. His hand lightly grazes her lower back as he leads them into the house.

She just wants to crash, but Blaze hopefully has news to report, which she wants to screen before Josh hears in case it's upsetting.

"We'll talk in the morning," she says when Blaze points him to the guest room. Josh was quiet for most of the drive, disappointed they didn't find Lily. Yawning, he drags his feet down the dark hallway. The light turns on and the door quietly clicks in its latch, casting the hallway into darkness again.

"Want a drink?" Blaze asks.

She shakes her head, covering a yawn. "I'm good."

She pats his chest and follows him into the bedroom. He toes off his sneakers and stretches out on top of the covers, fully clothed. Olivia changes into her sleep pants and a tank. She washes her face and brushes her teeth, then crawls under the sheets.

Blaze rolls toward her. He lightly skims his fingers down her arm. Skin sensitive to his touch tingles.

"How are you?" he whispers.

"Exhausted." Her eyes are heavy. It's an effort to keep them open. "I'm worried about Josh."

"I know." He weaves his fingers with hers.

"He was so angry when he got here, and now? I don't know. He was almost too quiet on the drive up. I'm worried he's giving up."

"Was the trip that much of a time waste?"

"No." Aside from Lily's name and proof Dwight found her, she might have a lead on Josh's father. If she can't locate Lily, or find her through Dwight, maybe she can find him. He might know where Lily could have gone. If she wasn't abducted, she could be there now. Before she and Josh left the CVS parking lot, Olivia finally looked at Dwight's photos. They were grainy, slightly unfocused, and appeared to be taken from across the street from wherever Ethan parked his truck, the one he drove in high school. It looked like the 7-Eleven. There were two people in the truck's cab kissing. At first she was shocked to see Ethan's truck and what that could mean. But one person was certainly Lily. She'd recognize her auburn hair anywhere. The other was a boy with light hair. For a second her stomach bottomed out and she feared Ethan lied to her. But this boy was definitely close to Lily's age. She could see how Dwight mistook him for Ethan, but he wasn't filled out like Ethan, who would have been twenty-one at the time. His face isn't visible in the photo, but even she could tell the shape of his head wasn't Ethan's. She did text Ethan the photos, asking if he could identify the guy in his truck. He hasn't texted back yet.

Then there's her dad. Tomorrow they're going to talk. About Lily, Josh, and whatever happened between them, fourteen years ago and now. If they never locate Lily, Josh remains in her care. Dwight might be dangerous, but she refuses to live in fear of her own father. Unlike Lily, she won't run. She won't let him bully her, or hurt Josh.

"Any luck with your calls?" she asks.

"Depends what you call luck. I called close to thirty hospitals and clinics. She wasn't registered as a patient. I'll call more tomorrow, cast a wider net. I didn't find a death certificate or missing persons report either."

"No one we talked to realized she was missing until we started asking questions."

"It's only been a few days," he reminds her. "And that Glenny woman thought she was out of town. Lily's friends probably think the same."

"Where could she have gone?" she wonders out loud. Tears fill her eyes and she quickly wipes them off. Josh is depending on her; she needs to keep her shit together.

Blaze fits his hand to her cheek. "You'll find her." His touch is comforting, his voice reassuring.

"Hope so." She owes it to Lily for not helping her when she needed it. For not seeing how difficult her childhood was compared to Olivia's. As much as she wants to find Lily for Josh, she wants a chance to make amends. Now that she's opened her heart to Blaze, she recognizes there's love in there for Lily, too. Always has been. She wants her sister back in her life.

His thumb wipes off a tear. Her breathing evens, and sleep starts to pull her under. He gently kisses her lips, then starts to get up, rousing her.

She grabs his arm. "Don't go."

"I was going to sleep on the couch. Josh—"

"Please?" She doesn't want to be alone; nor does she want to sleep without him. He's too much a part of this new world she's building for herself.

Their eyes meet and hold. The whites of his shimmer in the faint moonlight coming through the window. He stands and strips to his boxers, then slides under the covers with a contented sigh.

"Roll over," he murmurs. She gives him her back and he aligns his body with hers. His fingers caress her arm. His breath warms her neck.

A sob builds in her chest but she locks it up tight. She needs to tell him something she didn't get around to saying last night.

"I shouldn't have broken up with you."

"Which time?" His voice rumbles with a note of humor.

"Both, but I meant the first time. You tried to talk to me and I shut you down every time. I left at the worst possible time." Harold and Rhonda had finalized their divorce and Harold moved out of town. Blaze rarely saw him. Rhonda was just diagnosed with lymphoma.

"I messed around with Macey because I was screwed up. And—" He heaves a sigh like he's reluctant to share what he has to say next. "I was mad at Charlotte, not you."

"My mom?" she asks, surprised. She twists around to face him. "What does she have to do with it?"

He lifts his head and peers down at her. "You don't know?"

"Know what? What are you talking about?"

"She slept with my dad."

"She what?" she says, appalled.

"I can't believe you don't know."

"Of course I don't. She wouldn't—" She stops. She was about to say Charlotte would never cheat on Dwight, especially since she swears he's the one sleeping around. But didn't Olivia wonder about Charlotte just this morning? She swears her mom had a visitor. Someone was in her parents' room. Charlotte was flustered when Olivia arrived. She wasn't as put together as normal. Her skin had a slight sheen.

Olivia cups her mouth, mortified. "Oh, my god. I had no idea. I'm so sorry she did that to your family."

"She didn't do it alone. Takes two to fool around. My parents were already on the outs."

"But my mom was the tipping point, wasn't she?"

Blaze nods slowly.

"She's the reason summers stopped at the lake." Olivia is floored.

"One of them."

"All this time . . ." She stops. Guilt pulls her deeper into the mattress. "All this time what?"

"I thought it was Lucas's fault. Remember when he was caught shoplifting? Your parents had my dad take us home early."

"Your brother was an idiot. He got us into a lot of trouble. But no, my parents loved him."

She feels the burn of tears. "They didn't invite us back the following summer."

He brushes aside the fine hair draping her forehead. "That wasn't because of Lucas. My parents weren't getting along. They didn't want visitors."

Olivia's hand rests at her side. She rubs the duvet between her fingers and stares at the ceiling. She'd been wrong about Lucas. She just assumed it was his fault. Just like she assumed Lily betrayed her with Ethan. Olivia has always jumped to conclusions without listening to the facts. Running before she could get hurt worse than she already felt.

She returns to her side, her back to Blaze's chest, unsure whether to cry or yell. She's so damn angry with herself. How ironic given what she thought a moment ago. Running has been her MO. Her fear of betrayal has cost her so much.

"Ancient history, Liv," Blaze whispers in her ear. He rubs the tension from her back. "I don't blame you for any of it. I love you. Always have. Always will."

This time she believes him. She reaches for his hand. "Thank you for staying."

He buries his face in her hair. "I'm not going anywhere."

"Good." Her body molds into his. Blaze's breaths deepen, but sleep taunts her like a prank from Lucas, staying just out of reach.

"Our parents slept together," she whispers.

Blaze shivers. "Yeah, I know. Don't go there."

She quietly laughs.

———

Day 7

Olivia wanders into Blaze's kitchen at half past five. Blaze is still in bed. He took the day off to stay with them. He'll spend it making more calls. Josh is already sitting at the kitchen table with a glass of orange juice, surprising Olivia.

"What are you doing up?" she asks, filling the electric kettle with filtered water.

He peers at her with bloodshot eyes. "Can't—" His mouth clamps shut. He doesn't even try to act out what he wants to say.

"Can't sleep?" she guesses, setting the kettle to boil. She's noticed the more tired or anxious he is, the more his speech deteriorates. The urge to console him almost pushes her across the kitchen. But she doesn't feel equipped. She can't promise they'll find Lily, not with her own hopes diminishing. She wishes she could tell him his speech would improve, but that would be a lie because she flat-out doesn't know if it ever will.

Josh nods.

"Me either." She gets a box of doughnut holes from Blaze's pantry, one of many treats he keeps on the top shelf, and sits with Josh. She nudges the box. "They aren't Krispy Kreme, but they taste good when you feel like crap."

He smirks at her foul language and takes a doughnut, then another. Olivia pops one in her mouth just as the kettle clicks off at a full boil. She gets up from the table and pours the water over coffee grounds, relishing the toasted scent that doesn't in the least bit make her feel any more awake than she already is.

"I thought she—" He moves his hand in a circular motion instead of finishing his sentence.

"You thought she'd be there? Me too." A part of her had hoped Lily was home waiting for her son. But life is never that easy. And neither is finding Lily.

He sucks in a ragged breath and Olivia can't do anything but watch as the past week finally catches up with him. A tear drops on the table, and he buries his face in his arms, his elbow knocking over the juice. The glass rolls off the table. Orange juice splatters on the floor, the chair legs, and cabinet doors. Olivia gasps. Josh lifts his head. Embarrassment shutters his eyes.

"It's okay," she reassures. A week ago she would have flipped about the mess. This morning, it's impossible to be upset about anything. All of her worry centers on Josh. And she feels powerless since she hasn't been able to give him what he wants: his mom.

"Josh, look at me."

She rests a hand on his shoulder and he lifts his chin. She lowers to her heels so that she's looking up at him. "We're just getting started. We'll find her."

He nods, sniffling, and drags an arm under his nose.

"Why don't you go back to bed? There isn't anything you can do right now. I'll clean up, and I'll keep working on finding your mom. I'll wake you if there's any news," she adds when he seems reluctant to move. "Watch your step." She assists him over the glass, and he leaves the kitchen. A few seconds later she hears the bedroom door close.

Olivia's phone rings. The number is one she doesn't recognize. She drops the dish towel and grabs her phone.

"Hello?" she answers, hopeful it's someone with news about Lily.

"Olivia Carson?"

"Speaking."

"This is Gayle Pierson, Jenna Mason's publicist." Olivia clutches her phone. Excitement uncurls. Gayle knows how to reach Lily. She might have news. "She's missing, you say?"

"Yes, for almost a week."

"That would explain why her voice mail is full. I just tried reaching her."

"Have you texted her?"

246

"This morning, yes, after I read your emails. I haven't heard back."

"Is that unusual for her?" Olivia paces the kitchen as they talk, desperate for news, her emotions in a tangle.

"To not reply right away?"

"That and her voice mail. Does it always get full?"

"My clients can go days without responding when they're on deadline. So, no. It wouldn't have alarmed me if I didn't know she was missing."

"Did she mention anything about leaving town or where she'd go if she wanted to get away? Any indication she was in danger?" Olivia asks.

"No. We haven't talked in over a week. But if she did tell me anything, I wouldn't be able to disclose it to you." Her tone takes on a professional edge.

"This might sound strange, but I don't have my sister's cell. I'm not sure what she's told you about our family, but I haven't seen her in years. Her son is with me and we need to find her. Can I get her number?"

"Dear, I wish I could pass it along. But I'm contractually prohibited from sharing anything personal about Jenna, including her contact information, unless I have her permission."

A surge of frustration froths below her surface. "Even if it's an emergency?" she asks, refusing to lose any more hope.

"Even in emergencies."

"Her son is a minor. They got separated," she argues. "That seems like an odd clause to include."

"Not really. I have some high-profile clients who value their privacy, no matter the circumstances." She pauses. "Tell you what, I'll continue trying to reach her. When I do, I'll pass along your number."

"Please," Olivia begs. "Tell her Josh is with me, and that he's safe."

"I will. If there's anything else I can do to help, let me know."

"Actually, there is," Olivia says. "Have you met Jenna in person?"

"Not sure where you're going with this, but yes."

"Can you describe her for me?"

"Dear, that contract I mentioned—"

"Okay, okay. But this is life or death, Gayle," she rushes to say before the publicist hangs up. "Would you say she's five foot four, lean frame, auburn hair, brown eyes, and has a mole on her right jaw?" She doubts Gayle knows about the constellation of moles on the back of her right shoulder.

Gayle heaves a sigh. "I wouldn't deny it. Although . . . shit. Her hair is more red than auburn. She dyed it for Josh."

A rush of gratitude pours into her. "I can't thank you enough."

Five minutes later, Olivia has Officer Curbelo on the line.

"How can I help you, Ms. Carson?"

"I'd like to report my sister as missing."

"Name, please."

"Jenna Mason."

CHAPTER 32

Olivia walks across her parents' deck. The wind coming off the bay stings her cheeks, and the water is choppy. She can hear waves hit their dock. The eucalyptus trees rustle, the leaves sounding like rain. There isn't a cloud in sight.

Charlotte sits alone, bundled in a thick floral blanket Olivia recognizes as the throw from the end of Lily's bed. It's been years since she's seen it, and it's strange seeing it wrapped around her mother.

Olivia grabs a chair as she passes the patio table and sits beside Charlotte, checking her phone once more. Nothing yet from Lucas. She hasn't been able to reach Dwight either and she's been trying them both since early this morning. She wants answers. What happened to Lily? Where is she? What did he do to her? But Dwight's car isn't in the drive. Neither is Lucas's truck. Both should have been home by now.

"I was wondering when you'd come by."

There's a catch in Charlotte's voice. Olivia studies her mom. Her cheeks are a deep red from the cold, blotchy from the wind. She pulls the blanket tighter around her shoulders.

Olivia shivers. She should have worn a thicker sweater. She didn't expect her mom to be sitting outside. The wind always kept Charlotte in the house. But her mom didn't answer the door when Olivia rang, so she thought to check the back, worried something might be wrong, only to find her here.

"Where's Dad? I thought he'd be home by now."

"He's not coming home." Olivia breathes through the panic pinching inside her rib cage.

"Did he decide to stay longer?" He'd told her two days. That put his arrival as yesterday. What's the holdup? Did the conference go on for another day? Did he decide to visit a client?

Charlotte crumples a soiled tissue. She dabs the inner corner of her eye. Olivia leans forward to get a better look at her mom. The thin skin underneath her eyes glistens.

"Are you crying?"

Charlotte tsks. "For Pete's sake, Olivia, must you point it out?" She quickly dries her face with trembling fingers. Concerned, Olivia reaches for her hand. Charlotte recoils. "Why are you here? Is it because of Josh?"

"Yes. But—" She stalls as a thought occurs and she rests a hand on Charlotte's lap. "Is Dad with someone?" Have her mom's suspicions been right all along? Did Dwight stay because he's having an affair?

"I don't want to talk about it." Charlotte tears at the tissue, keeping her fingers busy.

"Is he with Lily?"

Charlotte's breath flutters like bird wings. She shakes her head.

Olivia presses on. "I found Lily's house in Oceanside. She wasn't there. I spoke with a neighbor. Lily changed her name to Jenna. Jenna Mason. I think it's pretty."

Charlotte doesn't react. She doesn't even blink.

"Why do I get the feeling you knew that already?" Olivia whispers. "You knew Dad visited her, didn't you?"

Charlotte plays with her fingers. She tugs at a cuticle. "Don't be ridiculous."

"Mom—"

Charlotte throws off the blanket, standing abruptly. "I'm going to open a bottle of wine. Do you want some?" She traverses the deck.

Olivia slowly stands, gawking at her mother.

"Get the glasses, will you?" Charlotte retreats into the house.

Olivia rubs her temples, feeling the early signs of a tension head-ache, and follows her mom into the house. Instead of retrieving the glasses, she trails her to the cellar, fed up with Charlotte's deliberate avoidance.

Why can't she talk about Lily? Is she scared? Did Dwight threaten her? Does she really not know anything? Highly doubtful.

Charlotte opens the cellar door with the lock on the outside, flips on the light, and carefully climbs down the narrow staircase. Olivia waits in the doorway.

"What do you think?" Charlotte asks. "The Sine Qua Non 2011 or 2012?"

"Sheesh, Mom." Both bottles are valued over four hundred dollars apiece. She must really be upset with Dwight. His client gifted him the bottles and he's been saving them for his and Charlotte's fortieth anniversary in another three years. "A cheap cab is fine." Drinking wine is not what Olivia had in mind, but she'll play along. It might loosen Charlotte's tongue.

"Really, Olivia. Don't insult me." Charlotte pulls a bottle from the rack and reads the label. "I need to make a point."

The spiteful inflection in Charlotte's tone prompts a memory. Lily locked in the dark cellar. Their mom's silhouette in the doorway. As far as Olivia knows, it happened only once. The punishment must have been effective. Lily must have told Charlotte whatever it was their mom wanted to know.

Charlotte will continue to find excuses not to share why Dwight pursued Lily, what happened between them, and whether Josh had been caught in the middle and physically and emotionally suffered the consequences. She'll blame it on the wine. She'll stall. She might even faint, just so she doesn't have to talk. She's just that stubborn.

"What about the Daou red blend?" Olivia suggests, backing away from the door. The last thing she sees before she closes the door is

Charlotte's alarm. Olivia tells herself she's not a bad person. Despite what Lucas thinks, she isn't anything like her mom. She isn't a daddy's girl. She just wants some fucking answers. Her nephew needs his mom.

Olivia bolts the door and turns off the light.

"Olivia? Olivia!" Charlotte shrieks.

Olivia presses her back to the door. "I'm sorry."

Charlotte races up the staircase and rattles the knob. "Olivia!" She knocks loudly. "Open the door this instant." She pounds on the door and Olivia's teeth rattle.

"Remember when you locked Lily in the cellar to get her to confess?" Olivia eventually found out her sister had put a dent in the hood of Dwight's car while playing basketball. She'd denied it was her fault until Charlotte locked her in the cellar. "I need to hear everything you know about Lily. Please, Mom, I just want to find her."

"Nothing I say will make up the years I lost with my little girl."

"Try me."

"You'll never forgive me."

Olivia turns her ear to the door. Her heart knocks against her sternum. "What won't I forgive? . . . Mom?"

Charlotte goes dreadfully quiet. Olivia imagines her mom on the other side of the door, huddled at the top of the stairs in the dark, sulking.

Olivia sinks to the floor, folds her arms over her knees, and rests her forehead in the crook of her arm wondering who will outlast whom, her or her mom?

———

A large crash startles Olivia awake. She lifts her head, rubbing her eyes. It's still daylight, and she's still leaning against the cellar door. She didn't mean to crash. But after a four-and-a-half-hour nap last night and a week of broken sleep, she can barely keep her eyes open. Her heart races. How much time has passed?

She glances at her phone, relieved it's only been thirty-five minutes as opposed to hours. There's a text from Blaze asking how things are going, and she loves that he's asking. He's making burgers for him and Josh. Will she be home for dinner? Does she want one?

She replies that she hopes to be home soon. Standing up, she lightly raps on the door. "Mom? You doing okay?"

Charlotte doesn't answer. Olivia presses her ear to the door. Did she hear a crash or was that a dream? It sounded like a wine bottle shattered.

Or a wave crashing on rocks, like the ones in her recurring nightmare. She hears them every time, right before she sees the glint of the knife in Dwight's hand. Had she been dreaming about that again?

Olivia unbolts the door and turns on the lights. "Mom?" She peers into the cellar. Charlotte isn't anywhere. "What the—?" Olivia climbs halfway down the stairs. Where could she have gone? There's nowhere to hide. There isn't a back exit. She does notice the floor is clean, so whatever she heard, it must have been in her head.

Olivia reaches the bottom of the staircase and moves deeper into the cellar. A knee joint cracks behind her. Something hard hits her shoulder.

"Ow!" Olivia whirls, rubbing the tender spot.

Charlotte stares at the bottle like she's baffled it didn't break and Olivia isn't passed out.

"Are you trying to kill me now?" Olivia blurts, shocked her mom attacked her. She yanks the bottle from Charlotte and reads the label. "This wine's half a grand. Trust me, I'm not worth it," she says, making light of this ludicrous situation. Her mom tried to knock her out.

With a wail unlike anything Olivia's heard come from her mom, Charlotte drops to her knees. She wraps her arms around Olivia and presses her cheek to Olivia's belly. "It wasn't me," Charlotte cries. "It was your father."

Olivia goes rigid, arms wide as if afraid to touch her mom. "What are you talking about?" she asks.

"Benton St. John. Lily overheard your father and me arguing. That's why she ran away. She believed your father would kill her just like he killed her father."

"What?" Olivia stumbles back. If Charlotte wasn't holding on to her, she would have fallen into the wine rack. "Benton St. John—"

"Is Lily's father."

The announcement smacks Olivia, leaving her breathless.

"I slept with him once. You have to believe me, Olivia. It didn't mean anything. But your father went insane. He couldn't take my cheating. He was afraid if word got out it wouldn't only ruin his reputation. My affair with Benton would ruin his chances during elections."

"So he killed him?" Olivia's breath escapes. She looks around the cellar, unfocused. The walls are closing in.

"Yes." Charlotte sobs.

Olivia shakes her head in denial but feels as if she's known all along. Her nightmare.

She has been dreaming about Benton's murder. Did she witness it? Impossible. It was dark, and she was only five. She wouldn't have remembered much, if anything at all. This revelation creates a cyclone of emotions. Her knees almost buckle with the weight of them. Is this why she's been so averse to being betrayed? Has she known deep down her father has been betraying her all along? *It's just a dream, Olivia.* She feels sick.

"The police questioned Dad. He wasn't a suspect after. What did he say to them? How did he get off?"

"He had an alibi."

"You? Oh god, Mom." Charlotte has been covering for Dwight for three decades. He's betrayed them all.

Olivia tucks Charlotte's tear-damp hair behind her ear. "Did you see him . . ." She chokes up.

Charlotte shakes her head. "I found blood on the knife."

Just like her dream. Olivia gulps.

"He threatened . . . He threatened me." She cries harder.

Olivia folds to her knees, her heart breaking for her mom, and takes Charlotte in her arms. "Shush." She cradles Charlotte's face, caresses her cheek. Rage burns inside Olivia's veins just thinking about her mom's suffering. How could she have stayed married knowing about the monster inside Dwight? Did she just not know how to leave him?

"He manipulated you." Olivia is sure of it. "Is this what you wanted to tell me? Why would you think I wouldn't have forgiven you?"

Charlotte looks at the floor. She plays with the hem of her blue cardigan. "I'm the one who told your father Ethan is Josh's father," she whispers.

Olivia falls back on her heels, reeling. Her hands drop in her lap. "Why would you do that?"

"You'll hate me."

"Try me," she says through her teeth.

Charlotte's lungs shudder. Her shoulders drop. "If you believed Lily betrayed you, you wouldn't go after her."

"You didn't want me to find her?" she asks, beyond shocked.

Charlotte shakes her head. "I had to keep her safe."

"From Dad. *My* dad." And at Olivia's expense. She broke up with Ethan because of that lie.

Charlotte nods.

"What about the photos Dad took of Lily and Ethan? It wasn't Ethan in the pictures. Dad thought it was. It wasn't the pictures that convinced him?"

Charlotte frowns. "What photos?"

"He didn't tell you? Do you know who Josh's father is?" Olivia still hasn't heard from Ethan about the photos she texted him.

Charlotte shakes her head and Olivia's eyes narrow. "I swear, darling," Charlotte says. "I don't. Lily wouldn't tell us." She covers her face and quietly sobs.

Olivia rises to her feet. She and Charlotte have plenty more to discuss, like where Lily might be and what they should do about Dwight. But Olivia isn't going to get anywhere while Charlotte's emotional.

Olivia helps her mom to her feet. Charlotte weaves.

"Go rest for a bit," Olivia says. "I'll make some tea and meet you in your room."

A shadow falls over the cellar. Olivia looks up, startled. Broad shoulders fill the doorway, and for a split second Olivia thinks it's Dwight and that he overheard their conversation. He could lock them in the cellar. They'd be stuck in here until Lucas came home or Blaze came looking for her.

Or worse. He'd come after her.

"What's going on?" A voice booms.

"Lucas!" Charlotte gasps, and Olivia wants to shout her relief. But Charlotte slips from her grasp and nimbly melts to the floor.

CHAPTER 33

LUCAS

While Olivia settles Charlotte in her room, Lucas sits in the hallway, his back to the wall, legs sprawled, an uncorked bottle of wine between his thighs. He found the bottle on the floor of the cellar. He glanced at the label once before opening, a Syrah from some winery south of here. He doubts he can pronounce the name right, but it reads like a foreign sports car.

Tipping back the bottle, he tries to remember what happened the other night when he last saw Dwight. He recalls sitting behind the wheel of his truck. Gang of Youths were singing about trying to love someone. The volume was dialed up enough that the windows vibrated. His jaw ached and back hurt. They still do. There was also a metallic taste in his mouth. He stared out the windshield wondering how the fuck he'd arrived there. Parked on the side of a narrow two-lane road that hugged a rock wall on one side and a wide, black abyss on the other.

The truck's motor was still running. He cut the engine and the music died. The night was silent. The sky blacker than sin. A car swerved around a bend and a band of light sliced through the cab of his truck like a searchlight outside an all-night club. Something shimmered on his hands.

"The fuck?" He turned on the interior light and held up his hands. Cut and bruised, knuckles swollen, they were sticky with dried blood. His stomach bottomed out.

Whose blood?

His legs tightened with the urge to run. The back seat and truck bed were empty. That was a relief. His vehicle was the only one in sight.

He rummaged through the junk in the center console and found his anxiety meds. Three pills were still left. He hadn't popped more than the prescribed dosage, which meant the pills hadn't caused his blackout.

How long had he been out?

Same amount of time he'd blacked out after Lily ran away? He'd been under for almost twelve hours, and he's hated himself since.

Lucas forced a deep breath and his hands blurred and vision went foggy. He slapped his cheeks. *Stay awake.*

What had happened? His mind raced.

He remembers his old man working the bar, schmoozing and canoodling, downing one finger of Blue Label after another. The guy had been wasted, and as Lucas watched him, years of pent-up rage brewed inside until he felt like he'd been burned alive.

He remembers Dwight finally picked a bed buddy and escorted the lithe creature half his age up to his room. Lucas hadn't blamed the blonde. Dwight was a catch. Wealthy, by all appearances, charismatic, and fitter than the average man in his early sixties. Dwight was skilled at letting others see what he wanted them to see rather than what lurked underneath the surface: a narcissistic asshole on the brink of bankruptcy who didn't give two shits about anyone but himself.

Lucas had waited outside Dwight's hotel room for the woman to leave. Dwight never let them stay the night. He didn't like his indiscretions staring him in the face the following morning. He preferred to start his days with a clean slate. A blank scorecard.

Blondie had finally left, and as soon as the elevator doors closed on her, Lucas had knocked on Dwight's door.

He clearly remembers his old man's look of surprise to find him standing there and not the midnight snack that had just left. He recalls forcing his way inside and closing the door behind him, flipping the bolt. The first punch had surprised them both. His fist connected with Dwight's jaw before he'd realized he swung.

One for Lily.

Dwight never should have scared her away. Lucas should have gone after her. Would he have if he hadn't blacked out?

Dwight's head had lurched back with the impact of Lucas's fist. He stumbled backward.

Lucas advanced, throwing the second punch.

"That's for cheating on Mom."

Dwight had dropped onto the chair, his momentum tipping it over. He crashed to the floor and his old man's legs flipped over his head until he lay sprawled on the ground. He started laughing maniacally.

"Shut up," Lucas growled.

Dwight lifted his head. "I'm the cheater? That what she told you? She's been cheating on me since we married." He laughed again, his forehead dropping back to the floor.

"Stop lying." Lucas flipped Dwight onto his back. He squeezed Dwight's throat, out of control. "You're a sick motherfucker." Charlotte would never cheat. Dwight's affairs tore her up.

"What are you doing?" Dwight gargled. He inhaled a ragged breath, struggling for air. He clawed at Lucas's hand.

"Remember when I was attacked in juvie? Remember when you wouldn't press charges? You wanted everything to go away? Well, it's your turn to go away."

"I don't know what you're talking about." Dwight gasped.

"Need to knock some sense into you. Maybe you'll remember then."

This one's for me.

He punched him again. Gratification pulled his mouth into a sneer. Years Dwight held back his love until Lucas, humiliated, stopped asking and acting out for it.

"Don't fucking come home. Ever. When Mom sends you the divorce papers, sign them," Lucas ordered, spittle raining on Dwight's face.

The last thing Lucas recalls before coming to in his truck was pummeling Dwight's face. He was shaking all over, sitting in his truck, parked on the side of the road. It was half-past three in the morning, so he'd only blacked out a couple hours.

He reached for the gym towel in the back seat and soaked it with water, emptying the plastic bottle. It bounced to the floor. He wiped the blood off his hands and almost threw the soiled towel out the window.

That's evidence.

The warning seethes in his head.

He stuffed the towel into his gym bag and threw open his door. He needed air.

The night was cool and he was sweating. He fanned his shirt. God, his back was on fire.

With a grunt, he twisted his torso to ease the ache. A car passed, its headlights splashing across the small valley below. Metal and glass reflected the light, winking at him like a joker card.

Shaken about what he might find, he leaned over the side railing to get a better look. He couldn't see a thing. He turned on his phone's flashlight, directing the beam below, and stumbled against his truck. He almost dropped his phone over the side.

Fresh sweat dripped into his eyes. Sick fear knotted his throat.

Dwight's car was down there.

How the hell did it get there? When had he left Dwight's hotel?

He didn't have the answers but his gut told him he's the reason Dwight crashed.

Panic pushed him back into the truck. Desperation had him firing the engine and gunning the gas. At the last second, he eased up on the pedal so he wouldn't burn rubber.

They'll track the make of your tires.

Dots would be connected.

With forced calm, Lucas eased from the roadside and left the scene.

Now Olivia closes the door to Charlotte's room and settles on the floor across from him.

"How's she doing?" he asks.

"She's resting. I gave her a sedative."

He could use one. Or three. He wants to forget what he saw, and that he's to blame.

She stretches her legs with a sigh. She sounds beat. Her boots meet his in the middle of the hallway. She knocks hers against his to say hey. There's dirt on the edges of his soles. Is that from a job? Or had he scaled the slope alongside the road to look inside Dwight's car and can't remember what he found? Shame heats his face. He should have taken them off at the door, but he heard Charlotte's muffled crying down the hallway. For a beat he thought Dwight had come home until he remembered his dad was dead and that he might have been the one who killed him. Dread is a brewing storm inside him.

"You owe me an explanation," she says.

"For what?" He chokes on the words, fearing she knows what he's been thinking.

"Not calling or texting."

"I said I'd text if Dad came home. He didn't."

Her face scrunches up at his reasoning.

Whatever. He brings the bottle to his mouth and tips it back. Glorified fruit juice. He'd rather have a beer but he's too tired to get up. His back still aches, as if he'd lifted his kayak overhead and javelin threw it into the water.

Or a body across a hotel room.

The thought lobs a tennis ball into his throat. What if the police come after him? What if he's sent to jail again? He swallows the wine roughly and winces. His face hurts, too.

"How's the nephew?" he asks so he stops thinking how he feels like a human punching bag.

"Josh"—she emphasizes his name—"is as well as a kid with a missing mom can be expected. We still haven't found Lily." She nods at the bottle. "What're you drinking?" He shows her the label and her eyes go all buggy. "That bottle's half a grand. Dad will kill you."

He makes a guttural sound and averts his face, but not before he sees how green hers is. He wouldn't be surprised if his looks worse. Gray like cremated remains. She cups her mouth and looks at the ceiling.

He drinks more. Seems fitting given Dwight can't kill him.

He wonders what she knows. Have the police notified Charlotte yet about Dwight? He didn't dare call her and chance someone pull his records. They'd see the timing of his call and from where he'd called.

Olivia reaches for the bottle. "Give me some."

He leans forward with a grunt, hands off the bottle. She takes a tentative sip. Her eyes close. "Holy shit, that's good." She drinks more and passes it back. "Mom tried to knock me out with that."

He stares at her for a beat, trying to picture his five-foot-three mom hitting his five-foot-seven sister over the head. "You serious?" She nods and he feels a strange tightening in his chest. "What did you do?"

"So it's my fault?"

He gives her a look.

Her eyes roll upward. "I locked her in the cellar."

A short laugh squirms out of him. Next thing he knows he's doubled over.

"Stop it." She kicks his boot. "It's not funny."

He laughs harder until he's crying. And then he's sobbing.

"Damn, Luc." He feels her hand on his shoulder. "What's wrong?" she asks.

"Get the fuck off me." He swats her hand.

"I just—"

"Back off." He shuts off the waterworks and downs more wine.

She scoots back to the opposite wall and glares at him. "You're an asshole."

Tell him something he doesn't already know.

"What happened to your face?"

"What's up with you and Mom?"

"I was asking about Dad and Lily."

"Work altercation." He grimaces.

Her lips pinch and he looks at the bottle between his legs. She knows he's lying.

"Dad isn't Lily's dad. Benton St. John is."

His head snaps up and jaw drops. Holy shit. That explained so much. No wonder Dwight couldn't tolerate Lily.

"Mom tell you that?"

She nods. "She also told me Dad killed St. John."

"Fuck me." Charlotte alluded to the idea that Dwight had offed St. John, but she didn't come right out and say it. His dad's a murderer.

So is he apparently. Fucking depressing.

A tear drops off Olivia's chin. "Did you know?"

"About Lily?" He shakes his head, shifting his gaze to the floor. He considers chugging the rest of the wine.

"What about St. John?"

His thumb picks at the label. "Mom might have mentioned something."

"When?"

"A few days ago?"

She nudges his leg. "And you didn't tell me?"

"I've been busy," he says tightly.

"Oh, yeah, that's right. Painting. Your baby sister is missing. Your dad is a murderer. Your mom is falling apart. Your big sis is about to have a breakdown. And what do you do? Bail. Good on you, Lucas. Always the dependable one."

"Fuck you." He hated when she held up her glossy mirror. He despised the sight of himself and everything he didn't do. Or, as of two nights ago, did do. If she only knew he hadn't bailed. He'll never tell what he'd been up to. But nothing was more important these past few days than righting the wrong he'd committed. He had to do something for Lily where before he'd done nothing.

"Your vocabulary is stellar, Luc. Give me that." She snags the bottle and guzzles the wine. Red lines leak from the corners of her mouth. She wipes them off with her sweater sleeve, staining the wool, and starts crying.

"I loved him," she whispers.

"I know," he says as gently as he can muster, fighting off his own tears.

"Where is he?"

Lucas shakes his head, praying she doesn't learn the secret he's hiding.

"We need to report him."

Panic, electric and hot, singes his veins. "To the cops? No way." He surges to his feet and weaves, light-headed. He slaps a hand on the wall. They start digging into the St. John case, they might see Dwight's death wasn't an accident. What if the driver of one of those cars that passed on the road remembers his truck? What if traffic cameras caught him following Dwight's car? Lucas won't spend another night behind bars if his life depends on it.

He needs a beer. And he needs to get the fuck out of here.

He also needs to get Olivia out of his face before she realizes what he did.

Olivia gets up. "Mom admitted it. Dad killed him. She confessed that she lied about being his alibi. Lily overheard them talking. She got scared and she ran." She hugs her stomach and leans over. "I can't believe he's a murderer. I feel so sick."

Lucas thinks of his old man picking up women at the bar. The way he fought back in the hotel room. No, he's not the man Olivia knew him to be. He's a mean sonovabitch. Lucas has known that for years.

He then thinks of the blank spot in his head. The two-hour time gap riding his ass like a nagging girlfriend.

"No cops."

She grips his hand. "You've got a thing against them. I get that. But shouldn't we do something?"

"It's a thirty-year-old murder case. Let it lie."

"But I'm worried about Mom. And what about Jean St. John? Don't you think she'd want to know?"

"No!" He bellows louder than he intended. Screw the beer. He's leaving.

Olivia puts a hand on his chest. "What's your problem?" His eyes dodge hers. "Lucas?"

His shoulders ripple with tension.

"No." She backs up a step, shaking her head. He doesn't meet her eyes. Hers drop to his hands and he sees her swallow hard. His knuckles are chewed up. "What did you do? Where's Dad? Why isn't he coming home?"

"I said leave it."

"What did you do?" she cries. "Please tell me. I have to know. Are you in trouble? Let me help you."

"I don't know." He fends off her hands and the faucet turns back on. "I don't know, I don't know." He covers his face and groans into his hands like a wounded animal. "Don't ask me. Please don't ask."

"Lucas." He can hear the tears in her voice.

He removes his hands from his face and stares at them as if they belong to someone else. Fingers curled clawlike, his hands shake.

Olivia's eyes leap to his. "Your face. Is Dad—" She stops, choking on her words. "I can't say it," she whispers, pulling at her hair. She walks a tight circle. "Oh, my god. This family." She hugs her chest and bends over like she's trying to crawl into herself. An agonizing wail slips through her lips and almost shatters his broken bits.

She loved Dwight so much. The truth about him is hitting her hard. She only saw the good in him, an unrealistic perspective given the monster he's turned out to be. Olivia was the old man's favorite.

He cups his hand beside her head, afraid to touch her, unsure how to comfort her or if he can. "I'll handle this. Just . . . stay out of it."

She hugs him fiercely. Her cheeks glisten with tears. "Do. Not. Get caught. I can't lose you, too. Not after Lily."

Her face falls. Too late. She lost him already. He faded away seventeen years ago. But of their own volition, his arms draw around her. He gives himself over to this moment to be her little brother. To let her love for him soak in.

"I don't know what to do," she whines into his shirt.

"Yes, you do. Be there for Josh. He needs you. Lily needs you to watch over him."

"What about Mom?"

"I'll stay with her."

She shakes her head and steps from his embrace. "No, that's okay. I have to get back to Josh. I'll take her with me. She shouldn't be alone."

If he had any sense of self-preservation, he'd tell her he shouldn't be alone tonight either. "Go pack her things. I'll help her to your car."

"Okay." She takes a deep breath and squeezes his hand.

Lucas follows her into the bedroom. His mom looks young and frail sleeping on her side. She's a formidable woman when she wants to be. Gorgeous, alluring. He was only three but he vaguely remembers that afternoon when she invited Benton St. John up to the apartment. Olivia was pissing him off, taking up the entire sandbox with her princess castle. That had to have been the day Lily was conceived.

"Hey, Mom." He nudges her shoulder. She mumbles incoherently. "Livy's leaving. She's taking you with her. Let me help you up."

She groans, her head lolling to the side. She looks up at him, eyes unfocused from the sedative, and smiles. "Luc darling. You're home."

He clasps her hand and eases her up. She doesn't argue as he walks her to Olivia's car. But man, she'll be spitting flames in the morning when she realizes she didn't sleep in her own bed.

Livy's problem. Not his. He'll be long gone by then.

Olivia joins them outside. She tosses Charlotte's overnight bag in the back seat. He opens the door for her.

"You going to be okay?" she asks.

He nods, his expression controlled.

She cups his jaw, forcing him to look her in the eye. "Don't do anything stupid."

"Never." He smirks.

"Lucas," she warns.

He sighs. "Promise." A lie. But sometimes, you gotta so you don't hurt the ones you love. Assuming he's capable of loving anymore.

"I'll call you tomorrow." She settles into the car. He closes the door. The engine turns over and she backs from the driveway. With one last look at him she waves, watching as if it's the last time she'll see him.

If she only knew.

He turns toward the bay and breathes in the ocean air, trying to cleanse what's rotting inside him. With one last lingering look at his parents' house, he walks to the water's edge with the weight of his and his father's sins on his shoulders.

CHAPTER 34

At Charlotte's insistence, Olivia drives her mom to her house. Charlotte doesn't feel comfortable going to Blaze's. Olivia doesn't argue. She calls Blaze, and he and Josh join them at her place. He wrapped up two burgers. Charlotte skips dinner. Groggy from her meds, she goes straight to bed. Noticing Olivia's blood sugar level is crashing, Blaze puts a burger in front of her. To her surprise, she wolfs it down. The burger is easier to swallow than what she just learned. She's a murderer's daughter. That was a lot to unpack, and it'll have to wait until she finds Lily, or whatever happened to her. Josh is her priority, and she needs to keep herself together for him.

After dinner, Blaze crashes on the couch, since Charlotte's sharing her bed. For hours Olivia paces her study. She isn't ready to talk. Numb, she doesn't know what to feel, let alone think about what Dwight did to Benton, Lily, and Josh. Three generations he's successfully silenced one way or the other. And she's having a hard time wrapping her head around that, so she spends the rest of the night with the Crimson Wave. By 5:30 a.m. she's a wreck. Her dad killed a man. He might have killed Lily. Lucas doesn't want to involve the cops. But she can't sit here and do nothing.

Settling on the edge of the couch, she nudges Blaze awake. Tears run freely down her face. This is it. She's losing it.

"Hey, hey, hey. What's wrong?" He sits up and cups the back of her head.

"I wasn't ready to talk last night."

"I could tell. What's up?" He caresses her damp cheek.

"It's my dad. He did something awful. He's a—" She stops. A sharp, acidic ache expands through her chest. Last week she had a loving, doting father. This week? He's the most atrocious person she's known. There's a gaping hole in her heart where she'd once felt her love for him.

"Let me make us some coffee," Blaze says.

In the kitchen, he brews coffee and she talks. She shares that Lily is her half sister and that Dwight isn't returning home. She can't explain why, but she has the feeling that she'll never see him again. It was the look in Lucas's eyes. Haunted. Something terrible happened to him while he was out of town and she suspects her dad was involved.

"Do you remember that case thirty years ago, the one where my parents' neighbor was murdered? He was stabbed multiple times with a kitchen knife? A couple of kids found his body washed up on the beach where the street dead-ends?"

"Vaguely. It was a big deal at the time, wasn't it?"

Olivia nods. She was only five. Most of what she remembers she read about years later in old newspaper articles.

"It wasn't solved. But everyone in the neighborhood was a person of interest and questioned. My dad was a suspect. Someone claimed they saw him out walking around the time of the murder. He got off because he had an alibi, my mom. The publicity ruined his chance of election. That was his first congressional campaign. He dropped out. He was very bitter about it."

"What does this have to do with Lily?"

Olivia looks at the knife block on the counter and her stomach revolts. Her hand circles her throat. Her dad gifted the set with the house. He said he and Charlotte received it as a wedding gift but no longer had use for them. They bought a new set when they finished the kitchen in the new house, the one Olivia grew up in. They held on to them for her, he said when she found them in the attic.

A rush of heat crawls up Olivia's throat. Her hand shakes when she lifts her coffee mug. She'll never be able to use those knives again, not without wondering if the cook's knife is the one Dwight used.

And what about Jean St John, Benton's widow? She moved to Texas almost ten years ago. Charlotte told her she remarried. Does Jean still think about her late husband or has she moved on? Lucas doesn't want Olivia to call the police and risk them reopening the case. What's he afraid of? And what if Olivia anonymously tips off Jean?

Her stomach wants to hurl the coffee she consumed. She presses a hand to her belly and Blaze is at her side.

"Are you all right? You look a little murky."

She gasps softly and nods, then returns her full attention to Blaze. "The man murdered was Benton St. John, Lily's father."

Blaze sets down his mug. "Holy shit. If the police had known."

"They'd have had probable cause against my dad. Things might have gone down differently for him. Here's the kicker, though. My mom confessed last night it was my dad. He did it. She's been covering for him."

His jaw falls open. No words come out. He cups his mouth, steps back, then forward as if rocking from the news, and yanks her into his arms. "I'm so sorry," he whispers over and over into her hair as she falls apart. Her body shakes, wrecked from the last forty-eight hours. "Where is he now?" he asks when she calms.

"I don't know." She sniffles, wipes her nose. "Mom says he's not coming home." Olivia thinks of Lucas again. The haunted look in his eyes. The cuts and bruises on his face and hands. He disappeared for three days. Dwight hasn't called her in the same number of days. He never did respond to her texts.

Blaze rests his hand over hers. "What do you need from me?"

She points at the knife block. "Those were a wedding gift to my parents. They came with the house. My dad stored them with a bunch of other junk in the attic. Can you get them out of my sight?"

His face loses color as the meaning of those knives sets in. "On it." He bags the block and takes it outside.

———

Olivia sits on the edge of her bed, watching Charlotte sleep. She nurses a tepid cup of coffee. As if sensing her presence, Charlotte stirs. She pushes up her eye mask and lifts her head. She looks around the room and squints at Olivia. "Why am I here?"

"You were upset. I didn't want you to spend the night alone."

She flops back on the pillow. "Take me home."

Olivia looks at her coffee. The cream has curdled on the surface. She needs to stir it. Instead, she asks the question that's been stirring in her head. "Is Dad dead? Is that why he's not coming home?" She stops short of asking if Lucas killed him.

To her side, she hears Charlotte's sharp intake of breath. Olivia looks at her, covers up to her chin. Petite and fragile, curled under a mound of blankets.

Charlotte scrapes her teeth on her bottom lip. She looks at the chandelier above the bed. "Did Lucas tell you?" she asks after a moment.

"Not so much in words."

A tear rolls across her temple and disappears into her hair. "It was a car accident. The police came by yesterday morning."

Olivia closes her eyes and lets Charlotte's words sink in with everything else she's heard in the last twenty-four hours. Relief washes over her. It wasn't Lucas's fault. She then waits for the sadness, and she waits for the rage. Her dad is dead. But the news doesn't surprise her. She doesn't react as she expected, crying until her throat hurts. She loved him like no other. But from her perspective, Dwight has been slowly dying all week. The more she learned about him, the more distanced she felt from the man who raised her. She was already pushing him away.

"Mom." Olivia takes her hand. Charlotte's fingers are Popsicle cold. "Why didn't you tell me yesterday?"

"I wanted to, Olivia. I didn't know how. You were so close to your father. His little girl. But he   he   " She turns her face into the pillow.

Olivia sets her mug on the bedside table. "Should we tell Mrs. St. John?" She can't stop thinking about Benton's widow. If Blaze had been murdered, Olivia wouldn't rest until the case was solved.

"No! Why would you do that?" Charlotte sits up. She grabs both of Olivia's hands. "It's been thirty years. She's moved away and remarried. Why dredge up bad memories? Do you want to put me in prison?" she asks, horrified.

"For what?"

"They'll accuse me of obstruction of justice. I lied about being his alibi. He wasn't with me at the time Benton was murdered."

Olivia's hands slip from her mom's. "But wouldn't you want justice if one of us was murdered?"

"It's not the same thing. Your father threatened he'd go to the police and blame me. I was scared," she cried. "I've been frightened of him for so many years."

"Oh, Mom." Olivia embraces her, wishing she could absorb her mom's pain. "We'll explain that he threatened you."

Charlotte pulls back. She grips Olivia's arms. Her nails dig into Olivia's skin. Her expression is fierce. "I can't risk it. Do you want me to spend the rest of my life in prison? That's what will happen. I'd die in there. Justice has been served. Your father is dead. God rest his soul." She does the sign of the cross. "This secret has to stay with us."

"But, Mom . . . It's murder."

Charlotte squeezes Olivia's arms. Olivia winces. "Promise me, Olivia. This doesn't leave the room."

Olivia drops her chin. It already has. Blaze knows. But she trusts him to keep their family's secret.

"Olivia," Charlotte says, insistent.

"Fine. I won't say a word."

"We take this to our graves."

"Jesus. All right," she says, trying to see this from Charlotte's angle. She's right. Olivia doesn't want to see her mom go to prison. It would break her.

Charlotte gently runs her fingers through Olivia's long hair. Her face softens. "You're the strongest of my three. Be our rock, Livy. Keep us steady."

"I'll try." Even though she feels like she's sinking in lies and secrets. "About Lily. Did Dad mention where she went?"

Charlotte shakes her head. "I told you the truth. He didn't tell me anything. I don't know where she is. I wish I did because I want her to come home now. You have to bring her back for me."

"I will." A tear leaks from Olivia's eye. Charlotte dabs it off with her pinkie, a sad smile tilting up her lips. Her eyes are misty.

"Josh is awake," Olivia says. "What do you say to a proper introduction?" With Dwight gone, they no longer have to fear what he might do to Josh.

"Well, I . . ." Charlotte's hands flutter from the sheets to the pillow to her knees as if she doesn't know what to touch.

"He's your grandson," Olivia says softly. "He wants to get to know his family."

"Not like this." Charlotte grimaces at the oversize sleep shirt with a beer-drinking cat and pink leggings Olivia dressed her in last night. She didn't pack her mom's pajamas. She only found negligees when she searched Charlotte's dresser and doubted her mom would feel comfortable wearing skimpy silk around her grandson. With Charlotte's messy morning hair, her outfit took fifteen years off her life. She could pass as Olivia's sister.

"I'm . . . unpresentable." She pats her head, touches her lips. "My hair isn't done. I haven't fixed my face."

Olivia smirks. Charlotte's upper-Bostonian is shining through the casual Californian attitude she never got the hang of adopting.

"He's a thirteen-year-old boy. I don't think he'll care."

"I do." She picks at the blanket. "He's afraid of me."

"Then show him otherwise. Until we find Lily, we're all he's got. He needs us, Mom. He's a great kid."

Charlotte huffs. "Oh, all right. If it means you'll stop badgering me. Let me freshen up and change into something less"—she plucks at the leggings—"pedestrian." She briskly walks into the attached bathroom and shuts the door.

———

Thirty minutes later, Charlotte sits across from Josh at the kitchen table watching him sketch. Olivia asked him to continue drawing the places he thinks Lily could have gone. She hopes keeping him engaged will loosen the words stuck on his tongue. After breakfast, she and Josh have an appointment with Officer Curbelo. Olivia wants to show her Josh's illustrations, especially the panel with Lily on the highway. Later today, they'll search the internet to match locations to his sketches while Blaze continues calling hospitals, extending his search area north of Los Angeles and east of Palm Springs.

Blaze stands beside her at the stove. He nudges her arm. "You okay?"

"For now." She pours egg mixture into the hot pan. "Just thinking what I have to do today."

"Theodore, the coffee's bitter." Charlotte pushes her mug away.

Blaze winces. Olivia shares a look with him. Charlotte is far from easy to please. She wonders if he feels awkward with her mom here. Charlotte has to be embarrassed. She about fainted again when Olivia first drove toward Blaze's house last night.

"I'll make another, Mrs. Carson," Blaze says, taking her mug to the sink. Charlotte returns her attention to Josh. She slides the pearl drop along its chain, watching as Josh's drawing comes to life.

"Sorry about that. She's picky with her coffee. She's also embarrassed."

"How so?" He turns on the kettle.

"She can hardly look at you."

He makes a face. "She shouldn't be. That was a lifetime ago."

"I still can't believe she slept with your dad."

"I can hear you," Charlotte says.

Josh snorts. Olivia cringes.

"Eggs." Blaze points at the pan she should have been watching.

"Shit." Smoke billows. The acrid smell of burnt eggs fills the room. Transferring the pan to another burner, she turns on the vent.

"Where is that?" Olivia hears her mom ask Josh. She glances over her shoulder. Charlotte flips Josh's sketch around to get a better look.

Josh scratches his scar with the pencil's eraser. "Um . . . place . . . log." He points at the mossy green shape that takes up most of the page. "Lake. It's a lake." He smiles, pleased to have found the word he wanted.

Charlotte's lips purse. "I know that, but where is it?"

Josh looks at Olivia for help. She approaches the table. "I asked Josh to sketch places his mom might be."

"It looks like the Whitmans' cabin."

"The what?" Olivia and Blaze say at once. They exchange a look. Blaze joins her at the table. Sure enough, Josh's drawing looks exactly like the view of the cabin from the lake. Excitement pours into her faster than Lucas used to dunk her into that lake. Could this be it?

"She's right," Blaze says. "It's the lake house. How would he know about it?"

"Because he's been there?" She watches Josh for an answer.

He shakes his head. "Never been. Ball . . . horn . . ." His face scrunches. "Picture. It was on the . . . bucket . . . fridge." He gasps like he's exhausted.

Olivia exchanges another look with Blaze. Josh sketched the lake house from a photo he remembers, is that what he means?

"We need to go, like right now. Today." The lake house was a refuge for Lily as much if not more than for Olivia. Those summers gave Lily a respite from Dwight.

Charlotte's phone buzzes with an incoming text. Her complexion pales. Moisture pools in her eyes. She clutches her phone, her knuckles bone white.

"What is it?" Olivia touches her shoulder, sensing her mounting panic.

"It's Lucas. He needs help."

"Is he okay?" she asks, remembering how she left him yesterday. His smile was strained, but he promised her he wouldn't do anything stupid.

"I don't know." Charlotte grasps her hand. "Take me home to Lucas, then go get my baby. Bring her back."

Torn between chasing down Lily and helping Lucas, Olivia agrees. "Promise you'll call if you need me."

Charlotte nods tightly. "I will," she whispers, on the brink of falling apart.

It must be bad, whatever Lucas has done. *Please, God*, Olivia whispers in her head. Keep her brother safe. She's as anxious as Charlotte to have her siblings together again.

CHAPTER 35

"This place hasn't changed at all." Olivia watches the scenery pass outside her window. Green Valley Lake, the best-kept secret high in the San Bernardino Mountains. Other kids went to sleepaway summer camps. The Whitmans' cabin was summer camp without counselors and KP duty. Campfires without corny songs. Canoe races without rules. While Lily and Tyler kept close to the cabin because they were younger, she, Blaze, and Lucas ran amok six weeks straight, year after year. She could hike the trails with her eyes closed. Bike the roads without Google Maps. Recite every flavor of Popsicle in the icebox at Decker's Market: Firecracker, Missile, Pop Ups, Orange Creamsicle. Looking back, she's surprised there weren't more trips to the clinic given all the trees they climbed and fell from or trips around the lake without life vests. They were stupid kids. But those summers held her best memories.

She absently plays with her fingers, wishing she had a cigarette. She's nervous. Blaze called the landline at the house. No one answered, but Olivia wasn't going to spend the day twiddling her thumbs if there is any chance that Lily could be there.

Josh's knees knock the back of her seat. He's been restless the entire drive.

"We're almost there," Olivia says over her shoulder.

"Yep." Josh cracks his knuckles, bounces his fists on his knees. Olivia prays this trip is worth the drive. She postponed her appointment with Officer Curbelo to go with her gut.

Blaze eases down their windows. The mountain air floods her with memories. Good ones of her and her siblings, like sharing a candy bar with Lucas or rowing Lily in the canoe, sticking close to shore under Harold's watchful eye. She leans her head toward the window and lets her hair go wild.

"Nervous?" Blaze asks.

"Mm-hmm." About Lily. Their mom and Lucas, too. Her brother's truck wasn't in the drive when they dropped off Charlotte. Her mom said she knew where he was and would call with an update. Olivia's worried about him and regrets she hadn't invited him to stay with them last night. She didn't apologize for blaming him for ruining their summers at the Whitmans'. He was never at fault, and he needs to hear that from her. He also needs to hear that she loves him.

"I can stop by Decker's," Blaze says.

Her gaze catches his and the drift of his offer. She shakes her head. "I'm good." There are other ways besides a pack of cigarettes to temper her anxiety. She looks across the lake's glass surface and has the urge to purchase a kayak. Once this is over, she'll ask Lucas if she can join him some days on his morning row. She misses the water at sunrise.

They turn onto the cabin's street and memories crash into her head like a blow from Titian Crimson. "Oh, my gosh, this place."

"I know, right? Maybe . . ." He stops and shakes his head.

"What?"

"No pressure, but maybe one day we could swing by the real estate office in town and check out some listings."

Her brows lift. "For us to go in on together?"

"Something like that." He pauses and smiles. "Yeah. Exactly like that. I want us to start our own traditions."

Olivia waits for the familiar twinge of panic that sours her stomach whenever she thinks about marriage and families. It never comes. She smiles. She could have her summers at the lake back. They could invite Lucas and Lily—Josh. Tyler, too, if he was up for it. They're too old to sleep in sheet tents under string light stars, but they can stay up all night talking around the campfire, or spend lazy days floating on the lake.

"Yeah, I'd like that."

"There!" Josh leans into the front and points at the cabin from Lily's picture.

There it is indeed. The place looks the same as it did the last time her family drove away. From the outside, the house is rustic with wood-stained siding. Inside, everything was top-of-the-line at the time.

"We've arrived," Blaze murmurs, turning into the driveway.

"Think she's here?" Olivia's heart is a helium balloon rising in her throat.

"Only one way to find out." His eyes are tender when he stops the Mercedes's engine.

Olivia looks out her window and her pulse throbs in her throat. The curtains are drawn and porch light on, exactly how the Whitmans left the house when they closed it up at the end of summer. If anyone is here, they're parked in the garage.

Josh is the first out of the car. Olivia and Blaze follow. Movement in the front window draws her eye. The curtains flutter, then the front door bolt releases. The door opens and a man appears. He's tall with broad shoulders and tawny hair.

"Ty?" Blaze shuts the car door and pockets the keys.

Olivia startles. She watches the man as he talks to someone inside the house. When he looks back at them, Olivia gasps. It is Tyler.

A woman appears beside him and Olivia bursts out crying. "Lily." Her sister's name is a whisper and Blaze is instantly at her side, his arm around her waist. She hoped with her entire being Lily would be here, but to see her in the flesh is a shock. She'd recognize her little sister anywhere.

Dressed in silver leggings with flame-red hair, the spitting image of Olivia's Dahlia Crimson, Lily stands frozen in the doorway. Olivia sees the moment she recognizes her son. Her face lights up, a heady combination of relief and elation. "Josh? Josh! Oh, my god."

"Mom!" Josh runs to her.

Lily flies down the steps and across the driveway. She's a blur, like pages flipping in a comic book. Olivia watches her sister with stunned wonder. She's alive, she's whole, and she's beautiful. Mother and son meet halfway. Josh launches into Lily's arms. She envelops him in a tight embrace and bursts into tears. "I thought I lost you." She sobs, holding Josh close.

"Okay, Mom. Okay. Okay."

It's okay, Mom. I'm okay. We'll be okay, Olivia interprets. She feels so much love for them both. Their reunion takes her breath away. Josh buries his face in Lily's hair and cries. They rock side to side.

Blaze touches Olivia's hand and she jerks, startled. "Are you okay?"

She shakes her head. Tears cloud her vision. "She's here," she whispers.

Blaze smiles. "Because you and Josh found her. You did this. Remember that."

"We did, huh?" She smiles. Whether or not Lily welcomes her, at least Olivia has that. She protected Josh when she hadn't protected her sister. She brought Josh home when she failed to do the same for Lily.

Lily's gaze meets Olivia's over Josh's head and her eyes round in shock. "Livy?"

Olivia wipes her face and lifts her hand in a short wave. "It's me," she whispers. She feels like an interloper. She also wants to hug Lily as fiercely as she hugs her son.

"How did he find you?" Lily asks when Josh's crying eases.

"I'm not entirely certain. He told me some. I guessed the rest. What about you? Where've you been? We've been so worried about you. Are you okay?"

"I'm fine now. Wonderful, actually." She cups Josh's face and smiles at him. "It's a long story. I'll tell you everything. But first—" She looks over her shoulder. "Come here, Tyler."

Tyler approaches them and Olivia gasps lightly. He's a wider, taller version of Blaze, and an unmistakable older version of Josh.

Lily whispers in Josh's ear and he lifts his head. He gawks at Tyler.

Her arm around Josh, Lily gestures at Tyler. "Meet your father."

Olivia's mouth falls open. Beside her, Blaze sharply inhales. "Holy shit."

"They've never met?" she asks. Josh mentioned it once, but it didn't occur to her it would happen in her presence. Right here and now. She's blessed to witness such a reunion.

"In person? No," Lily says.

She's going to start crying again. Olivia has so many questions about where Lily went after she ran away. How did she survive? Why hasn't Tyler ever met his son? And why didn't he tell Blaze anything when Blaze called him? Her questions are a dryer full of clothes tumbling in her mind but all she can do right now is watch and feel immense happiness for her nephew.

"Close your mouth, Liv." Blaze gives her hand a squeeze.

Tyler offers Josh his hand, looking just as nervous as his son. He keeps his emotions in check, his face tight when he says, "I've been wanting to meet you for a very long time."

"Me too." Josh grasps Tyler's hand and Tyler's smile is shaky.

Olivia and Blaze share a look. His blue eyes reflect what's on her mind. What happened when Lily ran away? Did Tyler even know she was pregnant with his child?

Lily looks away, her expression unreadable, and Olivia wonders exactly what is their story, when Lily notices Blaze standing beside her.

"Hey, Lily." Blaze lifts a hand.

"Hi." She looks at Olivia after a quick glance at Josh and Tyler to see how they're faring. "Can we take a walk?"

"You go," Blaze says when Olivia turns to him. "We'll stay with Josh."

Lily kisses her son. "I need a moment with your aunt. I'll be right there if you need me." She points at the dock and gestures for Olivia to join her.

Olivia is bursting with questions and Lily is looking around the place as if she's walking back in time.

"We made a lot of good memories here." Lily skims her fingers on a tree trunk as they pass. "It's really good to see you again, Livy."

"I can't tell you how good it is to see you. I have so many questions." About Dwight, Josh, the life Lily built for her and her son.

"Me too. So, uh . . ." Lily looks back at the guys. "You and Blaze?" She cringes. "Sorry. That's not what I meant. I mean, that's not where I meant to begin."

"That's okay." Olivia feels Lily's awkwardness as her own. Where do they begin when so many years have passed? But she can tell where Lily is going with this, and they need to get it out in the open.

"Mom told Dad that Ethan was Josh's father."

Lily looks at her, stunned. "That doesn't make sense. I never gave them a name."

Olivia knows that now. But it's reassuring to hear the truth directly from Lily after all the lies their parents told. "Mom wanted me to hate you. I wouldn't try looking for you. She said you were safer away than at home."

"That woman." Lily shakes her head.

"She was trying to protect you, that's what she told me." And Olivia firmly believes that. For all her faults, Charlotte loves Lily. "I only learned about it yesterday."

"You thought I told her it was Ethan?"

"At first, yes." Olivia nods. "And I hated you for years." She follows Lily up onto the dock. There's a light breeze over the lake that smells of moss and dirt.

Lily drops a leaf she plucked from a bush in the water. It floats on the surface. "I'm sorry about Ethan. I liked him. But you and Blaze? You're better together."

Olivia tilts her head. "Why didn't you ever tell me that?"

Lily shrugs. "We didn't tell each other a lot of stuff. I should have. Are you, though? Together?"

Olivia smiles. Her body warms in the early autumn sun. She nods.

"Good. I'm happy for you."

"You and Tyler?"

"I don't know what we are. We haven't seen each other in a long time. I was staying with a friend up the road and saw a car in the driveway yesterday." Lily watches the house. Josh appears on the deck. He waves when he sees them. Lily and Olivia wave back.

"This is going to sound terrible." Lily absently rubs her forearm and Olivia braces herself for the worst. This is it. Lily wants her to leave. She won't let Olivia see Josh again. She'll want to keep all ties with the Carsons severed.

Lily glances back at her son. Tyler and Blaze have joined him. "I never told Josh much about you. I didn't get the chance. I was going to. He was asking about his dad and my family. Then he had his accident and—" She chokes up.

"Hey, it's okay." Olivia touches Lily's shoulder, then stops resisting. She pulls her in for a hug and revels in how good it feels to have her little sister back in her arms. Questions about Lily and Josh and what happened to them, how they separated, Dwight's involvement, pound the walls in her head. But this, holding Lily, showing her the compassion she should have had when they were younger, has her momentarily biting her tongue. Olivia can never make up the years she neglected her sister, or for the years she pretended Lily was okay and she didn't search for her. But she can show her now what matters: having her sister back. "I don't care what you told Josh about me. All I care is that I get to see him again. And you. I don't want to lose you again."

Lily hugs her with a desperation that reminds Olivia of the little girl who used to hold her hand. She sniffles like a child. "It's been so hard."

Olivia gives her a bone-crushing squeeze. She can only imagine what Lily's been through. She steps back and takes a good look at her. Lily's grown up into a beautiful woman, flaming red hair and all. They're faint, but she still has freckles across her nose.

"How did Josh find you?" Lily dries her face with the base of her palm.

"He has an envelope from you addressed to me. I found it in his backpack."

She frowns. "What envelope?"

"It's old. Josh's birth certificate and a power of attorney dated a year after he was born. I take it you were going to send it to me but never did?"

Lily's brows pull together. She tilts her head. "I wonder when he found those. It had to have been before his injury. He has trouble reading."

"I think he showed the envelope to the woman who drove him."

"Who?"

"Some old lady. She dropped him off at my house and left before I could get her name. My guess is he hitchhiked."

She gapes. "Josh!"

"He's safe. He's been with me the entire time. All I wanted was to find you and get him back to you. I owed you that much."

"You owed me? For what?"

"I should have let you move in with me when you asked. I should have stood up for you when Dad was being an ass. I'm sorry I didn't. I didn't realize . . . No, I refused to accept how bad it was between you. But he had me believing you destroyed everything you borrowed from me when it really was him. He was manipulating us behind our backs." Olivia sees that now that she knows the truth about him and Lily's parentage. The prom dress—Dwight made her believe Lily ruined the dress, but she wouldn't put it past him to run her dress through the mud. She'd blame Lily, making her feel like a family outcast. He let Lily cut up Olivia's magazines, knowing they were her favorite and that she'd hate Lily for doing so. Everything he did pushed Lily away and kept Olivia close to him. As if he was afraid Olivia would find out what he was really like. And remember what he'd done. Dwight had been manipulating her for years, and she never saw it.

"I'm sorry I wasn't there for you. And I'm sorry I made you think I didn't love you."

"I didn't hate you, Olivia. You were Dwight's favorite, and he didn't like me. He scared me. I wasn't trying to keep my distance from you. I was trying to stay away from him."

Josh's laughter carries to the lake and they look up at the house again. Blaze and Tyler are smiling, a good thing. It's been a long time since they've connected.

"What happened? How'd you get separated from Josh?"

Lily's eyes brighten with fear. "Someone is after me. We were on our way here to hide when I had to pull over. Josh had to go to the bathroom. I was hit when I got out of the car. We were parked on the side of the road. When I came to, Josh was gone. I flagged down a passing car and the driver, a young gal, I think—I don't remember, it's hazy—she called an ambulance for me."

"Geez, Lily."

She tugs at her shirt. "I'd never been so scared."

"Was it Dad? I mean, Dwight? Did he hit you? Did he push Josh? Oh, my god, Lily. I can't believe he'd do this to you. What did he want from you?"

"He wanted to make sure I wasn't talking. I know things about him. But it wasn't him. He's not the one who's after me."

Olivia blinks. She falls back a step. "Who is?"

"I don't know who or why."

That doesn't sound good. "He's still out there?"

Lily nods. She and Josh are still in danger.

"Lil—" Olivia's chest hurts out of fear for them.

Lily touches her arm. "There's so much I have to tell you, but . . ." She looks back over her shoulder and Olivia sees Lily's longing plainly etched on her face. She wants to get back to her son, and Olivia doesn't blame her. Someone is still out there looking for them.

She rests her hand over Lily's. "Wait . . . Before we go back, there's something I have to tell you. I know about Dwight, that he's not your dad. I know he . . . that . . ."

"That what?" Lily folds her arms. "That Benton St. John was my dad?"

Olivia exhales roughly. "Yes. That."

"I found out the night I left."

"Mom mentioned that. She said you overheard them arguing. She also said you know Dwight killed him."

Lily blinks. Her mouth falls open. "Mom told you that?"

"Yeah, it's horrible, isn't it?" she asks, confused by Lily's reaction. Why is she shocked if she already knew?

"My god." Lily roughly rakes both hands through her hair.

Olivia's pulse pounds in her throat. Apprehension moves through her, starting at her toes and rising like a sealed room filling with water, threatening to suffocate her. "What's wrong? Is there something else?" She's not sure she can handle more revelations about her dad.

Lily stares at her, thunderstruck. "You've got it all wrong. Dwight didn't kill my dad."

"Then who did?"

CHAPTER 36
CHARLOTTE

Most parents teach their children honesty is the best policy. Charlotte's daddy taught her to lie.

"Deception is an art," she remembers him explaining once over a cup of Earl Grey and biscuits. His office was located near her high school. She'd meet him there every afternoon on her way home from class. He insisted what he taught her would take her further than any Pythagorean theorem or Byzantine Empire lecture could.

"Master it, and this will be yours." He gestured at his office space with the inlaid walnut paneling and plush steel-blue carpeting. Paintings from contemporary artists the likes of Nova and Gallegos that were as provocative as they were repulsive. Charlotte thought of them as hauntingly beautiful. She wanted her own art gallery in Laguna Niguel with its homes on high cliffs over sea-glass blue waters, not her daddy's square office in a steel tower. Stocks and REITs were interesting if one liked that sort of thing, which Charlotte didn't. Boston was an icebox in the winter and a sweatshop during summer, and neither was good for a girl's complexion. Her sights were set on something much grander in California, with its fast cars and sun-drenched men.

She escaped to California as soon as she was admitted into USC. Within a few years, she met Dwight Carson, someone who was suddenly shinier in her eyes than the art gallery she aspired to own, with his lofty political aspirations and charming personality. One day, he'd be in the White House and she'd be right beside him. She left campus without her diploma and followed Dwight and his dreams, making them her own.

Enraged that she'd waste her future, Charlotte's daddy disowned her. But she didn't mind. She and Dwight were going places she could never get to as Gilbert Dayton's daughter. She and Dwight married. They had a beautiful baby girl they named Olivia, and two years later, a son they called Lucas. Dwight launched his winery consulting business, meeting all the right people up and down the west coast, and Charlotte earned her real estate license, quickly rising to the top of her firm as the highest producing agent.

She then met Benton St. John. Gorgeous, athletic, looked at her just the right way, Benton. And for a brief bit of time he was the shiniest trinket in the window. She wanted nothing more than her neighbor. If her husband could have a little morsel on the side, she could have her treats, too.

Charlotte remembers the day Lily was conceived. She looked at her reflection in the mirror, smoothing her floral-print pencil skirt over her lush hips as anticipation warmed her blood. She undid one more pearl button on her pink silk blouse so that just enough cleavage showed. Tempting, not tacky.

Picking up the Manhattans she'd just mixed, she went out the back door of their custom-built home. It was an excessively hot July on the California coast, but the cool breeze coming off the bay and across the yard felt refreshing.

She rounded the corner of the house to the side yard, where Benton watched over her two children playing in the massive sandbox their daddy paid someone under the table to build. Benton smiled broadly, hands tucked in his trouser pockets, when he saw her, and her heart fluttered like his auburn hair in the wind. God, the man was beautiful. He took a glass from her, their fingers brushing. Electricity zinged up her arm, tightened her breasts. They had a connection. She'd felt it the instant he and his wife arrived at the house she'd shown, and eventually, sold to them. She'd bet the commission on her next deal that he felt the same. And now they were neighbors, three doors apart. So convenient, especially when she had a husband whose business kept him on the road more than off.

Benton's hazel eyes held hers over the rim of his glass. A single maraschino cherry bobbed in the well of the glass like a buoy in the bay. His gaze held delicious promises of what he planned to do with her. She shivered with delight.

Looking back, Charlotte should have turned around and walked back into the house. A fling to scratch an itch wasn't worth her marriage, children, and the fallout that followed. But she wouldn't have had her Lily. She also wouldn't have found herself in her current situation: a widow hell-bent on leaving town before her precious children returned home with the knowledge of what she'd done.

Instead, Charlotte had lured Benton up to the apartment above the detached garage.

"Olivia, Lucas," Charlotte said to her children who played in the sand. "Mommy and Mr. St. John have grown-up things to discuss. We'll be right there." She lifted her Manhattan toward the apartment, careful not to spill. "Follow me, Mr. St. John. I have some real estate I'd like to show you." She walked across the lawn, her weight on her toes so her heels didn't sink, and with a bounce in his step, Benton tailed her up the narrow staircase to the second-floor apartment.

She'd barely closed the door before he took her glass, setting both drinks on a nearby table, and crowded her against the wall. "Do you know how long I've waited for this?" He growled the words, boxing her in. "Weeks, Charlie. Fucking weeks." His mouth landed on hers and hips ground into the juncture of her thighs. His tongue swiped over her lips, dipped into her mouth. He tasted of cherry from the one sip he took of his cocktail, mints, and the lingering bitterness of coffee. He smelled of drugstore aftershave and nervous sweat.

"No need to rush. We have plenty of time," she said when he tore his mouth from hers and kissed a dotted line down her neck.

Hands she'd admired when he signed their real estate documents skimmed down her thighs. They pushed up her pencil skirt, bunching the material at her waist. He ran his finger along the edge of her silk lace panties, from hip to crotch and back. "You attached to these?"

Before she could answer, he tore them off. She gasped, her head banging into the wall at the suddenness of it. The skin on her hip stung like a rug burn. He gently rubbed the tender flesh and suckled at her bottom lip.

"Sorry," he murmured. "I can't seem to control myself around you. You make me wild."

"Then let's get wild." Her smile was seductive.

He took her against the wall just that once, because afterward Benton grew a conscience like a wart he refused to burn off.

The damn man.

Charlotte zips closed the suitcase that holds her shoes and glances at the clock. It's the fourth case she's packed and she doesn't have much time. Olivia will most likely be home tomorrow and she'll bring Lily, and everything Lily overheard about Charlotte before she ran away. Lucas could show up tonight from wherever it is that he went off to. Okay, so she lied. He didn't text her. Nancy did. She needed to borrow Charlotte's COACH tote, the pewter one that looks divine with her slingback heels. But Charlotte needed a viable excuse so Olivia wouldn't drag her up the mountain to face Lily. She was finally free of Dwight. She wouldn't risk her freedom altogether. So she told her daughter the text was from Lucas.

Whenever she threatened to leave him, he'd plead for her to stay. Then he'd get angry that she threatened to go in the first place. He told her he'd follow her. He'd tip off the police about what really went down the night Benton died. He'd sacrifice himself to keep her at his side. His shiny, well-connected arm ornament.

He would, too, so she bided her time until she knew he wouldn't come after her.

Fortunately, Dwight was never interested in monitoring their finances. Taxes made his eyes cross. It's why he kept draining his company's accounts. He spent more than he saved. Math wasn't his forte. He was grateful Charlotte didn't mind handling their books, making it too easy for Charlotte to send most of her earnings to the offshore accounts she set up when she received the inheritance from her mother Dwight never knew about.

Her daddy was right to disown her when she failed to graduate college and married Dwight. He told her Dwight wouldn't amount to anything. Admittedly, marrying him had been foolish and impulsive. But Dwight fit her mold of a perfect partner. She thought one day her daddy would be proud. He'd write her back into his will. Welcome her home with open arms.

He never did. But Gilbert Dayton didn't foresee his own wife, who was wealthy in her own right and concerned as any mother should be about her only daughter, divorcing him. Thanks to Val Dayton, Charlotte was set for life.

The doorbell rings and Charlotte scowls at the clock. Her ride is early.

"I'm still packing," she tells the driver when she answers the door. She gestures at the luggage nearby. "Take these. I'll be out when I'm ready."

"Yes, Mrs. Carson." He brings his department store aftershave odor with him when he steps into the house.

Charlotte returns to her bedroom and packs up the bathroom. She loads her satchel with makeup and perfumes. When she's done, she returns to the front door, passing decades of family photos in the hallway. She puts the satchel on the floor and takes their last family portrait off the wall, the one she reframed. She removes the photo and tears it in two. Dwight floats to the ground. Lucas, Olivia, and Lily circle her, proud and gorgeous in their evening attire.

Her lip trembles. She presses the photo to her chest. She'll miss her babies.

She closes the front door, leaving her house for the last time. She meant what she said to Olivia. She'll die if she's sentenced to prison.

"All set?" The driver opens her door.

She hands off her satchel and settles into the back seat of the sleek town car with blacked-out windows.

He rounds the car and gets in front. "Where to? SLO Airport?"

She smiles at her reflection in the window. Her plans are bigger than that.

"LAX."

His squinty eyes peer at her in the rearview mirror. "That'll cost you."

She peers inside her purse to check she remembered to empty the safe of cash.

"That won't be a problem."

"Yes, ma'am." He shifts the car into gear. It glides from the curb, away from her failures and toward something much better.

CHAPTER 37

Thirty years ago

Charlotte ran as fast as her condition allowed, one hand holding her bulging belly. She traversed her yard and the two neighboring properties. Their neighborhood was young, with empty lots scattered throughout the subdivision. One day, custom homes with floor-to-ceiling windows overlooking the Pacific Ocean and Morro Bay would sprawl across the open space. Tonight, they were empty and dark under a moonless sky. The dirt ground was treacherous.

Her eyes tracked the ground. One misstep and she'd fall. She could twist an ankle, or worse, lose her baby. She reached the end of the continent where land disappeared into the ocean and inched her way down the rocky berm. Standing in the knee-deep tide, he was right where the note he'd left taped to the refrigerator said he'd be. The ocean roared, smelling of brine and rotten fish. Moderate waves crashed into his legs, soaking his pants and spraying his back.

"Dwight, what are you doing?" she yelled over the ocean's anger.

Something struggled at his feet. The water receded slightly, and she noticed he had one foot propped on a rock. Or was it a fish? Whatever it was, it flopped around, as big as a seal.

"Teaching our neighbor a lesson." Dwight yanked up whatever was in the water. A very drenched, very beaten-up Benton St. John gasped for air. He blinked at her with one eye. The other was swollen shut. Salt water dripped off his eyelashes and watered-down blood off his chin from a split lip. The gash was deep. Dwight hadn't removed his Freemason's ring when he punched him.

"Help me." Benton's voice was hoarse, tearing through a raw throat. He probably swallowed a lot of salt water. If Dwight didn't kill him, that certainly would.

"Think about what you're doing, Dwight," she pleaded. "Consider the impact on our community. Your campaign! He's a schoolteacher. He goes missing, people will notice."

"Think of the impact that will have on me." He points at her middle. "I'm running for Congress, for Christ's sake. I can't be connected to anything scandalous. *We* can't be connected." Dwight had his sights on the Capitol, even the White House. All eyes would be on them, the perfect couple, with their two brunette, jade-eyed children, a boy and a girl.

But Charlotte had gone and ruined it and gotten pregnant. Dwight had gotten snipped right after she gave birth to Lucas and, until her, Benton had never slept with anyone since he married Jean, who was on birth control. In their haste to scratch that itch burning between them, she and Benton had forgotten to use a condom. And Dwight was positive people would know the kid wasn't his when he, or she, started to look more like the man living down the street than the man Charlotte was married to. There would be no mistaking Benton's auburn hair.

"How did you find out it was him?" She gestured at Benton, who struggled in Dwight's grasp. Her husband had him in a choke hold.

"Our little princess, of course."

"Olivia?"

"She tells me everything, Charlotte. She tells me about the visitors you've shown real estate to above the garage. Did you clip your lawn for all of them?" He sneered.

Charlotte grimaced. Dammit. She should have bribed the kids to keep their little mouths shut.

"Benton boy came sniffing. You weren't here but he was sure curious about that babe in your belly." The one she refused to abort. She couldn't kill her own blood.

"It's not like you don't sleep around when you're away on business," she accused.

"I don't throw it in your face." He jabbed a finger in the direction of her swollen belly. She was four months along. It was her third child, so she looked like a house. She'd better not be pregnant with twins. *Dammit, Benton.* She should ask if twins ran in his family.

"Don't you, though? I wash your clothes. I smell their perfume. I see their lipstick stains on your shirts. How many have there been, Dwight? Benton and I slept together once. Once!" she shrieked.

Benton struggled, almost slipping free before Dwight hooked his ankle and Benton face planted in the water.

"You can't kill him," she tried to reason.

"I wasn't planning to kill anyone, but you've left me no choice."

"No, I mean you can't drown him. He's competed in several Ironmans. He's trained to hold his breath. He'll resist you for as long as he can." Apparently, Benton was some sort of prodigy when it came to competitive swimming. He broke records at his university. It was one of the trivia bits he shared when she first met him and his wife. But if Dwight doesn't do something soon, someone is bound to stumble upon them.

Dwight makes an exasperated noise. "I'm doing this for you, Charlotte. Don't you see? I'm trying to curb your appetite before it gets out of control."

"My appetite? What about yours? It's just as bad."

"I'm discreet," he argued, and she knew he was right. He was subtle with his indiscretions, and this was a lesson she should take to heart if they wanted a life in the public eye.

Benton thrashed in the water and Dwight jerked him up again. "He won't die."

"Drowning isn't as quick as they make it in the movies, honey. Let him go."

"So he can run to the police and report us? You're in on this now. Think, Charlotte. You'll lose this life we've built together. You want more money and more prestige than you could ever inherit from your daddy, and I can give that to you. I *will* give that to you. We'll do this together, sugar. Don't let this fool take that away from us." He gave Benton a good shake and Dwight's gaze dropped to her hand. "What's with the knife?"

Charlotte looked at the kitchen knife she'd forgotten to put down after she read Dwight's note. "I was cutting onions." There was still translucent skin on the edge of the blade. Her husband was right. She did want that life he could give her. An illustrious, prominent life they could only achieve together, with his charisma and her connections. She knew people, wealthy people, through her parents. But thanks to Dwight's penchant for violence and her forgetfulness (The *fucking* condom!), not to mention her refusal to get rid of the baby (She was Catholic, after all.), Benton was now in the way. He would report Dwight to the authorities and see her as an accomplice. They would be ruined. Her dear children would grow up without their mommy and daddy. She'd give birth locked up in a cage like an animal. They couldn't have that.

She plunged the knife she'd just used to chop up dinner into Benton's gut. She'd recently sharpened the knife and the blade went in smoothly. His eyes widened in shock, and for a split second she felt mirth dancing in hers. *Fascinating.* Slicing through flesh is like carving a chicken.

She stabbed him again and again and again as Dwight watched on with horrified interest, as if he was stunned his wife could commit such a monstrous act, until he snapped out of his stupor and bellowed, "Enough!" He dragged Benton's limp, lifeless body farther into the ocean. They watched the tide take her lover away.

"We need to get rid of the knife," Dwight said when he returned to her side.

"But I have to finish dinner." She rinsed off the blade and her hand in the cold water.

He took the knife from her and helped her up the steep berm. "Afterward then. I'll hide the entire set in the old house's attic."

"Mommy?"

Charlotte froze. Dwight swore under his breath. He squeezed Charlotte's hand with a bruising grip. "What did she see?" he whispered harshly.

"How the fuck do I know?" Charlotte spat. "Olivia, darling, what are you doing here?" she asked, trying not to panic. Children talk. They always do. She'd tell on them. Not directly, but something or someone would trigger a memory and Olivia would start babbling.

Olivia's nightgown swirled around her ankles. She clutched her rag doll. Wise green eyes too big for her head blinked innocently at Charlotte. Olivia leaned to the left, trying to see behind them. She pointed at the water. "Who's that man?"

"Shit," Dwight muttered.

Charlotte was sweating. "That's a seal, darling," she said, her voice pitching upward.

Olivia's nose scrunched up. "Why's the seal wearing clothes?"

"Don't be silly, Livy. Seals don't wear clothes." Charlotte's laugh was maniacal.

Dwight jerked her arm. "What if she tells someone?"

"She won't because you'll get her to believe she didn't see anything and that we weren't here."

"Charlotte—" He growled. "I'm not gaslighting our daughter."

"You'll do whatever it takes to keep her from talking," she said through her teeth. She poked him hard in the chest. "None of this happened. You hear me? We never speak of this again, and that includes Olivia."

"She'll have nightmares for life. This will mess her up."

"No, it won't, because you're her daddy and she trusts you. Keep her close. Make her forget. She's only five for fuck's sake. Now get her out of here." Charlotte discreetly took back the knife, positioning her body so Olivia wasn't left with the image of her mommy carrying the murder weapon. If her daughter recalled anything, it wouldn't be her holding the blade.

"Upsy-daisy, Princess." Dwight picked up Olivia. "You must be cold."

"Really cold." She giggled. "I love you, Daddy."

"Love you, too, Princess."

Charlotte looked back at the ocean one last time. It was too dark to see Benton. Poor man. He never had a chance when he confronted Dwight.

Hair flew into her face. Wind slammed into her back. She stumbled. Spooked, she looked down at the water. The ocean wanted her. Too bad. It couldn't have her. Not today.

CHAPTER 38

Two weeks after Dwight's death, Olivia buried her dad's cremated remains with only Blaze at her side. It wasn't so much a funeral as it was a goodbye to a man Olivia barely knew. Dwight might not have murdered Benton St. John, but he had a hand in the man's demise.

Dwight's autopsy report showed his blood alcohol was above the legal limit. His death was ruled an accident. Whatever role Lucas played, only he knows. Olivia's brother isn't anywhere to be found, at least in the places she's looked. Lucas has bailed before without notice, but he's never been gone this long. It's been three months. She's worried about him and his frame of mind.

As for Charlotte, Olivia doesn't begin to know where to look for her, or if she should. She skipped town the day Olivia and Blaze drove Josh to the lake house. She watched the surveillance footage and saw the town car drive Charlotte away. But her mom left behind the deed to her house in her children's names: Olivia, Lucas, and Jenna Mason, proving Charlotte had known Lily's name all along. It's the only way Olivia could explain away the deed. Charlotte wouldn't have been able to change it on such short notice.

She left them each a bank account funded by an untraceable off-shore account with enough money to buy a house. Or in Olivia's case, a second home. In Oceanside. On the beach. If she wanted to have a place near Lily and Josh.

At least that explained why the husband of one of the county's most successful real estate brokers always complained about never having enough money. His wife was funneling it elsewhere.

It's been three months since Olivia found Lily, and she still hasn't fully recovered from Charlotte's deceit. Both parents betrayed her, but her mom crushed her soul. There are days when she's with her therapist that she wonders if she'll ever get over a betrayal of that magnitude. Does one ever fully recover? Her therapist has commended her for not shutting others out, which those who've been wronged tend to do, and as Olivia's done in the past. This time, she isn't alone.

Christmas is in four days. Day after tomorrow, Olivia and Blaze will drive to Oceanside to spend the holidays with Lily, Josh, and Tyler. She and Lily—she still isn't used to calling her sister Jenna—need to decide what to do about Lucas and Charlotte. Pursue them, or let them be? Lily is just as worried about Lucas as she is, but Olivia's reason for finding Charlotte is selfish. She needs closure, and she wants justice. She also wants to tell her mom that her recurring nightmare finally makes sense. As soon as Lily shared what she'd overheard the night she ran away, that Charlotte had wielded the knife, Olivia's mind filled in the blanks, from the beginning to its awful, bloody end.

"When will you get . . . here?" Josh asks during their daily phone call. He was the one who insisted he and Olivia regularly keep in touch. But when Lily mentioned Josh's speech pathologist encouraged him to talk as often as he could, Olivia suggested he call her daily. His aphasia has abated for the most part. Aside from a slight hesitation in his speech, it's barely noticeable. A relief given how his injury happened, which was almost as much of a relief as it was to hear from Lily that Dwight didn't push him.

In the last few months, Josh has made remarkable progress. He's learned to talk around a word if he can't find it. He's back in school and picked up reading again. The Crimson Wave graphic novels were the first two books he read. They probably don't need to talk every day anymore, but neither has bothered to change their routine.

"Blaze has to work on Monday, so we'll be there late." She's also waiting on a delivery from her publisher, a very advance, spiral-bound copy of book three in her Crimson Wave trilogy, one of many gifts she has for Josh.

Blaze remarked on the pile accumulating in the living room under their white pine Christmas tree. They'll have to take his truck instead of her Mercedes if she keeps buying Josh and Lily gifts. She just gave him a look. What does he expect? She has a lot of holidays and birthdays to make up for. Besides, she's an aunt. She's entitled to a little spoiling.

"I promise to call as soon as we get on the road. And don't forget to call earlier tomorrow," she reminds Josh as she walks into the dining room where Amber, Mike, and Blaze wait with a bottle of champagne. "Amber's wedding is at four."

Mike grunts. "Mine too."

Olivia winks at him and says goodbye to Josh.

"Love you, Aunt O."

"Love you too."

She sets down her phone on the table and Blaze pops the cork. Champagne foams at the mouth, leaking onto the table. Blaze gives a whoop and Mike grabs two flutes. Amber's ring sparkles and Olivia blots the spill with a stack of napkins. Blaze sheepishly grins.

"I might have shaken it up a bit. A toast to the happy couple." He lifts his glass. "May the roof over your heads be solid, the foundation underneath stable, and the love inside eternal."

"Well, shit. He kept it clean," Mike quips, and they laugh.

"Cheers to you guys," Blaze says.

"Here, here," Amber says, beaming, and kisses her fiancé.

Mike had proposed to her in the hospital cafeteria the day Olivia and Josh drove to Oceanside looking for Lily. Amber called to invite

Olivia and Blaze to dinner to share their good news but held off when she realized Olivia was in a panic to find her nephew after he left the car.

Olivia and Blaze eventually did join Amber and Mike for dinner. And just as Amber promised Olivia would one day pay her back for all those favors Olivia asked of her, Amber insisted on Olivia standing in as her maid of honor.

"I couldn't be happier for you." Olivia hugs her friend.

Hours later, after the champagne has been consumed, and the engaged couple has gone home for the night, Blaze kicks back on the porch with a glass of Knob Creek over ice and listens to the rain.

Olivia joins him, setting two shot glasses and the bottle of Fireball on the table between them.

Blaze sits upright. "I was wondering what happened to that. Thought you drank it with Miller," he teases.

Olivia thinks of the last text she received from Ethan, several days after she sent him Dwight's photos. Ethan didn't see whoever was in his truck with Lily. But the pictures had to have been taken one of the times Ethan picked her up. They were parked in front of the 7-Eleven where Lily had worked. If he were to make a guess, he'd say it was Tyler Whitman. He'd never seen Lily and Tyler together, but he did run into Tyler once in the parking lot.

If only Ethan knew how right he was.

Olivia scrunches her nose at the liquor. "I really hate this stuff."

"Then why'd you bring it out?"

She shrugs, unscrewing the top.

"I know why." His eyes flash with heat. He stands up, grinning, and grabs her hand.

"All right, all right." She laughs, yanking her hand away when he tries to draw her inside the house. They aren't going to go do the horny-teen thing. Not yet, anyway.

Pouring two shots, she says, "I want to make a point that I'm serious about us."

"Oh, I got that message loud and clear when you went in on the cabin with me." They finally found a place on the lake. The house closes in a few weeks and she can't wait for spring when Blaze starts the remodel. The place will be beautiful when he finishes.

She gives him his shot. "You said, and I quote, 'That's ours when you're ready. We'll get stupid drunk and—'" She grins wickedly, taps her glass to his, and tosses back the liquor. Blaze sucks air through his teeth and she cringes. "That's nasty."

"But you love me."

"I do, very much." Lips moist from the Fireball, she gives him a Hot Tamale–flavored kiss.

Blaze settles back onto the chair and kicks up his heels, resting his boots on the porch rail. Olivia sits beside him, drawing her legs underneath her. The air is winter crisp, but not intolerable. They watch the rain until it tapers off and the clouds part, revealing a star-speckled night sky. At some point, Blaze reaches for her hand.

"My heart is full," he says quietly.

Olivia thinks of her brother and how much she misses him. She thinks of her mom's deception and her dad's betrayal, and her heart grows heavy. But then she remembers Lily and Josh and how they're both in her life, and she couldn't be happier about that. She's battled her pain and fury over betrayal and came out a winner because she's learned to put faith in those who deserve it. And she knows now how to handle herself if she does get hurt. Because loving someone, whether a sister, a friend, or the man beside her, is worth the risk.

Looking over at Blaze, her heart has never felt fuller. She adores him. She kisses the back of his hand.

"Mine too," she whispers.

COMING SPRING 2022
No More Lies
Book 2 in the No More Series

AN EXCERPT FROM
NO MORE LIES

Editor's note: This is an early excerpt and may not reflect the finished book.

Jenna Mason crosses the Washington Middle School parking lot with her head down. If she looked up, she'd notice the small group of moms huddled around Beth Hopkins's sports activity vehicle. She might pick up snippets of their conversation or notice that they stop talking when she walks by. She would see them staring, and she wouldn't miss Leigh Duffy whispering in Beth's ear or Beth's shock. She would realize that she isn't as invisible as she believes. Not anymore. But Jenna is pressed for time. She needs to find her son Josh before the bell rings. He left his homework binder behind, again.

She knows she's enabling him. A responsible parent would let her son suffer the consequences of not turning his homework in on time. Some tough love would teach him to pack his book bag before bed and have it ready by the door come morning. Another parent would drop the binder off at the front office, but that would bring attention to both her and Josh. Marks on his grades would earn her an email from the teacher, something else she's determined to avoid. The less interaction with anyone through any means, the less people will remember them when they disappear.

Jenna has spent her entire adult life flying under the radar as much as humanly possible without fully disappearing off the face of the earth. An impossibility now that her twelve-year-old convinced her to stay put. Somewhat. He wants a normal life. He wants to surf and skateboard, hang out at the park or on the beach. He wants friends, real friends he doesn't have to abandon and never see again because Jenna forces them to move frequently and without notice. How many times has she picked Josh up from school, their trunk stuffed with suitcases and cardboard boxes, and left town? Too many to count.

Jenna cuts through the schoolyard. Kids congregate in their cliques like dolphin pods. They fiddle with their phones, Snapping and TikTok'ing or whatever it is kids do with their devices. Josh has tried to explain, but since she won't allow him a smartphone (too easy to track), she hasn't gone out of her way to learn more about social media. Though Josh has given her an earful about how embarrassing it is to be seen with a flip phone. He prefers not to use it than get mocked for having one, which is why he didn't answer when she called him about the binder a few minutes after he left the house to walk to school.

She beelines to the lunch tables under the green and gold canopy, the school's colors, where she knows Josh sits with his friend Anson before class starts. Anson sees her before Josh. He waves.

"Hello, Ms. Mason."

Josh swivels on the bench. "Mom!" His eyes bug then dart around to see who's watching. He hunches, trying to look smaller, invisible like her, but for a different reason. She doesn't want to make a lasting impression. Josh just embarrasses easily. She knows it's his age, but she can't help blaming herself. He'd be confident like his father was at twelve if he weren't afraid that she'd yank him from the life they've created for themselves over the last eighteen months.

Jenna smiles. "Hi, Anson. Josh." She stretches her son's name, softening the reprimanding undercurrents in her tone with a look and sets the white binder covered in vibrant shades of permanent marker on the table. Josh is a doodler, though his artwork is more realistic than her quirky characters. She still can't believe her YouTube cartoon went viral several years back. Some days she wishes it hadn't. She can never go fully underground again. But it pays the bills and then some. She can finally buy Josh Vans at the Shoppes in Carlsbad rather than worn sneakers with stained soles at the Salvation Army. They can eat out at restaurants with linen napkins, like the ones her parents took her to when she was young, rather than the reheated meals from canned food at the shelters she once frequented. All in all, their lifestyle has improved the last year and a half, though it hasn't assuaged the constant urge to look over her shoulder everywhere she goes.

Josh drags the binder toward him and stuffs it in his red backpack. "What are you doing here?"

"You didn't answer my call."

He grimaces. "My phone's dead."

She grips the edge of the table, channeling her anger into the metal instead of at her son. She doesn't cause scenes. She despises drawing attention. "You didn't charge it last night?" That's a hard, fast rule between them. From the day he could understand her, she's taught him to never be caught unprepared. They each have a packed suitcase under their beds for when they need to roll. And the need will come. She knows exactly where everything is located and what she'd take with them the next time they ditch town. Josh always knows to keep his phone charged and within reach.

The school bell rings, the sound shrill, and her heart lurches. She can hear that darn bell from their house five blocks away.

"No, I didn't," Josh grumbles, standing.

"Why not?"

"I forgot." He shoulders his backpack. Anson does the same, looking guilty he got caught in the middle of their squabble. Josh starts to back away. "Can I go now?"

Jenna lifts her hands to the side, walking toward him. "If you'd answered your phone, I wouldn't have had to grace you with my presence."

Josh's cheeks brighten. "Mom, stop," he loudly whispers, backing away faster. "I have to get to class."

"We could have met halfway, before you got to campus."

Josh rolls his eyes. "Okay, fine. Sorry, all right? I'll charge my phone tonight. Bye." He turns around and jogs to his first period science class before she can say anything further that would mortify him or scar him for life.

"Have a good day, Ms. Mason."

"You too, Anson."

He waves and jogs to catch up with Josh. She watches her son walk away with his best friend. He bumps shoulders with Anson, and they laugh. She smiles because he's happy, surprised by the accompanying burn of tears. Josh is growing up so fast. He looks more like his father every day, but his personality is all Lucas, his uncle. Thoughts of both men strain her chest. She misses them terribly, always has. She also misses the days when Josh was little. He was a total love bug. Today she barely squeezed a kiss out of him before he left for school and didn't even get a thank-you when she dropped off the binder.

"You're welcome," she mutters to herself. Blinking away the sting in her eyes, Jenna heads home. She makes it halfway across the parking lot before Leigh steps in her way. The move is sudden, and Jenna bumps into her.

"Sorry," Jenna mumbles and tries to move past Leigh.

Leigh steps to the side, blocking her again. Jenna bites the inside of her cheek and squints at Leigh, Washington Middle School's parents' club secretary and community gossip. Jenna didn't have to be actively involved with the other parents to know about Leigh. Josh came home with enough ridiculous stories he heard from Maggie Duffy, who got the latest dirt from her mom. Leigh's eyes are bright and her smile wickedly wide. The tip of her tongue touches the end of her incisor as her *Flashdance*-style sweatshirt slips off her right shoulder. Her arms are crossed under her chest. She wiggles her shoulders as if she can't contain her news.

"Is it true?" she asks, her brows arching high. Leigh is one of those people who makes eye contact and holds on, and not in a pleasant way. The feeling of Leigh staring into your soul is mighty uncomfortable, like leaving the house without pants and you don't realize so until you feel cool air against your nether regions. "Well?"

Jenna frowns, searching wildly for an escape route. "Is what true?"

Leigh rolls her head and gives Jenna a look as if Jenna should know exactly what Leigh is talking about. "They say you murdered some sixteen-year-old kid."

ACKNOWLEDGMENTS

Thank you, as always, to my team at Lake Union Publishing: Chris Werner, Nicole Burns-Ascue, Laura Barrett, Gabriella Dumpit, and Danielle Marshall. It's an honor to continue working with you. A special thanks to my editors Tiffany Yates Martin, Cheri Madison, Karin Silver, and Robin O'Dell, who work closely with Chris to bring out the best in all my books. This story shines because of you. And to my agent, Gordon Warnock, for being the best advocate this author can have. Thanks to Jessica Preeg, Kathleen Carter, Jaqueline Smith, and everyone in marketing and publicity who work tirelessly to ensure this book reaches my readers.

To the book clubs, reviewers, bloggers, bookstagrammers, and social media groups who've shined a light on this book and all my previous books, and who continue to support me and my work, thank you! I truly could not do this without you. A special shout-out to my top reader group, the Tiki Lounge. You make popping onto social media worth it. Your posts and fun anecdotes brighten my day. Thanks to Collette Sockel Joseph who won a contest inside the Tiki Lounge to Amber's boyfriend, Dr. Michael Drake. Thank you, Jen Cannon, for keeping my advance reader teams organized, and for standing in for me online when I'm stuck in my writing cave. You've been a life saver.

Special thanks to Ret. Lt. Jeff Bassett for his valuable time and insight, and for patiently answering my questions. This is a work of fiction. Any inaccuracies to fit within the confines of the story are my own. To my mom, Phyllis Hall, who gave me a more accurate picture of Josh's condition than anything I researched in books could have provided. To Orly Konig who never failed to listen when I whined or complained about the plot or my characters. Thanks for talking (and texting) me back to sanity.

To my husband, Henry, for being you. To Evan and Brenna for being there. You are my light.

And to you, dear reader, thanks for coming on this journey with me. Let me know what you thought of *No More Words*. You can connect with me through my website, www.kerrylonsdale.com. You can also sign up for my newsletter, Kerry's Beach Club, on my site. I encourage you to join my top reader group on Facebook, Kerry's Tiki Lounge (www.facebook.com/groups/kerrystikilounge) where you'll be privy to sneak peeks and deleted content. Taking *No More Words* to the beach or on a trip? Be sure to tag me (@kerrylonsdale) and the book (#NoMoreWords) on social media with your photos and I'll share. And finally, if you enjoyed Olivia's story, I'd be honored if you left a review on your favorite book review site.

ABOUT THE AUTHOR

Photo © 2018 Chantelle Hartshorne

Kerry Lonsdale is the *Wall Street Journal, Washington Post,* and Amazon Charts bestselling author of *Side Trip, Last Summer, All the Breaking Waves,* and the Everything Series (*Everything We Keep, Everything We Left Behind,* and *Everything We Give*). Her work has been translated into more than twenty-seven languages. She resides in Northern California with her husband and two children. You can visit Kerry at www.kerrylonsdale.com.